Estelle Ryan

The Uccello Connection

The Uccello Connection

A Genevieve Lenard Novel

By Estelle Ryan

First published 2017

Dedication

To RJ

Chapter ONE

"Seriously?" Francine, my best friend and one of the best hackers in the world, raised her eyebrows and stared at me. "Every night for the last two weeks? Why didn't you tell me this before?"

"Why should I?" I reached over and adjusted her knife so it mirrored exactly the setting of the fork. We were in *L'arbre Pourpre*, one of the four restaurants in Strasbourg Francine and I frequented when we went for lunch. The last few months had been uncommonly stressful and we had not been as consistent as before in meeting for lunch.

This morning, Francine had stormed into my viewing room and rudely interrupted me while I'd been analysing data we had found on Emad Vernet, a criminal we'd been trying to locate for the last six months. I had gasped at her audacity when she'd touched my computer without my permission and turned off the fifteen monitors in front of me.

She'd loudly bemoaned that she felt neglected and that I had to fix this. She'd insisted I needed a break and had to spend said break with her. The rest of my team had supported her. Much to my dismay.

But I had also missed our lunches and had not argued too much on our way to the restaurant. No sooner had the waiter placed a carafe of sparkling water on the table than Francine had started with her questions.

"Why should you tell me?" She threw her hands in the air, her bracelets jingling. "You should tell me all about Vinnie and Roxy because I'm your bestest best friend and because—"

"Your curiosity is stronger than your respect for their privacy?"

"How can you even think such a thing?" Her voice was a pitch higher in indignation, but her lips twitched when I lifted one eyebrow and gave her a look that she called the 'speak-the-truth-or-die' look. Her shoulders relaxed and she grinned. "Okay, sure. Who cares about their privacy? I want all the deets on Roxy and Vinnie. Tell me, tell me, tell me."

"I don't know the deet… details." I resented each time Francine's use of certain words slipped into my vernacular. "Vinnie and Roxy are romantically involved. That's it."

"Oh, no, girlfriend." She placed her palms on the table and leaned towards me. "This is so much more."

Vinnie was not only part of our team investigating art and other sensitive crimes, he was also a very dear friend. He was the protector of our team with a physique to match his self-appointed job.

Seven months ago, we'd had a case that involved several international leaders, one of whom had died from polonium-210 poisoning. During that time, Doctor Roxanne Ferreira had been of great help. Her knowledge of radiation poisoning and her high-level security clearance had introduced her to our team, to our lives. It was her engaging personality, curiosity and kindness that had made her inclusion into our group of friends the logical next step.

Our waiter arrived with our orders and carefully placed my soup bowl on the plate in front of me. My lips contracted in disapproval and I centred the bowl on the plate. Francine snorted, then smiled up at the waiter when he placed her bowl in the exact centre of her plate. "Thank you, sweetie."

Colour crept up the young man's neck at Francine's blatant flirting. His pupils dilated and he pulled his shoulders back, just enough to puff out his chest. Francine had this effect on most men. Her Brazilian-French looks and natural sensuality made it an interesting experience to be with her. It gave me ample opportunity to do what I was best at—analyse behaviour.

The restaurant was not as full on this Tuesday early afternoon as it would be later in the day. But there were enough patrons at the moment to give the restaurant a convivial atmosphere. In the ten minutes we'd been sitting at our table, I'd noticed the ardent interest of three men, two of whom were with women who could be their wives or girlfriends.

Francine's light laughter drew the attention of one of the three gentlemen and his eyes narrowed as he stared at Francine's legs. The waiter left us, walking with a touch more confidence that he had before. I frowned. "He's very young."

"Who?" Her confusion was genuine. It took another two seconds for her to comprehend my meaning. "The waiter? Why on earth wou… Aha. How many more times do I have to explain the difference between serious flirting and fun flirting?"

"No matter how many times you attempt to convince me, those are not technical definitions." I scooped the creamy broccoli soup onto my spoon. "And you *were* flirting with him."

"Pah." She smacked her lips and picked up her spoon. "You're not changing the subject. Tell me about Roxy staying over."

"You know she's been staying over. What else do you want to know?"

"Do you think it's serious between Vinnie and Roxy?"

"Define serious."

Her hand froze and she lowered her full spoon to her bowl. "Come on. You really want me to spell it out? Fine. I will. Do you think this is true L-O-V-E?"

"Why are you spelling ou…" I shook my head. "Don't answer that. I don't know what they are feeling."

Francine rolled her eyes. "What do you see?"

I considered her question. As a world-renowned nonverbal communication expert, I found safety in analysing people's body language. It made for much clearer understanding than merely relying on words. People seldom said what they truly meant.

I shared my apartment with Colin Frey, my romantic partner and a notorious thief who also worked for Interpol. Our side of the apartment had three bedrooms and the kitchen that was mostly used by Vinnie. He stayed in the connecting three-bedroom apartment and had claimed my kitchen as his 'kingdom'.

I thought back to yesterday morning when I'd left my bedroom to find Vinnie and Roxy kissing in my kitchen.

They usually kept such displays of affection private, but were always either holding hands or maintaining some form of contact. When I'd interrupted their kiss, Vinnie had leaned back and the micro-expressions I'd registered on both their faces had been very telling. "They care deeply for each other."

"I knew it!" Francine wiggled in her chair. "I knew it!"

"Then why did you ask me?" There was no malice in my question. I didn't even expect an answer.

"Because I wanted you to confirm what I've known for months." The smile lifting her cheeks was soft and genuine. "I'm so happy Vin found someone who can give him the love he deserves. And to top it all, I actually like Roxy."

"She's messy." I shuddered just thinking about my kitchen after the one and only time Roxy had helped Vinnie prepare dinner. Colin had laughed when Vinnie had pushed Roxy out of 'his' kitchen and said he'd rather have Francine with her evil spices helping him.

"But she's smart, bubbly, funny and treats Vin like a prince." Francine narrowed her eyes. "I do wish she would take me up on my offer to go shopping. That girl needs a serious wardrobe makeover."

"I don't care about her sense of fashion." I truly didn't. It was the acceptance she'd shown to everyone that had won my respect.

"Just because she's a doctor doesn't mean she *always* has to wear those ghastly, horrid, clunky running shoes." Her top lip curled and she shuddered. "Those things are an offense to every sexy, strong woman."

This was the eleventh time Francine had complained about

Roxy's choice of footwear. I ignored it and enjoyed the last of my soup. I was relieved when Francine didn't press for more information about Vinnie's relationship with Roxy. It had been an emotionally disruptive experience to watch Vinnie's romance grow.

It had been most confusing to be excited and happy for him, but at the same time wanting to protect him from potential disappointment. I didn't like the distressing emotions that accompanied friendships. Colin often reminded me that it was part of life, but I insisted my emotional being had been much less complicated before he, Francine, Vinnie and the others had blasted into my life.

These emotions were an unwelcome distraction. I resented spending time on trying to identify and then deal with the constant worry, affection and pride that interrupted my work. Before my life became saturated with friendships, I'd been much more focused on developing my career and knowledge base.

My existence had also been much poorer.

"Girlfriend." Francine tapped her bright orange manicured nails on the table. "Come back to me."

I blinked a few times and saw that my soup bowl had been removed. "Sorry."

"Were you thinking about Fradkov?"

"No." Although I should have been. Ivan Fradkov had been the mastermind behind the polonium-210 attack seven months ago. It had been the first time I'd ever heard of him, but both Colin and Vinnie had had previous encounters with him. Colin had authenticated paintings Fradkov had acquired for his Renaissance collection and

Vinnie had learned through an old friend about Fradkov's many successes at destroying corporate and political careers.

"Okay." Her expression alerted me that I was not going to like her next question. "So, were you thinking about all those magazines you've been receiving? Or were you thinking about the seven"—she leaned forward—"*seven* invitations to be keynote speaker you turned down?"

Francine had access to all our emails and even though she never abused it, she wasn't too shy to ask about our online orders or anything else she found interesting. At first, I had found it most disconcerting to have another person have such unlimited access to a part of my life, but she had proven herself both trustworthy and discreet.

"I wasn't thinking about that either." Although I still didn't know who'd been sending me academic journals. The first journal had been delivered to Rousseau & Rousseau five months ago. At first I had been suspicious. I hadn't subscribed to any academic journals, yet the plastic-wrapped magazine had been addressed to me.

Each week after that another journal had been delivered, much to my delight. The articles were all deeply researched and well written. Topics ranging from automated video analysis of nonverbal communication to the latest research on criminal psychology were covered in-depth. Reading these articles had made me long even more for the years I had spent researching and developing my academic career.

"Maybe you should be thinking about this." Francine studied me, her expression growing more serious. "I'm totally snooping now, but why don't you want to speak at these conferences and meetings? You used to do this a lot. Why not anymore?"

I took a sip of my water. Not because I was thirsty. It was both an avoidance and delaying tactic. I was internationally regarded as one of the best, if not the best, in the field of nonverbal communication. There had always been a high demand for me to lecture at symposiums, conferences and universities.

I'd used these events to overcome my fear of public speaking and had enjoyed the challenge of creating a fifty-minute lecture that would not only educate, but also entertain the mostly neurotypicals who'd attended my lectures. I missed it.

"Girlfriend?" Francine reached across the table, but didn't touch me. "Is there something bothering you?"

"I don't have the mental and emotional space for this," I blurted. I closed my eyes for a second and swallowed. "My mind is too consumed with the cases we have."

"Seriously?" She sat back in her chair and frowned at me. "I mean, we do have cases almost all the time, but the big ones only come once in a while. Surely these aren't that absorbing?"

I'd never had a best friend before. This was another emotional area I'd had to explore and find a way to cope with the emotional demands that went with this. Right now, I was feeling the pressure of that friendship. I wanted to tell her that it was the relationships that enriched my life that also held me back. But from previous experience, I knew that such a statement would hurt her.

I didn't want that. Nor did I want the long emotional

discussion that would inevitably follow, so I changed the topic back to Fradkov. "Has Manny received any feedback on our request for those bank accounts?"

"Mister Grumpy told me this morning that he doubts St Kitts and Nevis will give us permission to check into any account held by one of their banks." She raised both hands in pretend outrage. "Then he had the audacity to tell me off when I suggested hacking those accounts."

Colonel Manfred Millard was the only law enforcement agent on our team. He was also a very unlikely romantic partner for Francine. But after a year and seven months, they both still found intense pleasure arguing and their affection for each other had become stronger.

"I didn't expect the banks or the government to give us access. You just had that one pseudonym for Fradkov and a suspicion that he had an account in St Kitts and Nevis."

"A suspicion?" Francine pulled herself up and glared at me. "I'll have you know that I have a titanium-strong feeling that Fradkov is hiding money in that country. As if anyone can call those two tiny islands a country. There are so many rich criminals popping in and out of that place that I'm quite sure it would be easy to smuggle the remaining polonium in and keep it there until Fradkov is ready to do what he wants to do."

That was the problem. We didn't know if Fradkov had the remaining polonium-210. During our last case, we'd discovered that Emad and his late brother Claude had worked with Fradkov in attempt to set Russia up for numerous crimes. It had been an endeavour to damage Russia's standing with Europe. Despite our investigation, we had not been able to determine if or how he and Emad were planning another attempt. This was causing us and numerous law enforcement agencies great alarm.

Any further thoughts about Fradkov and Emad were interrupted by a tall man stopping next to our table. He was not one of the three men who'd shown an interest in Francine. He stared at Francine for a second, then took a chair from the empty table next to us and sat down at our table. The fear emanating from him caused my heart rate to increase exponentially. I leaned away from him and committed every physical feature and every nonverbal cue to memory.

His face was pale, his *depressor anguli oris* muscles turning the corners of his mouth down. His frontalis muscles pulled his eyebrows up and his widened eyes kept shifting from Francine to the door.

His fear was real.

His greying dark hair was messy as if he'd pushed his hands through it numerous times, his beard was a few days old and his nails were bitten to the quick. At least his trousers and shirt were clean and ironed.

"HotFrandeur88?" His voice shook and he cleared his throat. His eyes widened even more as he continued to stare at Francine. "You are HotFrandeur88, right?"

Francine didn't change her posture or expression. If it hadn't been for my expertise, I would not have noticed the almost imperceptible tightening of her lips and the slight increase in overall muscle tension. She leaned towards him, her expression sultry. "Ooh, aren't I lucky today. Some handsome stranger falls right in my lap. And he calls me the sexiest name ever. Do you really think I look like a HotFrandeur88? But before you answer"—she lifted one shoulder and pursed her lips, befitting her sensual retort—"what is your name, sexy?"

I watched as she first toyed with her dessert spoon and then started drawing circles on her smartphone with her manicured nail. It took me two seconds to realise she had activated the recording device on her phone while keeping the stranger off balance with her outrageous flirting.

The man leaned away from her. "If you're not HotFrandeur88, please tell me. I need to find her. Pasquier told me she could help me. I need help. Are you HotFrandeur88?"

Francine's eyes narrowed. "How do you know Joe?"

"He helped me a few times with a… project."

I pointed at his face. "Your blinking increased and you clasped your hands. You're lying."

He looked at me for the first time. "I'm not. I swear I'm not. I'm just… they're going to kill me and if HotFrandeur88 doesn't help me, they will also kill my family."

"Whoa, bucko." Francine dropped all sensual pretence and glanced at me. "This woman here is the best body language expert in the world. She will know the moment you are bullshitting me. That being said, tell me *exactly* how you know Pasquier."

I wondered who this person was, but didn't want to interrupt what appeared to be something very important. The stranger swallowed a few times and rubbed his hands on his thighs. Typical self-comforting behaviour. He looked at me, then turned to face me completely. "My name is Otto Coulaux. I fence stolen artworks and Joe Pasquier became a friend after many years of collaboration. A few times he helped me get into digital places I didn't have legal access to. And a few times I helped him sell things he got access to illegally."

"You're telling the truth." I studied every muscle in his face. "Whoever you are running away from is a much bigger threat than the possibility of being incarcerated for the crimes you've just confessed to."

"I'm not just scared for my life. They know everything about me, including where my ex and my two daughters live." His lips trembled. "The things they threatened to do to my little kids…"

"Who are 'they'?" Francine asked.

He turned back to her. "You are HotFrandeur88, right?"

"I will wipe any and all digital evidence of your entire existence if you ever tell anyone."

His shoulders dropped as he exhaled in relief. "Joe told me that you're the only one he would ever trust to do something good."

"So Joe is still as funny as he was when I almost sent him to jail five years ago." Her small smile was genuine. "A pity he's still working for the bad guys."

"He's a good guy in my opinion. He's the reason I know my life is in danger."

"What kind of danger?" I asked.

"Two days ago Joe phoned me." Otto lowered his voice even more and glanced around the restaurant. He looked around a second time before he was satisfied that the other patrons had no interest in our conversation. None of the three men were looking at our table. Otto leaned closer to

Francine. "He told me my name was on a kill list."

"What kill list? Who else is on this list?" Was this literal or figurative?

"He didn't say. He just told me that I should find HotFrandeur88 and that she would be able to help me."

Francine frowned. "How would I be able to stop someone from killing you?"

"By getting my name off that list and then helping us disappear."

"You're going to have to give me a lot more than this, Otto." Francine shook her head. "If you're involved with Joe and if someone wants to kill you, you're already on the wrong side of the law. So why would I help you?"

"Look, I know I break the law." Otto took a deep breath. "I facilitate the sale of stolen art, but I've always made a point of choosing clients who don't pay me with blood money."

"Ah, another criminal with a strong moral code." Francine's lips thinned. "Hon, if I research your client list, I can guarantee you that every single one of them has paid you with blood money."

"You can't make a guarantee like that." There was no way she could anticipate the results of such a search.

"Maybe not, but I hope to hell he's getting the point I'm trying to make."

"You're digressing." I turned to Otto. "Who's going to kill you?"

"Not just me. My family too." His voice broke. "Joe told me their names were on the list as well. He's going to kill us all."

I frowned. "Are you using the word 'kill' figuratively?"

"Yes. Maybe. I don't know!" He slumped in his chair. "It doesn't matter. I don't even know if you can help me. Maybe it's already too late." He turned to Francine, his expression pleading. "Just make sure my girls are safe."

"Okay. Take a deep breath." Francine waited until Otto inhaled and let the air rush out. "Send me the email Joe sent you and I'll do everything I can to see who's behind this list."

"I don't need your help to find out who's behind it. I know who's behind it. The sick fuck has everything in place to execute his psycho plan." His voice was now a barely audible whisper. "Seven months ago, he ordered me to get the best forgers money could buy. He gave me a list of names and told me to find out who were the top four forgers. He got them working fulltime to forge I don't know how many paintings. I was told in no uncertain terms that I was never to make contact with them again, but Lucy phoned me last week. Joe reckons that's what got me onto that kill list."

"Who's Lucy?" I had so many other questions, but this was the first that came out.

"A brilliant artist. Her forgeries are perfect, undetectable." He shook his head. "And now she's dead. The police found her body in a small park in Paris."

"What did she tell you?" Francine asked.

"That she'd been in contact with the other forgers. I have no idea how they found out about each other, but when they did, they compared notes. They realised that they were busy forging artworks that were all from one exhibition. One of them found out that these forgeries were going to be used in a wider strategy to cause a frigging world war." His eyes were wide with fear when he looked at me. "He's going to succeed, you know. He's going to blow up cities, kill thousands and start a war that we'll never come back from. I just want to be in a safe place when he does that."

I put both hands on the table. "Who's behind this? Who's going to start this war?"

He blinked a few times, then lowered his chin, his voice quiet. "Ivan Fradkov."

My breath left me and my heart rate sped up to a point where I felt lightheaded. Francine hid her shock much better, only raising both eyebrows and leaning slightly away from Otto as if trying to escape the mention of Fradkov's name.

"How do you know Fradkov?" Her voice was raspy from tension tightening her throat muscles.

"He's owned me for the last seven years of my life."

"You're his slave? Slavery is illegal in France." And I couldn't imagine a slave master allowing Otto to go to a restaurant alone.

"Not literally, but I might as well have been." He closed his eyes. When he opened them, fresh fear filled his face. "Once. It was only that once and he had me in his claws. I sold an Uccello painting to him. He really got it for a steal, but still insisted on having it independently authenticated. He didn't care about the money I'd spent on the art historian who'd given the painting a thumbs up. No. He wanted his own Professor So-and-So to make sure he bought an original Uccello for a measly hundred thousand euros. I could easily have sold it for double that price, but I needed the cash."

He swallowed a few times, but continued his story. "This Professor Whatever said the painting was a forgery and that was the end of my freedom. I have no idea how Fradkov found out every last detail of my life, but nothing connected to me or mine was secret any more. The worst is that he knows about Jordyn and Grace, my two daughters. Those girls have nothing to do with my life. They don't even know I exist. I told my ex that it was the best way. If she wanted to keep them safe and in good schools, clothes and a comfortable house, no one could ever know where I was or that the girls are mine. And now they're on that list."

"I can't decide whether you're an arsehole or a hero." Francine crossed her arms.

"Oh, I'm an arsehole. There's not a heroic bone in my body. That's why I need you to help me. I need my name off that list. I need to keep my twins safe." He straightened. "If you do this for me, I'll give you Emad Vernet. I know he and Fradkov have it in for some team trying to stop them from setting the world on fire. Emad is a little wuss. I have no patience for that jackass. But I really don't want to be part of their plan."

"What plan?" My question came out harsher than I'd intended, but I didn't apologise. This might be the key evidence we needed to stop Fradkov and Emad forever.

"Oh, they're talking about putting the hurt on everyone on every level—economic, social, even emergency services. That just pissed me off. I have great respect for firefighters. They are heroes."

"Do you know any specifics about this big plan?" Francine's sceptical tone caught my attention and I looked at her. She didn't trust Otto. "Anything that will make me believe that you're not just here to get some free ride or to set me up for something?"

"I know Emad is hiding in plain sight, closer than you think, and living in a frigging antique collection." He straightened even more in his chair. "I also know where Fradkov is holing up."

"Give me an addre…" Francine's eyebrows shot up as she looked at something behind me. Her mouth opened in a silent scream and her hands shot up in a defensive gesture.

As I started to turn around to see what had caused Francine such instant fear, I caught a glimpse of a slim man dressed all in black. His right arm rose and I wondered why he had a coat draped over it. In this elegant restaurant, all the patrons left their coats or jackets at the door.

The deafening report of a gun sent adrenaline flooding my system. Francine screamed, joined by other patrons in the restaurant, but I barely heard it. My entire being was focused on Otto slumped over onto the table, blood pouring from a hole in the back of his head, his face turned away from me. An even larger bloodstain forming on that side had to be from the exit wound. That was what Francine was looking as she slapped both hands over her mouth to stop herself from screaming again.

The familiar paralysis of a shutdown took over my body. I forced my eyes towards the door to watch the black-clad figure disappear into the street. It took a herculean effort to turn my attention back to Francine. She had left her state of shock and had her phone to her ear, furiously shouting into it. Anger pulled at all the muscles in her face. She was unharmed.

I slowly lowered my gaze to my hands resting on the table. It wasn't the dead man's head lying an arm's length from me that was my final undoing. It was the spray of blood on my hands that brought the darkness rushing towards me. I didn't fight it. Not this time. I simply couldn't cope with the innumerable tiny drops of blood on the back of my hands and even between my fingers.

I allowed the darkness to take me.

Chapter TWO

"Jenny?" A warm hand rubbed my forearm. Another warm hand was holding one of mine. "Come back to us, love."

I took a shuddering breath and tried to open my eyes. The message from my brain wasn't reaching my eyelids. Instead of becoming panicked, I focused on the familiar voice talking to me.

Colin. His was the only touch I'd ever tolerated while my mind shut down from being overstimulated. From the first day he'd broken into my apartment and sent me into a shutdown, there had been a calmness about him that my non-neurotypical brain had found appealing and acceptable.

Bit by bit, I became aware of my body. I was hugging my knees to my chest and rocking slightly. It took a few relaxing breaths and deep concentration to stop the rocking. At least I wasn't keening. Not now. As far as my shutdowns went, keening and rocking were the two most common traits.

I wiggled my toes and was glad when they responded to the message my brain sent. Now Colin was telling me about a book he was reading. He had bought it a few days ago and had been excited to learn more lesser-known facts about Vikings.

"I was really surprised when I read last night that the Vikings' horned helmets were at first worn for ceremonial purposes. Then it became trendy for the men to wear them when they were at sea. Did you know this? I meant to tell you, but then we"—he chuckled softly—"well, you know what we did last night."

His hand tightened around mine, the contact comforting. I opened my eyes. I was still at the table in the restaurant, on the same chair. Colin was sitting on a chair facing mine, concern embedded in every muscle on his face. All the tension disappeared when he saw my eyes were open. A genuine smile lifted his cheeks and crinkled the corners of his eyes. "Hey there."

"How long have I been in a shutdown?" I lifted one finger to stop his response. "Hey."

My delayed politeness intensified his smile. "Welcome back. You've been out for almost three hours."

This did not please me. Years of training my mind had helped in preventing and delaying shutdowns, but I had never been able to control the length of them. When my brain became overwhelmed with any form of stimuli, it shut down for as long as it needed to. Francine had once jokingly said that my brain was an entity on its own, working separately from me. Of course, I'd scoffed at that unscientific notion, but there had been plenty of times where I'd felt separated from my brain.

"Jenny." Colin shook my hand gently. "Don't go away again."

"I'm here." I inhaled deeply and lowered my legs to the floor. The next few minutes were undoubtedly going to be uncomfortable while blood circulation returned to my lower extremities.

Blood. The word rushed through my mind and I remembered the reason I'd gone into the shutdown. My eyes jerked down to my hands and my shoulders slumped with relief.

"I cleaned them." He took both my hands in his and looked pointedly at a bottle of disinfectant and a plastic bag filled with cotton swabs. "I am of the opinion that your hands have never been this clean. Heck, my hands have never been this clean."

I blinked a few times and managed to stop myself from asking him why he would do such a thing. We had been together for three years, but Colin still surprised me with the utter selflessness and patience he exhibited with my non-neurotypical behaviour. "I love you."

"Wow." His eyes widened with pleasure, his smile soft. "I love you too."

"Oh, for the love of all that is holy." Manny pulled a chair closer and sat down hard. "Stop staring into each other's eyes and tell me you're okay, Doc."

"I'm unharmed." I turned back to Colin. "Vikings never wore horned helmets. That was fabricated by painters towards the end of the nineteenth century. You are too intelligent to… you baited me."

Colin leaned forward and kissed my forehead. "It worked."

Manny shifted in his chair. "Stop snogging, Frey. We have a murder to solve."

"Did the medical examiner take the body?" I was glad that I'd missed the gruesome task of Otto's body being loaded onto a gurney and zipped closed in a black body bag. As much as I loathed shutdowns, they did protect my mind from being even more overwhelmed.

"Yes." Manny waved at the table. "The crime scene guys have also been here and took all the evidence."

"Where's Francine?" I wondered how she was dealing with having been so close to an assassination.

"She's gone back to the team room." Manny grunted. "I've never seen her so pissed off. Despite my dire warnings that I will arrest her, I'm sure she's hacking everything and everybody to find out what that Pasquier person sent Ollie."

"Otto." I knew Manny purposely got names wrong, yet I couldn't help myself correcting him. "Did Francine find the killer on the city street cameras?"

"We did." Pink, the IT specialist for GIPN—the equivalent of the United States' SWAT teams or Germany's SEK teams—took a chair from a nearby table and sat down next to Manny. He looked me over. "How're you feeling?"

"I haven't spent any time analysing my feelings yet. I would rather use that time productively by getting as much information as I can about what happened."

Pink smiled. "Okey-dokey. What do you want to know?"

"Has the killer been arrested? Did he say why he killed Otto? And who sent him?"

"Oh. Yeah." Pink's *platysma* muscles pulled his mouth into a grimace. "After Francine phoned Manny, she immediately got into the city's CCTV system and searched for the killer. It didn't take her long to find footage of him leaving the restaurant, but she lost him when he went into a street not covered by cameras. He must've known that and planned his exit from there. By the time she'd gone through all the cameras of surrounding shops and ATMs, I got here with the team."

"Where's Daniel?" I frowned and looked around the restaurant. Daniel Cassel was the leader of the GIPN team and had proven himself to be not only astute in reading people and situations, but also a great operational leader of his team. I respected him.

"Dan's out of town. He's running a course at some international exchange for emergency response teams." Pink shrugged. "I'm second in command, so I'm wearing the leader hat at the moment."

I looked at his uncovered head. "Where is it?"

"Where is what?"

"That hat?" I narrowed my eyes. "Daniel has never worn any head covering that indicated he was the leader."

Pink laughed. "My bad. Sorry, Genevieve. I was speaking metaphorically. Daniel really is better at this than I am, so please be patient when I say something that's not clear."

He was right. From our first meeting, Daniel had shown uncommon sensitivity towards my non-neurotypical behaviour and had made an effort to eliminate metaphors from his speech. My intellect allowed me to learn and understand metaphors and colloquialisms, but my first inclination was always to interpret someone's words literally. Trying to interpret a person's true meaning by analysing the many nuances and hidden meanings required such immense effort that I often missed the rest of that person's communication.

"Supermodel and P… he weren't able to find that killer anywhere." Manny glared at Pink when he stumbled over using the GIPN member's name. Manny frequently expressed his aversion to such a silly nickname. "And supermodel looked everywhere. That's one of the reasons she's so pissed off."

"Francine really didn't like the guy disappearing like that." Pink nodded. "I agree with her that he has to be highly informed about all cameras in the area to vanish into thin air." He winced. "I mean, *appear* to vanish into thin air."

"I saw the footage of him leaving the restaurant and blending into the foot traffic on the street," Manny said. "That bastard is good. The big guy thinks this killer is a pro."

"Vinnie?" I didn't like that I was slower than usual to notice the absence of my friends. "Where is he?"

"He went with Francine." Something in Colin's tone caught my attention. A sad smile lifted one corner of his mouth. "He's extremely upset at what happened."

"Why? Did he know Otto?"

Colin stared at me. "Really? Think a little bit more, my smart love."

I did. I considered Vinnie's personality and why he would be distressed. I sighed. "It's not his fault."

"You try to tell him that, Doc." Manny snorted. "I thought he was going to pop a vein when he got here."

Colin raised one hand. "Let me give you a quick rundown on what happened while you were out. Francine phoned Manny, who immediately phoned Daniel. Couldn't get hold of him and phoned Pink. By that time the three of us were already in Vinnie's pickup truck racing through the streets. Pink and his team arrived a few minutes after we did. The police a few minutes after that."

"It took us a whole two minutes to secure the restaurant." Pink waved his hand around. "A lot of the guests had fled the scene. A few others stayed out of morbid curiosity and Francine was ordering everyone to stay away from the table."

"You were curled up on your chair"—Colin squeezed my hand—"and Francine was working like crazy on her tablet."

Pink nodded. "I sent three of our guys to the last location where Francine had tracked the killer, but they came up empty… er, without any results. Then we got the crime scene guys in and the rest is history… er, a boring story."

Colin chuckled. "A boring story?"

"Whatever, man." A light shade of pink coloured Pink's cheeks. "I'm trying."

I didn't like witnessing his embarrassment. I put my hand on the table, reaching for him. "Thank you, Pink. It might be simpler if you continue your usual vernacular and I'll ask if something is unclear."

"No." He shook his head vigorously. "This is a good experience for me. It makes me consider my words better and makes me try harder to keep my explanations clear."

"Do you want to hug or can we get back to the case?" Manny knocked on the table top. "We know absolutely nothing about this killer and we need to find out why he killed Otto."

I turned to Colin. "Did you listen to the recording Francine made?"

"We did and that is why I disagree with Millard." Colin looked at Manny. "We don't have *nothing* on the killer. We have a possible motive. If what Otto said is true, then it could be Fradkov or Emad who ordered the kill. I can imagine they didn't want us to know whatever it was that Otto was going to share with Jenny and Francine."

"That's conjecture." I thought about this. "Although it's a reasonable conclusion to draw."

"We also know most of the killer's physical appearance," Pink said. "We have his height, his body type, his gait. What we don't have is his facial features. He was wearing a cap, has a hipster beard and was wearing large sunglasses. This obscured too much of his face to get any metrics."

"What's a hipster beard?" How was that different to any other beard?

"A stupid big beard." Manny rubbed his stubbled jaw. "It's not important, Doc. What is important is that we need to find this killer-for-hire and we need to find out who hired him."

"How can you be so convinced that he is a killer-for hire? That he didn't kill Otto for another reason?" I frowned. "Did you find evidence you haven't told me about yet?"

"No, Doc. This is just the most logical conclusion. And don't give me that look. Of course we will consider all possibilities, but my gut tells me that Fradkov and Emad are behind this." Manny scowled at Colin. "*Now* are you going to share with the class what you know about this Otto criminal?"

Colin smiled and winked at me. "Millard feels slighted because I didn't want to tell him until you could also hear."

"Hear what?"

"What I know about Otto. And what I was able to find out in the last two hours."

"Did you have any dealings with him?"

"No." Colin shook his head. "I'd never actually met the guy. I'd heard of him, yes, but our paths never crossed. Well, they kind of did, but not physically."

"Oh, just get to it, Frey." Manny shifted in his chair.

Colin ignored him. "Six years ago, Fradkov hired one of my aliases to authenticate a painting he'd bought. It was an Uccello that he'd gotten for about five percent of its market value. That in itself should've been enough warning for him, but he'd gone ahead and bought the painting."

"You were the expert Fradkov used. And then he blackmailed Otto because you'd proven the painting wasn't authentic." I wasn't surprised.

"Yup. It was me. The painting Fradkov had bought was for his Renaissance collection and I, as Professor Henry Vaughn, had a reputation for being an expert in this field. Especially if you wanted an off-the-books authentication. I'd agreed to meet Fradkov in Brussels and it took me less than thirty seconds to tell him the painting was a forgery. A brilliant forgery, but it was not a work done by Uccello's masterful hands."

Colin looked up and left—recalling a memory. "Fradkov was livid. He didn't shout or become aggressive. He's one of those quiet angry people. The most dangerous in my opinion. I asked him who'd sold him the painting and he told me it was Otto. I took my fee and left. As soon as I got home, I started looking into Otto.

"He was an art history graduate and really knew his work and his clients. The people I spoke to had a lot of respect for him. He'd mastered the skill of finding rare paintings for great prices. About half of these paintings were stolen or part of a disputed estate, but he also did a lot of legitimate deals. Yet he worked really hard to keep his name quiet. He didn't want to be recognisable or searchable, which was a very smart decision.

"When I listened to Francine's recording, it suddenly made sense why Otto started dealing more in Renaissance art after that incident. That must have been when he started working for Fradkov. Under duress, of course."

"What did your contacts say about him?" Pink asked.

"Pretty much the same. He was good at his job. Because so few of the paintings he sold ever turned out to be forgeries, people were willing to take the risk of losing thousands of euros. They more often saved hundreds of thousands, if not millions, buying works from him."

"Do you know where he found these paintings?"

"No, but I heard rumours that he had a list of art thieves he sourced artworks from. Apparently, he also had a list of the best Renaissance forgers. Well, it had been a rumour until Otto confirmed it on that recording." Colin tilted his head. "I would really like to find that list."

"Later, Frey." Manny sat up. "We have a lot of other things to do first. We need to find that killer. We need to find out what the bleeding hell Otto was talking about when he said that Fradkov plans to start a war. Hell, we need to find Fradkov and throw his murdering arse in jail and then throw that key in the bloody ocean."

Claudette Mécary, the only female member of Daniel's team, walked towards us, holding my handbag. I was about to reprimand her for taking my property without my consent when I noticed the rust-coloured dots on the light brown surface. It was a faux suede bag, one that had been treated to resist most stains. It had been an important feature when I'd bought the bag. I never wanted to touch it again.

"Your phone's been ringing for the last twenty minutes."

Claudette held my bag out for me to take. "The crime scene guys finished photographing and swiping it. We were able to convince them to give it back to us only until you removed everything inside. They still want the bag though."

I leaned away from the handbag, my eyes locked on the blood spatter. "I don't want it."

The familiar ringtone of my phone sounded from my bag. Claudette shook it lightly. "There it goes again. You might want to take this. I think it might be important, especially since it hasn't stopped for twenty minutes."

Colin reached over and took my bag. He looked at me. "May I?"

I nodded and watched as Colin took care not to touch the outside of the bag. As soon as he unzipped it, he reached in and lifted out my phone. He knew where to find it. I always kept my phone in the same place in my handbag. Now I was going to have to find another handbag and get used to everything being in different places. I hated change.

The phone stopped ringing just as Colin held it out to me, but started again immediately. I took the phone and looked at the screen. I didn't recognise the number and was tempted to decline the call. Yet I swiped the screen and lifted the phone to my ear. "Hello?"

"Doctor Lenard." A familiar male voice sighed in relief. "I've been trying really hard to get hold of you."

I still couldn't place his voice. "Who is this?"

"Oh, sorry. It's Alain Vernet."

My eyebrows rose in surprise. Alain was Emad's adoptive father. For more than two decades he'd been on the UN's advisory boards. When we'd confronted him with Emad and his biological son Claude's illegal activities seven months ago, he'd been horrified, but not surprised. He'd helped us in our case and I'd witnessed his internal battles as he'd betrayed his sons to do the right thing. After that case, he'd resigned and I'd not been in contact with him since. This call was a surprise. And suspicious in its timing. "Please hold. I'm with my team and am putting you on speakerphone."

"Even better." He paused a moment. "Can I speak? Can everyone hear me?"

I placed the phone on the table. "Yes."

"Manfred Millard here." Manny leaned towards the phone. "What's the problem, Alain?"

"I received a painting." His voice shook and I focused my attention. My speciality was in nonverbal communication, but sometimes I was able to glean clues from listening to people's tone of voice. Alain's conveyed fear. "And I don't know what to do about it."

"Colin Frey speaking, sir." Colin also leaned towards my phone. "What kind of painting?"

"I… I think my son painted this."

"Emad?" Manny's question came out loud. He cleared his throat. "You think Emad painted this? Did he deliver it? How did you receive it? When did you receive it?"

"A courier dropped it off an hour ago. I was surprised because I didn't order anything and wasn't expecting any delivery, but it was clearly addressed to me." He paused. "I can't be sure it's Emad. The address is printed out and the return address is a mailing service. I checked. I… I just have a feeling."

I needed to see his face. And I needed to see the painting. I was sure Colin would be able to tell more than I could from analysing the painting, which made this conversation moot. "Bring the painting to Rousseau & Rousseau. We'll meet you there in twenty minutes."

"Please, sir." Colin winked at me. "We can do a better job understanding this if we can look at the painting."

"Sure. Yes. Sure." Alain inhaled deeply. "I just want this nightmare to end. I'll be there in fifteen minutes."

Chapter THREE

The elevator doors to Rousseau & Rousseau's foyer opened, but Colin, Manny and I couldn't exit. The door was blocked by Vinnie's large frame. "Jen-girl! Why did it take you so long to get back here? I've been waiting for hours."

Manny grunted and pushed Vinnie out the way. "We're here now, big guy. Stop being such a girl."

Vinnie ignored him. He stared down at me as I exited the elevator. I stepped in front of him and looked up to study his expression. And I saw exactly what Colin had described. The scar that ran down the left side of Vinnie's face was more pronounced. It always gained colour when he experienced strong emotions. The contractions of the muscles around his mouth and eyes revealed a myriad of emotions, the dominant of which was guilt. But it was the underlying relief that I would focus on. "I'm safe, Vinnie."

"Now you are." Fear flashed over his features. "A few hours ago you weren't."

"That is true. It would, however, be a foolish loss of time to agonise over what could've happened."

Vinnie lowered his chin and stared at me for a second. Then he nodded. "Gonna hug you."

That was all the warning I got. Clearly Vinnie had determined that I was managing the stimuli well enough for him to add to them. I forced my body to relax as he embraced me tightly, almost lifting me off my feet. Vinnie was very kinaesthetic, something I found hard to deal with.

Yet I knew how important physical contact was for him. He held me even closer and whispered in my ear, "I'm glad you're okay, Jen-girl. I was terrified."

On a calming inhale, I put my arms around his wide shoulders and hugged him back. "Me too."

"Okay, you big wuss." Manny's voice sounded rough—the way it did when he witnessed something that touched him emotionally. "Let go of Doc before you crush every bone in her body. We're going to need her to solve this case."

Vinnie exhaled a slow and steady breath before letting me go. I took a small step back and resisted the urge to step behind Colin. Instead I stood next to him and reached for his hand. He squeezed mine lightly and an immediate calm pushed away the panic that had been building while in Vinnie's embrace.

Seeing the same calm now on Vinnie's face pleased me. It had taken a while to fully understand that something as simple as a hug could give that to my muscular friend. That was why I was willing to deal with the panic of being touched.

"Oh, for the love of all the saints!" Manny waved his hand in front of my face. "Doc! Can we go now?"

"Yes." I turned towards the reception area. "Where is Timothée?"

The heavy wooden desk was as neat as always, fitting in well with the rest of the affluent décor of the high-end insurance company Rousseau & Rousseau. Phillip Rousseau, the founder and owner of this company, had become the father figure I had never had. Not only was he a stable presence in my life, but his intellect, integrity and compassion were qualities I both respected and valued highly.

"I'm here…er, Genevieve." Timothée Renaud walked towards us from the kitchen, carrying a tray of coffee mugs. He'd been working as Phillip's personal assistant for the last three years and I'd watched him mature in that time. He had always been stylish, but a distinguished elegance now combined with his usual sense of fashion to give him a more confident and worldly appearance.

He had taken a long time to get used to my unconventional ways and only in the last three months started calling me by my first name. Most times it was preceded by hesitation, but I respected his attempt to treat me the same as he did Phillip and Colin. He was still uncomfortable around Manny and pretended to be brave around Vinnie. It was amusing to observe.

"I have another magazine for you." Tim glanced towards his desk. "Remember to pick it up before you go back to your viewing room."

"Thank you." I was pleased with this news. These journals were intellectually superior to most reading material available.

Tim nodded towards the large conference room. "Phillip and Monsieur Vernet are in there. I made coffee for everyone."

"I don't drink coffee, boy." Manny glared at the mugs and walked past Tim.

The younger man rolled his eyes and pulled up his lip while staring at Manny's back. Then he turned to us. "Colonel Moanfred Millard's disgusting milky tea is also on this tray."

Vinnie burst out laughing. "I'm going to call the old man that forever. Good one, dude."

Tim's chest pushed out and he flushed at Vinnie's praise. He tried to change his expressions to nonchalance as he turned and followed Manny to the conference room, but without success. Even Colin had seen his delight at being called 'dude'. I didn't know if Vinnie knew how hard Tim had been trying to gain the large man's approval. It certainly didn't seem so as the three of us made our way to the conference room.

Many an interview with suspects and victims had taken place in this space, many secrets revealed. I stepped through the door and as usual my eyes first went to the paintings lining three of the four walls. I had an uncontrollable need to adjust any paintings hanging at an incorrect angle, no matter how small.

Phillip periodically rotated the paintings in the conference rooms, something that I'd gotten used to, but still found jarring. No form of change was easy for me. Today three of the paintings from the smallest conference room were on the far wall, one of which I recognised as the Monet Phillip had purchased last year.

Once I'd reassured myself the paintings were all aligned, I looked at the two older men sitting at the end of the table. Phillip was wearing a bespoke charcoal suit, the wine-red handkerchief in his pocket matching his silk tie. Concern marred his usually confident features. He got up as soon as he saw me and came around the table.

"I'm so sorry, Genevieve." He stopped in front of me. "No one should ever have to experience that."

"I'm unharmed." I didn't know what else to say as Phillip studied me.

He appeared to come to a conclusion and rolled his shoulders lightly to remove the tension that had built up. "I can see that and I'm relieved."

"This is a shockingly bad copy of Uccello's *St George and the Dragon*." Colin was standing in front of an easel in the corner of the room and turned around. Distaste was evident in the way his *levator labii superioris* muscle raised his top lip. "The painting is inspired by a legend that goes back to tenth- or eleventh-century Cappadocia, where Saint George killed a dragon that terrorised a small town. This dragon had been poisoning the lake that provided the town with drinking water. The locals fed the dragon two sheep every day to stop it from doing so, but then ran out of sheep and started feeding it their children.

"One day, the king's daughter was chosen to be fed to the dragon. Saint George rode by when she was standing next to the lake awaiting her fate. Long story short, he injured the dragon very badly and took it on a leash into town. He then kindly offered to kill the dragon if everyone converted to Christianity and was baptised.

"Thousands of people converted, including the king, and the manipulating saint killed the dragon. Uccello is only one of many masters who painted this legend. Raphael, Giovanni Bellini and Peter Paul Rubens are a few others. Of course it's also been forged many times in various levels of mastery. But this?" He pointed at the painting behind him. "This is a bad copy."

I walked towards the painting, but stopped when I was next to Alain Vernet. He was looking at the painting, emotional pain and grave concern clear on his face. He looked older than when I'd met him seven months ago. Lines formed by the *corrugator supercilii* and *frontalis* muscles because of frowning were deeper, his hair significantly greyer. Combined with the dark shadows under his eyes, I concluded that he had not experienced a lot of inner peace since his biological son had been killed and his adopted son had turned against his country and against his father.

I thought of how Phillip would approach this and took a deep breath. "Hello, Monsieur Vernet."

"Doctor Lenard." He pushed himself out of his chair. "Thank you for responding so quickly. I really don't know what to do about this."

"What makes you think Emad sent this to you?"

"A feeling." His smile was sad and resigned. "Just a silly old man's feeling."

"You're not old." I didn't even try to hide the stern tone in my voice. "And you're not silly. You're sad because your sons betrayed their country and everything you taught them."

"Genevieve." Phillip's soft warning brought even more sadness to Alain's face.

"No, Phillip. She's right." He sat back down. "Emad might not be my blood son, but he's all I have left. Yet I know that I lost him many years ago. Most likely when he became a spy for France. He was such a great child. Such a happy child."

No one spoke. Alain's sadness affected everyone, even Manny. Vinnie reacted as usual to situations that distressed people, especially the vulnerable—he became angry. His nostrils flared and his stance widened. With effort he unclenched his fists and leaned against the doorframe, his attempt to appear relaxed not successful.

"He was a gentle child," Alain said softly as if to himself. "He was devastated when his mother died and his biological father's family didn't want him. When Claude and I arrived, he immediately took a liking to Claude and they played for hours with the action figures Claude had brought with him. Emad's family never gave him any toys. And when he came back with us, he was so happy to have his own room, play with Claude and be wanted."

Alain blinked and a tear rolled down his cheek. He angrily wiped it away with the back of his hand. "Claude was always the difficult one. When you found out that he was smuggling goods and he was involved in that radiation threat, I wasn't surprised. How many times did I bail him out of jail? Too many times. He never learned any lessons.

"But my Emad? He was such a good boy. And a brilliant lawyer. Brilliant enough for the CIA to take note and recruit him to spy for them. I often wonder if that was his undoing or whether he was also just a bad seed. Does the fault lie with me? Did I fail as a parent and now I'm suffering the consequences?"

No one answered his question. I considered it rhetorical, but the desperation around his eyes propelled me to answer. "There are many unanswered questions about the outcome of child rearing. There have been countless cases of children suffering from emotional and physical neglect and abuse, yet they grow up to be psychologically balanced individuals who rise above their circumstances and become great successes.

"The converse is also true. Children who grow up in emotionally and physically safe and stable homes can grow up to become abusive or even ruthless killers. The range in between is wide and fraught with variables. It is without a doubt that you made mistakes as a parent, but my research has shown me that there is no guaranteed outcome to raising children."

Phillip's expression was grateful as he smiled gently at me. He turned to Alain. "Genevieve is right. You did the best you could, Alain. You can't hold yourself responsible for the decisions they made as adults."

Alain just shook his head. Manny walked to the painting and scowled at it. "What did you say this was, Frey?"

"A bad copy of Uccello's *St George and the Dragon*. Have you not been listening to anything I said?"

"Hmm." Manny leaned forward, shook his head and straightened. "Yeah. No. I don't see any George or any dragon. Doc, maybe you should come and look at this. To me, it just looks like the artwork from a year six pupil."

I stepped to the painting and stood next to Colin. He was pinching his chin between his thumb and forefinger, his head tilted to one side as he studied the artwork. I turned my attention to the painting and blinked.

I had no expertise in analysing the skills of an artist, but I felt comfortable categorising this as undeveloped. To the left was a stick figure that I assumed was a woman. She held something in her hand that connected her to something to her left that could be any kind of monstrous animal. But since I knew the name of the painting, I once again assumed that this was the dragon. To their right was another stick figure on what I assumed to be a horse. Even in my limited knowledge of art, I would never have insulted any abstract artists by suggesting this fell in that genre. It was simply inept.

Something about this painting registered in my brain, but did not filter through to my cerebral cortex—my thinking brain. I stared at it, hoping for whatever anomaly my subconscious had noted to come to the fore. It didn't.

Conversation flowed around me. Manny, Alain and Phillip were speculating about the meaning of the painting. I stopped listening to their uninformed and amateur guesses at the psychology behind the colours and style used. Instead I started mentally playing Mozart's Symphony no.31 in D major.

As I listened to another rushing scale, my eyes narrowed on the horse. The strings continued, but I turned the volume down in my head as I searched the rest of the painting for a pattern. I found it. It was hidden all over the painting.

I turned to Colin, who had not moved. "What do you see?"

"I don't know. Apart from the obvious, that is." He inhaled deeply, shook his head and looked at me. His eyes widened when he registered my expression. "What did you find?"

"Show me the original painting first."

Colin reached into his trouser pocket. "Will the smartphone screen be big enough for you?"

"It will suffice." I waited patiently until Colin found the painting online and handed his phone to me. I tilted the phone to eliminate the glare from the overhead lights on the screen. The painting on the small screen bore little resemblance to the one on the easel in front of me.

The difference was staggering. The only similarities were in the princess and the dragon being to the left of the painting and St George on his horse to the right. In the original, the dragon's head was lowered to the ground, his head low in submission. The princess controlled him with a leash and St George defeated him with a lance, blood dripping from the dragon's wound. In the background behind St George, a storm was building and the princess and the dragon were standing in front of a cave.

"Should I get a tablet in here?" Manny asked.

"No. This is…" My mind was distracted by what I was seeing. I zoomed in on the photo on Colin's phone and compared it to the juvenile-looking painting on the easel.

Colin leaned in to see what was on the screen, then also looked at the painting. By the time I confirmed a fourth pattern, Colin's breathing changed. "In my life."

"What?" Manny got up and walked towards us.

"I would not have seen it." Colin shook his head. "If it had been on an original artwork, maybe. But on this? Wow."

"What the bleeding hell are you babbling about?" Manny stood on Colin's other side, not crowding me. "Talk, Frey."

"It seems like Emad has cleverly disguised letters in his painting." Colin pointed at the point of the princess' cloak. "See the lines that look like they are folds in her cloak? That is an elongated 'V' and that is an 'I'. That one is also an 'I'. Oh, wait. There's another one."

"Oh, my." Alain got up and sat down again. "When they were children, I often played Scrabble with them. The boys loved it and were both really good at it. They got a bit bored with it in their early teens, so I found a way to make it more interesting. We would hide letters everywhere in the house. It had to be in a clever place, not a sock drawer." His smile was sad. "Emad was the best at finding smart hiding places and also finding the letters that were hidden. On Mondays and Tuesdays we would hide the letters, Wednesdays and Thursdays were for finding the letters and Friday was the day we got to use the letters we found to have a head start at making words."

"Well, we're not going to make a word with one 'V' and two 'I's." Manny looked at me. "Any more letters, Doc?"

"So far I've found three bundles of letters." I pointed at the top of the painting, just right of the centre. "In the original, the clouds are further to the right, but here you can see an 'I' and two 'X's'."

"Want to tell me what you think this means?" Manny's tone was the one he used when he was losing patience with me.

"Not yet. I want to make sure I have all the numbers." I turned my attention back to the two paintings. I don't know how long I stood there comparing the original to the badly copied masterpiece. I turned to share the conclusion I'd reached and my eyes caught the fresh coffee on the table.

"You found it all, Doc?" Manny pushed a steaming mug towards me.

"Yes." I took a sip of the coffee and exhaled in pleasure. "There are six batches of letters. I believe these are Roman numerals. There are only X's, I's and V's on Emad's painting. On their own they can't form words. But as Roman numerals, they might have value."

"What value, Doc?"

I turned to Alain. "Did you play any mathematical games with your children?"

"They didn't enjoy number games. Scrabble was our thing."

When I was at university, an acquaintance had invited me to play Scrabble with them. I had liked the concept and had excelled in combining letters to form words. An unpleasant argument had broken out when I had formed a fourth word they had never heard of. They had been resentful of my vocabulary as well as my intolerance of their ignorance. I hadn't received a second invitation.

"And you played no other games?" Phillip asked. "Maybe some other word games?"

"We did, but like I said, Scrabble was something that bonded us for many years." Alain rubbed his hand over his mouth. "Just before all this insanity started, Emad uploaded a Scrabble-type app to my phone. I never used it. It just didn't seem right to be doing something that reminded me of the time when they were still good boys. The time before both my sons became traitors and criminals."

"What numbers did you find, Jenny?" Colin glanced at the painting.

"If I put them in the order they appear next to each other, it would be XXXIV, XXI, XIII, VIII, V and III." A small smile pulled at the corners of my mouth when Colin's eyes widened. "You recognise this."

"Yes." Excitement lifted the corners of his mouth. "What do you think this means?"

"Doc! Frey!" Manny slapped his palm on the table. "What are you talking about?"

"The Fibonacci sequence." Phillip raised his eyebrows and shook his head. "Is there a possibility that it could be something else, Genevieve?"

"There is always that possibility, but since those are the only numbers that appear in the painting"—I drew a spiral with my finger in the air—"and since they appear in what would be the golden spiral, I doubt that it could be anything other than thirty-four, twenty-one, thirteen, eight, five and three."

"The sequence is not complete though." Colin leaned back in his chair. "We still need two ones."

"I don't want to speculate on what we don't have or why we don't have it. I'd rather focus on these numbers." This excited me.

"For the love of all the saints, would someone please tell me what this Fibrazzi sequence is?"

"Fibonacci." I sighed and looked at Colin. He would explain this complex mathematical marvel in a way more suited for Manny to understand.

He winked at me and turned to Manny. "It's a series of numbers where a number is added to the number before it to form the next number. So, zero plus one is one, one plus one is two, one plus two is three, three plus two is five and so on."

"And the purpose of this bloody exercise in counting is…?" Manny lifted both hands, his expression confused.

Colin shook his head and looked at the opposite wall for a moment before he looked back at Manny with a sigh and a look of disdain. "This sequence is said to have first been observed in the Hindu-Arabic arithmetic system. Fibonacci grew up in North Africa and studied it while there. These numbers are all around us. You can see it in hurricanes, galaxies, but the most common example is in sunflowers. Their seeds are uniformly distributed not matter how large the seed head may be. It all adds up."

"Someone better tell me what the hell this has to do with that painting." Manny shook his index finger at Emad's artwork.

"Maybe nothing, but most probably a lot," Colin said. "These numbers are used in the Fibonacci spiral, which is an approximation of the golden spiral. This is a series of connected quarter-circles inside a square, using the Fibonacci numbers for dimensions. This can be observed in many paintings from the Renaissance era, including the Mona Lisa."

"It will be easier to show you." I looked at Colin. "But for that I'll need my computer or at the very least my tablet."

"Should I get it for you?"

"Not now." Manny waved his hand as if to remove the suggestion. "Doc, just draw with your finger on that painting and show me."

I reared back. "I'm not touching a painting."

"I'll show you." Colin stepped closer to the horrid copy of Uccello's masterpiece and pointed at the bottom left corner. "It starts here, then curves up to include the princess and the dragon, tops out where the clouds start." He groaned. "The clouds are not supposed to start there, but I suppose Emad needed to make his point. Anyway, it then curves down around Saint George and his horse. The Fibonacci spiral continues to curve inward and here the final curve ends between the horse's front legs. It's a perfect fit for the spiral."

"Huh." Manny slumped deeper into his chair. "That's quite something."

"Do you think Emad is sending me some kind of message with this?" Alain tried to hide it, but hope was evident around his eyes, his mouth, even his posture.

"To quote Doc, it would be speculation." Manny shrugged. "But knowing what we do about Emad? Yeah, he's sending some kind of message."

"The question though is what that message is," Alain said. "We never talked about this mathematical sequence and I can't remember him ever mentioning something like this. I'm so sorry I can't be of any more help."

"You helped us a lot by bringing in the painting." Phillip put his hand on Alain's shoulder. "We'll figure this out."

"Hi, everyone." Francine walked into the conference room and stopped in front of me. "I'm glad you're okay."

I studied her expression and saw her sincerity as well as her concern. It took me a second to remember why she would be concerned. The mystery of Emad's painting and the Fibonacci sequence had taken my mind off Otto being assassinated next to me. "I'm unharmed. Emad sent a painting."

"I know." She glanced at one of the hidden security cameras in the room. "I've been watching. And listening." She turned to Alain. "Would you consent to me cloning your phone?"

"Why?" Alain lifted both shoulders.

"I heard you say that Emad had downloaded an app on your phone." She paused. "Did he have full access to your phone?"

"Before all of this, yes." He took his smartphone from his trouser pocket and put it on the table. "This is my private phone. He would use it to search for something on the internet or update my apps and programmes. He never touched my work phone. And I gave that back when I resigned."

Francine looked at the phone on the table. "I don't want to take your phone and leave you without your device, but if I have an exact copy—a clone—I might be able to find something that we can use to track Emad."

Alain thought about this. "I no longer have access to any confidential information. And I have nothing to hide." He pushed his phone across the table towards Francine. "Clone it. Find my son. But please, don't kill him."

"I'm confident they'll do their utmost to bring him in safe," Phillip said.

"But we need to bring him in whether he wants to surrender or not." Manny's expression conveyed a warning. "We can't pussyfoot around Emad. He's a national, if not international, threat."

Alain's shoulders dropped. "I know. Just try. That's all I ask."

Francine put her laptop on the table and plugged Alain's phone into her computer. "This will only take a minute or two."

It took three minutes. As the seconds ticked by, I noticed his distress increasing. The moment Francine finished cloning his phone, he took it, made his excuses and left.

"Um? Genevieve?" Tim stood in the doorway and looked nervously from me to Manny and back. He lifted the cordless phone in his hand. "I have an Ivan Fradkov on the line for you."

Both my hands flew to my sternum, my head shaking from side to side uncontrollably. I didn't want to speak to Fradkov. Why did he want to speak to me? I took three deep breaths and concentrated on stilling my head.

"What the hell?" Manny jumped up and grabbed the phone. "Can he hear us?"

Tim took a step back. "No, sir."

"Supermodel."

"Already on it." Francine was working furiously on her laptop.

"Timmy, tell me everything this man said." Manny shook the phone at Tim.

"Um… He said that Genevieve would want to speak to him. At first I told him that she no longer works here, but he insisted. When he gave his name, I recognised it. So I thought I'd come and ask what to do."

Manny turned to me. "Doc?"

It took a lot of effort not to shake my head again. I crossed my arms tightly over my chest. "I don't want to speak to him."

"We might learn something, Doc." His gentle tone surprised me. Did I look as frightened as I felt?

I uncrossed my arms and pulled my shoulders back. "Okay."

Manny looked at Francine. "You got this?"

"On it."

He held out the phone. "Keep him on the line as long as possible."

"Just press the green button." Tim took another step back when we looked at him. "That will connect you and put you on speakerphone."

I took another calming breath, determined to use all the knowledge I'd accumulated over the years to get as much from the next few minutes. I pressed the green button. "Hello?"

"Doctor Genevieve Lenard." Fradkov's voice was deep, his speech relaxed and with a sophisticated British accent. "What a pleasure to finally speak to you."

"What do you want?" I ignored Manny's scowl.

"Just a quick chat." His words were so quiet that I leaned a bit closer to the phone. "I wanted to formally introduce myself and also tell you that I'm really looking forward to sparring with you."

"I don't spar." I'd never even entered a boxing ring.

"Maybe not." He inhaled deeply and sighed as if content. "But don't you think it will be fun for the two of us, two such great minds, to go against each other?"

"No."

Manny was waving his hands in the air, then walked away from me shaking his head.

Fradkov's laugh was soft. He sounded genuinely amused. "Well, I think it will be the most fun I've had in years. Make sure that you sleep with one eye open, Doctor Genevieve Lenard. Those people always around you might be in danger."

"What do…" I didn't continue. Fradkov had ended the call.

"What the fuck was that?" Vinnie put his fists on his hips. "He's phoning you to fucking threaten us?"

"Supermodel?" Manny's voice was tight.

She closed her eyes and shook her head. "He rerouted the call. I traced it to Iceland, but I doubt I would've found his location. It kept bouncing from one country to the next."

"Bloody hellfire." Manny swung around and glared at me. "What do you make of this, Doc?"

I swallowed a few times to get rid of the horrid tension strangling me. When I spoke, my voice croaked. I cleared my throat and tried again. "He's playing a game. This is his move to intimidate us. To scare us."

And it worked. The fear that had gripped me when he'd threatened my friends would not let go. His gentle, cultured tone had unnerved me in a manner that surprised me.

I ignored Manny, Colin and Vinnie discussing heightened security measures and focused all my energy on pushing the conversation and the fear to the back of my mind. I would not give Fradkov power over my thoughts. I would not allow this phone call to disconcert me, to distract me from investigating this case and finding him.

"Then that's that. We'll all be more careful until we catch this bastard." Manny got up and waved with his hand towards the door. "Let's go home."

"It's far too early." I glanced at my watch, then looked again. "It's almost six o'clock."

"Yes, missy. Time to go home. All of this can wait until tomorrow morning." Manny turned to Vinnie. "I'm hungry. I hope you're making enough food today."

My stomach rumbled at the mention of food, reminding me that I'd never finished my lunch. Manny was right. The painting with the hidden Fibonacci sequence would still be here tomorrow. The investigation into Fradkov would still be here tomorrow. I got up just as Vinnie pushed away from the door frame.

"As if I ever don't make enough food." Vinnie crossed his arms. "And who invited you anyway, old man?"

"She did." Manny pointed his thumb at me. "She and supermodel."

Vinnie glared at Francine as she closed her laptop. "Just keep your grubby hands away from my spices and my food."

Chapter FOUR

I opened my bedroom door leading to the living area and was greeted by noise. This had become the norm in my life. Vinnie was in the kitchen cooking, shouting at Francine to put the turmeric down and leave his kitchen. Legally, it was my kitchen. Yet I couldn't remember the last time I'd prepared any food there. Vinnie had taken complete control of that part of my apartment.

When we'd arrived home, I'd gone straight to my bathroom and had a longer and hotter than usual shower. I wished it could've removed the remnants of fear after Fradkov's phone call. It hadn't. I had scrubbed every centimetre of my body even though Otto's blood had only splattered on my hands and forearms. Wearing jeans and a light sweater, I now felt like my skin once again belonged to me.

"Doc G!" Nikki pushed herself up from one of the two sofas and rushed towards me as fast as she could. Had it been eight months ago, she would've run, but her protruding stomach prevented her from moving too fast. She stopped in front of me, her stomach almost touching mine, and stared at me. "Are you okay?"

Nikki had entered my life in a manner similar to Colin, Vinnie and the others. Unexpectedly. Her father had been a criminal who'd been killed during one of our cases. A sequence of events had led to her sharing the connected apartment with Vinnie and becoming an important part of my life.

"I'm unharmed." I glanced down at her stomach. "How's your back today?"

"Fine. Today it's not my back, it's my feet. They're huge." She leaned to one side and awkwardly lifted one foot. "Look!"

I raised one eyebrow as I studied her narrow feet with metallic green toenails. "They look the same size as usual."

She put her foot down. "Well, they feel huge. I feel huge."

"You're beautiful, little punk." Vinnie put the dishcloth on the kitchen counter and walked to us. "How many times do I need to tell you that?"

"Until I no longer feel like I'm a waddling hippo." She swallowed her last word and her eyes widened. Then her expression softened. She grabbed my hand and placed it on the left side of her pregnant belly. "He's moving. Feel."

The first time Nikki had pushed my hand to her stomach, I'd gone into a shutdown. Feeling the growing life move under my hand had overwhelmed my senses so immediately, there had been no fighting the darkness. That had been four months and sixteen days ago. After that, Nikki and I had worked together until I'd been comfortable, even curious, feeling her baby boy move around her uterus.

A pointy body part pushed against my hand. It pulled back and pushed again, moving a few centimetres to the centre of Nikki's abdomen. Nikki lifted her hand from mine. She knew her touch was distressing. She also knew I would keep my hand on the soft t-shirt stretched over her stomach. "Eric has been very busy today. I think it might be the pastry I ate after breakfast. I asked the big punk to make a boring bolognese tonight. Last time we had that, my little guy really liked it."

Vinnie laughed. "I would love to think that my nephew loves my bolognese, but it wasn't he who really liked it. *You* had a third helping."

"I'm eating for two!"

I didn't correct her. Eric was moving again, but slower, less jerky. Vinnie and Nikki continued to banter, but my attention was on the little person growing in Nikki's stomach. I'd read twenty-seven books on pregnancy, childbirth and the first year of an infant's life. But I didn't feel prepared for the change this little boy was about to introduce to my life.

It had been a difficult three weeks when Nikki had struggled with the decision whether to keep the baby or give it up for adoption or terminate the pregnancy. I'd had my opinion and had freely shared it with her, but had wanted her to make the decision on her own. Those three weeks had been difficult for everyone. Manny had asked me three to six times a day if Nikki had made her decision and Vinnie had been withdrawn until Nikki had told us what she'd decided.

Despite her youth and her vivacious character, Nikki was mature beyond her years. Growing up with a father who'd been a notorious criminal, well-respected and feared amongst his peers, she'd learned very early the value of carefully considering one's actions and words. Everyone, me included, had been relieved and proud of her when she'd decided to not only go through with the pregnancy, but also keep the baby.

I hadn't been surprised when Nikki had told us that she'd decided to name her baby after her father, using his second name since his first name was too closely connected to his criminal history. She'd always known about his illegal activities and she'd always loved him. His death had been hard for her, but it had also been the reason she was now part of this circle of friends who had become like family.

"This happens every time, Doc G." Nikki's smile was gentle. "Eric is going bonkers inside and the moment you touch him, he calms down."

"I'm not touching him. I'm touching you." I lifted my hand from her stomach and put it behind my back.

"Oh, you're touching that little man, Jen-girl." Vinnie put his hand where mine was. "You even look all gooey when you do it."

"What does that mean?"

Colin got up from the sofa to stand next to me. "It means that your expression changes when you feel Eric move under your hand, love."

I looked at him in alarm. "I'm no longer afraid. Surely you can see it. My expression is not one of discomfort."

Colin pulled me closer to him and hugged me. "Oh, we all know that, Jenny. When Vinnie says gooey, he means that you look like that."

I followed Colin's pointed index finger to look at Vinnie's face. The harsh lines on his face had softened, his eyes were relaxed and slightly closed, the corners of his mouth lifted. The depth of his affection was unmistakeable. "That's 'gooey'?"

"Yes."

"I look like that?"

"Just prettier."

I continued studying Vinnie's face until he snorted. He kissed Nikki on her head and returned to the kitchen. She put both her hands over her stomach. "I think he's gone to sleep. Thanks, Doc G."

I nodded. I didn't know what else to do or say.

"Are you sure you're okay?" She tilted her head, concern pulling at the corners of her eyes. "Francine told me what happened. That's like really brutal."

"I've told you I'm unharmed. If you need a more detailed explanation of my emotional well-being, you should ask a better question."

"Well, ouch." Her smile belied the expression she'd started using of late. "Okay, let me think. Hmm." She cleared her throat. "Doc G, are you processing the assassination sufficiently? Are you emotionally handling this?"

I didn't understand why Colin laughed softly or why Nikki's micro-expressions bore evidence of humour. I ignored that and nodded my approval of her carefully thought-out question. I considered my answer. "It was a most disconcerting experience, but after my shower I'm feeling much more in control. I've processed most of what has happened and now have a strong desire to understand the assassination as well as the painting."

"What painting?"

"Food's ready!" Vinnie carried a large serving dish to the table, his floral oven mitts contrasting with his muscular build. "Come, people. I didn't cook this just for myself."

We moved to the table and the only topic discussed for

the next ten minutes was Vinnie's food and its effect on Eric. I'd learned not to get involved in these nonsensical discussions. Wasting time on improbable and most often impossible scenarios was part of light-hearted social interaction. It was hard enough for me not to dispute every point made about the culinary expertise of a foetus. It would be impossible for me to partake in this conversation and not get involved in arguing my factual points until everyone relented.

Instead of listening to the content of their inane conversation, I watched my friends, observing their body language. The *orbicularis oculi* muscles contracted the corners of Francine's eyes and her lips twitched with suppressed humour. She teased Vinnie every chance she got, most often with outrageous suggestions of spice additions to his family recipes. Without fail, Vinnie responded with threats to her health and well-being while Manny appeared bored.

Manny's micro-expressions in reaction to a particularly strongly-worded rebuff from Vinnie or taunt from Francine were proof that he was indeed interested in the conversation and enjoying it immensely. He no longer tried to hide the subtle glances he sent Nikki, especially her stomach. In the beginning, Manny had been very gruff about the pregnancy. After I'd confronted him about the fear visible on his face whenever that topic arose, he'd made an effort to be more expressive about his concern and love for Nikki.

Nikki's response to that confrontation had been to throw her arms around Manny and tell him repeatedly that she loved him too. He'd grunted and huffed, but had hugged her back and I'd seen pride, concern and affection on his face.

Vinnie's cooking was delicious as usual and everyone teased Nikki when she took another helping. Even though she joked about eating for two, her appetite had not changed much from before the pregnancy. Early on, she'd joined fitness classes for pregnant women, but had changed to yoga in her sixth month. Not only was she working hard to look after the baby growing in her, she had worked even harder to finish her art degree.

The last few years had brought many changes in my life. What had once been a routine, predictable existence was now filled with unpredictable chaos. This was the main reason for the cognitive dissonance I frequently experienced about my friends who'd come to play such an important role in my life.

It was sometimes hard to reconcile that so much time had passed since Nikki had moved in with us. Two weeks ago, she'd received the results from her exams and now had a BA degree. She'd decided to take the next year off to spend with Eric as well as decide what her next step in her career would be. I had watched her study and had been envious of the focus she'd had. I missed the academic and cerebral challenges that had accompanied my own studies.

"Right, Doc G?" Nikki bumped me with her shoulder. When I didn't respond immediately, she sighed. "You weren't listening to anything we said, were you? Ooh, no, wait. Please don't answer. You're just going to tell me, again, that I shouldn't eat any fish."

"I showed you the evidence from numerous sources that only fish high in mercury should be avoided." I leaned away from her. "You're teasing."

She winked at me, then looked at Colin. "What painting were you talking about earlier?"

"A very, very, very bad attempt at a reproduction." Colin told her briefly about the painting Alain was convinced had come from Emad.

In the beginning I had balked at involving Nikki in cases. Technically, she wasn't allowed to know anything about the crimes we investigated, but too many times our cases had drawn her in and put her life in danger. A few times she had even given valuable insight into a case.

Colin's explanation was interrupted by my front door flying open.

"I'm here! I'm here!" Doctor Roxanne Ferreira rushed into the apartment, then ran back to close and lock the door behind her. She dropped her handbag on the sofa and hurried to the table. "I tried. Really! But the head of oncology wanted to talk to me about some experimental treatments. And then Doctor Héroult wanted to know if I was going to the conference in Brussels next week." She grabbed Vinnie's face between her hands and gave him a smacking kiss on the lips. "I'm really, really, really sorry." She sat down next to him and looked at us, her smile bright. "Hi, everyone! I'm so hungry. Ooh! Bolognese." She reached for the serving plate. "I know I interrupted something. Sorry about that too. I'm just going to shut up now and eat. Please continue."

Francine had once described Roxy as a whirlwind. The last minute certainly made me agree with that analogy. Especially the disordered state of her curly hair. At one point during the day, she must have attempted to put her hair in a simple braid. Countless strands had escaped and were framing her face and it looked like the hairband she'd used needed only one more head movement to dislodge completely.

Despite her incessant tardiness and messy hair, I liked her. I especially liked that she was the reason for the gentle smile softening Vinnie's features. He took the serving plate from her and handed her the salad bowl. "Good thing I doubled the recipe. There's enough for second helpings for you and third helpings for the punk."

Roxy giggled and winked at Nikki. "Eating for two again, are we?"

"Hey, gotta keep my strength up. Being on holiday is hard work."

"Holiday." Roxy sighed long and loudly. "Yes, I know that word. I'm even sure I once had this thing you call a holiday. Enjoy it while you can, babe. Ooh, there I go again. Interrupting things. What were you guys gossiping about before I came in?"

"Colin was telling me about a bad painting." Nikki turned to Colin. "Do you have a photo of it?"

"I do." Francine picked up her tablet from next to her plate and swiped the screen a few times before she handed it to Nikki. "Swipe to the right for the original."

Nikki's eyebrows shot up the moment she focused on the tablet screen. "Wow. You weren't kidding. It's like this guy didn't even try to make it look like an Uccello original."

"You know who painted this?" Manny asked.

"Yup. I mean, he's like only one of the best Renaissance artists ever." She curled her lip. "Not the person who painted this abomination. He's really not an artist. Uccello was a true master with a style that was so unique, a lot of scholars prefer to call it idiosyncratic." Her eyes widened in excitement. "Did you know he was also a mathematician? Cool, huh? He was obsessed with perspective and legend has it that he wouldn't go to sleep until he got the exact vanishing point of whatever he was painting. He did a lot to pioneer visual perspective with his focus on creating a feeling of depth in his paintings. If you look at the works before his, they appear to be flat."

Colin leaned back in his chair, his expression calculating. "Okay, Miss Know-It-All. Tell me what you see."

"A test! Lucky me." Nikki's sarcasm was easy to recognise. It was always accompanied by a contraction of the *orbicularis oculi* muscles in the corner of her left eye, followed by a badly hidden eye roll. She gave Colin a look that attempted to communicate her fake ennui and turned her attention back to the tablet. For the next minute, the only sound around the table was Roxy's cutlery against her plate as she ate her bolognese. Nikki's tongue protruded between her lips as she tilted the tablet this way and that. A few times she zoomed in on parts of the painting before zooming out and swiping to see the original.

I watched her expressions closely for any recognition of an anomaly. When her eyebrows rose and her head tilted, I smiled. She zoomed and swiped until her narrowed eyes and slight smile told me she had come to a conclusion. "I see it! The letters. They are in the princess' cloak, the clouds and the horse's front legs. For such a bad painting, they're quite well hidden."

"How many letters do you see?" I was sure I'd found them all, but there was a remote possibility Nikki might see something I hadn't.

"Um. Seven. But they're like bundles of letters. Hey, wait! These are all V's, X's and I's." She looked at me. "Could these all be Roman numerals?"

"That is my inference, yes."

"Inference, huh?" She winked at me. "So what do all these Roman numerals mean? And how do we know which order to put these letters to get the right number?"

"Often, the simplest answer is the right answer. For now, I'm taking the letters in the order they appear. On the cloak, we see three 'X's, a 'V', and an 'I'. I'm reading it left to right and am concluding that we are supposed to see thirty-four."

"Okay." She drew out the last syllable while processing my answer. "But what order are the numbers in then? And what do they mean? Is it an IP address? A GPS co-ordinate? A telephone number?"

"I'm running the six numbers through a programme, hoping we'll find out where they're supposed to lead us." Francine reached for her tablet and Nikki handed it over. "But I do know it's not an IP address, a GPS co-ordinate or a telephone number. I checked all of those first."

"Hmm." Nikki looked at me. "You found something else with those numbers, didn't you? I missed something, didn't I?"

"Could it be that all those numbers are part of the Fibonacci sequence?" Roxy pushed her empty plate away and reached for her wine glass.

"Fibonacci?" Nikki looked at Roxy, then at me and back at

Roxy, her eyes big. "Oh, my God! We like totally studied the spiral in my first year. It's amazing how many paintings can have that spiral overlaid to show how well the painting fits in each one of those squares."

"I know." Roxy leaned forward. "The Fibonacci sequence forms what is called the Golden Ratio, which is one point six one six. Apparently our faces are most attractive when they have the Golden Ratio. And it is said that the distance between our first and second knuckle, and second and third knuckle, all have that ratio."

"How cool!" Nikki stretched her fingers out in front of her and stared at them.

"You'll find this interesting, Nix." Roxy smiled at Nikki. "There's a gynaecologist from Belgium who measured more than five thousand uteruses and found that the uterus ratio in newborn girls is about two and shrinks down to one point four six in old age. But, in the most fertile years of a woman's life, the ratio is around one point six. Fibonacci's Golden Ratio. Even the spirals of human DNA embody these proportions."

It amused me to watch both Manny and Vinnie follow the conversation. Manny looked bored and annoyed, but was listening intently. I knew he would catalogue the information and use it at a time everyone else would least expect it. Vinnie looked proud. When Nikki gave more examples of the Fibonacci spiral in art and even nature, he leaned back, his chest pushed out. And when Roxy continued with how the Golden Ratio had also been used in the pyramids in Egypt, a smug smile lifted the corners of his mouth. It was as if he was taking credit for his loved ones' knowledge and intellect.

"Okay, you two smartarses." Manny shifted in his chair. "Maybe you two can come up with a way to make this Finobracci circle relevant to Emad and Alain."

"It's the Fibonacci spiral." Nikki rolled her eyes. "I understand why Doc G gets so annoyed with you."

"It is exasperating." Especially since I was incapable of ignoring it.

Manny shrugged. "Doesn't matter what the name of that spiral-thingie is. If we don't know what to do with it, that thing is completely useless to us."

"Maybe there's an app for it." Nikki giggled when Roxy held out her hand to give her a high five. A few days ago, Manny had complained about all the apps Nikki had been talking about. Her generation used mobile applications to find restaurants, hail taxis, avoid traffic jams, monitor the number of steps they took each day and even collect comic characters at landmarks all over the world. Roxy had joined Nikki in teasing Manny for only having one app on his phone—a news agency's.

"An app!" Francine's loud exclamation startled me. "Nix, you're a genius!"

She grabbed her tablet and began to tap and swipe with intent. Nikki looked at Francine for another second, then shrugged, her eyebrow raised. "Of course I am a genius. It took you little people so very long to figure it out."

"Ooh! Ooh!" Francine stared at her tablet, her eyes wide.

"What happened, supermodel?" Manny leaned to the side to look at her tablet screen. He scowled. "What does that mean?"

"Um, I think it means what it says, handsome." Francine

turned the tablet for me to see the screen. "I put the clone of Alain's phone on my tablet and entered the numbers into the app Emad had uploaded to his phone."

"Alain said it was a Scrabble application." Which I assumed would require words.

"It looks like it, but I entered the Roman numerals in the order they appear on the spiral of his horrid painting and this is what it gave me." She shook the tablet a bit.

I narrowed my eyes and studied the screen. Huge white letters filled most of the screen, a photo of the badly painted copy of Uccello in the background.

"'Well done, Dad! You've just made it to the next level. Another clue on the way.'" Nikki frowned. "Another clue? Does that mean another butt-ugly painting?"

I didn't answer her. I didn't know what it meant. But I did know that we had just received irrefutable confirmation that Emad had sent the painting. And that this game he was playing had only just started.

Manny phoned Alain, but the older man hadn't heard from Emad or received another painting. Francine tried more options with the app, but didn't get any other results. In the end it was Roxy who convinced us to stop talking about work and retire to the entertainment area to watch a movie together.

It was a mindless action film with outrageous inaccuracies and physically impossible feats, yet it didn't bother me as much as it usually did. I was distracted and used the opportunity to mentally go over everything we'd learned in the last nine hours.

I avoided thinking too much about Fradkov's soft-spoken

threats, Otto's death and that the assassin was moving around freely knowing that we'd witnessed him committing premeditated murder. Most of my energy was spent on trying to connect Emad, Fradkov, the painting Alain had received and the Fibonacci sequence.

I needed more data. I only hoped it would not come at the cost of more lives.

Chapter FIVE

I was most displeased with the change in my routine. Even though Vinnie had made a valid argument for me joining him, I felt disoriented. I hated the feeling. There was a certain morning routine I liked to follow. This morning, I hadn't even had the opportunity to finish my breakfast.

Vinnie had received an early-morning phone call from his friend Justine, inviting him for breakfast. He'd been surprised that she was currently in Strasbourg and immediately suspected that she wanted to talk to him about Fradkov. She hadn't admitted as much, citing insecure phone lines, but Vinnie was convinced that there was no other reason for her invitation.

He had insisted I join him. Colin had assumed that meant he was to come as well and now the three of us were in an elevator in the highest-rated hotel in Strasbourg. I crossed my arms and looked at the hotel employee standing quietly next to the buttons. The security in this hotel was similar to most high-end European hotels and we couldn't go unescorted to Justine's presidential suite.

The man was in his mid-thirties with a strong jaw, high cheekbones and light brown eyes framed by thick eyelashes. His build and height would make him attractive to women of all ages. I was more interested in the unobtrusiveness he had mastered. His movements were controlled, his arms kept close to his body, his head was lowered and he seldom made eye contact.

"Did she say why she's in Strasbourg?" Colin asked Vinnie, glancing at the porter, who showed no reaction.

"She's here for something to do with her granddaughter." Vinnie also looked at the porter, but when the younger man showed no signs of listening, he continued. "She didn't want to share her trip too early in case someone found out about it."

I was fascinated by this. Both Colin and Vinnie were extremely security-conscious, yet the porter had successfully convinced them that their conversation was confidential. I wondered how many secrets this man had heard while taking guests up to the rooms.

I had many questions to ask Vinnie, but was not going to be lulled into a false sense of safety by the man's nonverbal skills. The short ride continued in silence until we reached the eleventh floor. The porter held his hand in front of the opened doors to indicate we could exit. He escorted us to a set of double doors and rang the doorbell.

A few seconds later, both doors swung open and we were greeted by a girl I estimated to be around seventeen years old. Her eyes widened and a smile lifted her cheeks when she saw Vinnie. "You're really here! I thought Granny was kidding."

Vinnie opened his arms and the girl rushed forward and threw her arms around his waist. Colin glanced into the living area, his eyes pausing on each painting that adorned the walls. No one noticed the porter leaving.

"Vinnie, you ugly so-and-so." An elderly lady came from a

room to the left of the living area, her body language welcoming. She was wearing loose dark beige pants and a flowing dark green top. A pale-green scarf appeared to have been carelessly knotted around her neck, completing the natural and relaxed-chic look. She had aged very elegantly. "Alexis, let these people in. You can't let them stand in the doorway all day."

"Oops. Sorry." Alexis stepped out of Vinnie's embrace and waved her hand towards the luxurious living area. "Please come in."

"It's good to see you again, my friend." Justine hugged Vinnie warmly, then kissed him on both cheeks. She looked at us as she stepped back. "You brought friends."

"Not just friends." Vinnie pushed out his chest, the pride in his expression evident. "This is my best bud and her pretty boyfriend."

Everyone laughed. I understood the importance of jest in any social situation, even though I didn't understand why Vinnie would belittle his best male friend by reducing him to mere physical features. I decided to ask Colin about this later and followed everyone into the suite.

The living area was spacious, the furniture of top quality and the finishings of similar standard to Phillip's business and home. This was clearly designed for those scant individuals who could afford such luxurious beauty.

I studied Justine laughing with Vinnie over something Alexis was telling them. She looked to be in her mid- to late fifties. Being the grandmother of a sixteen-year-old, she was most probably in her sixties. Genetics were in her favour, her skin showing only a few laughter lines and her figure slim. She moved with the grace of people who did yoga or dancing.

"Alexis, go do your internet things." Justine waved her granddaughter towards a door to the right. "We're going to plan to take over the world."

Alexis giggled and walked away singing about a pinkie and a brain. There was so much about the last five minutes I didn't understand. Yet I didn't ask. Already, my non-neurotypical brain was struggling with the change in routine. Spending too much time trying to analyse illogical behaviour was the next step to overwhelming my senses and going into a shutdown.

"Let's go into the dining room." Justine led us into a room with a dark wood dining room table that could seat six people. A beautiful chandelier hung from the ceiling and the table was set for breakfast. Justine sat down and regarded the food laid out in front of her. "I didn't know what you guys and gal eat, so I ordered everything. Carnivores and vegans alike can feast on this."

She was correct. There was a plate with assorted dried meats, another plate with cheeses, one bowl with whole fruit and another with a mixed fruit salad. Pastries, bread and a selection of yogurts and cereals completed the generous breakfast. Even though I hadn't eaten, I was hesitant to eat the food from a hotel I was not familiar with.

Vinnie saw my reluctance and chuckled. "This hotel has won quite a few awards and is highly rated on the travel blogs and sites."

"You're still reading all those cooking blogs?" Justine put

the dishing fork back on the plate with meats, but changed her mind and put another two slices of ham on her plate.

"This is not just any cooking blog." Vinnie reached for the pastries. "This woman goes to the best restaurants and hotels and does an inspection of their kitchen. She's brutal! The hotels and restaurants love and hate her. If your kitchen passes her OCD inspection, there will be a crazy influx of new customers. People like to know that their food comes from clean kitchens."

Still I didn't take any of the food.

Colin took a banana from the fruit bowl and held it out to me. "It's not like they can touch and contaminate this, love."

Justine's laughter filled the room. "Never thought about bananas that way. Must be the most hygienic fruit to eat then."

"Bananas are the only fruit that contains tryptophan, an amino acid. It combines with the vitamin B6 in bananas to help the body produce serotonin. Bananas can make a person feel happier." I took the banana from Colin and nodded when he held the coffee pot over the cup on my right.

"Oh, my word! You're a walking, talking Wikipedia." Justine's eyes were wide with mirth.

"Wikipedia is not a source to be trusted. There are countless inaccuracies in many articles. The information I have is accurate, without dispute."

"Well, there we have it then." Justine pointed her coffee cup at me. "I know you're Vinnie's best bud, but I would like to know your name."

"I'm Genevieve Lenard."

"Doctor Genevieve Lenard," Vinnie said before I could continue. "She's the smartest of us all."

"Not smart enough if she's hanging out with you." Justine winked at me. "And why do I have the honour of your presence, Doctor Lenard?"

"Vinnie insisted that I accompany him." I put the unpeeled banana on my plate. "I don't want to be here."

Her eyes narrowed and most of the jovial welcoming cues left her face. "Feel free to leave, my dear. No one is holding you at gunpoint."

"Jen-girl is just pissed off that I messed up her morning routine." Vinnie didn't look concerned at Justine's unfriendliness. "She will be glad she's here once you tell me why you invited me for this fantastic spread."

Justine nodded at Colin and me, but looked at Vinnie. "Are these the people helping you find Fradkov?"

"They are. They're the best, Justine. If anyone's going to find Fradkov, it will be me and my team."

"Hmm." She turned to Colin. "So you're the one Vinnie told me I shouldn't ask about."

Colin smiled. "You can ask. We're on the same side here."

"Yeah. We'll see about that." She glanced at me. "Look, I don't care who you are and what kind of doctor you are. All I care about is catching that fucker who killed my two boys and their wives. I would prefer to catch him myself and spend a few hours torturing the shit out of him, but I'm a bit busy with my four grandchildren. They should not be left on their own because their grandmother is in prison."

"That is a sensible decision." Although I was disconcerted

by seeing her genuine desire for revenge. The hatred when she spoke about Fradkov and her sons' deaths was real and strong.

Justine looked at the closed door of her granddaughter's bedroom. "She's here for a final interview for university. Gads, I'm proud of that girl. Hell, I'm proud of all my kids. Being the youngest, Alexis took the death of her parents much harder than the others. We've had to work really hard for her to have any kind of enjoyable adolescence. Mind you, she's the one who did most of the work. I've never seen anyone fight so hard against the viciousness that is depression."

"Having you there fighting with her made it easier." Vinnie's voice was gentle, his expression revealing the respect he had for this woman.

She snorted an unfeminine laugh and put her coffee mug down. "I'm a fighter, Vinnie. You know me. But you don't know how much I want to… no, how much I *need* to find that fuckface and kill him. The thing is, I'm not getting younger and I need to choose who and what I'm fighting for. My grandkids come first. Which means I'm going to need you to fight this one for me."

"It will be my pleasure."

She turned her attention back to me. "I need you to understand why I want Fradkov to suffer before he dies. He didn't only kill my sons and their wives. He used them in a cruel game." She swallowed as her blinking increased. Then she pulled her shoulders back, her lips tightened and her bottom jaw jutted. "Adam was eleven months older than Evan. They grew up as if they were twins and had always been best friends. Adam was the numbers guy and

Evan the people guy. When they decided to start a business together, many people thought it might damage their closeness. It didn't.

"They ran their investment company for eighteen years and never had one argument." She laughed. "No, that's not true. They constantly argued about the brand of coffee and tea Evan was buying. Adam liked stronger flavours and Evan would always buy the milder roasted coffees and fruity or flavoured teas. Yes, they did argue. But it was never serious."

She picked up her napkin and played with the seams. "Eight years ago, they signed a contract to handle the pension fund of the Department of Justice in Romania. Their reputation, their integrity got them that contract. Man, they were good at their jobs. Evan would reel the clients in and Adam would make their money grow in ways that the biggest investment firms would never achieve and most definitely would never guarantee.

"Six months later, strange things started happening. Someone broke into their office, but didn't steal anything. Adam had their computers checked for possible malware. Nothing. Evan had the office checked for all kinds of electronic listening devices. Nothing. But it was there. Those little bugs were so far advanced that the security company didn't find them.

"They were pinhole cameras that allowed Fradkov to not only listen, but also watch Adam and Evan as they worked. That's how he knew everything. How he knew exactly what to do to destroy my sons' careers, reputations and business."

No one spoke. Vinnie's expression led me to believe that he'd never heard the full story of Adam and Evan's murders.

Justine took a shaky breath and continued. "In my investigation later, I discovered that Fradkov had been hired by the opposition party in Romania to discredit the president. He took what he knew about Adam's strategy and used it to develop his own. That bastard knew where Adam planned to invest the money and when.

"So he fed false information to the media about these companies where Adam was to invest, ensuring that their stock fell moments after Adam bought in. My sons lost three hundred million euros in eight days. Most of that money was the Romanian government's. Fradkov then sent the local media in Romania expertly and viciously edited videos that made it look as if Adam was conspiring with the president to steal the country's money."

She folded the napkin and put it on the table. "But my Adam wasn't stupid. He used that footage to determine where the cameras were and hired another security company to take them out. He also paid ridiculous money to a hacker to find out who had accessed those cameras. And that's how he found out it was Fradkov. That hacker traced the connection back to a hotel in Bucharest where Fradkov was staying and managed to get a video grab of his face. It was a side profile, but it was enough. He put that photo up on the dark net and very quickly got a name.

"By now, the Romanian government as well as the French government were launching investigations against my sons. One evening, my sons were putting all the evidence they had together to hand over to their lawyer. Adam's wife Jenna and Evan's wife Anne were in Adam's house helping them. We'd agreed that Adam's two kids and Evan's two boys would stay with me for a few days so the adults could work undisturbed."

She clenched her teeth and took a few deep breaths. "Adam's home security footage showed how Fradkov entered the house from a side door, walked into the dining room where they were working and shot each of them." Her voice broke. "Twice in the head and twice in the heart. Jenna was last to die. The bastard ignored her crying and her pleas, just calmly walked to where she was cowering and killed her too."

It was quiet in the dining room. Fury showed in Vinnie's lowered brows, his tightened eyelids and his clenched jaw. Colin's expression was not as strong, but beneath the anger I did observe deep concern. I didn't want to lose myself in the emotionality of what had happened. Instead I put all my mental energy into analysing Justine's words and everyone's expressions.

I was deeply affected by the intensity of this woman's emotional pain. It had been eight years and her grief appeared as fresh as that of a person who'd lost someone a few days ago.

"I have questions." But I didn't know if it was appropriate to ask yet.

"Good." Justine straightened in her chair, shook her shoulders and looked at me. "Ask me."

"How do you know that it was Fradkov who killed your sons? Did you see his full profile on the footage?"

"Of course not. He was wearing a cap, glasses and had a big scarf around his neck, almost up to his ears." She lifted one hand to stop my next question. "But I'm not without resources, Doctor Lenard. Once the haze of my children's funerals lifted, I got to work. I hired all kinds of experts to analyse the video. They compared it with photos and a few other videos I'd been able to get on Fradkov and came to a unanimous decision that it had been him."

"How did you know to look for Fradkov? Did your sons tell you that he was the person behind the market manipulation?"

"No, they didn't. Not before they died." She pulled her shoulders back even more, pride flooding her face. "A week after they died a package arrived at my home. It was their failsafe. They had given it to their courier company to deliver at that date, unless one of my sons cancelled it in person."

"They knew their lives were in danger," Colin said.

"Yet they were fighting for the right thing. All of them were fighters. Even the petite and usually weak Anne."

"Fighters like their mom." Vinnie leaned over and squeezed her shoulder.

"You betcha big ass they were fighters." She patted his hand and moved out from under the gesture of sympathy. Her gaze returned to me. "One man. Only one man was responsible for my sons losing everything they'd achieved, for my grandchildren being orphaned overnight and for me losing both my children."

"What about a police investigation?" I asked.

"Oh, there was an investigation, all right. But between Romania and France, everyone was so scared to cause any more scandals that they didn't want to look too hard. There had already been two huge revolutions in Romania and they didn't want to cause another." Her smile was triumphant. "They thought they could get away with sweeping all of this under the rug, but there was no way I was going to let my grandchildren grow up reading about their fathers being involved in some illegal dealings. Not in this lifetime.

"So I gave the prosecutor an ultimatum. Either he made sure France as well as Romania cleared my sons of any and all wrongdoing or I was going to go public in the biggest, loudest way possible. I have enough money to produce a movie about this and pay broadcasters to show it. They knew it and relented."

I studied her. "You're not completely satisfied with the outcome."

"Of course not. I mean, I'm really happy that there isn't a single black mark on my sons' names, but their killer is still running around hurting other families. In order to get my sons' names cleared, I had to agree not to pursue Fradkov's prosecution."

"Why not?" Surely the police would like to convict a murderer.

"I've never been able to find out exactly why, but I'm ninety-nine percent convinced Fradkov has some dirt on both the French and the Romanian head prosecutors. Either that or he promised a revolution that was going to put Egypt's and Ukraine's revolutions to shame."

"So you decided to look for Fradkov on your own." Colin nodded. "I would've done the same."

Justine sighed. "I didn't take into account that I would no longer have as much free time having four teenagers in my house. Previously, I would've dedicated every waking moment to finding Fradkov. Not the last few years. I had to go to parent-teacher meetings, go shopping for new shoes, deal with teenage outrage because the teacher dared give them homework, control their internet access, check that they speak to real friends and not just tap away to social media friends, remember to feed them and"—she touched her hair—"remember to go to the hairdresser once in a while. So no, I didn't have much time to get that motherfucker."

"But you have people helping you." Vinnie leaned back in his chair. "And I'm willing to bet that someone came through with something."

She raised one professionally shaped eyebrow. "Money buys a lot of information and even loyalty. All I did was offer some criminal a nice monthly stipend and he keeps his ear to the ground."

"Why would he do that?" No one could get useful information from such an action.

"It's an expression, love." Colin took my hand and looked at Justine. "What did your guy find out?"

She looked from us to Vinnie and back. "Well, I suppose Vinnie has told you everything I've found out before, so I'm not going to bore you with that."

"I would like to hear it again." Mainly because I wanted to see her nonverbal cues as she shared the information. I might learn something of great value that she didn't tell Vinnie.

"Huh. Very well." She scratched behind her ear, her expression revealing her bemusement at my request. "Ivan Fradkov was born in Cuba, spent most of his childhood in that area, but went to the US to study politics. I've confirmed a few rumours about him working for national security agencies. So far, my guys have only been able to confirm his connections to the CIA and to the old USSR's KGB, but we're not sure about MI6, Germany's BND, Israel's Mossad or Iraq's INIS. But we do know that most of these places showed an interest in him as soon as he graduated. I reckon that one of them got him then. That's why he disappeared for such a long time."

She took the jug with orange juice, filled her glass and took a few sips. "Then, about seventeen years ago, he started his… er… career in politics. Something in those years must have triggered his interest in changing the course of history. His first big success was in Belgium in 1999. He was the power behind the push for the government to admit that there were dioxin-like toxins in the feed, eggs and tissue of millions of chickens. You should read about it. It's quite an interesting story. But for brevity's sake, I'll just say that the end result was that seven million chickens and fifty thousand pigs were slaughtered and discarded. It caused a food crisis in Belgium to the cost of around six hundred and twenty-five million euros."

Vinnie whistled, his eyes wide. "That's a shitload of money."

"Yes. Not only did many Belgians shop for meat and dairy products in neighbouring countries, but they had totally lost faith in the governing party. The CVP lost spectacularly in that year's elections, which ended their eight-year reign.

"Then he got really into it. One day I'll tell you all the detail. Hey, I might even write a book about it, but for now you only need to know that I have concrete evidence that Fradkov was behind the first campaign in Kiev that started the 2001 Ukraine-without-Kuchma mass protest campaign. Fradkov got a few people very heated about journalist Georgiy Gongadze's disappearance.

"The protesters went to the main plaza of Kiev in December 2000, insisting that there was a proper investigation into that journalist's disappearance and also that President Kuchma stepped down. Fradkov incited a few more such events which ended up in the prime minister being fired, but more importantly, it was the precursor for the big Orange Revolution in 2004."

She drank the rest of her orange juice and filled her glass again. "The list of all his conquests is long. I hate to say it, but Fradkov is a hugely intelligent and very successful man. He's never claimed responsibility or taken credit for any of the revolutions he's caused. He always works under the radar and is smart enough to know when he needs to outsource."

The slight contraction of her *orbicularis oculi* muscles around her eyes gave her secret away. I leaned back in my chair. "The person giving you information about Fradkov is someone he's outsourcing work to."

"Yes." She looked straight at me. "And that's all I'll say on the topic. To continue about Fradkov, he's been this successful because he's not greedy. He does maybe one job every twelve to eighteen months. But those are huge jobs. I have not been able to establish the exact fee he charges, but you can imagine."

"No, I can't." I had no frame of reference for remuneration related to criminal activities.

"Oh, I can, Jen-girl." Vinnie snorted. "I bet his fees are seven figures, if not more."

"That would be my guess as well." Justine nodded. "The kind of changes Fradkov's work brought made new presidents and new CEOs very rich and powerful. Or I should say, richer and more powerful. They already had more than enough money to part with a few million before they had their competition ousted. Now to get to the reason I invited Vinnie for breakfast." She pushed her glass away and leaned her forearms on the table. "Over the past few months, Fradkov's behaviour has changed. To the point of being so obvious that it's gotten a few mentions amongst his people."

"You've used far too many generalities and unclear expressions." I needed detailed information. "What about Fradkov's behaviour has changed? And who are 'his people'?"

Justine's eyebrow lifted and her eyes narrowed. She did not appreciate my need for clarity. "If you give me a moment to explain, I will tell you. Firstly, Fradkov used to communicate periodically with his people. Okay, okay. I'll first explain who 'his people' are." The way she rolled her eyes was befitting her grandchild, most definitely not a woman in her sixties. "As far as I've been able to figure out, there are five people who frequently work with Fradkov. Even though he has something very powerful to control them, they have proven their worth to him a million times over.

"And when I say a million times, I should actually say millions of euros. These guys have helped Fradkov infiltrate companies and government organisations through hacking, spying and all kids of subterfuge. Like I said before, he's been this successful because he's had a lot of help. As for knowing these five people's names, I don't."

"Tell me about Fradkov's change in behaviour."

She tilted her head and studied me. "Do you know that you sound really rude most of the time? I know I'm a bitch and that I'm rude and sarcastic, but your rudeness is different."

"My intention is not to be rude." I didn't want to explain my non-neurotypical mind to her. "But I do want that information."

"See? Rude in a not really rude way." She leaned back in her chair and waved with one hand. "Never mind that. Fradkov's behaviour. So, the last seven and some years I've had him on my radar, I've gotten to know his habits quite well. Like I said before, he's in contact with his people frequently. And when I say frequently, I mean at least once every two weeks. That's changed. In the last six months, he's gone as long as six weeks without making any contact.

"My guy was beginning to get happy because he thought that Fradkov was maybe dead and that would mean freedom. But he did make contact, only to go quiet again for three weeks, then five weeks. His communication was never predictable before, but it was within a two-week period.

"Another thing that has my guy scratching his head is that Fradkov has never gone this long without planning someone's demise. The contact he's had with my guy has not been about work, research or some criminal activity. It has just been to touch base."

"Touch base?"

"Ah, it's mostly an American expression. It means Fradkov has only been phoning his guys to stay in touch and make sure they're still living in fear of him. He's not been asking them to do actual work and all of them are waiting for the other shoe to drop."

"When did the first shoe drop?" And what did shoes have to do with Fradkov's change in behaviour?

Justine laughed and Vinnie chuckled. He leaned towards the older woman. "It's better to cut out most idioms and weird expressions, else you'll realise just how silly most of them are."

Her laughter disappeared and her eyes widened. She turned to me, regret in her expression. "You're autistic, aren't you? Dammit. If you'd told me, I would've been more careful with what I said. One of Alexis' friends is on the high end of the spectrum and it certainly taught me a few things about communication. Hmm. You make a lot more sense now."

"The shoe?" If this was an expression, I needed to know what she'd meant with it. I didn't need to have a long discussion about autism.

"Right. Back to business." She winked at me. "These guys are waiting for the real reason Fradkov has been this quiet. They suspect that something big is coming and that this 'something' is going to be big *and* bad. Especially since they started doing some covert investigation."

"Do these guys know each other?" Colin asked.

"Now they do, yes. In the beginning each one though he was the only one under Fradkov's control, but as time went on, they figured it out. They might be criminals and they might have landed under Fradkov's control, but they're not stupid. They suspect there are more, but these five have been able to find only each other.

"Anyway, one of them heard a rumour that Fradkov has been getting a lot of artwork forged. I have no idea what that's about, but knowing Fradkov as I do, it's important.

Apparently, there are also rumours that he's in contact with some fringe, fanatic, extremist group in Belarus. No matter how hard they tried, they've not been able to verify it. They're scared to push too hard for intel in case Fradkov gets wind that the men he controls are investigating him."

"Gets wind means that he might find out." Colin squeezed my hand and nodded for Justine to continue.

"Gads, I didn't even realise I'd said that. Huh." She shook her head. "Anyway, the guys are still looking into this Belarus rumour. It's not like Fradkov has never taken on a country at war or a country with ties to Russia. There should be no reason for him to withhold this if he has plans for Belarus."

"Will you let us know if they find anything?" Vinnie asked.

"For you, Vinnie?" Her smile was genuine. "I'll do anything."

"And if you have any other pertinent information," I added.

Her expression sobered. "I'll give you everything I have as long as you get that fucker. I've spent more time in psychologists' waiting rooms than any grandparent should ever have to. My grandchildren have suffered immensely because of one man. A man who has so much power that he's managed to never leave prosecutable evidence behind. Or if he has, he's been able to make it disappear or make his accusers disappear. He should be stopped. Not just because I want him wiped from this planet. But because he's a threat to the political and economic stability of this planet."

Justine had nothing else of value to share with us and after three more minutes of her expressing her desire to see Fradkov die and another five minutes of her boasting about her grandchildren, I was desperate to leave. Fortunately, I was not the only one who wanted to get back to the team room. Another long three minutes later, we were in Colin's SUV, Mozart's Symphony No.15 in G major quietly filling the interior.

The sound of my phone ringing interrupted the light-hearted music. This morning, I'd used a handbag that I had bought last year and had never used. It was one of the few purchases I'd regretted. In the shop, I had thought the extra pocket worked into the lining would be useful. It had not been. Every time I'd put my wallet or smartphone in my bag, this gaping pocket would get in the way.

The same way it did now when I reached into this bag to get my phone. I glanced at the screen and wondered why Roxy would phone me and not Vinnie. "Hello?"

"Oh, God. I'm so glad you answered. I thought I would have to phone a million times like before."

"What do you want?"

She giggled. "Are you with Colin? Maybe Vinnie?"

"I'm with both." I glanced at Colin as he turned off the music.

"Put me on speakerphone. Everyone's going to want to hear this."

I tapped on the speakerphone icon and held the phone between the driver and passenger seats. "We can all hear you now."

"Hi, guys!" She didn't wait for them to answer. "So, I've had an interesting morning so far. I had just waltzed into my office when a nurse came rushing in. They brought in some diplomat who was on death's door. Ooh, sorry, Genevieve. The guy was a few minutes away from dying. So, off I run to his bed to see what was wrong with him and guess what?"

My eyes widened when her pause indicated she genuinely expected us to guess. I inhaled to tell Roxy precisely what I thought of her inane tactic, but Vinnie spoke first. "What?"

"The man had radiation poisoning."

"You could make that determination by just looking at him?" I found that hard to believe.

"Well, no." Her tone was the same as Nikki's when she was overstating the obvious as if we were dim-witted. "At first it looked like a rash and some exhaustion, but then I remembered that Gallo guy and that's when I knew. Radiation poisoning!"

Seven months ago, Marcos Gallo had poisoned himself with polonium-210 in a convoluted effort to help Fradkov achieve his goal of causing dissent in Russia. I still shuddered when I thought about the effects of the radiation poisoning on Gallo's body. "Have you run tests to confirm?"

"I have and here's the scary part." She paused for dramatic effect. "It's polonium-210. The same that poisoned Gallo."

"What did the man say?" I turned to Colin. "Let's go to the hospital."

"Don't bother. He died two hours after they brought him in." Even though Roxy tried to hide it, I could hear the distress in her tone.

"Who was he?" Colin asked.

"Aleksei Volyntsev. Apparently some Russian diplomat."

A myriad of thoughts rushed through my mind. It would be too great a coincidence if this death, this polonium-210 poisoning, was not related to our case. Otto's murder, Emad's painting, the Russian diplomat's death were somehow connected. But how I didn't know. Not yet.

Chapter SIX

"Doc, I need you to promise me that you'll be diplomatic." Manny glared at Colin when he snorted. "Bugger off, Frey. This is serious."

We were standing on the pavement outside the consulate general of Russia in Strasbourg. After Roxy's call, I'd phoned Manny and told him about the diplomat's death. He'd told us to go straight to the consulate general building and wait there for him. Strangely enough, he'd insisted on Vinnie giving his word that the men would keep me in the car and wait until Manny arrived before we spoke to anyone.

"Doc!" Manny wasn't slouching or hiding his hands in his trouser pockets. He was genuinely concerned. "Promise me."

"I am intelligent and informed enough to know that France's and Europe's relationship with Russia has always been delicate. I also understand that giving offence to someone as important as the consul general would not only be insensitive so soon after losing a colleague, but could potentially block our access to their assistance in this case." I mirrored Manny's body language by raising both eyebrows, leaning forward and placing my fists on my hips. I didn't look in his eyes though. "I will be careful with my interaction."

Immediately, Manny's posture lost some of its tension. He stared at me for a few more seconds before he pushed his hands in his pockets, his shoulders slouching. "Good. I'm counting on you, Doc. We don't know what kind of reception we're going to get in there and I want to get as much information out of those Russkies as possible."

"Who's undiplomatic now?" Colin shook his head. "Jenny's got this, Millard. Maybe *you* should worry about not offending the Russians."

"All I'm saying is that we don't know why this Alex Volyntsev died of polonium-210 poisoning. Maybe he was poisoned or maybe he worked with it and that's how he got sick. Maybe he was the poisoner."

"Too much conjecture." I hated it. "Our time would be put to better use speaking to the consul general."

"True dat, Jen-girl." Vinnie smiled at Manny, but it wasn't a sincere smile. It was smug and provoking. "Let's go chat to those Russkies."

Manny turned to Vinnie, a smirk pulling at his lips. "You're not going, big guy. Privott only got Frey's alias, Doc and me in. You're going to have to stand out here and look pretty. Well, look unpretty."

"Prissy Privott?" Vinnie didn't have much patience for the director of public relations for the president of France. At times I agreed that Julien Privott seemed to spend more time lecturing us about political fallout and optics than helping us when the president assigned us a case. Vinnie's top lip curled. "That little brown-noser will fall over in a light breeze. If I'm not going in, who's going to protect Jen-girl in there?"

"Since I'm totally useless, I assume Frey will have to do it."

"That's not what I meant and you know it, old man." Vinnie's anger was masking the fear I wasn't surprised to see.

I stepped in front of him, but couldn't get myself to touch

him. I did manage to move a bit closer than my usual personal space allowed. It got Vinnie's attention. Most neurotypicals would've made eye contact at this point. I didn't. I stared at the *depressor anguli oris* muscles pulling the corners of his mouth down. "I'm safe, Vinnie. Colin and Manny are with me. We are going into an official building and as far as I can recall, no murders have been reported at these premises."

"Ever," Manny added. "Doc is safe, big guy."

Vinnie didn't take his eyes off me. "What should you do when someone starts shooting?"

"I should drop to the floor and seek shelter." I blinked a few times. "But what I should do and what my brain allows me to do in challenging situations are not always the same thing, Vinnie."

"Not helping, Jen-girl." Vinnie swallowed. "You stay safe in there, you hear?"

Neurotypical people often needed lies to placate them. I couldn't offer this to Vinnie. "I promise to try my best to be careful what I say and be watchful."

"You do that." He looked at Colin. "Bring her back, dude."

"Oh, for the love of all the saints!" Manny looked up to the cloudless sky. "We're not going into battle."

"And what about me, Vin?" Colin pressed his palm against his chest, his expression of emotional hurt insincere and exaggerated. "You're not worried about me? Your best bud?"

"Oh, fuck off." Vinnie huffed and took a step back. "Just watch your back in there."

"Love you too, Vin." Colin slapped Vinnie hard between the shoulders and pointed with his chin to the beautiful building. “So? Are we going in or do you also want me to promise to be a good little boy, Millard?”

“Don’t irritate me, Frey. I only need Doc in there with me. Give me more grief and I’ll leave you with the gorilla out here.” Manny nodded at Vinnie. “Wait here for us, big guy. And stay in touch with supermodel. I’m still waiting for her to send me everything she’s found on Volyntsev.”

I hiked my handbag strap higher on my shoulder and followed Manny to the beautiful wrought-iron gate. A small sign next to the gate stipulated the opening hours. Today was Tuesday, which meant it wasn’t open to the public. Manny didn’t press the button to ring the bell. Instead he looked up at the camera situated above the gate. “Colonel Millard and Doctor Lenard to see the consul general.”

Four seconds later a buzzing sound came from the gate. Manny pushed it open and waved me through. “After you, Doc.”

Colin followed me through the gate and we walked to the large wooden doors. Colin lifted his hand to ring the bell, but didn’t get the chance. One of the two doors opened. The nonverbal cues of the obese man standing in the door did not communicate welcome. His tight lips and narrowed eyes clearly conveyed his displeasure with our presence.

He first assessed Colin, then gave me a furtive look before studying Manny. Either he was under the misconception that women didn’t pose threats or he was uncomfortable with my presence. His lips thinned when Manny hunched over and pushed his hands in his pockets. He stepped back with an irritated sigh. “Mister Millard, I assume. Come in.”

“Ah, that would be Colonel Millard, old chap.” Manny’s

smile was wide and would look sincere to someone who didn't know him or who wasn't an expert in nonverbal communication. He walked past us and the large man into the entrance hall. "I'm much obliged that you could fit us in so quickly."

Colin shook his head and gestured that I should follow Manny. The large man was not paying attention to us at all. His eyes followed every movement Manny made. So, I went inside and Colin closed the door behind us.

The rubber soles on Manny's shoes squeaked on the light marble entrance hall floor. He walked to one of the many paintings on the wall and nodded as if he knew what he was looking at. "Such a pretty picture."

"It's a masterpiece. Not a picture." The clipped words carried no friendliness. "My name is Roman Kuvaev. I'm the head of office and assistant to the consul general."

"Ah, so you're going to take us to meet him now." Manny's tone and micro-expressions communicated his low opinion of the man in front of us. I wondered why Manny was acting contradictory to the manner in which he had insisted I should behave. He was rude and his passive aggression was inviting loathing from the obese man.

Roman turned to a corridor to our left. "If you'll follow me."

Again Manny waited for Colin and me to go ahead of him. When Colin passed Manny, he raised his eyebrows. "What the hell, Millard?"

Manny's only response to Colin's whispered question was to slouch even more. I suspected he intentionally dragged his feet so his shoes would squeak even more on the beautiful marble floors.

The corridor was long with doors on both sides. Numerous paintings filled the exposed walls and a few times Colin's eyes widened in recognition. It would be no surprise if many, if not all, of the paintings were originals.

Roman entered the second-last door to the right without looking back to make sure we were following him. I gave one last look at the corridor behind us before I followed Manny and Colin into a richly decorated office. Roman walked to the desk and waved at the antique chairs lining the wall. "Wait."

Manny sat down hard in a chair and raised both shoulders when Roman glared at him. I was most definitely going to ask Manny about his behaviour as soon as we left this place. I sat down, leaving a chair open between us. Colin walked to a painting hanging above a small table with a vase holding twenty-six white roses. Again, his eyes widened as he looked at the painting and his lips parted as he leaned in. Another original.

Roman picked up the phone on his desk and pressed a button. It was fascinating to watch the change in his micro-expressions. Where his *depressor anguli oris* muscles had pulled the corners of his mouth down, they now relaxed until his lips were fuller and lifted in a slight smile. His *procerus* muscles no longer pulled his brow into a scowl. Now the *corrugator supercilii muscles* moved his eyebrows slightly into what was called a thinker's brow.

Combined with the tension in his shoulders, it was easy for me to surmise that he was paying careful attention to someone he held in high regard. My Russian language skills were such that I understood when he replied to the other person, agreeing to making us coffee after he showed us into the consul general's office. He ended the call and walked towards us, his expression less severe when he looked at Manny. "Tea or coffee?"

"Tea would be grand, old chap. With a dash of milk, if you please."

Roman nodded and turned to me, eyebrow raised. I just shook my head.

"A cup of coffee would be fantastic." Colin's smile was genuine when he turned to face Roman. "It would only add to the pleasure of looking at all these breathtakingly beautiful works of art."

Colin had said the right thing. Roman's posture relaxed, his expression softening even more when he focused on the landscape. "Victor Borisov-Musatov was my grandmother's favourite. We couldn't afford art, but she had posters of his paintings, including this *Still Life with Flowers*. All of them were in beautiful frames. This one she put in her bedroom because she said she wanted that beauty to watch over her as she slept. The other two paintings were in the living room. She always made sure our guests noticed and appreciated the paintings."

"Your grandmother had great taste. Borisov-Musatov is known to be the creator of the Russian symbolism style. He did such amazing post-impressionistic work and was a master of bringing symbolism, realism and pure beauty into each painting."

Roman regarded Colin for a few seconds, trying to keep his expression neutral. But I noticed the interest as well as respect his micro-expressions revealed. The large man might not like Manny and might disregard me, but Colin had won him over. He nodded. "I will bring your coffee, sir. If you'd please follow me. The consul general is ready to see you."

Colin held out his hand to me and waited until I joined him. Then he looked at Manny and scratched his nose with his middle finger. Manny uttered a rude noise as he got up and joined us. Roman walked to a heavy wooden door to our left, knocked once and opened it. He looked at Colin. "Please enter."

We stepped into a spacious room. To the left was a table with six chairs, clearly designated for small conference meetings. Behind it, a dark wood bookshelf filled most of the wall. Cream and gold curtains hung on each side of the large windows. The cream carpet covering the floor was lush and of obvious quality.

The desk in front of the windows was larger than the conference table. It was void of any clutter. Only a leather-bound daily planner, computer monitor, keyboard and mouse populated the surface. The man sitting at the desk studied us for another two seconds before he got up. "Colonel Millard?"

"That would be me, sir." Manny straightened, stepped past Colin and extended his hand. "Let me start by offering my condolences for your tragic loss."

"Nikolai Guskov." The consul general came around his desk and shook Manny's hand. "Thank you for your kind words, Colonel. This tragedy came as a great shock to us."

"Let me introduce my team." Manny turned to Colin and me. "This is Doctor Genevieve Lenard and…"

"Isaac Watts." Colin stepped forward and shook the consul general's hand. "I'm so sorry for your loss, sir."

"Thank you." Nikolai Guskov's brows lowered, the corners of his mouth pulling down. His grief was genuine. He waved at the conference table. "Shall we?"

No sooner had we settled around the table than Roman came in, carrying a silver tray. The tea and coffee were in silver pots, the crockery fine cream porcelain with gold around the rims and ears. Judging by the quality and opulence of our surroundings, I was confident that the teaspoons were real gold.

As soon as Roman established that he was no longer needed, he left the room and closed the door quietly behind him. Nikolai Guskov stared vacantly at the polished silver coffee pot in front of him. "Al was a good man."

"Al?" I had no idea who he was talking about.

He jerked as if startled into wakefulness and looked at me. "My apologies. Aleksei Volyntsev was not only one of the best diplomats I ever worked with, he was also a friend. A good friend."

Since the moment we'd walked into his office, Nikolai had not once exhibited signs of insincerity. I studied him as he struggled to control his emotions. He was of average height, and his fit body looked like he led an active life. I couldn't estimate his age, but his youthful looks were a genetic advantage that would always make him appear younger than he was. His manicured hands, elegant suit and styled hair were evidence that he valued his appearance.

"It's never easy losing a friend." Manny's tone was gentle, his nonverbal cues sincere. I found the change in his behaviour jarring. And fascinating. I wanted to understand what it was in Roman that had elicited Manny's contempt.

None of that was now visible. He leaned closer to Nikolai. "When did he get sick?"

"A few weeks ago, he complained that he got a head cold." A sad smile pulled the corners of Nikolai's mouth sideways. "He always suffered terribly from seasonal allergies and was happy when winter finally arrived. So when he felt like he had a cold, he was quite angry. He loved spending the weekends with his kids skiing and this cold made it hard for him to enjoy anything."

"Was he at any meeting or conference or did he travel somewhere before he caught this cold?" Manny asked.

Nikolai frowned and looked up at the ceiling. When he looked back at Manny, he shook his head. "No. Al was busy with the exhibition and didn't go anywhere for about three months. So travelling is out of the equation. But meetings? All the time. We spend three to seven nights a week at some event and twice or three times a week during the day. There's always something."

"Could you tell us more about the exhibition?" Colin's dilated pupils indicated that he was interested and wanted to absorb as much information as possible.

"Oh, that is something I'm very proud of." Nikolai's chin lifted, his shoulders pulled back. "This was just one of the many reasons Al and I became friends. We shared similar passions, similar visions. Both of us want Russia to become a leading power in the world when it comes to culture. Music, art, poetry, writing—Russia has always produced some of the best works in the world. Al and I envisioned Russia empowering her people by channelling the creative arts as well as academia into something more mainstream."

"I assume you have a great passion for the arts." Colin nodded at the three paintings on the wall facing the windows. "Those are great reproductions."

"Thank you." His eyes narrowed. "How did you know they were not the real thing?"

Colin chuckled. "The fact that the artist signed his name under the original artists' names. I've always believed it takes a master to produce a masterpiece, but a gifted master to reproduce that work. Jacques Prouvé is well known in the art world as one of the most gifted masters when it comes to reproducing post-impressionist paintings."

"You know your art." Nikolai leaned towards Colin. "Al would've loved chatting with you. He was the one who gave me Prouvé's name. My wife has not forgiven him for that. I've spent far too much money on spoiling myself."

"Collecting beautiful artworks can be very addictive." Colin paused. "I assume the exhibition was only authentic artworks?"

"Oh, yes." Nikolai nodded. "Al insisted on it when Lev came to him with the proposal. You see, Lev Markov is a close ally to the president of Belarus as well as a good friend to Al. After a scandal involving Lev's father-in-law, he was no longer welcome in his own country and settled here in France. As a matter of fact, he lives here in Strasbourg. Despite the distance, he still remains friends with President Pyotr Grekova."

Art, exhibitions, polonium-210 poisoning and now politics? I paid close attention to everything Nikolai said as well as every accompanying micro-expression. All these factors were related to Fradkov, so I didn't want to miss even the smallest detail.

"A bit more background." Nikolai sat back in his chair. "Last year, Al and I started UTA, the Unity Through Art project. We have the Russian government's full backing to grow this so we can reach as many people as possible."

"What is this project?" Manny asked.

"In short, we aim to bring music, art, poetry, writing and acting to the EU, but especially to those territories previously part of the USSR. There are a lot of people and politicians in Russia who would like the image of Russians being warmongers to change. We are lovers and poets. Artists and musicians."

"The darker side of your history is difficult to deny though," Manny said.

"True. Al and I hoped to use the UTA project to be a step towards healing some rifts. We organised one classical music concert and two jazz concerts here in Strasbourg. Both were huge successes. That's when Lev heard of us. A day after the first jazz concert, he came to me with the idea of an art exhibition. It turned out that President Grekova wasn't the only influential person he knew. He has countless contacts in the international art world.

"Within two weeks Lev was able to secure paintings from Renaissance artists from seven different museums in five different countries. Together with Al we planned the exhibition. It opened here in Strasbourg, then moves to Belarus, Ukraine, Georgia, and so on."

"Those are countries closest to Russia with a more recent history of war or political uprising." I followed the news closely and these countries all had recent volatile political situations. "What about Poland, the Czech Republic, Slovakia,

Estonia, Latvia—"

"Russia has as much damage control to do in those countries as elsewhere, but we had to prioritise." He didn't look pleased with it. "I wanted to include all the old Soviet states, but we were not permitted. So we decided to take it one step at a time, one battle at a time."

I inhaled to ask about their war strategy, but Colin put his hand on my forearm and shook his head. I thought about it for a second and nodded. An interesting expression to use, especially from someone who wanted to change the perception of his country.

"Where are the paintings at the moment?" Colin asked. "Still here in Strasbourg?"

"No. Our exhibition here ended two weeks ago. The next one is in Belarus. In Minsk. Some of the paintings are already there and some are on their way there now. It's a logistical nightmare to move these valuable works across borders."

"How many paintings do you have in the exhibition?" Colin shifted in his chair to lean even closer to Nikolai, closer to the topic that always brought more colour to his complexion and expression to his face.

"Two hundred and seventy-three." Nikolai smiled. "I still can't believe we actually got so many amazing artworks together. There are two Gozzolis, one Pisanello, two Clouets and works from Bellini, Tintoretto and Donatello. It's a breathtaking exhibition."

"Yet I didn't hear anything about it." Colin's tone was neutral, but I saw the suspicion around his eyes. "Why not?"

"The exhibition here in Strasbourg was an unofficial opening. Lev hosted it in his home and didn't want it open to the public. Only a few selected people were invited to three separate viewings. And since France wasn't part of the USSR, it didn't make sense to fight for an open exhibition. Belarus will be our official opening and from then on it will be open to the public in each location."

"Could you be so kind as to send us a list of the paintings as well as the planned exhibitions?"

"I'll get Roman to do it as soon as we're done here." Nikolai frowned. "You know, Monsieur Privott only told me that you would be here to ask me about Al's death. He didn't say anything about the exhibitions."

Manny cleared his throat, drawing Nikolai's attention. "I'm sure your government is also looking into this since Aleksei died from radiation poisoning. Surely you can understand that we need to investigate every detail to make sure that this is not something that could be a threat to national or even international security."

Nikolai looked at Manny for two seconds before smiling. "Your answer is one I would give when I didn't want to show my hand. You know something about Al's death, don't you?"

Manny slumped slightly. Barely visible expressions revealed his inner debate. He looked at me. "Doc?"

"Yes?"

Manny's lips thinned. Then he took a deep breath and turned to Nikolai. "My apologies, but I need to know if I can trust you." He looked at me again. "Can we trust him?"

"I don't know." I sighed when Manny's nostrils flared. "I only have the context of our conversation. Based on that, Consul General Guskov has been truthful most of the time."

"Most?" Nikolai moved his arms from their relaxed position on the arms of the chair to cross in front of him. "And you'd better call me Nikolai if you're going to call me a liar."

"I didn't call you a liar. You said there are a lot of politicians and people in Russia who would like Russia's image to change. When you said 'a lot', your blinking increased and you touched your neck. You don't believe there are a lot of politicians and people… ah, so only politicians then." It had been easy to see his different reactions to the two groups. I found it fascinating to meet someone so closely connected to politics who exhibited such a strong loathing for politicians. "You don't believe politicians are interested in promoting peace."

"Who are you?" Nikolai's brow lowered and he stared at me.

"Doctor Genevieve Lenard." I thought about our conversation so far and added, "You may call me Genevieve."

"She's the best body language expert the world has to offer." Manny nodded once. "And to answer your earlier question, we don't have specific information about Aleksei's radiation poisoning. But we are investigating another case that we suspect might be connected to your friend's death."

"Could you share anything with me?"

"Not at this time." Manny pulled his smartphone from his trouser pocket and frowned at the screen before he put it back. "Can I rely on you to give us your full co-operation?"

"Absolutely." Nikolai glanced at the door, closed his eyes for a second and took a deep breath. "I love my country. Russia is unlike any other place in the world. But there are things that I'm not proud of. I suppose everyone feels like that about their countries. I'm hoping that I can bring some change, no matter how small. It might just snowball into a bigger change that could make Russia the country I believe she can be." He chewed the inside of his cheek, his internal debate visible on his face. "What I'm trying to say is that I want to stop bad things and make good things happen."

Manny lifted one hand to stop Nikolai. "I understand. Enough said."

"Thank you." Nikolai's shoulders lowered in relief. He got up, walked to his desk and came back with a business card. He handed it to Manny. "If you need any more information, please don't hesitate to contact me."

Chapter SEVEN

"You'll have to ask Millard, love." Colin waited until I exited the elevator and followed me into our team room. On the way here, we'd talked about our impressions of Nikolai Guskov and his assistant Roman. Vinnie had eagerly listened and had asked intelligent questions. This had helped me to organise my observations in my mind.

"Ask me what, Doc?" Manny was standing next to Francine's desk, his hand on her shoulder. As Colin, Vinnie and I got closer, he put his hands in his trouser pockets.

"Why did you act like a buffoon in front of Roman, but treat Nikolai as a respected peer?"

Francine turned to look at Manny, her eyes wide. "A buffoon, handsome? I'm shocked."

I didn't know why Francine was lying, but was more interested in Manny's answer than confronting her about it.

Manny took a step away from Francine and shrugged. "That Roman pissed me off."

"Why?"

"Why, Doc?" Manny huffed. "He looked at us as if the cat had dragged us in, dismissed you as a nobody, then fawned all over Frey about a stupid painting. And you're asking me why that pissed me off?"

"Yes."

Manny's nostrils flared when my simple answer caused Vinnie

to laugh. Manny's lips thinned even more and he walked to the round table. "I'm not getting into this with you now, missy. I'm hungry and I want to eat."

Francine got up and stretched. "I ordered Chinese from that place you like, girlfriend. We might as well go and eat before Manny gets hangrier."

I pulled my lips between my teeth to prevent myself from commenting and joined everyone at the table. The familiar smell of Gong Bao chicken brought the realisation that it was twelve minutes past one and I hadn't eaten anything since the one piece of toast and coffee I'd had at home this morning. I hadn't even eaten the banana in Justine's hotel suite.

I sat down in my usual chair and just couldn't contain it anymore. "Hangry should never have been accepted as a word. I accept the evolution of language, but this is a ridiculous word."

"For once we agree, Doc." Manny opened one of the cardboard containers and inhaled. "Ah, sweet and sour pork. Thanks, supermodel."

It was quiet around the table for a few minutes while everyone ate. This Chinese restaurant was one of three places in Strasbourg from which I accepted takeaway food. The owner was a rude, small Chinese woman who spoke in staccato sentences. Despite complaining both times I'd insisted on inspecting the kitchen, she had proudly showed off what happened behind the closed doors.

Her staff's body language had revealed their fear of her temper, but they had been proud to give me a demonstration of completing an order. The fresh products, gleaming surfaces and obsessive cleaning had placated all concerns I'd had about their food.

I took another bite and watched Francine as she once again swiped her tablet screen. Something was causing her great concern. When we'd walked in, I had noticed her biting the inside of her bottom lip the way she did when she fretted about something.

My first thought had been that Fradkov had phoned again, but I'd dismissed it immediately. She would've told us if he'd phoned. I'd put her disquiet down to the frustration of Emad and Fradkov still evading capture. I looked at her closely as she tapped the screen again. She chewed a bit longer on her bottom lip, then glanced at Manny.

Even though I needed to know what was worrying Francine, I first needed to understand Manny's behaviour. I put my chopsticks down and looked at him. "I would like an answer that is not sarcastic or irritated. Why did you treat Nikolai like a peer and Roman like a suspect?"

Manny finished chewing, his expression annoyed. "Roman is a pill."

"What's that?" Surely he was not referring to medicine.

"It's someone I don't trust as far as I can throw him, missy." Manny sighed and stabbed his chopsticks into his meal. He blinked, a brief and surprising expression of grief moving across his face. "Nikolai, on the other hand, made me think of a partner I had many years ago. I was still working at Scotland Yard and George was my second partner that year. He was the most strait-laced person I'd ever met." Manny glanced at Colin, his top lip curling. "He always wore these well-tailored suits, classy ties and shiny shoes. Not the typical look for a lowly copper."

"Wasn't he a detective like you?" Why would Manny's partner be an officer when he was an inspector?

"He was, but we're not talking about George right now." Manny picked up his chopsticks again. "Nikolai has the same look about him, but also the same no-nonsense approach. There is something about that man that tells me he's not your typical Russian. And before you ask, Doc, I don't know what that 'something' is. All I know is that my gut tells me that I can trust him a hell of a lot more than I can trust his assistant."

I nodded. Even though it still irked me whenever one of my team told me that their internal organs were giving them information about a person, I'd learned to accept this. Very often people received nonverbal information that was processed on a subconscious level to give them a good or bad feeling about a person. It was unreasonable to expect most people to translate those signals into words. Not everyone had a high enough self-awareness and knowledge of psychology to understand what they were feeling.

"What's your opinion about Nikolai, Doc?"

"He was truthful in most of his exchanges. His passion for Russia's art, music and poetry was unmistakeable, as well as his dedication to sharing it with other cultures."

"But can we trust him?" Manny lifted his right hand as if to stop me. "And I'm not talking about trusting him with state secrets. I'm talking about trusting him to be honest and co-operative."

I thought about this. "Not once did I observe any calculation in his answers. His grief for his friend was genuine as well as his desire to help." I thought about this some more. "I don't like your definition of trust, but from the short time we were with Nikolai, I feel confident that we can expect him to be forthcoming with information that could help us find his friend's killer."

"And I think he would be even more helpful if we can do something to help him with his art project," Colin added. "I agree with Jenny about his passion. I think he would go against what certain elements in the Russian government want him to do if it were to benefit his cause."

"Hmm. I'll keep that in mind." Manny pointed his chopsticks at Francine. "What did you find on the radiation poisoning diplomat?"

Francine moved her shoulders and rolled her head as if to regain composure, then swiped her tablet screen. "Aleksei Volyntsev would've been fifty-two tomorrow. He was born and educated in St. Petersburg. His family was extremely well-connected during the USSR era. After the Iron Curtain came down, they moved all their interests into the aviation industry and have become not only disgustingly rich, but also very powerful.

"I haven't found anything that raised red flags either on Aleksei or his family. Aleksei was a diplomat for sixteen years and made friends everywhere he went. It sounds like everyone loved working with him. The US Secretary of State described him as the only Russian she could take at his word. I've tried to dig up dirt on him, but couldn't find anything. All he did was build good relationships and take Russian artists and performers to every country he was stationed in."

"So Nikolai was right about his desire to show the softer and more beautiful side of Russia," Colin said.

I stared at Francine. Her distress was becoming a distraction. "Did you find any connection to Fradkov or Emad?"

"Nothing, but I set up a search, so maybe it will come up with something."

In an uncommon show of affection, Manny put his hand over Francine's. "Tell them what you told me, supermodel."

"About what?" Francine looked up from her tablet. "Daniel?"

"What about Daniel?" Vinnie crossed his arms. "He's not been answering my SMSes."

The downturned corners of Francine's mouth and the anxiety around her eyes brought a tightening to my chest. She pushed her food away. "Daniel is missing."

The food I had swallowed pushed back up my oesophagus. I hunched my shoulders at the surprising adrenaline burst entering my veins. I had become used to experiencing this with many aspects of Nikki's life. Having the young and often vulnerable woman enter my life had countless times caused this rush of fear flooding my system.

I had known Daniel for the last four years and had not considered him a close friend. Vinnie, Francine and Manny were my close friends. Nikki was someone I deeply cared for and Phillip was the only person I now considered a father figure in my life. It had taken a long time for me to admit that what I was feeling for Colin was love. But Daniel? I had only ever considered him an acquaintance. At best. It would appear I had been wrong.

I cleared my throat to get rid of the suffocating feeling. "What do you mean missing?"

"I mean neither Pink nor I can get hold of him." She lifted her tablet. "I'm running searches on all Daniel's devices in case they go online. His phone, tablet and computer are all turned off. I can't even turn his phone on remotely, which tells me that either he's removed his phone's battery or there is no phone or internet reception where he is."

"How long has he been missing?" The words came out a pitch higher than I'd intended.

"Four hours."

Manny straightened. "You didn't tell me that. Four hours is nothing, supermodel. Maybe he's watching a movie or he just wants some away time from everyone always meddling."

"Pah! I don't meddle, handsome. I protect." Francine's response didn't hold the same energy as usual. "And if you would quit interrupting me, I'll have time to tell the whole story."

"Could you please do so factually and in chronological order?" I found her tendency to interrupt herself with irrelevant information most annoying.

"Okay, okay. Daniel was supposed to check in with Pink almost five hours ago."

"That's not chronological." I leaned forward. "Pink is not the type of person to overreact to a situation. What is causing him to be so concerned about Daniel's wellbeing? Where is Daniel? Why would Pink need to reach him?"

"Fine. I'll speak in bullet points." She rolled her eyes and started counting off her fingers. "Daniel left Strasbourg at seven this morning on a flight to Paris. From there he caught a flight to Minsk."

I jerked. "Minsk? What's he doing in Minsk?"

"He's on an exchange with the Belarussian equivalent of

GIPN." She wrinkled her nose. "They wanted expert training."

Vinnie crossed his arms. "Daniel mentioned something like that, but that was weeks ago. I thought nothing came of it."

"Well, Pink said that Daniel is there to train with their team and their team leader is here to train with Pink and the others." The concern on her face intensified. "His plane was supposed to land in Minsk four hours ago. Daniel told Pink he was going to turn his phone on the moment they landed in case Pink needed him for something. He hasn't switched on his phone and he hasn't been in contact. I also can't find any evidence that his plane has landed."

Manny turned to me. "Doc? Is this all connected?"

"I have no idea. We don't have enough data. But I'm not prone to believing in coincidences."

"What coincidences?" Vinnie asked.

"I've only told you about the art exhibition." Colin's eyes were wide. "I haven't yet told you where."

"In Belarus?" Vinnie's eyebrows rose high on his forehead.

"Give me all you've got." Francine tapped her manicured nail on the table. "If I have more information, I might be more successful tracking Daniel."

Colin told them about the official opening of the Renaissance exhibition in Belarus. "And to top it off, the man who organised a lot of the art and had a small VIP exhibition here is a good friend of the Belarussian president."

"This has to be connected." Francine's eyes lost their focus. "I wonder if… hmm… maybe I could…"

"Supermodel!"

"Huh? Oh, sorry. I'm just thinking about how I can use this

to narrow the search for Daniel." She looked at me. "Tell me more about the politics. How do you think Russia, Belarus and France can be connected with Daniel being missing?"

"I have no idea how the politics between these three countries could have any link to Daniel being unreachable." I thought about an article I'd read in one of the journals that had been delivered. "Even though Belarus gained their independence in 1989, they still have very close ties to Russia. Since they're neighbours, Russia is to date still Belarus' biggest and most important political and economic partner. That was only one of the reasons the EU didn't want to admit Belarus into the union.

"They have an unfortunate history of human rights abuses and interference in democratic elections. And this happened recently as well. Belarus accused the Polish ethnic minorities of trying to cause a similar revolution to Ukraine's Orange Revolution in 2004. They targeted Polish people living in Ukraine, including closing down a Polish-language newspaper. In 2005, the EU declared its concern about this situation and France expressed solidarity with Poland a day later. Ukraine also frowned upon Belarus' handling of the Polish minority."

"Holy Mary." Manny rubbed his hand over his face. "I hate politics."

"And politicians." Vinnie tilted his head. "Maybe not all of them. President Godard and his wife are cool."

The elevator doors pinged and Phillip walked into the team room. "Afternoon, all. I hope you finished eating."

Another rush of adrenaline entered my bloodstream when I noticed the tension around his eyes. "What happened?"

"Alain is in my office. He got another painting." He looked around the table. "You looked worried before I came in. What's going on?"

"Daniel is missing." I got up, then sat back down. Confusion warred in my mind. On the one hand, I felt an almost painful need to go to my viewing room and do whatever I could to find Daniel. It would be a futile use of time since Francine was much better equipped and skilled to run legal and illegal searches.

On the other hand, I wanted to see this second painting and solve the mystery behind these artworks. Why was Emad sending them to his father? Was he merely playing a game with his dad or was there a more malevolent motivation behind it all? I didn't know what to do.

"This is what we'll do." Manny got up. "Supermodel, you keep looking for Daniel. Do whatever you need to. Get the big guy to help you."

"With computers?" Vinnie snorted, but I saw his frustration.

Manny's look of impatience was genuine. "Quit pretending you're only good with your fists. You have many connections. Get on your bloody phone and start finding out things."

Vinnie's eyes widened, the lines around his eyes relaxing marginally. "On it, old man."

"You two." Manny pointed at Colin and me. "With me. We're going to see what Emad sent."

Colin grabbed my tablet and three minutes later we were in the large conference room in Rousseau & Rousseau next door. A second painting was on an easel next to the first painting Emad had sent Alain. Colin nodded a greeting towards Alain and walked straight to the painting.

My attention was focused on Alain. Distress was clearly visible on his face. The professional and emotional toll of his sons' actions had changed him from a dynamic and life-loving middle-aged gentleman to a tired old man. I stepped closer to where he was standing, wringing his hands. "When did you receive the painting?"

"Around one o'clock. I had just finished lunch when my doorbell rang and the courier handed me that." He pointed accusingly at the painting. He stared at his shaking index finger, then dropped his arm and sat down slowly. "I just want this to end. I don't know how much more of this I can bear. How can one father have gone so very wrong with both his children? Was I misguided in thinking that I was providing my children with a safe, stable environment, teaching them to respect the lives of those rich and poor? Did I spoil them by sending them to private schools? What did I do wrong?"

Phillip sat down next to Alain and poured tea from the setting on the table. "This is not a question that has an answer, Alain. Surely you know that it is pointless to go down the what-if road."

"It's human nature to try to understand that which doesn't fit into our perceived frame of normal." I shook my head when Phillip lifted the teapot, offering to pour me tea. "It's been clear from the onset that your sons did not function within the framework of societal norms. Like the vast majority of people, their behaviour came from a confluence of influences, not excluding their own psychological profiles and psychiatric makeup."

"Jenny, come look here." Colin didn't turn away from the painting, only reaching with his hand behind him as if I would take it.

I didn't. I did, however, join him at the easels. "Do you know which painting this is?"

"Oh, yes." He straightened. "This is Uccello's *Scene from the Life of the Holy Hermits.*"

"Huh." Manny shrugged. "Does this painting have any specific meaning?"

"Beyond possibly holding more Fibonacci numbers that we can enter into that app, none I can think of." Colin touched his chin. "Uccello painted these saints who lived as hermits in the Egyptian desert as belonging to a religious order that was more common in Florence. The rocky landscape with caves and forests and animals was quite unusual for that time."

Alain put his teacup down. "Phillip explained that you entered those numbers into the app and that is why I received the second painting."

"Hmm." Manny pushed his hands in his trouser pockets. "Doc, do you see the Fibrochino numbers?"

"Fibonacci." I ignored Colin's soft laugh and turned my attention to the painting.

"I think I got two numbers." Alain got up to stand next to me. He pointed at the different places on the canvas. "Top centre where the saint is on his knees praying, and there on the pulpit in the bottom right."

I moved away from him, closer to Colin. "You are correct. Those are well-hidden numerals."

"I can see an 'X' and 'V' here." Colin pointed at the praying saint in the bottom left.

"Show me the original." I waited for Colin to turn my tablet on and find the painting. He handed it to me and I looked at the colourful masterpiece. It was a busy painting with a lot of people in what seemed like different forms of religious practice. It was beautiful not only in its composition, but also in the amount of information conveyed.

The differences between Uccello's original and the attempted copy on the easel were vast. It was clear that Emad hadn't even tried to copy the style or brush-strokes or specific colours. The saints were painted with the skill of a child and the building in the top left corner resembled the simple line-drawings found in kindergarten art.

I tilted my head and mentally called up the overture of Mozart's *Die Zauberflöte*. Even replaying it in my mind, I always found it to be both exciting and helpful for my focus. I followed the Fibonacci spiral on the painting and inspected those parts of the painting closely. When the overture reached its end, I saw the number that had been eluding me and pointed at one of the priests sitting around the altar. "There."

"Are these Fibonacci numbers?" Manny asked.

"Yes." I frowned. "But they are in the wrong order. This is incorrect. It should follow the sequence."

"Could it be that the numbers should be entered into the app in that order? Not the true sequence?" Colin leaned closer to the painting. "That means his codes are quite simplistic."

"What are the numbers, Doc?" Manny lifted his index finger to halt my answer. "In the sequence they appear here?"

"Thirty-four, three, eight, fifty-five, one."

Manny looked at the security camera above the door. "Do

your thing, supermodel."

"This might not be the correct order for the app." I found it difficult to agree with Colin's suggestion. Surely Emad would not make it this easy.

Manny's phone rang. He raised an eyebrow and gave me a look that I'd come to know as telling me that I'd been wrong. He answered his phone and put it on the conference table. "You're on speakerphone."

"Okey-dokey. Hello, Alain."

Alain leaned towards the phone. "Hello, Francine."

"So I ran the numbers through and what do you know. Bing, bang, boom, we got to another level of the app."

"Should I be expecting another painting?" Alain's raised upper eyelids, tensed lips and open mouth revealed the fear he experienced just thinking about this.

"Yes." Francine cleared her throat. "I'm sorry for all of this, Alain."

"So am I, Francine. So am I."

From experience I knew that Francine had not apologised, but had sympathised with Alain's situation. He had apologised. I did not blame him for his sons' actions. It had been their choice to become involved in criminal activities that had led to Claude's death and Emad currently being a fugitive.

Once again, I looked at the two paintings. Why was Emad sending them to his father? Was he yearning for a connection with his dad? Was he playing a nefarious game? If so, what was the outcome he was aiming for? Were the numbers themselves important or was their only purpose to take us to the next clue? Where were all the clues leading us to? What would happen if Alain received another painting and entering the Fibonacci code we found on it triggered something—a bomb, an event, something catastrophic?

"Um, guys?" Francine's tone held a tension I recognised. It only had that pitch and tightness when adrenaline had entered her system.

"What?" Manny asked.

"You better get up here right now." She took a deep breath. "I've got Pink on video call and you'll want to hear this."

Manny got up and took his phone. "We're on our way."

"I'll take care of Alain." To the untrained eye, Phillip was relaxed and confident. But I saw his deep concern. "Please keep me updated."

I hurried after Manny, focusing on my breathing. The tightness in my chest was preventing me from inhaling deeply enough to relax the tension in my muscles. For a brief moment, I wanted to go in the opposite direction. I didn't want to hear the bad news I was about to face in the team room.

Chapter EIGHT

"What the hell do you mean the plane is missing?" The *masseter* muscles in Manny's jaw tensed, his fists on his hips. "A plane doesn't just disappear into thin air. Why isn't this on the news? Does the airline even know that the plane is missing?"

"Give him time to finish, handsome." Francine put her hand on Manny's shoulder. We were in my viewing room. Colin, Manny and I were sitting on the three chairs in front of the fifteen monitors. Francine was standing behind Manny and Vinnie was leaning against the doorframe.

The moment Pink had given us the news, I had frozen. My mouth didn't want to form any of the words rushing through my mind. Francine was right. Pink had only told us that Daniel's plane had gone off radar when Vinnie had let off a long and very strongly-worded sentence. Manny had bombarded Pink with questions. Me? I'd pushed Mozart's Clarinet Concerto in A major into my mind to drive away the darkness that was threatening to overtake my mind and leave me in a complete shutdown.

Pink swallowed a few times, his face pale. "I phoned the airline. I'd checked Daniel's flight to Minsk before I even asked for Francine's help. They told us that the plane was on schedule and there was nothing wrong."

I pointed at his face, words still not forming in my mouth.

Colin took my hand in his and rubbed it as if I was cold. "Jenny's seeing something on your face, Pink. What?"

"I don't know." Pink blinked a few times. "Maybe the fact that I'm monumentally pissed off with myself for not following my gut. When they told me everything was fine and that we shouldn't look for terrorist attacks under every bush, I knew something was up. I had a feeling and I didn't go with it. I thought I was overreacting. I checked three of the apps that follow all flights. Two of them showed Daniel's flight, but one didn't. It's not impossible to manipulate that information to look like the plane is there. Or not there. I don't know what to believe."

I shook my head. Colin squeezed my hand. "I agree with Jenny. You're not a drama queen, Pink. You don't overreact."

"I wish I'd pushed them for more info three hours ago." Anger and regret pulled at the corners of Pink's mouth. "Now they won't tell me why they didn't reveal that the plane had lost contact earlier. I know they're protecting something or someone, but I—*we*—simply don't have the kind of security clearance to be told what or who is on that plane. Not without warrants."

"*Daniel* is on that fucking plane." Vinnie stepped into my viewing room, breathed a few times loudly before returning to his place in the doorway.

"I'll get a manifest of everything and everyone on the plane." Francine started tapping on her tablet, but stopped when Manny turned in his chair to look at her.

"Let's do this right, people." He rubbed one hand over his face. "I'll get in touch with Privott. We're not the president's special little team for no reason. He'll get us everything we need to know about this flight, its cargo, the passengers and the staff. Leave the hacking for when someone decides to stonewall us."

Francine nodded and Manny tapped on the screen of his smartphone. While everyone listened to the short and mostly one-sided conversation Manny had with the director of public relations for the president of France, I filled my mind with the beautiful sounds of the clarinet concerto, hoping it would remove the panic that was blocking the signals from my brain to my mouth.

Manny finished his call with an order to have the flight details within ten minutes, then stabbed hard at his smartphone screen with his finger.

I inhaled deeply and addressed the monitors. "What is the timeline of the plane? When did it take off? Do you have a minute-by-minute report until they lost contact?"

Pink looked down to something in his hands and nodded. He lifted his tablet until it was in view. "The airline sent it to me a few minutes ago."

"Tell me."

"Uh"—he looked at his tablet—"flight 602 took off at exactly eleven thirty from Paris, they climbed steadily until eleven forty-five, entered German airspace and when they went over Cologne they were supposed to make contact with the air traffic control tower. They didn't. The tower tried to establish contact with them eight times, but still they didn't respond. The plane simply wasn't where the radar showed it was." Pink stopped, his eyes wide. "Shit."

"Are you thinking what I'm thinking?" Francine's nonverbal cues fluctuated between shock, excitement and disbelief. "Can this be real? The first time?"

"I don't know, Francine." Pink put both his hands on his head. "This would be huge."

"What the bleeding hell are you two on about?" Manny knocked on my desk. "What would be huge?"

"Hacking a plane." Francine shifted from side to side, excitement bringing colour to her cheeks. "In theory it is entirely possible and a few hackers claim to have done it, but it's been shot down by the airlines, national security experts and cybersecurity experts as impossible."

"How else could Daniel's plane show up on radar, but not be there?" Pink asked. "Someone must've gotten into the system and is controlling it. That would certainly explain why the airline is not forthcoming. It would also explain why two of the apps showed Dan's flight path."

Francine nodded as if she'd just confirmed a fact. "It's a cover-up. They wouldn't want the public to know about the plane hacking. I don't think any aviation authority would like that juicy little titbit to be public. Can you imagine what it would do to airline stock, travel plans, etcetera?"

"People are going to start asking questions very soon." Pink leaned back. "I'm surprised it hasn't hit the internet yet. When it does, it will cause a shit-storm all over these people holding back information."

"Holy hell!" Manny slumped in his chair and stared at my desk. He picked up one of my academic journals lying on the top of seventeen others, glared at it and put it back. Sighing deeply, he rubbed his hands over his face. "Hacking cars and planes. What's next? No, don't answer that. Supermodel, tell me what you know about the possibility of hacking a plane.

Surely your criminal pals talk about it on the underweb."

"There's a lot of discussion about this on the *dark web*, but it's mostly speculation and hypotheticals." She looked up and left, remembering. "I can't recall any conversation that would hint at it being done here in Europe."

"Is it possible?" Manny asked again.

"Very." Pink swallowed. "Even though they use micro-segmentation in modern, fully computerised planes, it doesn't mean that it's impossible to get to the plane's avionics system, the beating heart of a plane."

"Micro-segmentation?" Vinnie asked.

"Separating the different packets on a common wire." Francine rubbed her hands together. "This is one way of keeping data exactly where it needs to be. Out of the hands of hackers. But Pink is right. It's not that hard to get in there."

"An attacker wouldn't be interested in getting into the passenger information or entertainment services domain, unless it's to get to the more important domains," Pink said. "If a hacker can compromise the satellite communication equipment, he or she will be able to progress into other, more critical systems on the plane."

"And the easiest way to do that would be through the on-board Wi-Fi." Francine lifted one manicured finger. "Fortunately not all planes have that in place yet. Hacking a lot of older planes would be as useful as hacking a brick. It would have to be a more modern plane to make this work."

"Bloody hell." Manny's phone pinged and he looked at the screen. "I've got the flight manifests."

"I'll put it up on the monitors." Francine swiped her tablet screen.

"No sense of privacy," Manny mumbled, but I didn't detect any resentment.

Francine tapped on her tablet a few times until she accessed my computer and monitors. She moved Pink to the centre monitor and arranged the different files on the other monitors.

My first interest was the passengers. I zoomed in on that monitor and scrolled through the two hundred and thirteen names. This was an Airbus A340-300 with a maximum capacity of two hundred and sixty-seven people.

Manny was scrolling on his smartphone. "Huh. Fifteen of the passengers are US teenagers. They're taking part in the IAAF World U18 Indoor Championships in Minsk. What the blazes is this IAAF World U18?"

"The IAAF is the International Association of Athletic Federations," Pink said. "It's like the Olympics, but for track and field events for kids seventeen years and younger."

"Let me check that." Francine tapped on her tablet. "The U18 Championships are taking place this week and next. I didn't know about this. All European countries are represented there. The US, Russia, China, Japan and Australia also have teams taking part."

"Who's this Venessa Neveu?" Manny squinted at the passenger list on the monitor. "She has a star next to her name."

"It's not a star. It's an asterisk, handsome." Francine worked on her tablet for three seconds. "She's the French minister of culture. It looks like she often goes on diplomatic trips. Whenever France is represented through music, art, sport or any such thing on an international level, she tries to be there.

She believes that these are the best ways to break down barriers between cultures, religions and races."

"Sounds like she would get on well with the Russian consul general." Colin's phone pinged and he took it from his pocket. "Both of them using something—art and sport—to build bridges and strengthen society."

Pink entered the entire passenger list into a search engine that gave us more detail on each passenger. There were businessmen, a scientist, Belarussians returning home, people on tourist visas, the US youth athletic team and the French minister of culture. Pink paused, his eyebrows lowered, his lips tense. "And Daniel Cassel."

"Dammit." Manny shook his head. "Anyone suspicious on the plane? Anyone flagged?"

Pink took a moment to answer. "Nothing at first glance, no. This system is quite reliable, so if some terrorist is on that plane, they've done a good job hiding themselves."

"Or they're using a false passport."

"Could it be that they targeted that plane because they knew Daniel was on it?" Manny asked.

"I doubt it." Colin was scrolling through some document on his phone. "I doubt it very much."

"Would you like to share with the class why you think this?" Manny's lips compressed as he glared at Colin's phone.

Colin tapped his phone screen a few times, then pointed at one of the monitors with his phone. "Because of that list."

"Which list?" Pink frowned. "I can't see what you guys are looking at."

"No way, dude!" Vinnie stepped closer, his eyebrows raised as he stared at the second monitor from the left. It displayed information that hadn't been there before. "It's a list of paintings."

"Remember Nikolai told us about the art going to Minsk for the grand opening? Well, it's on this plane." Colin shook his head. "My God. I understand the reasoning behind having goods of extremely high value on a flight that would normally only transport goods of lesser value, hiding it in plain sight and all. But this? This makes my blood boil."

I found that expression most disturbing, but looking at the list of artworks was of much more interest. "Eighty-seven paintings. The combined value of those must be staggering."

"No, love. They are invaluable. Priceless. Without measure." Colin pushed his fingers through his hair. "The Sandro Botticelli, Giovanni Bellini, Caravaggio and Lorenzo Lotto alone could never be replaced. God, there's also a Jean Clouet and a Pisanello. This is a treasure trove."

Something Colin had said earlier bothered me. "How do you know these are the paintings for the exhibition Nikolai was talking about?"

"Oh. Yes." Colin lifted his phone. "He emailed me a complete list."

"Ooh, let me put it up here with everything else." Francine tapped on her tablet a few times, undoubtedly accessing Colin's email. Three seconds later another monitor lit up with a document.

I slowly scrolled through the list, looking for a possible anomaly. I found it on the second page. "Uccello's *Saint George and the Dragon* is on that list."

"Shit." Colin leaned closer. "Is the *Scenes of the Life of the Holy Hermits* also there?"

I ran a quick search and found it listed near the bottom of the third page. "It's here."

"The originals of Emad's bad forgeries are on that plane?" Manny rubbed his hands hard over his face. "Holy bloody hell!"

A stunned silence filled the room for almost a minute. Question after question flowed through my mind until they were running on a loop. I turned Mozart's clarinet concerto on in my mind to continue the Adagio. The harmony of this composition was great to help me focus. I needed to stop the rotating questions and thoughts. If I didn't, experience had taught me that it would result in a shutdown that lasted longer than most.

I inhaled deeply and shifted in my chair. "Has Emad somehow had access to these paintings? Is that how he was able to copy them, albeit badly?"

"He could've done it from one of the gajillion photos on the internet," Francine said.

"Hmm." Colin shook his head slowly. "I don't know. Taking everything that has happened into consideration, I'm thinking that he had access to them."

I waved my hand to dismiss their speculation. "I should not have asked a question that had no certain answer. A better question might be how Emad had access to this list. Does he have a connection to this exhibition?"

"Well, the list of paintings in this exhibition is no secret." Colin lifted his phone and shook it lightly. "You can find it on the internet. Nikolai Guskov's UTA has done extensive marketing to create awareness of this exhibition. The biggest draw, of course, would be listing the most famous Renaissance painters in order to attract people."

Colin's answer led to more questions joining the loop in my mind. Mentally, I turned up the volume of the clarinet concerto.

"Doc's not going to say it, so I will." Manny slumped lower in his chair. "We have all these Renaissance artists, so I'm convinced that Fradkov and his Renaissance fetish would be interested. If Fradkov is interested, then he most likely got Emad involved in this. Those two must have known that the art would be transported today."

"I agree." Francine nodded enthusiastically. "And I wouldn't clutch my pearls in shock if Fradkov has hacked that plane to get to the art. I like your theory, handsome."

"That's no ringing endorsement." Manny grunted. "Doc? What do you think?"

"I think that we should look for more facts and spend less time speculating." I observed Manny's irritation without surprise. He liked speculating. He called it brainstorming. I sighed. "Instead of guesses, here are a few questions." I stared at the top monitor without seeing what was on it. "Has the plane been hacked? Has it been hijacked? If either of those are true, was it done for the art? Or is Daniel the target? Maybe the French minister of culture? Is it a terrorist attack to instil fear and is unrelated to any of this? Is the US U18 team the target? Is there something or someone else on the plane that is not on the manifest that could be of interest to whomever took control of the plane? Or"—I swallowed—"is it technical failure and a simple plane crash?"

Manny raised one eyebrow. "Do *you* believe that it could be anything not related to Fradkov, Emad, the paintings or Daniel?"

"No." It would mean I would have to believe in a myriad coincidences. "But I don't know who fits in where or what their desired outcome is."

"Well, my desired outcome is to find Daniel." Pink had been quiet for so long, I'd forgotten about him. His expression was dire. "We must do it now. We must find Dan."

I agreed. The urge to find Daniel and see his easy smile overrode my curiosity over the badly copied paintings Emad had sent his father. I thought back to yesterday's associations. "Otto told us that Emad had plans to target emergency services. Could it be that he had Daniel and his team in mind?"

"Shit." Pink lost some colour in his face. "You guys really think Dan was targeted?"

"I don't know." I didn't. "But I'm going to need your input if we are to find him. We need to know everything possible about Daniel Cassel."

Chapter NINE

"This really doesn't feel right." Vinnie grimaced and took a step away from the table.

"I feel exactly the same, Vin." Francine sighed, but didn't stop working on her computer.

"That makes three of us." Pink was sitting next to Francine at my dining room table. I had taken the wooden bowl I'd bought in Peru from the centre of the rectangular wooden table to make place for the four laptops currently displaying various parts of Daniel's digital life.

Pink had insisted in joining us as we looked into Daniel's life. He'd also asked if we could do this away from anything official. At first, his reasoning had seemed illogical. Whether we worked in my apartment or in the team room, our investigations always remained official. It had only been when I'd taken a few moments to analyse his micro-expressions that I had understood his distress. He didn't want Daniel's private life to be viewed by anyone else but us.

"Each part of Daniel's life is only that. A segment." I waited until everyone looked at me. Each face displayed high levels of disquietude. "We are doing this to get a holistic view of his life in the hopes that we will find something to determine if Daniel was specifically targeted."

"I might have something." It looked like Francine was

about to cry. She inhaled, but stopped when the front door opened.

Nikki stepped into my apartment and her eyes widened when she registered the sombre tone around the table. Some of the laughter around her eyes and mouth disappeared. "Is this about that plane?"

"How do you know about the plane?" Manny's tone was accusatory. He'd been in constant contact with the aviation authorities as well as Julien Privott, all of whom had told him they were keeping the disappearance of the plane quiet.

"It's all over Twitter. And Snapchat. And Instagram." She walked closer and stopped next to Manny. "And for the old fogies, it's all over Facebook."

Vinnie jumped up and stormed to the other side of the apartment, the part he and Nikki shared. A second later, the drone of the large-screen television sounded. "It's on the news!"

As one, we got up and walked to the entertainment area Nikki, Vinnie and Colin frequented. Vinnie was standing a few feet from the television, clutching the remote control. He shook it at the television. "It's breaking news. Everyone knows about it now."

"Bloody hell." Manny left the room, his smartphone already against his ear.

"Um…" Nikki looked at everyone in the room, then came to stand next to me. "What's happening, Doc G?"

"The control towers lost contact with this plane seven hours ago. There are eighty-seven paintings on this flight, a group of American students and Daniel."

"Wait. What?" Her *frontalis* muscles raised her eyebrows high, widening her eyes. "Daniel? Our Daniel? Daniel with the shaved head and the sweet smile? He's on that plane?"

"Yes." Pink's tone was strained.

"Oh, Pink, I'm so sorry." She walked up to him and threw her arms around him. "You must be so worried."

Some of the tension left Pink's muscles as he returned Nikki's embrace. He rested his cheek on the top of her head and sighed deeply.

Manny walked back into the room, a deep frown furrowing his brow. "Privott says they had to give the media something. The people waiting for the plane to land were threatening legal action if they weren't informed."

"Seriously?" Not letting go of Pink, Nikki turned her head to stare at us. "I mean seriously. They really thought they could keep this information from the public? People have all kinds of apps to track planes en route and check if there are any delays."

"At least they're not revealing too much." Vinnie hadn't taken his eyes off the television. "Only the flight number, how many people and when it lost contact."

"You guys are really worried." Nikki gave Pink another hug, stepped away from him and looked at Francine. "Especially you. Why?"

I was becoming used to the pride that welled up in me when Nikki proved to be observant, sensitive and mature. I also turned to look at Francine and saw the same fear I had observed earlier. She nodded towards the dining room. "I'd better show you."

"Do you need me to be there?" Nikki rubbed the side of her pregnant belly, something she did when the baby was pushing or kicking.

"No, doll." Francine shook her head. "You go and have a nice long bath. If we need you, we'll call."

"Good." Nikki grunted. "Today has been one of those days when it feels like I haven't slept in seven years."

"That's physically not possible." My shoulders dropped slightly. "You're exaggerating again. That means you're not feeling very bad."

"Only like I could sleep for like three years." She winked at me and turned to her room. "Go find Daniel, Doc G. Bring him home."

I watched her walk to her room before I followed Francine to the dining room table. I sat down in my usual seat, Colin next to me. He'd been very quiet since we'd arrived home. I could easily see his attempt to hide his deep concern. Even though his body appeared relaxed as he leaned back in his seat, the constant contractions of the *orbicularis oculi* muscles around his eyes and the *depressor anguli oris* muscles pulling the corners of his mouth down revealed his inner turmoil.

Francine sat down heavily in her chair and pointed to her laptop monitor. "The logical first place I looked was Daniel's emails. Like most people he has his work and two private email addresses."

"I don't have two private email addresses." What was the point?

"Yeah, but you're not like everyone else, girlfriend." Francine winked at me, yet her usual playfulness was not present. She looked back at her laptop monitor. "Daniel received an email sent to his work address and one of his lesser-used private addresses yesterday."

"What kind of email, supermodel?" Manny asked when Francine didn't continue.

"A threat."

"What the hell?" Pink rushed to her side and looked at the monitor. The longer he read what was on the screen, the wider his eyes became. His lips parted in an expression of breathless shock. "This… this can't be true."

"Speak. Now." The worry in Manny's voice was more pronounced than his annoyance.

Pink looked up, his eyes wide in disbelief. "This email says that the sender will reveal all the payments Dan received from Isabelle Godard. They knew that he got money from the president's wife to hide evidence of certain crimes and to plant evidence in selected crime scenes. All this to help advance President Godard's career."

"Dan would never do this." Vinnie picked up a dining room chair and for a moment I thought he was going to throw it across the room. He didn't. With visible control, he turned the chair and straddled it. "He wouldn't. Not Daniel."

"I concur." I felt comfortable in my assessment of Daniel's character. He had shown honesty and integrity time and again. "I've been meeting Isabelle for the last two years and it would also be completely out of character for her to be complicit in something like this. She wouldn't jeopardise all the work she's done to establish her charities and help the president by committing such atrocious crimes to supposedly advance his career."

"They have evidence." Francine's voice sounded broken. "It's here in the attachment."

"Fucking hell." Manny walked to the kitchen, stood stiffly

in front of the coffee machine for a few seconds and walked back. "What evidence?"

Francine clicked a few times and turned her computer to Pink. She didn't want to speak.

"Bank statements." Pink leaned closer and scratched his head. "It looks legit."

"It's not." There was no doubt in Vinnie's tone or on his face.

"Show me." I needed to see this evidence. Someone needed to look at this objectively and judging by the distress on all the faces around the table, I was the only person capable of putting my emotions aside.

Pink turned Francine's computer around and pushed it across the table to me. I lifted it and placed it exactly parallel to the edge of the wooden table. Only when I was pleased with its placement did I look at the monitor. I was looking at the first of a series of screenshots. These were online bank statements and I agreed with Pink that they looked real.

But since I'd started investigating insurance fraud and later art crimes, I had learned how very easy it was to forge any document, online or not. I scrutinised each screenshot before I went to the next one. Francine opened the screenshots on another computer to show Manny and Vinnie. Colin was quiet next to me, but I knew he was also looking for the smallest detail that could lead us to where this had originated.

A few lines were highlighted on each of the statements. Those were the alleged payments Daniel had received from Isabelle. And each of those looked authentic. I was sure

Francine was already looking into the account that had sent those payments.

I went back to the first screenshot and inspected all the other transactions. There were the usual monthly payments to Daniel's mobile phone service provider, transfers to pay his utilities, his car payment, a magazine subscription and his mortgage. Other transactions showed his preference for a specific café close to the GIPN offices, the odd new piece of clothing and numerous online payments for e-books. He seemed to read a lot of science fiction and action thrillers.

"Can we get into Daniel's bank account?" I needed to see more.

"Um." Francine looked at Manny, then at Pink, back at Manny, then at me. "Yes?"

I stared at her. "Why are you asking me? Can you or can't you access his bank records?"

"It's not legal, Doc." For once Manny didn't show any disapproval. He was merely making a statement.

"I know. That wasn't my question."

"Then I can do it." Francine immediately got to work on her second computer. It didn't take long. "There will be no trace of this hack."

"Good." Manny took her computer and held it out to me. "Until we have no other option, everything we learn about Daniel stays in this room."

"Please, God." Pink closed his eyes for a second. When he opened them, his internal struggle for control over his emotions almost appeared to cause him physical pain. "He can hate me forever, but right now I don't care about his privacy. As long as none of this ever leaves this room."

Colin took the computer Manny held to me. He moved Francine's computer with the emails and put this one in its place. I took a moment to align it precisely, but this time I didn't waste time on it. I needed this data. While the others discussed the many ways Daniel would never betray his country, his morals and the trust of his friends, I carefully went through his bank account, examining each transaction.

It took me only eleven minutes to come to a conclusion. "Francine, could someone have hacked his account like you just did?"

"Of course. This bank's security is good, but not really hard to bypass."

"Could Emad or Fradkov have done this?"

"I don't know if their skills are up to it, but Joe Pasquier definitely could've done this." She shuddered when she talked about the hacker who had sent the man who'd been assassinated at our lunch table. She took a deep breath and held out her hand for her computer. "Give me a moment with my computer. I have an idea."

While she typed on her computer, biting her lower lip, I went back to Daniel's emails. I found only that one email he had received. "This was sent during the time his phone would've been switched off."

"What do you mean, love?"

I pointed at the time stamp. "His flight was at eleven thirty. We know the flight took off on time, which means Daniel's phone would've been unable to receive any calls or any emails."

"Unless they have wireless on the plane." Pink immediately shook his head. "They didn't. We checked that when we looked into the possibility of the plane being hacked. This is an older plane and doesn't have those features."

I thought about this for a short while. There were many loose pieces of information I suspected were all connected. Our job now was to find the links between Aleksei Volyntsev's death by polonium-210 poisoning, Fradkov, Emad, the exhibition, the missing plane, Daniel, the apparent payoffs from the president's wife and the paintings on the plane.

That gave me pause. There was no conceivable way to categorise as a coincidence Daniel's presence on a plane with paintings that in some way were connected to Fradkov and Emad.

Before I could follow that thought, Francine gasped. "Ooh, you're so right. The bastards! They hacked Daniel's account. And guess what? Huh? Guess."

"Supermodel."

"The transfers into Daniel's account comes from an account in the name of Isabelle Godard. And this account is from a bank in"—she paused dramatically—"St Kitts and Nevis. I told you Fradkov had accounts there."

I frowned. "I don't understand. Is this Isabelle's account or Fradkov's?"

"Isabelle's. Or at least it is in her name." She straightened and lifted her chin. "I'm willing to stake my shoe collection that Fradkov has an account at the same bank and that he opened this one."

"Can you find out when this account was opened?" Colin asked.

"Of course I can." She winked at Manny. "I'll do it when

this handsome man isn't glowering at me. But I'm sure it is recent. Why, you may ask? Because all the transfers to Daniel's account was added yesterday. They were backdated to make it look like it's been over time, but it's all from yesterday."

"That's why he wouldn't have noticed it." Pink's lips were in a thin line. "Like most people, he almost never checks his bank account. Only when he pays stuff once a month does he go online. He definitely wouldn't have checked when he was packing and getting ready for his trip to Belarus."

"Can you see what time they hacked it?" I needed to make sense of the timeline.

"It was done early this morning. Before Otto was assassinated." Francine tapped her chin with a manicured finger. "Why target Daniel?"

"Hmm." Manny scratched his jaw. "So the email was sent at a time Daniel would not have been able to open it. The transfers were done at a time he would not have noticed it. They knew he was going to be on that flight."

I read the email again. "This is very vague. If Emad or Fradkov wanted to blackmail Daniel, what is it that they wanted? The sender is threatening to show everyone the proof that Daniel's been receiving payoffs from Isabelle, but doesn't make any demands."

"Check his spam box," Colin said. "Maybe they sent another email and it went to Daniel's spam folder."

No sooner had Colin said that than I opened the folder. There were eighteen unopened emails, the very top one sent from the same email address as the threat. "It's here. It was sent four hours before the other one."

"Well? Read it, Doc."

I opened the email and started reading it. Manny threw his hands in the air and Colin put his hand on my forearm. "I think Millard wanted you to read it out loud, love."

"Oh." I glanced at Manny's irate expression and started reading. "'You took away from me everything that was important in my life. Now I will take away what's important in your life. I've been watching you, Daniel Cassel. I know how you value your precious integrity, your moral codes, your honesty. I will strip you of all that you treasure. I will annihilate everything you are. You will be nothing. You will have nothing. No one will respect you, care for you, support you or help you. You will no longer exist. In the end, I will win.'"

"Motherfucker!" Vinnie got up and grabbed the back of his chair until his knuckled turned white. He let go of the chair and walked to the kitchen. Halfway there he turned around. "This is Emad. It has to be. He thinks Daniel killed Claude and wants revenge. That motherfucker has to die."

"Take a breath, big guy." Manny watched Vinnie through narrowed eyes. "We're not in the business of killing people, remember? We're the good guys."

"You're a good guy. I'm not." Vinnie thumped his chest with one fist. "I've never claimed to be a good guy. And I'll be very happy to get rid of this evil motherfu—"

"You're right." Nikki's soft admission stopped Vinnie. He hadn't noticed her come into the kitchen. She walked right up to him and cuddled under his arm. "You're not a good guy. You're one of the best people I've ever met." She took his hand and put it on her round stomach. "This baby will be so lucky to have you as an uncle. From your example, Eric will learn loyalty, friendship, honesty and love. And I know he will be the safest baby in the world."

"Aw, fuck, Nikki." Vinnie closed his eyes and clenched his teeth so hard, the *masseter* muscles in his jaw bulged. Slowly he relaxed and opened his eyes on a sigh. He kissed the top of her head and whispered, "Thank you."

"Now if you don't mind, I'm going to make some hot chocolate." She winked at Vinnie. "The baby needs chocolate."

"I'll make it." Vinnie tapped her on the nose with his index finger and walked to the fridge.

"I'll be in my room." Nikki looked at me and waited. When I didn't react, she rolled her eyes. "Are you okay? Do you need me to stay?"

"I'm well. I don't need you."

"Of course you do. You all do. You're all lost without me. I'm the sand to your beach, the froth to your cappuccino, the violin to your Mozart." Her words had no meaning to me, but the infectious smile she was trying hard to hold back affected me. She whooped and pointed at my face. "You smiled. I saw it. You did. Woo-hoo!"

"Go to your room, young lady." Vinnie took her by the shoulders and pushed her out the kitchen. "We've got some ass-kicking to plan."

"Don't forget my hot chocolate!" she called over her shoulder as she walked to her room.

I was grateful for the lightness Nikki had brought with her. Especially since I hadn't finished reading the email I'd found in Daniel's spam box. "There's more to this email."

Manny slumped deeper into his chair. "Read the rest, Doc."

I cleared my throat and read. "'This is going to be fun. I'm the puppet master and you are the most insignificant of my puppets. My other puppets are important, more important than you'll ever dream of being. Maybe not as honourable as you, but with thousands of years of history behind them and one of the biggest powers in the world, who cares about being honourable? Soon you will be like them. No honour. Stripped to the bone.'" I cleared my throat again. "This is everything. And there's no other email from this email address."

"Shit." Pink had his hand over his mouth, his eyes wide. "Who do you think this superpower is?"

"It has to be Russia," Francine said. "If you think about the most powerful countries in the world, Russia is the only one that makes sense."

"How do you figure that?" Vinnie put a tray with steaming mugs of coffee in the centre of the table. He took a mug and walked towards Nikki's room.

"The United States has no connection to any part of this case, to Fradkov or to Emad." I stopped when I realised I'd answered a question aimed at Francine. She waved her hand for me to continue and I nodded. "Neither does China, Great Britain, Germany or any other country. France has significance to Emad because this is where his brother died."

"And to Fradkov?" Manny asked.

"From the information Justine shared about Fradkov and also from my own analysis, I truly don't think there is a country that offers Fradkov any emotional value. People, and in this case countries, only have value to him if they benefit Fradkov is some way." I thought about it some more. "Fradkov has an obvious connection to Russia, being born there. This could be the closest to an emotional connection he has to a country. Knowing his history, it would be befitting that he would include Russia in some scheme to overthrow a government or change the political landscape in some form."

"But how does Madame Godard fit into all of this?" Manny asked. "I need to brief Privott, but I don't know what the hell to tell him."

"I'll ask her." I took my phone from my handbag and dialled the seventh last number in my call history. Isabelle was one of the few people not on my team I called.

"It's close to midnight, missy." Manny tapped on his empty wrist. "You can't phone her now."

"Genevieve?" Isabelle sounded awake, but confused. "What a surprise."

Suddenly, I didn't know what to say.

"Genevieve? Is everything okay?" Now she sounded worried.

"No." My voice cracked and I realised that I had come to value her more than just a person to share lunch with. "Your reputation is about to be destroyed and I don't know why I'm feeling so distressed about it."

"Holy Mary and the saints!" Manny got up just as Isabelle gasped in my ear. He grabbed the phone from my hand and gave it to Francine. "You speak to her."

Francine took the phone and swiped the screen. "Isabelle, it's Francine. I've got you on speakerphone. Manny, Vinnie,

Colin, Genevieve and Pink are here."

"Francine? What's going on? Do I need to call Raymond?"

Francine looked at Manny, but he had his back turned to her. She blinked a few times. "Um, maybe we don't have to involve the president yet."

"Okay." There was a short pause and it sounded like Isabelle took a deep breath. "Tell me."

"This is a long story, but let me first ask you this. Do you have a bank account in St Kitts and Nevis?"

"No." Her answer was strong and without hesitation. "I have three bank accounts. All of them are held in France. My finances are open for anyone to inspect at any time. Why?"

"Do you remember Daniel Cassel?" Francine gave an impressive summary of what we'd found, including the damning evidence and the fact that Daniel's account had been hacked. There was a moment of silence when she finished.

"Are all of you in agreement that Daniel is innocent of accepting bribes from me?"

"Not only that"—Francine leaned closer to the phone—"we don't believe that you paid those bribes."

"But you have evidence that I have an offshore bank account."

"Nowadays evidence means squat." Francine ignored Manny's warning gaze. "I will prove that your so-called account was not opened by you. That is if it actually exists."

"Manfred Millard here, Madame Godard." Manny rested both palms on the table and spoke into the phone in Francine's hand. "The bigger question here is why Ivan Fradkov and Emad Vernet want to destroy your husband's reputation. Why they want to use you and Daniel to do it and whether it will be effective."

"Of course it will be effective. It doesn't even have to be true." Anger entered her voice. "We saw what happened after those falsehoods were revealed seven months ago. It was easy to prove that not one of those accusations had any basis, but the damage was done. Another non-scandal like that and I don't know if we will be able to recover."

"Where are you now?" I asked.

She hesitated. "Oh, what the hell. I know I can trust you guys. We're in Brussels for the night."

"Meeting about the mess Europe is in?" Manny asked.

"No."

"Russia?"

"I really can't disclose anything, Manny."

"You just did." I leaned away from Manny when he glared at me.

"No, you didn't tell us anything, Madame Godard. Let me ask you this—and please feel free to answer in the same way you did before. Does this meeting have anything to do with a peace agreement between Russia and previous USSR territories?"

"I can't disclose that."

"I see." Manny straightened. "Thank you for your time, Madame Godard."

"Oh, for goodness' sake, Manny, call me Isabelle. Your girlfriend does."

"Yes, ma'am."

"Francine?"

"Yes?" The smile around Francine's lips sounded in her answer.

"Is this line secure?"

"From our side, yes."

"Good. This cloak-and-dagger stuff is ridiculous." She inhaled. "I wonder if the plane disappearing was about more than just the paintings, if Fradkov was involved."

"Why?" I asked.

"Two weeks ago, Raymond contacted Daniel. Julien was so angry about it."

"Privott gets angry about everything," Manny said. "Why this time?"

"Because Ray asked Daniel's advice about certain security measures and Julien took it as a personal attack that he and Ray's security detail weren't doing a good enough job."

"Privott is such a girl." Vinnie cleared his throat. "Vinnie speaking, Isabelle."

"I agree with you, Vinnie." There was no humour in Isabelle's laugh. "But Julien is good at his job. Really good at it."

"Do you know what security measures they discussed?" Manny asked.

"No. Sorry."

"Dammit." Manny rubbed his hand over his face.

"I need to tell Ray about this. The last while, he's been getting more concerned about Fradkov and Emad still being free. After what happened, you know." Isabelle had been held captive by Emad's brother before he'd been killed. The president had been grateful that we'd kept Isabelle safe, but also furious that her life had been in danger. I didn't hear anger or fear in her voice now. Only determination. "Manny, will you speak to Julien or must we contact him?"

"I'll brief him, ma'a… Isabelle." He looked at me. "Any other questions, Doc?"

"Not now." I raised my voice slightly towards the phone. "I will work very hard to make sure your reputation is not affected by this new development."

"I know you will, Genevieve. Thank you for looking out for me." She took the time to say goodbye to everyone around the table before ending the call. I liked her.

"I was wrong about Daniel not being a target." Colin didn't take his eyes from where he was staring at the ceiling. "This adds another layer to him being on the plane."

"What do you mean, Frey?"

He looked at Manny. "I mean that they could've hijacked the plane to kidnap Daniel."

"And extract security information about the president from him." Pink started shaking his head before he finished his sentence. "No, that doesn't make sense. If they did their homework on Daniel, they would know he would never reveal secrets. No matter how they tortured him."

I blanched at the mention of torture. I didn't know what to think about the missing plane or about any of this, but my mind had not yet gone to such dire scenarios. Now I could only hope that it would not become an unending loop playing in my mind.

"Okay, people." Manny closed Francine's laptop and lifted one eyebrow when she complained. "It's really late and I think we all need a few hours' sleep so we can get at this fresh and early in the morning."

"We need to look for the plane." Vinnie crossed his arms.

"God, I wish I could." Pink put his hand over his eyes for a second. "We're good at *this*, Vin. The people who are the best at finding missing planes are working around the clock to find Daniel and the other two hundred and twelve people on that plane. I agree with Manny. A few hours' sleep will give us new perspective."

"I don't like it."

"I don't care." Manny pulled Francine from her chair. "Come, supermodel. We're going home."

"I need my computers." The fact that Francine didn't use Manny's order to make some inappropriate sexual comment confirmed how this case was affecting us all. This was personal.

Five minutes later, only Vinnie, Colin and I remained around the table. I didn't know if I would be able to sleep tonight, but I knew that my body needed to rest. If I were to find the missing elements that connected all these many pieces, I had to be in optimum physical condition.

Chapter TEN

"What?" It was the tension in Colin's sleepy voice that brought me to wakefulness.

Our bedroom was dark, but enough light from the street spilled into the room for me to see Colin's outline. He was leaning on one arm, his smartphone against his ear throwing an eerie light against the side of his face. This allowed me to see his micro-expressions, first relief, then concern. His frown intensified as he sat up and turned on his bedside lamp.

I also sat up. "What's happening?"

"We'll be ready." He lowered his phone and swiped the screen. "Millard and Francine are on their way. Privott is most likely already waiting downstairs for them. They'll come up together."

"Why? Did they find the plane?" The muscles in my throat tightened. "Did it crash?"

"It didn't crash." He took my hand in both his and squeezed. "Millard only told me that they found the plane and they'll be here in a few minutes."

I glanced at the clock on my bedside table. It was eleven minutes to four. I pulled my hand out of Colin's and got up. "Nothing about Daniel?"

"Millard didn't even give me a chance to ask." He got up and walked to his wardrobe. "I was still talking to him when he ended the call."

It took us less than three minutes to get dressed. As we left the room, I noticed that we both wore jeans and black shirts. Mine was a three-quarter-sleeved t-shirt, simple in design and comfortable. Colin was wearing a tailored shirt of the highest quality. I'd grown used to him always dressing with the utmost care. It was his way of preparing for whatever challenge he was about to face.

"I'll go wake Vin." He walked to the other side of our joined apartments and I went into the kitchen. Vinnie would want to be the one making coffee, but I couldn't just sit and wait. I needed to be busy.

Colin returned a few seconds later. I stopped when I noticed his expression. "Why are you amused?"

"He should be embarrassed, not amused." Vinnie walked into the kitchen, pulling a t-shirt over his head. The muscles in his torso stretched and moved with this action, drawing my eyes to the scar that ran over his shoulder. I'd known Vinnie for four years, but had only found out about the origins of his scars recently. He pulled the t-shirt down and walked to the coffee machine. "And he should've knocked."

"Oh, get over yourself, snookums." Roxy walked into the kitchen, her hair an abhorrent mess. She patted it once, shrugged and finished buttoning her shirt. "We were not naked, we were not doing fun things and Colin didn't know I would be in bed with you."

"He should know by now."

"Pah!" She slapped his shoulder and turned to me. "How're you holding up?"

I stared at her. Her question was too generic to answer. And I simply couldn't keep my observation to myself anymore. I pointed to her shirt. "Your buttons are not aligned."

She looked down and giggled. "I do this all the time. I mean, really! How hard can it be to put the first button in the first button hole, right? Okey-dokey. I'll go fix this on the other side of the wall so I don't make Vinnie blush."

As she walked out the kitchen, I called, "Your socks also don't match."

She giggled again and disappeared behind the wall separating the two apartments. I'd come to truly like Roxy. She was intelligent, astute in her observations and without any pretence. I did find her chaotic nature hard to accept though. I constantly had to remind myself that she had not once judged my many non-neurotypical behaviours and that the least I could do was accept her as she was. It was hard.

The beeping of our security system followed by the sound of a key in the front door interrupted my thoughts. Vinnie and Colin both walked to the door, Vinnie reaching behind his back for the handgun he had put there.

The front door opened to Manny and Francine bickering, Julien Privott standing behind them.

"Hacking it would be so much faster. You're just being a ninny."

"A ninny?" Manny's lips were in a tight line, his glare focused on Francine. "That's the best you can come up with?"

"Where's the plane?" I walked to Manny and stared at him. "Is Daniel alive?"

"Let's all sit down, Doc."

"No." I crossed my arms. "Is Daniel… Is Daniel dead?"

Manny inhaled deeply. "We don't know. Everyone else on the plane is fine. Now let's sit down so Privott can explain everything."

I looked at the president's director of public relations. He was wearing suit pants and a white shirt that looked like it had just been ironed. His face was clean-shaven and his hair carefully styled. None of this hid the exhaustion around his eyes and pulling at the corners of his mouth. He nodded at me. "Genevieve."

"Julien." Only recently had our working relationship progressed to a first-name basis. "What do you know about Daniel?"

"Not much." He pointed at the dining room table where Francine and Manny were seated. "Shall we? I'll tell you everything I know."

"You'd better." Vinnie put the tray with our coffee on the table, straightened and looked at Julien with such menace that I crossed my arms over my chest before I realised what I was doing. He took a step towards Julien. "Now."

"God, you people are wound even tighter than the airline people and the president's security." Julien sat down at the table, took a mug of coffee and took a long sip. I couldn't muster sympathy for the unmistakeable stress visible on his face. I needed to know about Daniel. Julien took another sip before putting his mug down. "Just before one this morning, the local authorities on both the Belarussian and Russian borders found the plane. It had landed on a road on the Russian side, but only eight hundred metres from the north-eastern border line between Belarus and Russia. At last count, eighty-four passengers managed to get into Belarus before the Russian authorities stopped anyone else from crossing the border."

I had so many questions. "Did the plane crash?"

"No. It made a perfect landing on the road."

"Where is Daniel?" I asked before he could say anything else.

"We don't know." Julien lifted his hand when Vinnie, Francine and Manny all spoke at the same time. "Just give me a chance to tell you what we know. From the few witness statements we've gathered so far, two men got up about twenty minutes after take-off and pulled out automatic weapons. One went to the front and ordered the flight attendant to open the door to the cockpit. Despite what all protocol dictates, when you have a gun aimed at you, people do what they're told. The flight attendant opened the door.

"The other gunman told the passengers that no one was going to get hurt. They would be inconvenienced, but if no one tried to be a hero, everyone would go home or wherever they were planning on going. Or something to that effect. The witnesses had a few versions of this. Anyway, the passengers just sat there quietly. The gunman even told them that they were going to land on a road that would be able to handle the landing. And when the time came, the landing was indeed executed perfectly and still none of the passengers had acted or tried anything heroic.

"The moment they landed, a group of men came from three different SUVs on the side of the road. The gunmen opened one of the plane's doors and one SUV drove a ladder to the door. There is conflict in the witness statements whether it was three or four other men who joined the first two gunmen. The newcomers held the passengers at gunpoint while the first two ordered the pilot to open the cargo hold.

"The men on the ground then took the paintings that were being transported to Minsk from the containers they'd been packed in and placed them in one SUV, which drove away as soon as they loaded forty-three paintings. One passenger counted carefully and was sure about the number. He was amazed how quickly they worked to fit all the smaller paintings in the vehicle. They then loaded a second SUV with the larger paintings. This SUV was out of sight and the passenger wasn't sure of the exact number, but estimated it to be about the same as what was put in the first SUV."

"That means they got away with all the paintings." The tension in Colin's throat raised his tone. "My God, the combined value. This is…" He scratched his head. "This is definitely the biggest heist in known history. Even if they took the least valuable of the paintings that were on that plane, their combined value is more than the Gardner museum heist."

"What was the value of that?" Roxy asked.

"Around five hundred million euros." Colin's skin had lost its colour. His eyes narrowed, his top lip raised in disgust. "This is going to devastate the art community."

It was difficult for me to witness the man I loved being distraught. I needed to focus on something else and looked at Julien. The tension around his eyes and in his shoulders caught my attention. "What's wrong? What else happened?"

"The gunmen eventually left and didn't hurt any of the passengers, just like they'd promised."

"They took Daniel." My words came out in a whisper.

"What the hell?" Manny slapped his hands on the table and half-pushed himself out of his chair. "Is Doc right? Why didn't you tell me this?"

Julien only nodded. "The passengers say that the first two gunmen sought out Daniel and another passenger, a woman."

I pointed at his face. "You're very distressed. What did they do to Daniel?"

Julien closed his eyes for three seconds. Typical avoidance behaviour. He didn't want to talk about this, but then he inhaled deeply and looked at me. "They beat him pretty badly."

"How badly?" Colin asked.

Julien swallowed. "He was unconscious when they put him in the third SUV."

"Fuck!" Vinnie got up and stormed into the kitchen. He opened the fridge and stared inside. After a few seconds he slammed the door shut. "We have to go get him."

"We've already got people on the ground." Julien pulled his shoulders back and turned to face Vinnie. "We have assets from three different countries starting a search. The president and the director of foreign intelligence have both called in a lot of favours. I've also called in one. My guys are following up on the SUVs. The registration plates came back to non-existent people in a shell company in Russia."

"Shit." Colin interlaced his fingers and rested his hands on his head. "Vin's right. We need to get Daniel back. It doesn't feel right just sitting here."

I looked at Julien. "Are these people who are currently searching for Daniel competent?"

"They are the best people we have." He straightened. "I didn't know we had so many people on the ground in that area. Not until a few hours ago."

When I looked at Vinnie, I was unsettled by the raw emotions displayed on his face. "The most prudent use of our time, skills and energy would be to continue our investigation."

"Fuck it, Jen-girl. I can't just sit around and look pretty."

"You're not pretty." I waved my hand to avoid an inane discussion. "You will not be sitting around. You have valuable resources that you can use."

"Like what?"

"Finding out if there have been any rumours or communication about a plane being hijacked or about an influx of art on the illegal market." I turned my attention back to Julien. "Tell me more about the woman the gunmen took. Who is she?"

"We don't know. Yet again, there's conflict in the witness statements. We're trying to determine exactly where she was seated. I'm expecting a call any moment now with her identity."

"Was she also beaten up?" Roxy asked.

"No, but she was handled quite roughly when she refused to go with them. Hopefully, we'll know soon who she is." Julien took his phone from his trouser pocket and glanced at the screen. "Nothing yet. Madame Godard and the president have been up all night trying to smooth things over."

"What does that mean?" I asked.

"President Godard will hold a press conference in a few hours. With all the recent terrorist attacks, the bombings at airports and crashed planes, he hopes to keep everyone calm."

"People's minds most likely already jumped to terrorism the moment the first report came out about the plane being missing." Roxy pushed some of her wayward curls behind one ear. "I don't know what the president would have to say to convince people to think otherwise."

"As soon as the president was briefed about the missing plane, we started working on a way to deal with this."

"In other words, spin it." Francine lifted one eyebrow.

"Call it what you want. We need the public to believe that we have the situation under control." He inhaled deeply. "That's a bit difficult since some of the passengers managed to contact their loved ones. Apparently they barely have phone reception where they are."

"What's their exact location?" Manny asked.

Julien looked from Manny to Francine to her tablet. "Search for Lake Osveya. The border crossing is right next to it."

"Got it." Francine tilted her head. "It really is in the very north-eastern corner of Belarus. And Latvia is right there too."

She held out her tablet and I took it. The road where Daniel's plane had landed was a few kilometres from where the borders of Russia, Belarus and Latvia met. "They're very close to the EU border."

Julien nodded. "Yes. I think if the passengers had known how close they were, they would've opted to walk through the forest at night in order to reach the safety of a European Union country rather than walk fifty metres to enter a country that still has such close ties to Russia."

Francine tapped her manicured nail on the table. "Well, I can tell you now that this Lake Osveya might be in the middle of nowhere and might not have any signal, but believe you me, the moment those gunmen disappeared, people took out their devices. And the moment they got within range of a signal, they most definitely connected with someone."

"Or put it on one of those bloody social media places. The news of Daniel's kidnapping is most likely everywhere." Manny pressed his palms against his eyes. "That means there's no containing it."

"And that means we have to use what we have." The calculation in Julien's expression confirmed his skills at turning any situation into positive publicity. "And that means that we're going to play up the art theft. We're feeding this to the media, making it a shocking heist."

"What about Daniel?" Vinnie asked.

"No doubt that will come up. The passengers are going to talk about this, but we'll find a way to play it down. It will be much better for Daniel if no one knows his identity and therefore his true value."

"Or the value of the woman." I wondered how she connected to Daniel, Fradkov, Emad, the threats to Daniel as well as Aleksei Volyntsev's polonium-210 poisoning.

A foreign ringtone drew my attention to Julien's phone. He swiped the screen before it could sound a second time. "Privott… Who…" His eyes widened and he paled. "Shit… Yes… I'm on it."

"Who is she?" Manny sat down, his body braced as if expecting impact.

"Amélie Didden."

I jerked when Roxy gasped loudly. "Oh, my God! I know her."

"What do you mean you know her?" Manny glared at Roxy. "Who is she?"

"She's a nuclear specialist. One of the best in nuclear chemistry and nuclear physics." Roxy scratched her head, which dislodged more riotous curls to fall around her face. "I was at a conference last year where she was the keynote speaker. She talked about the key implications in radiation, nuclear processes and nuclear properties. She's an incredible scientist."

An uncomfortable insight settled in my mind. "Would she be able to weaponise polonium-210?"

"Oh!" Roxy's mouth hung open for a second while she processed the full impact of my question. "Oh, this is not good. You're talking about the polonium-210 that's still missing from the last case with Fradkov and Emad, right? Oh. Oh, this is not good."

Manny threw his hands in the air. "Stop saying 'oh' and tell us if this Didden woman can use the polonium-210 to cause mass casualties."

"Watch your tone, old man." Vinnie crossed his arms, the look he gave Manny menacing.

Roxy chewed her thumbnail, ignoring both men's posturing. "Huh. Polonium-210 is not impossible to weaponise, but people have to ingest or inhale it, since a piece of paper would be a sufficient shield against any external exposure. Getting people to ingest it would be the best way to deliver a deadly dose."

"Could she do it, Rox?" Vinnie asked softly.

"Yes. Oh, most definitely yes." She nodded so hard her curls were bobbing. "If anyone could create an effective weapon that could kill thousands, even tens of thousands, it would be Amélie Didden."

"Holy, bloody hell!"

"What else do you know about her, Doctor Ferreira?" Julien asked.

"She is a leader and spokesperson for ISOLDE at CERN."

"Who's Isolde?" Julien narrowed his eyes. "Or is Isolde a what?"

"It's the On-Line Isotope Mass Separator. It is a facility located at CERN, which is the European Organization for Nuclear Research in Switzerland. ISOLDE started operating in 1967 and has numerous applications, including the production of radioactive nuclei." Roxy twisted one of her many wayward curls around her finger. "She's also a prolific researcher and has published many important articles. I can think of three of those articles that might be of interest to criminals like Fradkov and Emad."

"I have more." Francine pointed at the monitor of her laptop. "She's frequently lectured at three universities in Russia. And the topics she lectured on? The threats and implementations of a hydrogen bomb, based on lithium deuteride. She also had a session on how to obtain electricity from controlled thermonuclear reaction. Then there were a few more lectures and meetings about all kinds of fusion things. Russia has kept some of those lectures and discussions from being accessed by the public."

"Another element pointing to Russia being guilty of

some sort of conspiracy." I ignored the burst of envy at Amélie Didden's lectures and academic papers. It was a foreign experience for me and most unwelcome, so I kept my focus on the topic. "Aleksei Volyntsev's polonium-210 poisoning pointed to Russia, the plane landing in Russia and the SUVs registered to a Russian company all point to Russia."

Fradkov had started his campaign against Russia which had brought him to our attention seven months ago. If he had succeeded then, it would've had devastating political implications. My research into Ivan Fradkov had led me to believe that he possessed not only a higher intellect, but also impressive strategising skills.

What confounded me was this second attempt to aim for the same outcome. His profile didn't indicate repetition of mistakes or even taking action to rectify a failure. So why was he so determined to put the blame on Russia for these events? Was this more than a paid job for him?

"I'm totally working on the assumption that Fradkov and Emad are behind every single thing that's connected to this case." Francine winked at me. "So now my question is, why would they want Russia to look guilty of things that could start a war? Oh, my God! Is that it? Does Fradkov want Russia to start a war?"

I thought about this. "I can't claim to know what Fradkov is thinking or what he is planning, but this would be in the realm of possibilities. His history has shown us the many times he's changed the course of a country's political future by causing a scandal or assassinating a key opposition leader."

"Dammit." Julien leaned back in his chair. "This has to do with this peace treaty we're busy negotiating."

"Can you give us more specifics?" Manny asked. "The president's wife only told us… don't you bloody look at me like that, Privott. The president's wife trusts us and she knew that whatever she said would not go anywhere."

Julien shook his head. "Sorry. I'm just really shocked that she would say anything. She's usually the one reminding everyone to watch what they say and to whom."

"Well?" Manny lifted one hand palm up. "Are you going to tell us or do I need to phone the president?"

"You can really be an unpleasant bastard."

"Says the pot to the kettle." Colin chuckled, even more so when both Manny and Julien glared at him.

Julien pressed his lips tightly together for a second before turning to me. "In the last few years, Russia has turned the freeze up on friendships with the West. Their indiscriminate bombings in Syria that have killed hundreds of vulnerable civilians and their annexation of Crimea are only two examples of actions they've taken in complete disregard to any peace discussions they've had with the West.

"Europe, the US and other entities are concerned about the direction Russia is taking. This is the biggest reason for this classified and immensely important peace deal being discussed at the moment. Whatever Fradkov has got up his sleeve to make Russia look bad will be disastrous. It would get Europe pissed off with Russia for killing people with polonium-210 and stealing art worth millions. It would get Russia pissed off because they'll know they're being set up and all hell will break loose."

I thought about this. "This is in the same tone as the threatening email Daniel received."

"What do you mean, Doc?"

"From what you just said, it sounds like Fradkov wants Europe to lose respect for Russia, no longer care for, support or help Russia. The same as the threats."

"Huh. You might be onto something there. We already suspected Emad sent Daniel those emails. And we know that Emad is working with Fradkov." Manny sighed. "And who the blazes says, 'I will annihilate everything you are' when they threaten someone? Annihilate? Hmph."

Roxy jerked and lost colour in her face, but no one else noticed. She looked at Manny, her frown intensifying. Her left hand immediately lifted to twist a wayward curl round and round her finger. The insight I'd gathered into Roxy from spending time with her in the last seven months taught me that she twisted her curls for many reasons, one of those being when she tried to make sense of something.

I interrupted a disagreement between Julien and Francine when I knocked on the table. I waited until Roxy looked at me. The moment she registered the expression on my face, she rolled her eyes. "Sometimes you're fun, but sometimes you're not."

"What's going on, Rox?" Vinnie asked.

"Doc?" Manny asked me, but I didn't take my eyes off Roxy.

She sighed dramatically. "She saw me react when you said 'annihilate'."

"Why would you react?" Vinnie moved closer to Roxy, lowered his head and stared at her. "Did someone use those words with you?"

"Yes." I saw it on her face.

"I'll answer for myself. Thanks, Genevieve." Her tone was annoyed, but fear was the predominant expression on her face. "Twice now, I've received emails telling me that this person was going to annihilate everything I am. I thought it was some nutcase. Or spam. Or some Russian beauty who wanted me to download her naked photos so I can have a sexy virus on my computer."

Everything in me stilled. This was adding another element to the case that didn't quite connect. Roxy was connected to us, therefore indirectly connected to the president. Her work in exotic diseases and her expertise in polonium-210 poisoning was another connection. The strongest link was the fact that she was the one who'd killed Emad's brother.

The official report stated that Emad had been killed by Daniel. It had been a unanimous decision to keep the reports simple as well as to keep Roxy safe. But now she was in danger. I shifted in my seat, most displeased with the emotional weight of the irrational desire to protect the people in my life. This time, my protective instinct was aimed at Roxy.

I was not the only one displeased. Vinnie's lowered brow, tightened lips and flared nostrils conveyed anger, fear and frustration. I was not surprised when he got up and towered over Roxy, his jaw jutted and his hands fisted. "Rox, what the fuck are you talking about?"

Chapter ELEVEN

"Don't growl at me like that, snookums." Roxy gently rested her palm on Vinnie's cheek. "I'm safe."

Vinnie leaned in closer. "Safe? Really? Then why the fuc… why are you receiving threats from Emad?"

"We don't know who sent the emails." I would agree that it was likely to be Emad. But we didn't yet have irrefutable proof it was him.

Vinnie ignored me, his expression not softening. "Why didn't you tell me about these threats?"

"Because this would happen."

"This what?" Vinnie straightened. "This, the fact that an international criminal is probably now looking to add you to his kill list? This, the fact that your life is in danger?"

"No." She shook her head. "This, the fact that I didn't want to be a worry, a burden to you."

"What the fuck?" Vinnie took a step back. "A burden? How can you think that?"

"You worry about everyone all the time, snookums." Her emotional guilelessness astounded me. I detected no awareness on her face for the audience listening to their private exchange. "I want to give you a respite from that."

Her expression told me that she didn't see the hurt that flashed over Vinnie's features. I couldn't let that go unaddressed. "By giving Vinnie a respite from protecting you, you are robbing him of the biggest gift he could give you. He's a protector by nature, Roxanne. If you don't allow him to be who he is, you're not accepting him."

At first, Roxy was offended, but by my last statement her eyes had grown wide. She looked at Vinnie. "Is she right?"

"She's always right." Vinnie glared at me. "Even when she tells the whole frigging world I'm a pussy."

"I didn't—" I stopped when Colin put his hand on my forearm and shook his head. I didn't know why he was smiling. Vinnie was clearly upset.

Roxy got up and stood in front of Vinnie. The top of her head only just reached his chin. She raised herself on her toes and kissed him lightly on his lips. "I didn't know. I'm sorry."

"Good, now give us access to your bleeding email." Manny mumbled something else about soap operas. I didn't ask him to explain because I recognised his irritated scowl.

Roxy gave Vinnie another soft kiss and sat down again. "Um, you want to have full access?"

"You have something to hide?" Manny lowered his chin and stared at her from under his brow.

"You are such a drama queen." Roxy rolled her eyes at Manny and turned to Francine. "Are you in my email yet?"

"Yes." Francine's smile was genuine and without apology. "Do I have official access?"

Roxy laughed. "Yeah. Just ignore all the online shopping confirmation emails."

"Show me the emails with the threats." Only if I read them would I be able to determine if it was the same person who had sent the threats to Daniel.

"They're in my 'Other' folder." Roxy put her index finger

on her lips. "Or maybe my 'Crap' folder. Oh, shit, I don't remember where I put it."

"Got it. It was in your 'WTH' folder." Francine looked at the laptop in front of me. "I sent it to you."

I thought of asking what 'WTH' could possibly mean, but didn't want to waste any more time. I opened my email and clicked on the first unread email. Colin leaned in closer to read it as well. I read it three times before I opened the second email.

I leaned back in my chair and studied the second email, allowing my mind to run through all the information we had gathered so far. The first email was a generic threat that Roxy had to stop keeping company with 'ill-chosen people' and that it would end her career. She had received the second email six days after the first. This one had information that interested me. "What happened in 2011?"

"Oh, yeah." Roxy tugged on a curl. "Is that the part where he tells me that my actions from 2011 will come back to haunt me?"

"Those weren't his words." I looked at the email. "The email reads, 'Doctors so often have a god complex and you are no different. The difference is that you are a bad god. The world needs to know what you did in 2011. And soon everyone will.'" I turned my attention back to her. "What did you do?"

Julien grunted loudly when Roxy glanced at him. "Roxanne Ferreira, do you really think I don't know who you are? The moment you started hanging out with this bunch, I had you thoroughly vetted. Only to find out you had already been vetted. Top-secret clearance and all. Not surprising, really.

Not when you know more about biological weapons than most of the numerous agencies that sang your praises. I'm the director of public relations for the president of France. In order to do my job, I'm privy to highly sensitive information and secrets that range from threatening national security to threatening every single moral value on this planet. Your little secret is not going to impress me. Really."

Roxy bit her bottom lip, then nodded and looked at me. "In 2011, I prevented an assassination attempt on the president of Moldova and killed the opposition leader."

A shocked silence followed her statement. Vinnie sat down hard on his chair, his expression a combination of respect and awe. Francine looked giddy, Manny's scowl was severe and Julien's eyebrows were raised high on his forehead. "I stand corrected. I'm impressed."

"Speak." Manny's tone mirrored his scowl.

"I was part of a six-month work exchange in Chişinău."

"What? Where?" Vinnie squinted. "It sounded like you sneezed."

Roxy smiled. "Chişinău is Moldova's capital. I was working at the academic hospital and also lecturing at the university. Five months in, I published a paper on improving the functions of important protein molecules to use in medical diagnostics and therapy. While doing my research, which was fascinating by the way, I came across a few things in the university's data that didn't look right to me. But the paper had to be published and I focused my attention on that. Once it was out in the big wide world, I returned to those things that had caught my attention.

"I did most of my research in their molecular biology lab,

which is in the biomedical engineering department, and I noticed that the numbers didn't make sense. The laboratory's inventory showed that they'd had two hundred grams of anthrax and they'd used a hundred and fifty. Yet their records showed that they had ordered and taken delivery of two hundred and fifty grams. That means there were a hundred grams unaccounted for."

"Dear Mary and all the holy saints." Manny sighed heavily, shaking his head.

Roxy straightened in her chair. "Anthrax is one of the easiest ways to off someone from a distance. You don't need all that much inside an envelope to give someone a lethal dose. Provided of course they open said envelope. Anyway, I looked a little deeper and found that the opposition leader's brother was a researcher at the lab. He was the one who had ordered the anthrax and also had full access to the stock.

"To make a very long story short, my discovery triggered an investigation that revealed a plot against the president. I helped the special investigations unit get enough solid evidence against the opposition leader to arrest him. When the guys went to arrest the leader, the idiot pulled out a gun. The rest is history."

"No, it's not." Manny leaned towards her. "I've never heard about this."

"Because it was kept very hush-hush. At that time, Moldova was at a bit of a delicate stage in politics and something like this would've resulted in an uprising. Not the good kind of uprising. So the death was explained away as a suicide."

"You said you killed him." Vinnie leaned towards her, his posture exhibiting anger. "You didn't."

"Technically I didn't." Remorse flashed across her features. She tightened her lips and pulled her shoulders back. "I know I shouldn't feel guilty, but I became a doctor to save lives, not cause the end of anyone's life."

"Your reasoning is flawed." I didn't like the sadness that had crept into Roxy's usually cheerful expression. "Were you there when this person was killed? Did you order him to be killed? Did you have any control over the situation that could make you responsible for the outcome? Did you tell the leader to pull out a gun when faced with law enforcement officers who are all well-armed?"

Roxy's smile didn't reach her eyes. "The answer to all those questions is no, but somehow my heart doesn't want to accept it."

The softness in Vinnie's expression when he reached over and pulled Roxy into a hard hug distracted me from being annoyed at people using an organ to explain their emotional centre.

"Ooh, I've got something!" Francine bounced in her chair, but didn't take her eyes off her computer. "This is just…"

"For the love of all that is holy." Manny slapped his hand on the table. "Would you for once finish a sentence?"

Francine looked up, her faux embarrassment ridiculous in its exaggeration. "Handsome, don't flirt like that with me in front of all these people."

Manny's lips tightened even more as his cheeks gained extra colour. "Supermodel."

She winked at him and smiled when Roxy giggled. "Okay,

fine. I've traced the two emails sent to Roxy. They were both sent from 3G internet from a phone. But that's not the really interesting bit. What has me all excited is that there is a connection between the SIM used to send the emails to Roxy and the SIM used for the phone and internet to send those emails to Daniel."

"What connection?" Vinnie straightened.

"Emad is smart. He didn't buy the SIM cards from the same store or on the same day or with the same credit card. As a matter of fact, he didn't use a credit card when he bought the SIM cards. But both these cards connected to the same four cell towers. So I installed some software that pushed an installation in both the devices to give us a location."

"And?" Manny shifted in his chair. His feet were already pointed at the door, his hands on his knees, ready to push him up.

"Both devices are at 316 Rue de Nami."

"That's seven blocks from us." Vinnie got up. "Let's go."

"Wait." I closed my eyes and thought about everything Otto had told us before he'd gotten killed. When I opened my eyes, I looked at Francine. "Bring up a map of the street."

"Give me a sec." She worked on her computer for a few seconds. "What are you looking for?"

"I want to see what the building looks like." I thought some more. "It most likely won't stand out. And it's already close to us."

"Close to us?" Manny asked. "What the hell, Doc?"

I saw the realisation dawn on Francine as she got back to work. I turned to Manny. "Before Otto was assassinated, he said that Emad was hiding in plain sight, closer than we think."

"Got it." Francine stared at her computer with wide eyes, then turned it around. "Look."

I leaned closer to see the building on her computer monitor. It was beautiful, but fitted in so well with the neighbouring buildings that it became nondescript.

"Anyone coming with me?" Vinnie walked to the door. "I'm going to gut that motherfucker."

"Hold your horses, big guy." Manny rubbed his hand over his face. "We've got to do this right."

"Yeah, you should put some thought into this first." Julien flinched only slightly when Vinnie looked at him with great aggression. "This is not only about your friend. It is also about a politically delicate situation, about the president's reputation, about his wife's reputation, as well as about the lives of Daniel and Amélie Didden."

"Fuck!" Vinnie glanced at the door, his fists tight, his arms away from his body. "I can't just stand here."

"We're not going to." Colin got up. "But if we want to do this right, we should get Daniel's team in on this."

"Is that wise?" Julien shook his head. "I mean, they're all emotionally invested in this. Won't it cloud their judgement?"

"They are the best for this job." Colin looked at Manny. "I'll get them up to speed. They can converge here and you can take it further."

Manny nodded at Colin, then turned to Julien with one eyebrow raised. Three seconds later, Julien threw his hands in the air and leaned back in his chair. Manny's smile was triumphant. "Thought so."

Vinnie shifted on his feet, restless. "Let's do this."

Chapter TWELVE

I pressed my thumb hard against my little finger. Usually it worked to trigger a response I'd conditioned myself to feel. Yet the expected calm didn't come at this moment. I hated feeling this powerless and anxious for the lives of those I cared for. At least Nikki and Roxy were safe at home and Colin was sitting next to me. I shifted a bit closer to him.

My non-neurotypical mind screamed at me to get away from this highly distressing situation. Another part of me wouldn't allow me to leave the GIPN operational truck. My eyes were glued to the monitors showing the body cameras of all the team members.

Vinnie was wearing a GIPN uniform, complete with body camera. Manny had donned a bulletproof vest and two holsters around his thighs. I watched him through Vinnie's body camera as he talked to Jean Bonnard. He was third in command after Daniel. Pink was still in the GIPN truck with us, but as their second-in-command and now the one in control, he would leave soon to guide the team as they entered the building down the street.

We were parked three houses to the west, blocking the street. Not that it was a problem at this hour. Very few people were awake at five thirty in the morning. Most would only wake up in another hour and leave for work an hour after that. The street was quiet in the glow of the streetlights.

This was one of the older areas in Strasbourg. The houses in this street, in this area, had been built for the affluent who'd wanted to have a few floors as well as a back entrance for the servants. Most of these buildings had long since been subdivided into apartments, the original layouts lost.

Francine had researched the owners of the house we'd tracked Emad to, while Pink had found the blueprints for the building. This was one of the very few houses that had never been subdivided and it appeared to have been in the same family for the last hundred and twenty-three years. It was a four-story mansion squeezed in between similar buildings from the same era.

It was most uncommon for a large residence in such a sought-after neighbourhood not to have been monetised by subdividing it. The plans showed large rooms, high ceilings and a wide staircase leading from just past the entrance all the way to the top floor. Pink had forwarded the plans to his team's devices and they'd planned their breach.

"Bonnard and Mécary are in place." Jean's voice was quiet and controlled. I glanced at the monitor of his partner Claudette's body camera and saw his posture was alert and ready for action. A quick look at his camera confirmed that Claudette was just as focused as Jean. They were at the front door, already having picked the lock. They were ready to open the door and enter.

"Meslot and Gautier in place." They'd used the neighbouring building to get to the roof and now were on a small balcony on the top floor. The two glass doors had been easy enough to force open without making too much noise. They too were ready to enter.

"Millard and the big guy are in place." Manny's tone was crisp. Again I glanced at Vinnie's body camera and saw Manny standing upright, his vigilance unmistakeable. They were at the back of the house, at what used to be the servants' entrance.

All of them, including Manny, were wearing night vision lenses over one eye. While strategising the breach, they had decided to only turn on the house's lights at the very last moment.

"That's my cue." Pink got up and turned on his communication unit. "I'm exiting the truck. One minute. Francine will monitor the infrared and update us."

"The target is still sleeping." Francine had taken Pink's seat and clicked through a few monitors until she settled. Pink had sent up GIPN's drone with the infrared camera to monitor the house. Only one body was visible in the whole building. It was on the third of the four floors and had moved only once since we'd arrived. The sleeping figure had gone from lying on his left side to lying on his back.

Francine was convinced it was Emad sleeping in the house, but I was careful not to make assumptions. If it were indeed Emad and GIPN safely captured him within the next few minutes, I would experience great relief. The last seven months with the threat Emad and Fradkov posed not only to me, but also to my team and the political stability of Europe, had added stress to my life that I did not find easy to process and control.

Francine clicked once and all the images on the monitors changed from the dark shadows to the eerie green from night vision. I could see a lot more now. The detail from the night vision devices didn't allow me to see micro-expressions, but I caught the changes in posture and larger nonverbal cues.

"Positions." Pink's voice came over the system. On screen, he joined Vinnie and Manny at the back door. "Breach in three, two, one. Execute, execute, execute."

I was fascinated by the stealth with which the big men moved through the house. Meslot and Gautier opened the balcony's two glass doors and quietly moved from room to room on the top floor while declaring each area secure as soon as they went through the room thoroughly, looking behind and under furniture and opening all cupboard doors. Still with minimal sound.

Pink, Vinnie and Manny entered the back door and met with Jean and Claudette at the staircase. Vinnie, Manny and Pink went straight to the room with the sleeping figure, leaving Jean and Claudette to secure the lower floors.

"Target still asleep."

I jerked at the sound of Francine's voice. She was taking over the role of Pink, keeping the team updated with any and all changes she observed from the truck. The few times I'd been in the truck during a GIPN operation, I'd been astounded at the wealth of information Pink received from the electronic surveillance and how quickly he relayed it to his team.

On Vinnie's camera, Pink was leading them up the stairs, Manny behind him, their weapons raised, one finger resting next to the trigger, ready to take action. At each landing, they checked the area before taking the next flight.

The walls along the stairs were filled with artwork that had Colin leaning closer to the monitors. He didn't say a word, but the tension in his muscles increased with each new painting that came into view. The unexpected cache of art was not a priority at the moment, but I knew Colin would not wait a second longer than necessary to enter that house and analyse the paintings that looked like masterpieces to my untrained eye.

Pink, Manny and Vinnie passed the second floor, paused to check the next flight and quietly made their way up the stairs. On the third floor, they moved towards the room they had earlier determined held the sleeping person.

"Still asleep." Francine's voice was a bare whisper and I wondered if they'd heard her. They moved quietly along the hallway, clearing three open rooms, two on the left and one on the right. Before they reached the second door on the right, Pink held up his fist and they stopped.

"Still no movement," Francine whispered again.

Pink raised two fingers and waved them forward. Manny immediately tapped Pink on his shoulder and moved past him to the other side of the open door. Vinnie's hand moved past his body camera to also tap Pink on his shoulder.

They waited until the other four members declared all the floors secure. Meslot and Gautier remained on the stairs while Jean and Claudette came from the second floor to join Manny, Vinnie and Pink. They approached the room from Vinnie and Pink's side. Claudette tapped Vinnie on his shoulder, who responded immediately by tapping Pink on his shoulder.

Pink raised his open hand and with his fingers together pointed three times into the room. Vinnie and Pink entered the room first. Manny followed them and didn't even look at the figure lying on the bed. From Claudette's body camera, I saw Manny sweep the room until his posture relaxed marginally and he positioned himself at the far side of the bed.

"Lights." Pink's soft, yet audible command was followed immediately by chaos. Jean switched on the bedroom's lights. There was a momentary flash of white on the screens before Francine clicked once to change the cameras back from night vision to normal viewing.

The monitors were filled with jerky movements and a lot of shouting came through the system. Pink and Vinnie's voices were the loudest, ordering the person on the bed to remain still and not even move his hands.

Most of the movement settled to show Manny not having moved from his position, his assault rifle trained on the person in the bed. Vinnie was standing next to the bed, his handgun pressed against the person's head. I leaned forward to get a better view and exhaled a breath I didn't even know I'd held.

It was Emad.

His eyes were wide, his pupils pinpricks as he jerked his gaze from gun-wielding man to gun-wielding man. I saw the moment he realised there was no escape for him. The tension around his mouth relaxed into an almost-smile and his shoulders sagged back into the mattress. "What do you know. You found me."

"Move and I'll maim you." Vinnie moved his weapon from Emad's head to press against his shoulder. If Vinnie were to shoot, he wouldn't kill Emad, but the injury would be painful and could cause permanent damage.

Pink pulled the light duvet off Emad to reveal the criminal's pale, naked body. He didn't move, didn't even attempt to hide his exposed genitals. His body was well-toned, but not very muscular. Knowing the human psyche, I wasn't surprised to see a micro-expression of vulnerability flash across his features. Even though clothing couldn't stop bullets, that layer gave us a certain subconscious protection against the world.

"Get up, asshole." Vinnie tapped the gun against Emad's shoulder. "We've got a lot to talk about."

Manny moved around the bed to stand next to Vinnie, not taking his aim off Emad. "You heard what the big guy said. Get up."

My entire being was focused on the monitors in front of me. Reading Emad's nonverbal communication was both surprising and illuminating. His facial muscles relaxed even more as he looked from Manny's rifle to Vinnie's expression of rage. He turned his head to look at the gun against his shoulder, the smile that tugged at the corners of his mouth genuine. "I might need a little bit of space to get up, gentlemen."

Manny nodded at Vinnie, but didn't step back. It took Vinnie another two seconds to rein in his anger and lift the muzzle of his handgun from Emad's shoulder. The smile lifting one corner of his mouth was not genuine. It was filled with malice. "Please do something stupid so I can shoot you. Please."

"My stupid card is filled up." Emad lifted his hands palms out and slowly sat up. "Tomorrow is another day. Right now, I think getting some trousers might be the best move for me.

Unless you like looking at my junk?"

"That's just the kind of thing that might get you shot, asshole." Vinnie lowered his weapon until it was aimed at Emad's crotch. "Although I might need binoculars to get a good aim."

Emad laughed loudly and shook his head. Still holding his hands up, he got out of bed and walked towards a large antique wardrobe and pointed at the door. "One of you might want to open this and get me a pair of trousers. And preferably some boxers too. I don't really like the whole free-in-the-air commando thing."

Pink looked at Manny and Vinnie. "You got him?"

"In my sights, dude." Vinnie rolled his shoulders, his top lip curled.

Pink nodded and walked towards the wardrobe. He studied Emad for a few seconds. "Step away from the wardrobe."

Emad nodded and walked back to the bed. I'd never paid close attention to Pink's observation skills. If Daniel had been here, I knew he would've noticed the lack of anticipation and excitement in Emad's body language. Emad was exhibiting none of the usual cues that would have led me to believe that there was a trap in the wardrobe. Pink seemed to have picked that up as well, the tension in his shoulders relaxing marginally as he reached into his backpack.

He took out a device that he'd used on a few occasions when securing a room from any electronic surveillance equipment. He'd proudly told me that he'd modified his device to not only register any surveillance devices, but also anything that had an electronic trigger or switch. I had to ask him three times before he'd admitted that it wasn't without limitations, but he had convinced me that he trusted his device to keep him and his team safe.

He slowly moved the device along the beautifully carved doors of the wardrobe, then swiped it across every centimetre of the wooden exterior. It took more than a minute before he nodded in satisfaction and opened the door. He put the device back in his backpack and took out the first pair of trousers, boxers and t-shirt he saw.

"Get dressed." Pink threw the clothes on the bed and stepped into the hallway. "Report."

"We checked the entire house." Meslot's voice was calm. "There's not a single trace of any radiation. If they have the polonium-210, it's not here."

"And we double-checked the rooms," Gautier said. "All clear. It's a huge place, this. And only a few rooms appear to have been lived in."

I glanced up at the monitors and saw Manny facing Vinnie's camera. "Get your butt in here, Doc. We've got work to do. Oh, and bring Frey. There are more paintings than I care for. Maybe he can make sense of it all."

"I've got the truck, Francine." Bernard Cosse, the newest member of the GIPN team, walked from the front of the truck to where we were sitting. "I'm not as good as you and Pink on the electronics, but I'll hold the fort here."

Francine jumped out of her seat. "Are you sure? That would be great."

Bernard smiled and nodded.

Francine waved impatiently at Colin and I. "Come on. We have a whole house of treasure waiting for us."

"If the paintings I saw on the walls are originals, it really is a house of treasure." Colin got up and held out his hand to me. "Coming?"

I inhaled deeply and got up without taking Colin's hand. I didn't want to go into the building that housed Emad. Even though I felt relief that he was now in our custody, it didn't bring the peace of mind I had hoped for. I reached into my mind to find out why the restlessness I had been feeling suddenly held an urgency to it. Nothing came to me. I ignored Colin's questioning look and walked past him to follow Francine out the truck.

We walked in silence to the house. I noticed only three of the extra officers Pink had requested as backup. I didn't know where the others were, but knowing we were surrounded gave me some form of comfort. Gautier opened the front door for us, light from the entrance spilling into the street. They had turned on every light in the house.

Francine pushed past Gautier, her mouth agape. "Oh, my God. What a beautiful place. Wow. Otto was right. Emad is really living in an antique collection."

I agreed with her. The entrance to the house looked like it could be a display room for an auction catalogue. Francine disappeared into the first room to our left and I walked to the staircase, leaving Colin behind. He was standing in front of a painting hanging over a fragile-looking table that I estimated dated from the seventeenth century.

Gautier locked the front door and followed me. "Vernet is on the third floor, Doc."

I stopped and looked at the tall man. "Doctor Lenard or Genevieve. Not Doc."

"Um. Okay." He raised one eyebrow. "So, Genevieve, are you going to the third floor?"

"Not yet." I recalled his earlier report to Pink. "Show me the rooms that you said looked lived-in."

His face relaxed with a genuine smile. I had not realised he was hoping for my approval or acceptance. He pointed at the room Francine had disappeared into. "I think he used that as a living room."

Francine was no longer in the room when I walked in. On the far side of the large space was a door that led to another room and I assumed she'd gone through there. I took my time looking around the room, registering every magazine and newspaper on the coffee tables, the placement of the remote control for the large flat screen television as well as every piece of furniture, rug and decoration.

When I was ready to leave, Gautier led me to a room on the first floor. As with all the other rooms, the high ceilings made it appear even more spacious than it already was. But in contrast to the room I'd been in and those I'd passed, this was not decorated with antique furnishings.

A large chrome and glass desk dominated the left-hand side of the room, whereas a computer station with four monitors and a mess of wires dominated the right. Behind the gleaming desk, a bookshelf took up most of the wall. I estimated there to be only fifty or so books. The rest of the shelves were filled with artworks of all eras. The wooden floor was bare and industrial-style light fittings decorated the other walls. There were a lot of lights in this room.

Instead of the heavy designer curtains that covered the other rooms' windows, this room had two sets of blinds. I looked closer and my suspicion that it blocked out all light from the outside as well as from within was confirmed. From my position by the window I looked around the room, thinking how very different it was from the almost cosy feel of the living room.

"Here you are." Manny walked into the room and stopped with disgust lifting his top lip. "What the hell is this?"

"A home office, me thinks." Gautier pointed at the desk and the piece of equipment next to it. "With this kind of industrial shredder, this can only be an office."

"What do you think, Doc?" Manny gave Gautier one last look before walking towards me.

"Gautier is most likely correct." I looked again at the bookshelves. "The lack of literature is a mystery though."

"Jenny!" Colin walked into the room, a painting in each hand. "You will not believe what I have here."

Colour rode high on his cheeks and his eyes were wide with excitement. He looked around for a suitable place to put the paintings on display. He decided on the clear desktop and carefully put the paintings down. I stepped closer and lifted both eyebrows. "Are they authentic?"

"These babies are as authentic as they come. I'll stake my entire collection on it."

Manny huffed and came to stand next to me. Then he gasped. "Bloody holy hell, Frey! Are these the Uccello paintings that are supposed to be on Daniel's plane?"

Colin nodded his head slowly, not taking his eyes off the paintings. "This here is Uccello's *Saint George and the Dragon* and that beauty is *Scenes of the Life of the Holy Hermits*. Aren't they magnificent?"

"They're very pretty, Frey. Now tell me why the hell they are here and not on that plane."

"I think that's a question better answered by Emad." I looked at Gautier. "Where is he?"

Gautier turned to Manny. "Sir?"

Manny groaned. "He's in the washroom tossing his cookies."

"Why would he do such a thing?" And who had given him cookies?

"He's vomiting, love." Colin frowned and looked at Manny. "What's wrong with him?"

"He claims that he's not sick or infected with anything."

"He says that it's relief," Gautier said quietly. "He's been saying 'It's over, it's over' the whole time he's been… vomiting."

Interesting. Every human being reacted differently to stress and also to the abrupt ending of a stressful situation. These reactions were far too numerous to spend valuable time considering at the moment. All I cared about was that Emad not only reacted in a very interesting manner, but he claimed something to be over. I turned to Manny. "Bring him in here when he's ready."

Manny nodded to Gautier who left the room immediately. Then he turned back to the paintings and stared at them for a few seconds before slumping. "Are you very sure these things are real, Frey?"

"As sure as you are that those shoes actually look good with those trousers. What am I saying? You most likely believe those shoes look good with everything."

"What the hell is wrong with my shoes?" Manny looked

down, then glared at Colin. "They're comfortable."

"And as ugly as sin." Colin pointed at the art on the desk. "These on the other hand are beauties that deserve to be in a museum, protected. Not in some international criminal's hideout. And yes, I'm completely convinced they are authentic. I don't know what was being transported to Minsk, but it was not Uccello's originals."

"Could the paintings on the plane be the forgeries that Otto and Justine talked about?"

"Huh." Colin blinked. "Very possible. If Otto and Justine were right and Fradkov got these masterpieces and others forged, maybe the forgeries were good enough to make it past inspection and get on that plane."

To what end, I wondered. I placed that question in the back of my mind and stepped closer to the bookshelf. "What do you think about the artworks here?"

"Oh, my." Colin walked to the left of the bookshelf, his eyes wide. "This is a Gian Lorenzo Bernini sculpture." He leaned in closer. "And it looks real. If it is real, the value of this will be… it will be unimaginable. Oh, my."

I waited. Colin was slowly walking along the shelves, inhaling sharply every time he focused on a different piece. He stopped in front of a sculpture of two men, one older and one younger. The older man had his arm around the younger man's shoulders, appearing to pull him forward. The younger man had his arm around the older man's waist, looking away. Colin was clearly in awe of what he was looking at. When he turned around to face me, his face had lost some colour. "This is *Daedalus and Icarus* by Antonio Canova, Jenny. He made this masterpiece in 1779. Without tests, I can't tell if it is authentic, but it sure looks like it. And knowing Fradkov, it most likely is. This should be in a museum with its own private guards. The value of this alone is in the millions of euros."

"Bloody hell." Manny sighed heavily and pushed his hands in his trouser pockets.

Loud footsteps sounded in the hallway and I glanced at the door. All the GIPN members had been quiet and light on their feet throughout the entire operation. The only reason I imagined they were stomping their feet was to alert us to Emad's presence.

No sooner had I thought that than Gautier came into the room, followed by Emad. Meslot and Pink were behind him, their hands on their holstered weapons. Emad was fully dressed, his hands cuffed behind his back. The slight movement of his shoulders indicated discomfort as he glanced around the room. His eyes widened when he noticed the two paintings on the desk. Then he smiled. "You found my inspiration."

"I'm pretty sure a four-year-old can paint better than you, Vernet." Manny pushed his hands in his pockets. "Where did you get these paintings?"

"They came with the house." Emad glanced at the bookshelf and took a step back. "There's a lot of inspiration in this house."

I stilled. Emad was not acting the same as when he'd been in GIPN custody seven months ago. Then, his only response to every question had been, "Lawyer." Now he was answering questions. He was also not attempting to hide any of his nonverbal cues. It was easy to read his relief, his fear and his sadness. I narrowed my eyes to register as much as possible.

"How long have you been here?" Manny asked.

"About six months." He smiled at me. "It was nice to be so close to the people who changed my life."

Manny snapped his fingers in the air until Emad looked at him. "Whose house is this?"

"Don't you know?" He glanced again at the bookshelf and lost some colour in his face. Inhaling deeply, he turned so he was no longer facing the desk and the wall behind it. "The house is still registered to the family who gave this place to Ivan."

"Ivan Fradkov?" Manny spoke through his teeth, his jaw clenched.

Emad swallowed a few times and I wondered if he was going to vomit again. But he appeared to regain his composure and faced Manny. "Yes. The house and everything in it belongs to Ivan Fradkov."

There was so much to read in Emad's nonverbal communication. When Manny was going to ask another question, I held up my hand to stop him. I took my time studying Emad until I felt I had a grasp of what I'd observed. I lowered my hand. "Are there any recording devices in this room?"

His relief at my question was almost comical. "Video only, no audio."

"In the rest of the house?"

"This is the only room that doesn't have audio."

I resisted the urge to search for cameras aiming at us and was impressed that none of the others looked up either. "Do you know where the cameras are?"

"I'm facing away from all of them."

Manny looked at me, his expression questioning. I nodded. Emad was telling the truth. "Any cameras aiming at me?"

"Only from the side." He glanced at Manny. "Everyone else is in full view."

Which meant that no one would be able to accurately read my lips if they later analysed the footage. I thought of all the questions I had for Emad. But the most important had to be asked first. "What do you know about the plane?"

"What plane?" His confusion appeared genuine.

"What do you know about Daniel Cassel?"

"The man responsible for my brother's death?" Sorrow and anger battled for dominance on his face. "I know that I'm conflicted about him. He did his job, but he took my brother from me."

I decided to change my tactic. "Did you kill Daniel?"

Emad's eyebrows rose high on his forehead, his mouth slightly agape. It was highly improbable, but not impossible to fake shock this immediate and this accurate. "He's dead? What? How? When did this happen?"

I leaned a bit closer to him. "Did you kill him?"

"No! No, I didn't." He shook his head vehemently. "I'm done with that. No. I didn't do any such thing. I swear. I haven't even left this house for the last six months."

It was so quick, I almost missed that micro-expression. "Have you been here voluntarily?"

He swallowed, his face losing colour again. "The first two weeks, yes."

There was more I wanted to know, but our safety was first priority. "What is behind the bookshelf?"

He closed his eyes and breathed slowly four times. When he opened his eyes, he looked exhausted. "Fradkov's panic room. I haven't been in there, but you'll most likely find the answers to all your questions in there."

Everyone in the room stood frozen, but I was sure they were tempted to look at the wall behind the desk. "Is it protected?"

"Booby-trapped?" Pink added.

"Yes." He lowered his head, his nonverbal cues begging me. "Please get me out of here."

"First tell us what to look for if we want to get into the panic room." Manny moved his lips to the minimum, no doubt to make it harder for someone to lip-read. "What kind of booby-traps are we talking about?"

"I don't know." He looked at me, imploring. "I really don't. He told me what he would do to my father if I ever came in here."

"You're lying." It was easy to see. "Your fear is real, but you do know how to enter that room."

His nostrils flared. "Get me out of here and I'll talk. Maybe. But I won't say another word while in this house."

He was being truthful. The way he pressed his lips tightly together confirmed that he would not co-operate while on Fradkov's property. I nodded to Manny. With a sigh, he waved Gautier closer. "Take this arsehole to Rousseau & Rousseau."

Chapter THIRTEEN

"This was… okay." The resentment on Vinnie's face as he looked at the empty serving dishes on the round table in our team room surprised me. He lifted one shoulder in a half-shrug. "I mean, the spinach had a bit too much cream and not enough mushrooms."

"Do you really think so?" Nikki stared at the large bowl that had contained the creamed spinach. "I followed your recipe exactly the way you made it last week."

"Ignore him, Nix." Francine lifted her chin and looked down her nose at Vinnie. "At least Nikki's food didn't need any cumin or a touch of rosemary."

"You can't put those things in any of these dishes, woman." Vinnie crossed his arms and exhaled loudly.

"There was absolutely nothing wrong with this food." Pink leaned back in his chair and rubbed his stomach. "It was possibly the best spinach I've ever eaten."

Vinnie inhaled sharply. "Then you've never had *my* creamed spinach."

Roxy shook her head and a few more curls escaped her loose braid. "You're just put out that we made fabulous food and you didn't have anything to do with it." She threw her arms around Vinnie in an uncomfortable-looking sideways hug and rested her head on his shoulder. "We didn't try to steal your job, snookums. We just wanted to help you a little bit on this crazy day. I know this has not been easy for you."

The tension in Vinnie's shoulders eased and he kissed Roxy's chaotic curls. When he raised his eyes to Nikki, his apology was clear on his face. "I didn't mean to insult your cooking, little punk."

"Well, you did." Her faux-distress was outrageous in its exaggeration. "And I'm telling Eric about this."

Vinnie snorted. "The tiny punk won't be interested in my food for at least the first six months and then only mushy versions of my family's masterpieces."

I found their bantering both soothing and confusing. After Manny had sent Emad to Rousseau & Rousseau, Pink had used his device to test the bookshelf and had determined where the door to the panic room was. But a lot of red lights had started blinking on his device. The entrance to the panic room had numerous unnamed electronic devices that Pink and Francine were convinced were better left alone for the moment.

Manny and Pink had called the bomb squad and had asked Edward Henry, their best explosives ordinance disposal technician, to join us at Fradkov's house to ensure there were no explosives. Edward had arrived with his team and had declared the premises secure after a forty-minute inspection.

In a rare show of stubborn resistance, Colin had refused to leave. He'd counted twenty-seven original works of art and hadn't wanted to leave them in the house. While Vinnie and Pink had helped him load the paintings in his SUV, Francine and I had confirmed six of those paintings were on the manifest from Daniel's flight. They were supposed to be on their way to the exhibition in Minsk.

Thirteen of these paintings were on numerous international lists for stolen art. Colin believed that Otto had helped Fradkov acquire these artworks illegally. Only eight of the paintings had been bought legitimately.

We now had twenty-seven authentic works of art in our team room, which meant some on the plane were forgeries. I refused to speculate how many more were forgeries. Colin estimated that the four forgers Otto and Justine mentioned could easily have forged between thirty and fifty paintings in the last seven months. It added yet another layer to this case.

When we'd arrived at Rousseau & Rousseau, Roxy and Nikki had already been waiting for an hour and a half with our lunch. Nikki had been especially proud to have done something to help while we were looking for Daniel. From the nonverbal cues I'd observed on Roxy's face, I'd surmised that she'd helped Nikki more for Nikki than for us. It made me like her even more.

The bantering continued while I looked around the table. Colin was quietly watching everyone, but his eyes kept moving back to the paintings from Fradkov's house on the other side of our spacious team room. Twelve of those paintings were arranged on easels, two of the smaller ones sharing one easel. The others were leaning against the wall. These masterpieces were awe-inspiring in their combined beauty.

Francine kept teasing Manny in an obvious attempt to lighten the mood, but she was not successful. Her wit was misplaced, her deep concern evident in the way she would bite down on her thumbnail when someone else dominated the conversation.

I looked at Julien and put my knife and fork down loud enough on my plate to get everyone's attention. "You told Manny earlier that none of your 'people on the ground' have reported any sightings of Daniel. Can these people be trusted? How do you know they're trying hard enough to locate Daniel?"

Julien looked at me for a few seconds. The lines around and the dark rings under his eyes were more prominent than last night. "I slept only three hours last night. Two of the four teams looking for Daniel did not sleep at all. One team is going through every single video recording they can find of ATM, shop security and city or town CCTV cameras in a hundred-kilometre radius from where the plane landed. So far they haven't found any sign of Daniel or of the nuclear scientist Amélie Didden. But they're not giving up. We've sent more of our best people to assist them."

"Isn't that a bit OTT?" Roxy glanced at me. "Over the top. Daniel is important and all, but so many people looking for one man?"

Julien studied Roxy for a long while. "What do you think it means?"

"That he's important in ways we don't know about."

Manny slumped in his chair. "Daniel's recent discussion with the president regarding national security issues is causing a panic that Privott here doesn't want to talk about."

I hated feeling so conflicted. On the one hand, I wanted to interview Emad and find out anything he knew about

Fradkov's plans. And to determine whether Emad truly wanted to be free of Fradkov or whether it had been a ruse. To what end I didn't know.

On the other hand, I had an extremely strong and utterly irrational urge to leave everything else, get in my car and drive to the border of Russia and Belarus to start looking for Daniel myself. It surprised me how my concern for him overrode my dislike for changing my environment. I was even considering entering the shockingly unsanitary interior of an aeroplane to reach the border quicker.

But there was something more to Julien's comment about the increased intensity of the search. "This is no longer just about Daniel, is it?"

Julien didn't answer. He just shook his head.

"Is the concern about Doctor Didden?" I nodded when I saw his reaction. "It is."

"The whole of Europe is up in arms about her disappearance. Together with Daniel, this makes for a nightmare. Not only because of the political implications, but because of the far-reaching and long-term effects any kind of nuclear action would have on global peace efforts."

"It would be every conspiracy theorist's wildest dreams all rolled into one." Francine shrugged. "Or so I imagine."

Vinnie snorted, but it wasn't his rude sound that caught my attention. There was something else in his body language. I pointed at his face. "What are you hiding?"

"I'm not hiding anything, Jen-girl." He rolled his eyes when I lifted one eyebrow. "I'm *not*. Okay, okay! Stop looking at me like that. I didn't share anything simply because there's nothing to tell."

"Talk, big guy." Manny lowered his chin and glared at Vinnie.

Vinnie cleared his throat. "I asked Justine if she had anyone who could help us find Daniel. She did. And she phoned me when we were on our way here to say that her people haven't found any trace or even any mention of a kidnapping attempt on Daniel and this Amélie chick. See? Nothing to tell."

"Hmph." There was no censure in Manny's response.

"Lev Markov." The two words came out louder than I'd intended, but this was a part of the case that I wanted to know more about, but had been too distracted by Daniel's kidnapping to pursue.

"Who?" Nikki asked.

"He's the Russian consul general's pal who organised all these paintings for the exhibition." Manny straightened. "Hell, Doc. I'd all but forgotten about him."

"Who is he?" Nikki asked again.

Colin put his knife and fork down. "Apparently a close friend of the Belarussian President as well as that diplomat who died from polonium-210 poisoning."

"Aleksei Volyntsev." Roxy leaned towards me. "Have you spoken to Lev Markov?"

"Not yet." I was disappointed in myself for this oversight. I looked at Manny. "We need to find out everything we can about him. I would prefer to speak to him as well. If he was indeed the person who secured most of these paintings for the exhibition, I would like to see his reaction when confronted with the news that the paintings on the plane were forgeries and that Fradkov had the originals in his home."

"And I would like to be the one confronting him with

that." Manny took his phone from his trouser pocket.

"Um." Julien leaned forward, his hands stretched towards Manny as if wanting to grab his phone. "Don't phone anyone. Let me contact the Russian consul general and set up a meeting. Things are so delicate at the moment, I don't want to risk the peace talks with you running your mouth and ruining the president's hard work."

Manny's lips thinned as his chin jutted in anger. He breathed a few times loudly through his nose, then shook his index finger at Julien. "You irritate me."

"Thank you."

"Hellfire." Manny slammed his phone on the table. "You better set up a meeting with that Markov guy or so help me, you'll regret ever meeting me."

Julien huffed a laugh. "I regretted it five minutes after meeting you. But here we are, working together. Just let me do my job so we can all keep ours."

"The sooner I can speak to Lev Markov, the better." The more I thought about it, the more questions I had.

"I'll see what I can do. I have some questions about that Russian company that owned the hijackers' SUV in any case." Julien got up and walked to the sofa in front of the window. He was speaking on his phone before he reached it.

"What about all these paintings?" Nikki tried to hide her excitement, but she'd never been good at deception and now was no exception. Her eyes were wide with appreciation as she looked at the easels. "I mean, seriously? Caravaggio, Veronese and Tintoretto? All right in front of me? This is the best exhibition I've ever been to. It's like a totally private show. How cool is that?"

"I checked all of them again and have only seen one that is a forgery. A brilliant forgery. One of the paintings that were supposed to be bought legitimately. I almost didn't see it wasn't authentic." Colin's tone was hushed, his slack jaw muscles and raised eyebrows confirming the awe he was experiencing. "Twenty-six original Renaissance masterpieces. Nikki is right. This is a private show and it's astounding."

Julien walked back to his chair, but stopped to look at the paintings. He turned to face Colin. "Were these all the paintings in Fradkov's house?"

"No." Colin shook his head. "We left behind at least another forty paintings—"

"Forty?" Julien sat down, his eyes wide. "How could you leave such valuable work there? Why didn't you bring it here?"

"Because I didn't consider paintings done by the hand of Ivan Fradkov to be of any worth." Colin's voice had lost all its warmth, micro-expressions of disgust quickly disguised under a neutral expression. "I was not going to allow art created by a psychopathic murderer to be anywhere near the works of these masters."

Julien nodded, but didn't apologise. He looked at me. "Couldn't you get any information from those paintings? Tell something about his personality?"

"I got that insight from the entire house." And Pink had gone through it with me to record everything so I could view it again later for further analysis. I hadn't wanted to be in the house longer than absolutely necessary. "Those paintings represent only a part of Fradkov."

"So what did you learn, Doc?" Manny leaned back in his

chair and glanced one more time at the paintings on the easels.

"I find it hard to believe that this is Fradkov's primary residence. The only personal touches in the house were in the rooms he hadn't changed. Those rooms still represent the previous owners."

"How do you know he didn't change anything?" Roxy asked.

"I found an article about the house that was published before Fradkov got the house." Francine lifted her tablet and waved it in the air. "I love archives. This article is from an interior design magazine and there are a gajillion photos to go with it. They were going on and on and on about what an exquisite example the house was of a blend of Romantic and Victorian-era design, arranged in a manner that is both warm and elegant. Twelve pages of photos and flowery descriptions."

"I compared those photos with the rooms and found only four rooms unchanged."

"How many rooms does this house have?" Nikki asked.

"Including the kitchen and bathroom?" Francine narrowed her eyes and looked up at the ceiling. "Um, twelve?"

"Fourteen." I had counted them all. "One of the four rooms that were changed was the room Emad slept in. He moved the chair and the two rugs were swapped. The room with the television was the other room. The furniture was moved and the photos in the article showed no reading materials on the coffee tables at all."

"There were magazines and newspapers everywhere when we got there. And not the kind of magazines Genevieve reads, if you know what I mean. These were not academic journals." Pink rolled his eyes. "Looked like my sister's teenage son's room."

"The home office where his panic room is also bears no resemblance to the room that was featured in the magazine." The difference had been significant. "Emad's reaction when he came into the room and stood there, combined with the décor of the room, convinced me that this was Fradkov's space. Emad's bedroom and the living room was untidy. It is clear that he doesn't need the spaces he occupies to be arranged in visually pleasing lines."

"What did that office look like?" Roxy asked.

"Sleek." Colin leaned back in his chair. "Very modern, all glass and chrome, and… sleek. That's the best word I can think of."

"The placement of the furniture, paintings and ornaments on the shelves reveal an organised mind. Maybe organised to the point of obsessive-compulsive behaviour." This was something I was intimately familiar with. It took a lot of effort not to give in to compulsions.

"What about the fourth room?" Nikki rubbed her protruding stomach on the left side and winced. Eric must be kicking again.

"A small room on the top floor. It had only a bed and a wardrobe. No rugs, no ornaments, nothing to personalise it."

"Not even paintings on the walls?" Nikki asked.

I raised my index finger. "One. Above the bed."

Colin pointed at the paintings on the easels. "It's the first one on the left."

"It's beautiful." Nikki's voice mimicked the awe visible on her face. "Is it authentic?"

"As far as I can tell, yes." Colin narrowed his eyes. "This is Uccello's *The Adoration of the Kings*. It's the perfect example of Uccello's work. The visual perspective, the feeling of depth. Yes, this is undoubtedly his work. I can't find a single brushstroke that doesn't line up with his style."

Something was bothering me. Something about this painting. I got up and walked to the easel, ignoring Manny and Colin's questions. I studied it, yet it didn't render any insights. I allowed Mozart's Quintet in A for Clarinet and Strings to clear my mind of all other thoughts and simply focused on the harmony and the painting in front of me. When a hand touched my forearm gently, I turned to glare at whomever had the audacity to interrupt me. It was Colin.

"Alain is here, love." He stared at me a bit longer, then nodded as if satisfied that I was okay. "He received another painting and is waiting for us in the conference room."

"With Emad?" I would be furious if Tim had put Alain with his son in a room and I hadn't been there to observe their reactions.

"No. He doesn't even know we have Emad here. Speaking of which." Colin nodded towards the elevator. "Emad finished his lunch and was demanding to talk to you."

"No." I glanced one last time at the painting. "I want to talk to Alain first."

Chapter FOURTEEN

I stepped into the conference room and inhaled to greet Alain, but froze. Something had caught my attention and was now much more important than being polite. I slowly turned my head towards the easel standing in the far corner of the room. The air rushed out of my lungs and I took a step forward.

I barely registered the familiar throat-clearing when Phillip tried to catch my attention. I ignored him and walked to the easel, my eyes trained on the terrible reproduction of the painting I had just studied in the team room.

This was undoubtedly Uccello's *The Adoration of the Kings*. It had the rocky background, the people in colourful attire congregating in front of a building in ruins. Directly in front of the building was a couple, the woman dressed in blue, holding a baby. Similar to the other two paintings, this one also looked like the efforts of a child. The colours were similar, the horses and people were mostly in the same places as the originals, but it didn't resemble the reverent scene Uccello had brought to life.

The connection my brain made filtered through to my cerebral cortex, bringing with it a rush of adrenaline. It caused my index finger to tremble when I pointed it at a badly painted person standing by the horses. "That's the key."

"What's that, Doc?" Manny was leaning against the table to my right.

"There's something in that man's beard."

"Frey, what is she talking about?"

Colin stood next to me and leaned forward. "How on earth did you see that?"

"Speak." Manny's tone conveyed frustration.

Colin straightened. "There's writing in the beard."

"What? This painting doesn't have numbers?" Manny didn't move any closer and I was grateful.

"I haven't looked for numbers yet." And I first wanted to confirm my suspicion. There was something more than just the numbers. I turned to Colin. "Did you bring your tablet?"

He nodded at a tablet on the table next to Manny. "I brought yours."

"Oh." I took the tablet and quickly found what I was looking for. Then I zoomed in. I tilted it at an angle for Manny and Colin to see.

"Genevieve." Phillip stood up and walked around the table. "Now might be a good time to greet our guest."

"No, no." Alain Vernet waved both hands in the air as if he was wiping something away. "Don't worry about me. Do whatever you need to do to end this."

"Genevieve." Phillip's voice was soft.

I sighed impatiently and turned to Alain. "Good afternoon, Alain. Thank you for allowing me to do my work."

Phillip cleared his throat and waited until I looked at him. Then he raised one eyebrow and widened his eyes pointedly. I knew what this meant. Again I sighed, but this time in resignation. "My apologies, Phillip. Alain, I also apologise for not acknowledging the difficulty you must experience receiving all these paintings." I looked back at Phillip. "May I continue?"

He nodded and I tilted the tablet towards Colin and Manny again. I zoomed out of the image and with my index finger followed the spiral above *Saint George and the Dragon* that Emad had painted. My finger ended between the white horse's front legs. "This is where the spiral curls in on itself. Look what happens when I zoom in."

With my index finger and thumb I stretched the image until only the horse's legs filled the screen. "Look at the inside of the legs."

"Honestly, love. I don't know how you saw that without first zooming in."

"I closely studied this painting as well as *Scenes from the Life of the Holy Hermits*. I just didn't recognise that what looks like dots is micro-writing." I turned the tablet again and brought up the painting with the hermits. Again I stretched the image where the spiral curled in on itself. "Here it ends on the priest by the pulpit. The micro-writing runs along the outside of the pulpit."

"What does it say?" Phillip asked. "Is it understandable?"

"It's gibberish." Manny straightened. "Or do you understand this, Doc?"

I stared at the tiny lettering, then returned to *Saint George and the Dragon* and took my time looking at the writing. "This is written in code."

"And you'll decipher it." Manny pointed at the painting on the easel. "But now we need to look at that one."

"I looked, but only found one number on that painting." Alain's soft question pulled me away from the additional clues Emad had included in these paintings. Why would he hide so many keys? I didn't trust his sincerity when he expressed his relief at escaping from Fradkov. Emad had spent too many years honing his covert skills, of which deception was the most important.

Colin held his hand out to my tablet. "May I? I'll overlay the Fibonacci spiral over the original. The numbers should be on the connection points."

I looked at the tablet when he finished and made a mental note of where the spiral lay. Colin handed the tablet to Phillip and stood next to me studying Emad's reproduction of *The Adoration of the Kings*. At first I thought Emad had not included any numbers in this painting. Then I saw the first one.

I pointed at the different patterns on the bottom right area of the painting. And frowned. "There's the 'V' here, and here and here are the 'I's. This is a seven."

"Is it just me or did he do a better job hiding the numbers?" Colin tilted his head and stared at the kneeling person's head.

"These numbers are much better concealed." But I found another one. I pointed at the shoulder of a man. "There is a fourteen."

"And here is a twenty-two." Colin pointed at the rocks.

It took us fifteen minutes to find one more number and determine that there were no more hidden numbers. Even though Emad's artistic skill had not improved with the paintings, he'd taken more care in hiding the numbers in the lines of the rocks and clothing of the worshippers.

"So what are all the numbers, Doc?"

I turned around and was surprised to see Francine in the conference room. I hadn't heard her enter. She winked at me and held up her tablet. "Totally ready to put those numbers into the app."

"I'm not sure of the order of the numbers, but they are twenty-two, seven, fourteen and nine. That's the order they appeared on the Fibonacci spiral in this painting."

"Only four numbers?" She tapped on her tablet, but stopped suddenly. "Hey, wait. Those aren't the numbers of the Fibonacci sequence. Right?"

"Correct." I didn't know what to make of it. "It is anomalous. That and the fact that they were much less visible than in the other two paintings."

"Huh." She shrugged and returned her attention to her tablet. "Let's see what this brings us then."

Alain crossed his arms in a full-body hug, his eyebrows pulled in and down, his lips thinned. I felt an uncomfortable twinge of empathy.

Instead of reacting to this troublesome emotion, I turned my attention back to Francine. She tapped a last time and waited, her hand hovering over the tablet screen. Her eyebrows shot up, then she blinked a few times. "Wow. Okay, I didn't expect this."

"What, supermodel?" Manny glared at her tablet.

"Let me put this up on the system." She tapped and swiped her tablet's screen a few times. The white display screen started rolling down against the far wall and the projector whirred to life. Three seconds later a photo was projected against the wall, only coming into full view as the screen rolled completely open.

Alain's gasp drew my attention away from the photo. Tears filled his eyes and his chin quivered with suppressed emotion. He swallowed a few times until he appeared more in control. "The boys always agreed that this was the best holiday we ever had. They were so happy."

He fell silent and a tear rolled down his cheek. I looked at the photo again. Analysing nonverbal cues from a photo often led to erroneous conclusions. One moment caught in time never revealed the full context of whatever preceded or followed the taking of that photo.

But going on what Alain had just revealed, it was impossible not to come to the conclusion that the man and the two young boys on this photo were undeniably happy. There were no indications of any negative emotions, their postures revealing relaxed and happy individuals.

The way the two boys had their arms around each other's shoulders in one-arm hugs and were leaning against a much younger Alain showed their affection and trust for each other. I estimated the boys to have been in their early teens, making this photo around thirty years old.

"Where was this taken?" Phillip's tone was gentle.

"A small village in the south of France." Alain cleared his throat and pulled his shoulders back. "It was the cheapest holiday we had. That year I had been very busy and had forgotten to book one of my favourite places. By the time the summer holidays were upon us, all the better holiday resorts that catered for busy boys were fully booked. On a whim I decided to rent a villa on a farm.

"There was a small lake that the boys swam in every day, there were fruit trees that kept their bellies full and farm animals that gave them hours of entertainment. They were constantly dirty and covered in scrapes, but I never saw them without huge smiles on their faces. They loved it."

"How old were they? When was this taken?" Manny asked.

"Thirty-two years ago. Emad was nine and Claude fourteen." A small smile pulled at the corners of his mouth. A sad smile. "Those were wonderful years. Their fun and adventures didn't end, not even when Claude was the reason for Emad breaking his arm."

This caught my attention. "Why did you flinch? How did Claude cause Emad's injury?"

"I flinched?" He leaned away from me. "I suppose I would. Claude was a rough boy. He was more physical than Emad. More active. Claude had found a rope in the barn and had tied it around one of the higher branches of a tree next to the lake. Then he used it to swing himself at a ridiculous height until he finally let go when he was over the lake.

"Emad didn't want to do that, wisely saying it looked too dangerous. If I'd been there, I would've put a stop to that immediately, but I didn't want to be one of those over-protective dads. I wanted to give them their space." He inhaled sharply and looked at me. "Do you think that was the reason Emad and Claude turned out to be these horrible men? These murderers? Should I have been more protective?"

"These questions are counterproductive. You'll never have answers to them." I softened my voice when Phillip cleared his throat in the way I'd come to know as a warning. "It's like asking why children die from hunger or why bad things happen to good people. There is no answer."

Alain turned his attention to the painting and swallowed. "Emad always followed Claude. Even when he thought it was dangerous or when his first reaction was to do something different. So when Claude called him a coward, he grabbed the rope and started swinging back and forth to build up even more momentum and height than Claude had done. He wanted to show his brother that he could do even better. On one of the backswings, the rope came loose and Emad fell to the ground. Fortunately, he only broke his arm. It could've been so much worse."

I thought about what Alain had just revealed. "Was Claude responsible for many of Emad's mishaps?"

"Excuse me?" Alain tilted his head and frowned in confusion.

"Was Claude responsible for many of Emad's mishaps?" This time I spoke a bit slower.

"Yes. No. I don't know." His eyes moved up and to the left. Recalling a memory. "Claude was the instigator. Emad often bested Claude, but he almost never started something. Claude was the one looking for ways to get into trouble. Emad then usually got them out of trouble or suffered the consequences alone. He never blamed his brother."

"Didn't he?" I found that hard to believe. "Did he never show any resentment towards Claude, who escaped punishment so many times?"

Alain thought about this. "He never said it in so many words, no. But now that you mention it, I can think of many situations where it was clear that Emad was angry with Claude, but he wouldn't point any fingers at his brother. So, yes. I suppose Emad did take a lot of blame for Claude's behaviour."

"If he never instigated something, does that mean he always followed Claude?"

"Oh, yes. Emad was always a follower. Once he was pointed in a direction, he would take initiative to follow through, but he needed guidance."

"Or a mentor?"

"Yes."

"Where is this leading, Doc?" Manny's frown had deepened with every question I'd asked Alain.

"If Emad was this strongly influenced by Claude during his childhood, it explains a lot of his behaviour. Without guidance he's without a purpose." I looked at the painting. "Sending these paintings could very well have been a cry for help."

"What?" Manny snorted.

"Really?" Alain put his hands on the table and leaned towards me. "He's asking for help?"

I swallowed. Four years with Manny and the others and I had finally succumbed to speculating.

"Just give us your thoughts, love." Colin took my hand. "It doesn't have to be without flaw and foolproof."

"I don't feel comfortable with that."

"Well, suck it up, Doc. Is Emad asking for help?"

It took three deep breaths before I could push the words past my lips. "I would venture it to be so. From our last case we know that Claude was a constant in Emad's life. He was there to guide Emad even though Emad had a successful career. He most likely depended on Claude's advice on assignments, cases and people."

"Then Claude died," Alain said softly. "Does Emad not know he still has me?"

"Did you have a close connection with him?"

"I want to say yes. God, I really want to say yes."

I saw the truth. "You didn't."

"No. We got on very well. We definitely had fewer arguments than Claude and I had, but I never felt that close to him. I always thought it was because he didn't see me as his real father."

"He wouldn't have been able to accept the guidance of more than one person. It would've confused him."

"But his brother was only a few years older than him. Definitely not capable of guidance."

"And you think that he now feels adrift without a mentor?" Manny slumped deeper into his chair. "You think he used the emails to Daniel and Roxy so we could find him? And he used this app and crap to… what? Give us some clues? A message?"

"I would feel more comfortable saying that after I've spoken to Emad." I was starting to feel nauseated from the stress of speculating. Even though this was a distinct possibility, I was certain there were nuances to Emad's behaviour I had yet to uncover.

"Oh, you'll get your chance, Doc." Manny looked at Francine. "You put in those numbers. Where's the follow-up message?"

"There is none." Francine picked up her tablet and tapped the screen a few times. "Yup, nothing at all. Strange."

A soft knock drew our attention to the conference room door just as it opened. Tim walked in, his posture straight. His confidence had increased significantly in the last year. "Genevieve, our… um… other guest is demanding to see you."

"He's being difficult?" I saw it in Tim's micro-expressions.

"To say the least." He glanced at Phillip. "What should I do?"

"Doc? Any more questions here?"

I took a moment to consider everything Alain had revealed about Emad and Claude, the photo Emad had sent to Alain and the painting on the easel. I got up. "I don't have any more questions for the moment."

Only Phillip and Alain remained seated as we got ready to leave. Phillip put his cup on the tray. "We'll be here in case you need us."

I nodded and left the room, already organising my thoughts to effectively question Emad. I needed to know if I were correct in thinking that he'd deliberately led us to Fradkov's house. That he had made it easy to track that address. Had he done that because he had wanted us to free him from Fradkov? Or was he pretending to have been an unwilling guest in Fradkov's house? The many questions floating in my mind were rudely interrupted by a loud argument in front of the conference room where Emad was waiting.

"What the bleeding hell?" Manny uttered a rude noise and pushed past me to the three men arguing.

Colin stopped next to me when I decided to wait until Manny had the situation under control. In front of the conference room door, Julien Privott was exhibiting body language more aggressive than I'd seen before.

His voice changed from an angry whisper to a loud demand. "How dare you prevent me from speaking to Vernet? Do you really want me to pull rank and let the president know that you're—"

"Following orders?" Manny stood behind Julien and waited until he turned around. "These GIPN officers are following orders, Privott. You have no rank here. You're only a little PR person."

Colour crept up Julien's face and his nostrils flared. "Little? *Little*?"

"Oh, get over yourself." Manny looked past Julien at the two GIPN officers from the other team. "Emad is still good?"

The taller of the two men glanced at the tablet in his hand and tilted it towards Manny. "He's leaning against the door, trying to hear what's going on here."

"And I'm pretty sure he doesn't want to speak to you, Privott."

Julien's bottom jaw moved as if he was chewing something hard. "I just want to protect the president. Nothing more, nothing less."

"What the bloody hell else do you think we're doing here?" Manny threw his hands in the air. "We're trying to find a team member who also advises the president. We're trying to protect the negotiations with Russia and God knows what else. You're in the perfect position to screw it all up." Manny leaned closer to Julien, his eyes narrowed. "Now listen to me, you *little* PR person. Either you observe quietly or so help me I will make sure you don't have a job tomorrow."

"He really shouldn't have tried to get into that room without Millard's say-so." Colin sounded amused. I glanced at him in surprise. How could he find this entertaining? The amount of animosity being displayed was most disconcerting. I felt a strong urge to escape to the safety of my viewing room.

"Okay, okay." Julien held both his hands up, palms out. "You're right. I should've waited for you. But you were taking so long. I need to know what this Fradkov idiot is planning. We can't risk Russia reneging on the talks. We need to stabilise the current situation and it will only happen if Russia works with us, not against us. We need Emad to tell us everything he knows."

"Emad is in there? My son is here?" Alain's shocked question came from behind me. I turned around to see his face void of colour. "Can I please see him? No. No, I wouldn't know what to say to him." A shudder shook his body. "Yet I really want to see him."

"I can't allow that." Manny shook his head. "Please go back to the conference room."

Alain looked at me. "Genevieve? Please? I need to make sure Emad is okay."

My immediate reaction was to deny him. Mostly because I didn't know the legalities involved. But then I thought about it some more. "We might need your help if Emad is not co-operating."

"Not co-operating? Oh, please tell me you won't hurt him." He pressed both fists hard against his chest. "I know he's done a lot of bad… a lot of evil things. But he's still my son."

His distress was visible in every nonverbal cue. "He will not be physically harmed."

"Thank you." He looked back towards the conference room he'd been in, then turned to me. "I… I really want to see him."

"You heard what Doc said." Manny's tone was gentler. "Wait for us. If we need you, we'll call for you."

We watched as Phillip walked Alain back to the larger conference room. As soon as they disappeared around the corner, Manny sighed heavily. "Okay, Doc. How are we going to do this?"

"I don't understand your question. You of all people know how to conduct an interview with a criminal."

Manny closed his eyes and rubbed his hands hard over his face. After three slow breaths, he opened his eyes. "How do you suggest we interview him, missy? Should Privott stay outside, should all of us go in, should only you and I do this? I'm asking for your bloody expert opinion."

"You weren't." I inhaled and held my breath to prevent myself from pontificating. It was hard. Instead I focused on the best way to get as much information from Emad as possible. "Physical intimidation won't work with Emad. He would respond to authority, so I think Julien should join us."

"Who's us?"

"You and me."

"Then let's do this." Manny put his hand on the door handle, but turned to Julien. "You might be the president's right hand, but here you follow our lead. Got it?"

Julien raised both hands and nodded. "I'm smart enough to know my strengths, Manny. This is your show."

Manny sighed heavily as he opened the door.

Chapter FIFTEEN

Emad was sitting at the far end of the conference table. His face was wan, his eyes bloodshot and his hair untidy as if he'd pushed his hands through it numerous times.

"Where's Daniel?" Manny pulled out a chair and sat down heavily. If I had not known him well, I might have been convinced that he wasn't really interested in the answer.

Julien sat down on the opposite end from Emad, not making eye contact. He was quite successful in not attracting attention. I sat down next to Manny, putting my entire focus on Emad.

He shrugged. "Where's my coffee? I asked for a latte at least an hour ago."

Manny's eyebrows rose high on his forehead. He looked at me. "Did you hear that? He's demanding service."

I clenched my teeth hard to resist answering Manny's question. Of course I'd heard Emad's request. I was sitting right next to Manny. I assumed his ridiculous question had a different purpose.

Emad sighed, shook his head and put both hands on the table. "I apologise. It feels like days ago that you got me out of Fradkov's house, yet it's only been a few hours. I'm just really tired. It's been a hard few months."

"Hard how?" Manny slumped deeper in his chair.

"Losing my brother, then being held against my will by a

psychopath. I think that qualifies as hard, don't you think?"

"What do you mean being held against your will?" Manny's question pleased me. I'd been wondering about Emad's claims when we'd found him this morning.

"Exactly what it implies. I didn't have freedom to leave the house."

"You couldn't open the doors?"

Emad rolled his eyes. "Of course I could open the doors. It was even okay for me to go to the small grocery store two blocks away, but Fradkov had made it very clear that I was not to consider going further than that. He promised to make my death a very slow and painful one after he'd made me watch my dad's very slow and painful death."

The most important thing about analysing body language was context. A lot of novices made the mistake of thinking they knew exactly what crossed arms, a shaking leg, a fist against the mouth meant, but without knowledge of the larger context, it was easy to err.

I couldn't ascertain Emad's truthfulness. All of his nonverbal cues agreed with what he was saying. Yet his background as a covert operative who excelled in deception kept me from feeling confident in anything I observed. I narrowed my eyes and watched as he glanced at all three of us. Was it to make eye contact to establish a connection or was it to determine how believable he was in his deception?

"I'm sure you know I've not been close to my father in a long time, but I didn't want him to suffer for Claude's bad judgement." Emad held up one hand towards Manny. "I know what you're going to ask. And my answer is that Claude was the one who made contact with Fradkov. It was

Claude who convinced me… No. Not convinced. Claude threatened me until I agreed to work with Fradkov. I didn't want anything to do with that man.

"Throughout the years working for the French government, I'd heard more than a few rumours about Ivan Fradkov. I knew that most people who'd ever been associated with him didn't get to live very long and anyone who ever went against him lived even shorter lives. But Claude didn't care about this. He was attracted to one last job and convinced me with that promise."

"The polonium-210 poisonings were supposed to be the last of your criminal activities?" I found that hard to believe.

"I really wanted it to be our last. For two years, I told Claude that our operations had to come to an end. No matter how careful we were and how we would never ever have been caught because of negligence on our side, we still worked with people. Idiots, actually. Idiots who had no loyalty towards us if their lives or livelihoods were being threatened. They would've given us up to the authorities in a heartbeat if it meant they would get out of an arrest or get a cosy deal."

His angry sigh and thinned lips were convincing. "But Claude insisted we continue. We had more customers than we had time, so the typical supply-demand thing happened and we offered our services at a premium. And these idiots were happy to pay. At least they knew they got value for their money. We always delivered on time and never got caught."

"Were you a willing participant in this business or did you also feel that you had no choice?" I didn't bother softening my voice to sound sympathetic. Emad could've, and most likely had, researched me and would know that I was trying to manipulate him.

"Both." He lifted his shoulders in a careless shrug. "At first I wasn't willing. Claude had managed to get himself into trouble with some drug dealer in Croatia of all places. I was on assignment in Bosnia, so it was easy for me to hop across the border to Croatia and deliver the dealer equipment that he needed for his… er… business. And no, I'm not going to tell you who the dealer was or what equipment. All you need to know is that it was our first job and it was much easier than I'd ever thought it would be."

"Then you became willing."

"Not yet. It was after a job that netted us over half a million euros that I realised how profitable this could be. Claude and I only had to do a few of these to have us both set for life. I became less willing again once we had a few million each stashed away. But Claude was greedy. As always. Enough was never enough for him. He always wanted more."

"What did Fradkov promise that made Claude willing to hang it up after that job?" Manny asked the question also on my mind.

"If the poisonings had gone as planned and you hadn't interfered and killed my brother—" Emad took a deep breath and slowly exhaled. "If all had gone according to plan, we would've each received ten million euros."

I ignored Julien's gasp and glanced at Manny. I only caught one micro-expression that indicated his shock. To anyone else, he would appear bored.

He raised one eyebrow. "And that was enough to retire?

What did you two jokers plan to do? Live on an island?"

"We were going to buy an island." Emad huffed a laugh, but there was no humour in it. "Now, I'll have to buy it alone. I don't have a brother anymore, you know."

This was it. This was the unguarded micro-expression I'd been waiting for. Well-hidden between his grief, anger and concern was contempt. His laugh would have convinced me of his resignation to these circumstances had it not been for his *levator labii superioris* muscle pulling his mouth into a sneer.

This put everything he had said in doubt. On the one hand I found it frustrating that I couldn't read his true communication as easily as most people's. But on the other hand I revelled in this challenge. It was not often that I couldn't read someone's nonverbal cues and ascertain the truth behind their words.

I made sure to control my own micro-expressions not to give away any of my observations. "If you plan to buy an island, you must feel confident that you won't be incarcerated and that Fradkov won't find you."

"I feel much more confident that I won't land up in prison than I do about Fradkov not finding me." He blinked slowly and tilted his head. His attempt at appearing pensive was almost convincing. "You know what would be perfect for me, for the French government and for your precious reputation? Killing Fradkov."

"You want us to do your dirty work?" Manny snorted. "Doc, I think we have ourselves an egomaniac here."

"No, it's not my dirty work." Emad swallowed. "The French government would never put me in prison. I know too much about too much. They're going to either kill me or send me to some black site and I'll disappear forever. And that's pretty much the same reason no government would ever put Fradkov in a prison. He knows too much about too many powerful people. Hell, he's the one who made them powerful. And leaving him running around as a free man is obviously not an option either."

"But we should let you run free?" Manny shook his head. "How stupid do you think we are?"

"Very." His flinch was genuine. "I apologise. I don't think you're stupid. You were smart enough to track me down. I'm just desperate to get out from under Fradkov's control."

"Why did Fradkov threaten your life? Hold you against your will as you said?" This really bothered me.

"He thought I was betraying him."

"Were you?"

"No." His lie was well-concealed, but I saw it. His shoulders dropped. "I wish I had the courage to betray that psycho. He's just too powerful. I was—I *am*—scared of what he'll do to me. If I ever betrayed him, the things he would do to me would break me."

"You are betraying him now."

He blinked once, then immediately widened his eyes in fear. He was convincing. "Oh, no. You have to protect me."

Manny inhaled to respond, but stopped when I raised my hand. He got impatient when I took too long to say something and raised both eyebrows. "Doc?"

I didn't want to reveal my idea in front of Emad, so I got up quietly and walked to the door. When I opened it, I wasn't surprised to see Phillip and Alain quietly talking a few metres from the conference room. Alain had been distressed and would've wanted to be immediately available if we'd needed him. Now I did.

I left the conference room, closed the door behind me and waited for Alain and Phillip to join me. Alain's eyes were wide, his face pale. "Is he asking for me? Is Emad asking for me?"

"No." I paused when I saw disappointment and pain flash across Alain's face. I looked at Phillip for assistance.

"But I'm sure he'll be happy to see you." Phillip rested his hand on Alain's shoulder and turned to me. "Do you need Alain's help?"

"No." I only realised Phillip's strategy when he widened his eyes. I cleared my throat. "Yes. Alain, I need your help. Emad is not being truthful and I believe your presence would help us."

"Anything." Alain glanced at the door. "I'll do anything to help."

"I'll be in my office if you need me." Phillip squeezed Alain's shoulder and smiled at me.

I nodded and opened the door. I walked in first so I could see Emad's reaction when his father entered the room. I was not disappointed. Emad stopped in the middle of a sentence, his face immediately losing colour when he noticed his father.

Micro-expressions were called such because of their fleeting nature. The happiness, hope, sadness, fear and worry on Emad's face could have easily been missed if I had not been trained to see it. No sooner had those expressions flittered across his face than he straightened his expression to something more neutral. His smile didn't reach his eyes when he watched Alain sit down next to Julien. "Hi, Dad."

Alain blinked a few times, but it didn't stop a tear from running down one cheek. "How are you, son?"

"Been better." Emad leaned forward. "I really need these people's help, Dad. I got in over my head and I need their help to get out."

"What are you into?" Alain's concern was genuine. As a father, he was not going to be objective.

"I can't tell you most of it, Dad." Emad sighed. "A lot of classified shit, but there's this man who's controlling my life at the moment. He's making me do things I don't want to."

"Like Claude did?"

Emad nodded. "Like Claude did."

"The photo you sent." Alain swiped the back of his hand over his wet cheek. "That holiday you broke your arm."

Emad's laugh held sadness. "Only one of many examples."

"Did you agree to Claude's ideas because he was your brother or because he manipulated you in some manner?" I almost smiled when I saw the brief appearance of Emad's tongue between his lips. Triumph. He thought he'd swayed us.

"Claude was very good at getting people to do what he wanted."

"The same way Fradkov is manipulating you now?"

"Yes." He glanced at Alain, then back to me. "Look, I know I have done a lot of illegal shit, but it never endangered people's lives before. This… Fradkov… I don't want to have any part in his plans anymore."

"Why does Fradkov terrify you so much?" The fear I'd seen was real.

"His plans… someone like him should never have a lot of power." He shook his head, looked at his dad, at Julien, then at Manny. "You are wasting time talking to me. You need to find Fradkov and stop him."

"Stop him from doing what?" Manny asked before I could. I was too distracted by what I'd observed.

"I don't know." His lie was well-disguised, but I'd seen it. "Really, I don't know what he's planning. All I know is that you are part of this plan. Your whole team, including that guy who went missing on the plane."

"What do you know about the plane?" Manny's tone was hostile.

"Nothing. I swear." He looked at me. "Fradkov spent a lot of time in his office talking to someone on the phone about the exact location where they put that plane down. And he was speaking in Russian. I heard him talk about this Daniel person, but I never heard anything about what he was planning after the plane landed."

"Doc?"

"He's telling the truth." But I wasn't. I watched as Emad's *zygomaticus major* muscles contracted in a tiny smirk. He thought he'd outwitted me. I wanted him to believe that. I still didn't know how much credit to give to anything he'd told us, but I needed to consider every word and nonverbal cue with great care if I wanted to get to the truth.

I was growing tired of this game he was playing and listened to him answer a few more questions from Manny. It became harder to keep my thoughts to myself, so I got up and left the room. A minute later, Manny, Julien and Alain joined me. Alain looked even more distraught than before.

"He's… he's not the boy I raised."

"We know that." Manny pushed his hands in his trouser pockets. "Thanks for your help, Alain."

"Did I help?" Alain looked at me. "All I did was sit there and wonder what I'd done wrong."

"Your presence helped." I relaxed when I saw Phillip coming towards us. He took one look at us and escorted Alain to his office.

Manny watched them leave with a deep frown. "Did he help, Doc?"

"Not much, but I did get a better read on Emad's nonverbal cues."

"I don't know how you people can think that was a successful interview." Julien exhaled heavily. "He didn't tell you anything. You don't know where Daniel is, you don't know what Fradkov's plan is, you don't know what's happening with the leftover polonium-210. You know nothing."

"That's not true." I thought about it. "You are correct that we don't know about those specific details, but I've learned something very important. Emad does have knowledge of Fradkov's plans, even if it is not detailed knowledge."

"Then we need to get back in there and get it out of him."

"What do you plan to do, Privott?" Manny grunted. "You're going to get your little bag with torture tools? Get real. That man is a trained spy. He's trained in deception and has most likely aced more interrogations than you've ever seen on TV and the movies."

"Manny is being facetious, but he's correct. Emad won't share with us what he knows."

Manny turned to me and narrowed his eyes. "You saw something else. What did you see, Doc?"

"Whatever Fradkov is planning might put him in a position of power different from what he's enjoying at the moment. Outside of a select few law enforcement agencies, Fradkov is an unknown entity. Emad revealed something I think he now greatly regrets." I'd seen it, but didn't yet know what it meant. "He affected his fear of Fradkov most of the times he talked about manipulation and plans. But when he said that someone like Fradkov should never have a lot of power, his fear was real."

"What do you make of it, Doc?"

"I'm not sure and don't want to speculate." I lifted my index finger. "But I know you want me to, so I will say this: I think that Fradkov is working towards something that would put him in a more powerful position than any of the people he's ever worked for."

Manny pressed his fists against his eyes. "What on God's green earth does that mean?"

I shrugged. I wasn't going to speculate any further. "I believe Daniel plays an important role in this and we need to find him."

Chapter SIXTEEN

"Do you know where Daniel is?" I stared at Nikolai Guskov's image on one of the monitors in front of me. "Have you found him?"

"I'm sorry, Genevieve. This is not why I called."

My shoulders dropped and I swallowed the disappointment pushing up my throat. When the Russian consul general had unexpectedly Skyped me, I had answered with irrational hope. Anger replaced the hope and disappointment. "Why did you call?"

Colin pushed his chair closer to mine to fit into the camera's view. "Good afternoon, Nikolai. We truly appreciate your help."

Nikolai studied Colin for a few seconds. "I assume you are the polite member of the team?"

"Amongst other duties." Colin's smile was evident in his tone. "Now if you could be so kind as to wait a second while I call…"

"No need to call me," Manny said from behind us. "I'm here."

"Good afternoon, Manny." Nikolai leaned back in his chair.

"Nikolai." Manny cleared his throat. "Do you have news for us?"

"Yes." Nikolai lifted one hand, palm out. "But before you get excited, I don't know where Daniel Cassel is."

Not taking an active part in the conversation and having

had a few moments to contain my emotional response, I was focused enough to register Nikolai's micro-expressions. "You're not being truthful."

"Actually, I am." His lips tightened and his tone lost some of its warmth. "I don't appreciate being called a liar. And if you would give me time to finish my thought, you would hear the whole truth."

"We apologise." Colin put his hand on my forearm and squeezed. "We're just very worried about our colleague."

"I understand that." Nikolai glanced away from his computer toward where the door would be. "This is not an official call, so I would appreciate your discretion."

"Noted." Manny shifted behind me. "Your news?"

"I'll start with Lev Markov. Your Monsieur Privott phoned to ask if I could set up a meeting. I called Lev, but he's in Ukraine. Since he's not well-received in Belarus, he went to Kiev to prepare for the exhibition's next stop. It's still two months away, but he wants to do what he can to get as much publicity as possible."

"What are you saying?" Manny frowned. "He's not going to speak to us?"

"He's available for a video call like this any time, but he said he doesn't know if he could be of any help."

"How well do you know him?" I made sure to register every one of his non-verbal cues.

"Well enough to seriously doubt he had any involvement in the art heist and kidnapping of your friend."

He was being truthful, but it didn't mean he was right. "It would be preferable if I could speak to him."

"I'll set it up. I assume as soon as possible?"

"Yes." I thought about his micro-expressions at the start of our conversation. "How do you know about Daniel's kidnapping?"

"Your Monsieur Privott also asked me about a Russian company." He glanced towards his office door again and lowered his voice. "I cannot and will not betray my country, but I will tell you that our best people have determined that the plane has not been hacked. Two apps had been hacked to give false information about the plane's location, but not the plane itself. Hijacked, yes. Not hacked. My government is suspecting a specific group is responsible for this."

"Who? Why?" Manny asked.

Nikolai didn't answer immediately. I saw the moment he came to a decision. He leaned closer to the camera. "I want my country to be the great Russia she can be. There is a lot in our past and unfortunately also in our present that I wish we can do away with."

"What did you find out?" I understood his need for the preamble, but it was not pertinent. Or helpful.

"As we speak, the hijackers are being brought in for questioning."

"You found them?" Colin asked.

"Yes. I gave Monsieur Privott their names. He said he'll give them to you. These men are not Russian." He lowered his voice. "Our people found them quite a distance from the border. No one is supposed to know that we have them or that we're questioning them."

I wondered how much trouble Nikolai would be in if his superiors knew he was confiding in us. "If the hijackers reveal any pertinent information—"

"I'll let you know," he finished. "I don't know if it will be of any use. Our people will already have acted on it by the time I hear anything."

"What about the paintings?" Colin straightened. "Were they recovered?"

"Yes and they're already on their way to Minsk. This time accompanied by armed guards."

"What about Daniel?" Manny asked. "Did your people see him? Do they know where he is?"

"It would appear that the hijackers didn't get what they wanted from your colleague."

"Is he dead?" Manny's question was so quiet, I was surprised Nikolai heard it.

"No." He was telling the truth.

"Is he free?" The thought of Daniel being captured and probably tortured brought dark edges to my peripheral vision.

"I don't know." He paused to look at the camera, his expression revealing the truth. "I'm not even supposed to be privy to this information and it would seem that certain entities have tried to keep even this intel away from me. There are apparently nuances to this situation I have not been aware of. What I know now is the men in custody are not the only ones who'd hijacked the plane, but they're part of a…" His eyes widened and he looked towards the door again. "I can't tell you anything else. If I have any more news, I will contact you. Please don't contact me."

He ended the call before any of us could respond.

"Bloody hell!" Manny's expletive was muted and sounded as if it came through a tunnel.

I closed my eyes and pushed Mozart's Sonata for two pianos in D major into my overwhelmed brain. It took the whole Allegro before I felt more in control and opened my eyes.

I had pulled my legs onto the chair and was clutching my knees against my chest as a last keen left my throat. I mentally wrote the next two lines of the Sonata and unlocked my arms.

Colin touched my forearm as I lowered my legs to the floor. "You okay, love?"

"Daniel's escaped." My voice sounded raw as if my keening had been loud enough to hurt my throat.

"Holy Mother of all." Manny pulled a chair closer and sat on my other side. It was only when I turned towards him that I saw Francine, Nikki and Vinnie in the viewing room as well. They were spread out to give me more space, but their nonverbal cues indicated that it was hard for them to keep their distance. "Doc! Come back to me. Why do you say Daniel's escaped?"

I shook my head and looked at Manny. "It was in Nikolai's expression when I asked him if Daniel is free. He made an effort to show me his expression. It was genuine. He thinks Daniel is free."

"Fuck!" Vinnie pushed his hands hard against his temples. "I hope you're right, Jen-girl. I hope you're right."

"But where is he?" Nikki was sitting on the floor between two of my antique-looking cabinets. She put her sketchpad on the floor and rubbed her stomach. "And why hasn't he contacted us yet?"

"Those are good questions." Francine tapped her finger on her lips. "If I were him and I escaped capture? And I knew there was some conspiracy going on that included the president of France? And possibly Russia? And my team? Huh." She rested both hands on her hips and nodded as if coming to a conclusion. "I would not contact you guys, because I wouldn't know whether your phones, homes, cars, computers are being monitored. I would try to make my way to you staying totally under the radar."

"Should I let Pink know about this?" Vinnie took his smartphone from one of the many pockets in his black combat trousers.

"Not yet, big guy." Manny lowered his chin and stared at me. "What else did you see, Doc?"

"Nothing else that will help us find Daniel or help us stop whatever it is that Fradkov is planning."

"Hmm." Manny exhaled loudly and slumped in his chair. "If Nikolai knows that Daniel escaped, then Fradkov most likely knows this too."

"How can you be certain of this?" I asked.

"We have to work on the assumption that"—Manny started counting on his fingers—"Fradkov orchestrated this plane fiasco and that he knows things even before anyone else knows them."

"Which means that Fradkov will most likely push his plans forward." Colin scratched the back of his neck. "Something like this usually results in an acceleration of whatever strategy the mastermind has in place."

"And that means we have to push even harder to figure out what the holy blazes Fradkov is up to." Manny looked at everyone in the room. "What do we know so far?"

"I got us some extra juicy stuff," Francine said over her

shoulder as she rushed to her desk in the team room. She returned with her tablet, tapping on the screen. "So I looked into all the passengers, but then I decided to first look at the crew. The pilot popped with some delicious questions." She raised one eyebrow. "For example, why would he have an account in St Kitts and Nevis?"

"The same bank as the account in Isabelle's name?" I asked.

"Another bank, but it's affiliated with Isabelle's bank." Excitement lightened her expression. "So the pilot has this account, right? Why do you think said account received a lovely two hundred and fifty thousand euros the day before Daniel's plane was hijacked? And this is my favourite question"—she gave an exaggerated shudder—"why would the very same account receive another two hundred and fifty thousand euros six hours after Daniel's plane disappeared? Huh? Why do you think?"

After four years of friendship, I was mostly convinced her questions were rhetorical. "Is there a history of payments into this account?"

"Oh, yes, my bestest bestie." She winked at me. "I traced these payments back to the company that owns the hijackers' SUVs. Paporotnik is registered in Russia. Weird name, right?" Her tablet pinged and she frowned. "Hmm. Julien just sent me the names of those hijackers. Give me a sec."

"First I hear about that company's name being Papaya." Manny scowled when Francine ignored him and continued tapping on her tablet. "It's a ridiculous name."

"Three of these guys' tickets were bought by Paporotnik." Francine looked up from her tablet. "I haven't yet hacked this account, so I'm only able to check online info about the tickets. But the pilot's account is an open book. This pilot has received five payments from this company in the last six years."

"Fradkov's pilot on call. Which makes this Fradkov's account." Manny turned slowly, his expression severe when he glared at Francine. "Tell me that no one will ever know how many laws you broke to gain that information."

"Me breaking laws?" She pressed her palm against her chest, the shock on her face false. "Why, handsome, I would never ever in my life do such a thing. And if I ever did, it would never ever be discovered."

Manny grunted. "Make sure it stays that way."

"Wanna know what else I found out?" She puckered her lips, her tone the one she used when her flirtation turned outrageous. "Huh? Wanna know how good I am?"

"Oh, just get on with it." Manny rubbed his hand over his face. "You're exhausting me."

Francine laughed, then turned to me. "I looked into Amélie Didden and couldn't find any dirt on her. I got Pink to look into her as well and nada. Everything we managed to dig up on her points to a righteous girl. She seems to be working her butt off to make sure that nuclear power is being used safely and has invented a few ingenious ways to safeguard nuclear power plants. I won't bore you and I don't want to confuse the men, but these safeguards are simple, elegant and effective."

"What was she doing on the plane?" This was a question that had been bothering me for a while.

"Ooh, this is where it gets interesting. She was on her way

to speak at a symposium in Belarus. Some kind of expert exchange. Sounds familiar? Well, the similarities to Daniel's trip don't end there. Her ticket was bought for her by no other than Paporotnik, the same shell company who paid for Daniel's ticket. It took Pink and me some time to trace all the tickets and such, but there we go."

My longing to be part of academic symposiums no longer held the same attraction. This was dangerous. I thought about everything Francine had revealed about the Russian shell company. "Has Paporotnik bought tickets for anyone else?"

"Ooh. Huh. I haven't looked that far yet. I just got confirmation of the tickets when the Russian consulate general called." She cupped her hand against the side of her mouth, glanced at Manny and whispered loudly, "He's quite good-looking for a Russian diplomat."

I didn't have the mental energy to attempt to understand her strange behaviour, so I maintained my focus on the case. "Can you find out if any more tickets were bought by that company?"

"Is the pope Catholic?" She started tapping on her tablet. "It's a yes, my bestest bestie. I'm checking."

Manny glared at her tablet before turning to me. "Do you agree that this is a set-up, Doc?"

"If by set-up you mean that the plane hijacking, the art heist, Daniel and Amélie Didden's abductions have been meticulously planned, then I agree. Moreover, this planning had to have been put in place months in advance. This is not impulsive."

Something that I had observed in the last thirty-eight hours was niggling in the back of my mind. We had gathered so much information about so many different aspects of this case, a lot of these bits of information seemingly disconnected. Yet I knew that it all linked together and would form a complete picture if only I were able to access the information my brain had registered but was still hovering in my subconscious.

The others were discussing different theories, but I lost interest when Francine suggested neuro-implants as a government experiment, now being used to control people to do whatever the government wanted them to do.

I leaned back in my chair and picked up mentally writing the rest of Mozart's Sonata. It didn't take long until disconnected threads untangled, smoothed out and rolled together to become a faultless rope. Before I could attempt to explain this to anyone, I had to get the confirmation and then organise my thoughts. It took sixteen minutes before I was ready.

I turned away from the fifteen monitors in front of me and wasn't surprised to find the team behind me. What did surprise me was that each of them had a coffee mug in their hands and were eating pastries. "You're getting crumbs on my floor."

"I'll clean it, Jen-girl." Vinnie nodded with his chin to my desk. "I take it you didn't see yours."

To the right of my keyboard was a plate with three of my favourite pastries and a steaming mug of coffee. My stomach contracted with hunger and I picked up the plate. "Thank you."

"Whatcha got, Doc?" Manny had pulled the third chair to the end of my long desk and was sitting with his legs stretched out in front of him.

"Fradkov's address."

Manny inhaled sharply and immediately started coughing. It took him a full minute and a few sips of coffee to regain his composure. "What the bloody hell! Where is he?"

"I don't know if he is at this address, but the location is here. In Strasbourg." I put my half-eaten pastry back on the plate and turned to my monitors. "Look here."

"Those frigging paintings again." Manny coughed once more and sighed.

I pointed at the first painting. "The micro-writing between the horse's front legs is a list of numbers."

"Please tell me you know what these numbers are?" Manny tilted his head. "I'm too tired to try to figure this out."

"Those sixteen numbers are GPS co-ordinates." I entered those numbers into the computer and brought the result up on another monitor. "And that's where it points to."

"Bloody hell." Manny straightened. "That's Fradkov's house. Where we got Emad."

"And the numbers for the second painting?" Francine asked.

I brought up the *Scene from the Life of the Holy Hermits*. "The spiral ends by the priest's head and gives us two sets of numbers. The first sixteen are exactly the same as the first painting. It's Fradkov's house. The next six numbers are not enough to be a phone number or GPS co-ordinates or an IP address."

"But it could be the code to that locked room in Fradkov's home office." She clapped her hands. "We could get in there."

"That's speculation." But I agreed with her assumption. It would be worth trying to get into that locked room. We might find paintings, documents, computers that could help us determine Fradkov's plan.

"What about the third painting, Doc?"

Again, I zoomed in on where the spiral converges. This time it was the shoulder of a man looking at Mary, Joseph and Jesus. "These numbers are also GPS co-ordinates."

"Where does—" Manny stopped when I brought the results up on the far right monitor. He squinted at the map. "Show us the street view."

I clicked on the icon and Rue de Gare filled the monitor. I dragged the view until it stopped on a specific building. "This is the exact location."

"It looks like a dump." Vinnie pushed away from the doorway and stepped closer. "That is not the type of neighbourhood I would imagine Fradkov lives in."

"That's a good reason for him to be there," Colin said. "If everyone expects him to live it up, living it down might just be the best way to hide."

"We need blueprints for that building." Manny turned to Francine.

"Already on it, handsome." She tapped and swiped her tablet. "I'll send it to your devices in the next two minutes."

"Dan's team is ready for this." Vinnie had his smartphone in his hand. "I'm calling Pink."

Manny got up. "The big guy and I will join the team at this address. Doc, get us everything you can on the owners, the street. Supermodel, get access to any cameras in the vicinity and see if there has been activity in that building in the last forty-eight hours. We are going in, but I don't want us to go in blind."

Chapter SEVENTEEN

We were not at the address I had uncovered in the third painting. Colin had suggested we first visit the locked room in Fradkov's house before anyone went to that address. It had taken eighteen minutes of debate until everyone agreed.

Colin and I were standing by the open front door of the house. A shiver shook my body. The weather had changed in the last two days and it was uncomfortably cold tonight. My jacket had been warm enough for the daytime weather, but was not appropriate for a lengthy wait on the street. Even though our vehicles and the GIPN truck were all parked nearby, I couldn't sit there waiting for the bomb squad to clear the locked room.

"Damn, it's cold." Colin blew into his cupped hands. "How much longer are these guys going to be?"

"We're done." Edward, the explosives ordinance disposal technician, came down the hallway, his protective helmet in his hand. "We cleared the house this morning and now we double-cleared it. Not a hint of explosive material."

"Have you opened the door to the room off the home office?" What if there were explosives in there?

"We did. It's safe to go in." He looked at Colin. "Colonel Millard said that you're going to think it's Christmas."

"Who?" Colin's eyes widened. "Me?"

"He sure wasn't talking about Doctor Lenard." Edward

winked at me and waved us in. "He did say that he wanted you there as well. Something about making sense of this psycho."

"Thank you, Edward." Colin grabbed my hand and entered the house.

We walked into the home office and once again I took note of how different it was from the rest of the house. The modern furnishings seemed out of place, but I wasn't interested in that. It was the open door and what lay beyond it that had my attention.

Vinnie was standing at the entrance to the room and smiled at Colin. "Dude, this is all your birthdays and Hanukahs rolled into one."

"Colin isn't Jewish." I grunted in annoyance that I'd taken Vinnie's comment literally and walked past him into the room. It was about three times larger than I had expected. As with the home office, this room was minimalistic in its décor. There was no desk or any other office furniture. Only a comfortable-looking chair and a small side table. The rest of the room looked like a store room in a museum or art gallery.

"Oh. Oh, wow." Colin's breathless words came out as a whisper. "This is… oh, wow."

"Yeah, yeah." Manny turned away from one of the paintings he'd been looking at. "You're getting a full dose of art-porn now, aren't you, Frey?"

"This is…" Colin frowned and went on his haunches in front of a colourful landscape. He tilted his head, then carefully took the painting by the frame and got up. He turned the artwork towards the light and studied it from a few angles. When he looked at me, his face had lost colour. "This is an authentic Uccello, Jenny. This is another one of the paintings that were supposed to be on the flight to Belarus."

"The hell you say." Manny pushed his hands into his trouser pockets. "I've counted sixty-one paintings here. Are all of them the real deal?"

"I've only checked this one, Millard." Colin raised the painting in his hands a bit higher, then put it back where he got it. He took another small painting and spent a few seconds inspecting it like he had the first one. "This is also authentic. This is a Caravaggio though. But this is also one of the paintings from the plane."

Three of the four walls in the room had paintings leaning against them. It was clear that the paintings had been carefully placed so as not to damage the frames and, more importantly, the paintings themselves. I walked along the wall to the left of the door and stopped in front of the second last painting. "This looks like Tintoretto's work."

Colin rushed to my side and, with the same care he'd taken with the other paintings, lifted the artwork. After a few seconds, he shook his head. "I can't believe it. This is also authentic."

"How sure are you, Frey?"

The stark gravity of Colin's expression was worrisome. "I'll stake my name on it. My real name."

"Holy fucking hell." Manny scratched the stubble on his jaw. "You know what this means, right?"

Colin nodded once. "This painting was supposed to be on the plane. That means the one on the plane is another forgery, most likely by the people Otto and Justine talked about. Those forgeries were good enough to pass as the originals."

"What do you think this means, Jen-girl?" Vinnie was leaning against the doorframe, his right hand resting on the gun holstered on his hip.

I considered the implications of finding an entire collection of Renaissance art in the house of a criminal who was an incredible and immediate threat to Europe's political stability. "To steal these paintings, replace them with passable forgeries, and hijack a plane that was transporting all these artworks takes strategic planning like I've not come across before."

"But what is his endgame, Doc?"

I raised both shoulders. "I don't know. So far everything he has done has been calculated. Which means that Daniel and Amélie Didden both being on the same plane as the forged paintings has significance. We need to find out why Fradkov needed both of them. Did he need them individually or is there something they can do together that will help him reach his goal?"

"The problem is that we don't know what his bloody goal is." Manny sighed loudly. "Hell. We don't know if he's trying to overthrow a government, endorse some official, kill all the migrants, save all the migrants, kill ISIS, destroy Russia, stage a coup in Belarus or assassinate President Godard."

And we were not going to discover Fradkov's motivation by standing in this room. I looked around the room "Is there anything else in here besides the paintings?"

"Nope." Vinnie pointed at the chair. "Pink and the team think that Fradkov used this room as a storage space for obvious reasons and as a quiet room to conduct business. This room is soundproof and has a satellite connection that could be used for internet or calls. Pink says it would be harder to trace if you're looking for usual cell phone and internet activity."

"Doc?" Manny waved around the room. "Does this give you any insight into Fradkov?"

"The room only indicates his desire to keep his communication secure. The paintings are much more revealing of his strategic planning skills. But I've already said that. I would prefer for us to move on."

"To the other address?" Manny asked.

I nodded.

"These paintings…" Colin sighed. "Millard, the artwork in this room is priceless. Individually, we're looking at hundreds of thousands, but more likely millions a piece. These need to be taken to the team room and be handled with the utmost care."

"I thought you would want to be the one to oversee this." Manny lowered his chin, glaring at Colin. "You're coming with us?"

Colin looked at the art, then looked at me. "I'm going where Jenny is going."

"Aw." Vinnie drew out the word, the teasing smile around his eyes negating his affected adoration. "He's such a romantic."

"Shut up, Vin." Colin took my hand. "You are going to the other address, right?"

"Yes. We might learn something that will lead us to understand his motivation."

"Good." Manny nodded once. "Pink sent their second GIPN team to the address already to secure it and the bomb squad is on their way to make sure there are no nasty surprises for us."

"Where is Pink?" Colin asked.

"With Frannie in the truck." Vinnie rolled his eyes. "They were geeking out about getting blueprints and other shit for that new building. The two of them are getting all excited about using GIPN's infrared again. Nerds."

"If it keeps us safe, they can be as nerdy as they want to be." Manny took his phone from his trouser pocket. "I'm going to get Privott to mobilise a specialised team to transport all these paintings to the team room. We're rolling out in ten minutes, so Frey, check as many paintings as you can in that time. Doc, start Mozarting. We need to figure out why Fradkov has authentic paintings here and hacked a plane to steal the fakes."

"Mozart isn't a verb," I said to Manny's back as he left the room. He was already talking to Julien on his phone and didn't respond.

Colin squeezed my hand once, then let go to pick up another painting, his expression fluctuating between awe and horror. "The value of this art is beyond money. It's the cultural heritage that should be treasured. How else will future generations be able to see how Uccello, Caravaggio and Lippi viewed the world during an era that bridged the Middle Ages and modern history?"

"Dude, *you're* geeking out now." Vinnie snorted. "If it weren't for Daniel and the team, I'd totally lose my manliness around you bunch."

Colin lifted another painting and stepped back, not taking his eyes off the still life. My eyes widened and I pushed him aside as I pointed at the computer on the floor. I wanted to take it and immediately search it for any information, but caution prevailed. "Vinnie, is it safe to take this computer?"

Eleven minutes later, we were sitting in the GIPN truck, the computer on the desk in front of Francine. It had been a flurry of activity to ensure that the computer had been simply a computer. Edward had patiently reassured us that even the smallest traces of explosive would've been detected when they'd meticulously cleared the room.

"Fradkov might be a genius in other ways, but his computer security really isn't all that." Francine puffed air through her lips. "Took me a whole three minutes to bypass all his attempts at keeping his computer safe."

"Stop bragging and tell us if there's anything useful on it, supermodel."

"Hmm… let me see." She tapped on the laptop's touchpad and entered a few commands. "Well, what do you know."

"Supermodel."

"Okay, okay." She waved her hand impatiently towards Manny. "You need to give me a minute to understand what I'm looking at."

Francine's expressions of time were incorrect. She never took the minute or the second she said. This time was no different. In less than thirty seconds she leaned back in her chair and pointed at the computer monitor. "Who's the queen of the world's computers? Huh? Who?"

"Bloody hell." Manny leaned forward to look at the four security camera feeds that now filled the small monitor. "Are these live?"

"Yes, they are, my handsomest handsome." Her smile was self-satisfied as she watched the video footage of Fradkov's second address. I recognised the building entrance and façade from the street-view we'd looked at when I'd found the second GPS co-ordinates on the third painting.

"Are there any recordings of the feeds?" I asked

"Ooh, that's a good idea." Francine worked on the computer for a few seconds, then bounced in her chair. "Here they are. What are we looking for?"

"Fradkov." I narrowed my eyes at the small monitor. "Is it possible to put that up on one of the bigger screens?"

"Use monitor five." Pink pointed at the largest of the monitors lining the truck's wall. He was sitting next to Francine, the monitor in front of him displaying a blueprint.

"This will take a minute." Her tone was distracted as she fast-forwarded the footage. I was convinced she didn't even realise that she was yet again expressing inaccurate time forecasts.

I stared at the still image on the large monitor. The only indication that the recording was playing at an accelerated speed was the change of light from night to day and again to night. It took seven minutes before I noticed movement. "There. Slow it down."

Francine reacted immediately and slowed the recording to normal speed. One camera was pointing at the door of the building, the second camera at the entrance and the other two cameras at the interior of a large room.

It was the man standing at the door who had caught my attention. The winter coat and wool hat didn't successfully disguise the posture and movements that I'd come to know as uniquely Fradkov's. The hat also didn't completely cover his face. There was enough of his jawline and mouth visible to make a positive identification. "Ivan Fradkov."

"When was this?" Manny asked.

Francine pointed at the time stamp in the top left corner of the monitor. "Yesterday morning at twenty-three minutes past two."

"Bloody hell. He is here."

On screen, Fradkov unlocked the door and entered the building. The door and the lock was commonplace enough that it would not attract anyone's attention from the street. It was the second door, a metre and a half from the front door, that had the security I expected from Fradkov. He unlocked three heavy-duty locks, then pressed the doorbell to the left of the door. A small panel opened under the doorbell to reveal a keypad and he entered a very long code into the pad. The thick metal door slid open.

"We got you." Francine rubbed her palms together. "You smug bastard. We got you."

"I'm just glad it's not a retina scanner or thumbprint or palm print or such thing." Pink shook his head. "That's a crazy long code he entered. If we hadn't found this recording, it would've taken us a long time to hack the code. Now it's all there."

I took a step back and crossed my arms tightly over my chest. "No. This isn't right."

"What do you mean, Doc?"

"This is too easy."

"You think Fradkov is setting us up? This is a trap?"

"I don't know." I rubbed my arms. Loose bits of information were niggling in the back of my head, but I couldn't point to the key element they were trying to reveal. "Fradkov is too thorough in his planning. To make this kind of careless mistake does not fit in with the detailed strategy we've witnessed so far."

"Okay then." Manny looked at Pink. "Extreme caution. We'll breach, but only after Edward gives us the green light and even then, I want everyone tiptoeing around."

An hour and a half later we were standing in Rue de Gare, in front of Fradkov's second address. It was cold. I crossed my arms and looked at Edward as he opened the back of the large bomb squad van. "Are you sure?"

"You've watched us clear that ground floor apartment and the rest of the building." Edward put a large device into the van, then pointed at the vehicle. "We have state-of-the-art tech in here and we didn't pick up any hint of explosives. It's safe to go in."

I turned back to the building and stared at it. The same as the other buildings on this block, it was an art nouveau design. The bomb squad and Daniel's team had worked in tandem to clear the building. They'd first determined that there were no other occupants inside. The infrared images had shown red sleeping figures in both neighbouring buildings, but had not shown any heat signature in the one I was reluctant to enter.

"Doc!" Manny stood in the open doorway and beckoned me with an impatient wave. "Let's get this done before midnight."

I had all the data to reassure me that it was safe to go in, yet something in my subconscious strongly resisted the idea.

"Jenny?" Colin put his arm around my shoulders and pulled me against his side. "Why don't you stay here? We'll check out the apartment. If you want to join us, you can. If you don't, then you just wait in the truck with Francine."

"No." I stepped out of his embrace. "I'll go in."

"At bloody last." Manny snapped his fingers. "Come on then. Let's do this."

I walked past Manny into the building. The front door and short entrance hall looked exactly like the video footage from the computer we'd found in Fradkov's secret room. The door to the right was standing open. I'd watched from the GIPN truck when Pink had keyed in the long code. The same tension I'd felt then now tightened the muscles in my throat until it felt like I was suffocating.

"Come on in, Jen-girl." Vinnie was standing on the other side of a spacious room. "You're gonna wanna see this."

I started playing Mozart's piano concerto in my mind as I took three calming breaths. I straightened my shoulders and stepped into the room. At one point this might have been a one- or even two-bedroom apartment. Now it was one large open space. It was decorated in the same minimalistic, modern style as the home office in Fradkov's house.

The kitchen against the wall to the left was utilitarian. There was nothing decorative or extra to suggest that food had ever been prepared in that space. Next to it an open door led to a well-lit bathroom. Even though I didn't like the modern finishings, I did appreciate the simple and clean appearance of the all-white room.

The only window would've opened up to the street if it had not been solid, triple-glazed glass. I recognised the small cream plastic containers in each of the corners. Vinnie had put the sound maskers on all of the windows in our apartments, the team room as well as every window in Rousseau & Rousseau's offices. Their sole purpose was to distort any sound made inside, preventing anyone from using laser microphones or parabolic listening devices to listen in on confidential, or in our case top-secret, conversations.

Only a large white sofa, a king-sized bed and a long wooden table furnished this apartment. These few pieces of furniture looked lost in the open space. I narrowed my eyes when small dots on the walls caught my attention. I walked closer to the wall opposite the door to have a closer look.

"Nails." Vinnie flicked one with his index finger. "We're guessing ol' Fradkov had the walls here full of paintings."

"You would most likely be right." Colin stood next to me, also looking at the wall. He turned around and inspected the other three walls. "So many nails."

If each nail had held a painting, the apartment that now appeared Spartan would've been alive with artwork.

Colin rolled back on his heels. "And I'm willing to bet my bottom dollar he had his panic room collection here."

"He's cleaned out this place." Pink adjusted the assault weapon slung over his shoulder and pointed at the open cupboard. "That is the only storage space in this apartment and as you can see, it's empty."

"What about the other apartments?" This building had four floors. I would be surprised if all the apartments were completely empty.

"Nothing." Pink shook his head. "My guys went through every single one of them and found only dust balls."

"They're quite well-maintained though. None of them look like they've been empty for a long time." Vinnie had joined the GIPN team when they'd cleared the building.

"But it's such a waste of space. He could make extra money renting out all these apartments."

"Hmm." Manny walked to the centre of the room and slowly turned in a complete circle. "Is there anything worth seeing here, Doc? Anything that can help us?"

I took my time looking around the open space. Similar to his home office in the house, this apartment also didn't have much to reveal Fradkov, the man. That in itself offered a great insight. He must have expected us and therefore had removed the only things of value to him. I was sure that if he'd had more time, he would've removed the nails and painted the walls to remove all traces that he'd had his collection in this space.

I joined Manny at the centre of the room, next to the sofa. The only insight the furniture offered was that Fradkov had expensive and modern taste. I tilted my head and looked at the ceiling. Immediate recognition sent a shudder through my body. I wrapped my arms around my torso and stared at the difference in the paint. "Turn off the lights."

"Say what now?" Manny asked.

I didn't take my eyes off the ceiling. "I think it might be phosphorescent paint."

"Glow-in-the-dark paint?" Vinnie walked to the light switch at the front door.

Colin joined me, also looking up. "It's hard to see that there's different types of paint. Well spotted, love."

"Hit the light, Vin." Pink was leaning against the far wall, next to a mirror that was fixed to the wall. He took two steps to the centre of the room and looked up. "I'm very curious to see what we have there."

Vinnie turned off the lights, but the room wasn't completely dark. The soft yellow light from the street wasn't enough to diminish the effects from the paint though. I gasped at the beauty and the craftsmanship that covered most of the ceiling.

"This is Uccello's *The Battle of San Romano.*" Colin's tone held a reverence that reflected my response to what I was seeing. "And it's an incredible facsimile."

But something wasn't right. My subconscious had picked up on a nuance in the painting that was causing my heartrate to increase. I studied the many men on their horses, most of them covered in armour. The man on the white horse in the centre of the painting and the man to the right of him were the only ones not wearing full armour.

"That's not right." Colin pointed at the top of the painting, close to the wall where Pink was standing. "In the original painting, those lances are pointed in different directions."

Colin was correct. All the men had lances that were pointing towards the same point. Even the two flags held by two of the horsemen pointed there. I followed the direction and gasped. They were all pointing to the mirror behind Pink.

My chest contracted and breathing became almost impossible. My throat had tightened so much that I couldn't make a sound, so I pointed. When no one reacted, I pointed with both hands and tried to utter a sound. A high-pitched keen filled the room.

"What the hell, Doc?" Manny turned towards me, then looked at where I was pointing just as the mirror slid to the side. "Gun!"

Colin grabbed me and dove to the floor. No sooner had he landed on top of me than the room exploded in gunfire. It sounded as if an entire army was opening fire on us. My mind struggled to comprehend what was happening and refused to obey Colin's shouted demands to, "Move!"

He grabbed my jacket and pulled me behind the sofa a moment before the floor by my feet shattered under automatic gunfire. I couldn't move. I tried to focus on the angry shouting that was barely audible above the non-stop shooting. Where had the guns come from? How many guns were there? Why didn't Edward's team find them? How many more bullets did these weapons have?

And who was pulling the triggers?

Wood splinters flew across the apartment as the weapons moved around the whole space. I didn't know if the sofa would protect us for much longer and wondered if I would see Nikki's baby.

The shooting stopped with the same suddenness as it had started. The silence was deafening. But it only lasted three seconds.

"Sit rep!" Manny sounded close.

"I'm good. Jenny? Are you okay?" Colin was sitting next to me, patting me as if looking for injuries. "Vin, we need light in here."

The lights were blinding, but it gave me something to focus on. I didn't want to surrender to the blackness that was closing in on me. I inhaled deeply, kept the air in my lungs for three seconds and exhaled. "I think I'm unharmed."

"I don't see any blood." Colin's hand was shaking when he took mine. "Vin? You okay?"

"Alive." Vinnie ran past us just as two of Pink's team members entered the apartment. "Pink. Pink!"

The unfamiliar panic in Vinnie's voice caused adrenaline to flood my system. I got up and looked around me. The apartment looked like a warzone. The walls were riddled with holes, only a few places on the floor had not been shattered and the furniture was also wrecked.

"Fuck!" Vinnie's pained shout drew my attention to the far wall. He was kneeling next to a body lying prone on the floor. Pink. "Get a fucking ambulance now! He's still alive."

Manny was already speaking into his smartphone. He was cradling his right arm, his dark blue coat preventing me from seeing any damage. As if in slow motion, I turned my attention back to Pink. His black uniform was shiny with blood, a dark red pool around his torso growing in size.

"Don't you fucking die, you motherfucker." With one hand, Vinnie was pressing hard against a wound on the side of Pink's neck. His other hand was pressing against Pink's left thigh. "I need more hands here. He's bleeding out."

The apartment filled with the rest of Daniel's team, people flowing around us. I could only watch. It felt as if my muscles had locked into place and I would never be able to move again. I took comfort in still being able to feel Colin's arm around my shoulders, holding me tightly against him. I couldn't even ask if he was uninjured, only hoping that his easy movements indicated that he was well.

Manny dropped to his knees next to Vinnie and pressed his one hand on Pink's hip, the other on the inside of his left arm. "Medics are two minutes out."

"Come on, man." Vinnie wiped his cheek against his

shoulder. "Hold on. Help is coming."

"What the fuck happened?" Claudette stared at the open space the mirror had covered. "We'd cleared this place."

"Manny!" Francine ran into the room and staggered to a stop next to Pink. "No. No. Oh, God, please no."

The emotional pain on Francine's face, the heartbroken look on Vinnie's face when he pressed harder and shouted profanities at Pink and the tightness around Manny's eyes and mouth became too much for me.

I had never experienced the loss of someone close to me. First, it had been Daniel's capture and subsequent disappearance. Now Pink. My mind couldn't handle this.

I sank to my knees and gave in to the safety of a shutdown.

Chapter EIGHTEEN

I jerked when Nikki took the cold mug from my hands and replaced it with a steaming cup of tea. I'd been sitting in the dark on my sofa and hadn't even heard or seen her moving around the kitchen. I lifted the cup and smelled the camomile tea. "Thank you."

"Drink it." She sat down next to me, her legs tucked under her, holding a mug in both hands. She was having hot chocolate again. "You didn't even touch the other one."

"Hmm." By the time I'd come out of my shutdown, Pink had already been transported to the hospital. He was still in surgery.

Manny and Francine had joined half of the GIPN team at the hospital, while Vinnie and the others had stayed at the apartment. They'd been there to secure the property while the crime scene investigators collected evidence. Vinnie had insisted on staying in the apartment to make sure Colin and I were safe. It had taken me longer than usual just to gain enough control and focus so I could get up from the floor.

The crime scene investigators had by then already processed most of the apartment and had been pleased when we left. The rest of Pink's team had then gone to the hospital, not only to wait for him to come out of the operating theatre, but also for security. They were still there.

Everyone had decided that it would be best for us to return

home and try to get a few hours' sleep before we continued our investigation. I had not been able to fall asleep at all. Every time I closed my eyes, I saw the pool of blood surrounding Pink, the helplessness on Vinnie's face and the trauma on Francine's.

I'd never been one to waste time trying to sleep when I knew it wasn't going to happen. That was why I'd made tea in the hopes that some revelation would come to me if I sat quietly, mentally writing Mozart's Symphony No. 8 in D major. It hadn't worked.

"Doc G?" Nikki bumped me with her shoulder. "I want to ask if you're okay, but it's such a stupid question under these circumstances. Um… are you… I don't know what to ask. Maybe I should ask what you are feeling at the moment."

"Feeling?" It was almost impossible to separate the chaotic emotions nullifying the usual effect Mozart's music had on my mind. It was this that had been preventing me from pursuing academic development in the last four years. "Too much."

"I know." Her voice broke. "Pink is the coolest geek I've ever met. He has to make it. He just has to."

"The doctors weren't very optimistic when they examined him." The loss of blood had been so extensive that they'd been amazed he hadn't died at the scene. But it wasn't that or the bullet that had gone straight through the trapezius muscle—closer to his shoulder than his neck—or the bullet in his thigh that had caused the pessimism.

One of the seven bullets that had entered his body had lodged in his spine. It was one of his lower vertebrae and the doctors had told Manny that we should be prepared for this to be a life-altering injury. Manny hadn't asked what that meant, but I knew. An injury to the lumbar nerves could result in loss of function of the hips and legs. Pink might never walk again.

Manny's injury had been a superficial flesh wound. I'd been with Colin in his SUV when Francine had phoned to tell us they were also on their way home. Manny had sounded annoyed when she'd gone into unnecessary detail about how handsome the young doctor was who'd treated Manny. He'd called that doctor a man-child. I'd been so relieved to hear him sound his normal self that I hadn't confronted him about that phrase.

Nikki shifted a bit closer to me, her body heat warming my side. She liked and often needed physical contact. I didn't. Yet I didn't find her presence distressing at the moment. Especially since she didn't talk. I needed the quiet to try to filter through the maelstrom of emotions overwhelming me. If I were to be effective at analysing all the data we'd gathered so far, I needed to gain control over my emotions.

We sat in silence for the next twenty minutes, sipping our beverages. With each minute, I felt my focus returning. And I desperately needed to have my focus, my control back. I needed to be able to look at everything that had taken place in the last four days with a high level of rationality and emotional distance.

Piece by piece, I went over the events. Otto Coulaux's assassination in the restaurant, all three paintings Emad had sent to Alain, the hidden messages in those paintings, Justine's observations that Fradkov's behaviour had changed over the last few months and the evidence I'd seen thereof.

There was also the death of Aleksei Volyntsev, bringing radiation poisoning back into our case, Aleksei's friendship with the Russian Consul General Nikolai Guskov, their friend Lev Markov, the threats issued to Roxy, the art exhibition, the hijacked plane that was supposed to transport the art, Daniel's kidnapping as well as Amélie Didden's.

They all flowed together with the fake transfers we'd found in Daniel and Isabelle's financials, the peace discussions between Russia and the EU, the art we'd found in Fradkov's house and the shooting in his apartment.

The crime scene investigators and the GIPN team had been quick to determine the guns had been placed in the wall compartment as a security measure. Apparently, there had been some countermeasure that prevented any detection device from picking up the traces of gunpowder as well as any electronic signals.

The guns had been remote-controlled, which had led to a few conclusions. Manny and Vinnie were convinced that Fradkov had expected us and that he'd fitted two guns to swivel while the automatic setting meant the bullets had reached most of the flat. They were also convinced that Fradkov had been the one remotely pulling the trigger, causing Pink's grave injuries. It was conjecture, but I silently agreed. Fradkov had known we would find that flat and had been waiting for us.

There was something about the flat and the incident that truly bothered me. I sighed deeply. There were many things about this case that bothered me. The ease and convenience of finding and getting access to Fradkov's flat was only one of them. And everything was somehow connected.

Deep in my subconscious the connection was already made, but I simply couldn't reach it. Not yet. I needed more time, but I also needed more data. More than that, I needed Pink to survive the surgery and I needed Daniel to be back in Strasbourg. I sighed again at the unwelcome return of emotions.

"Having a pyjama party?" Vinnie asked softly from the kitchen. Nikki had left on one sunken light, which gave off just enough light to find one's way. Vinnie looked at my mug. "Want more of what you're having?"

"I'll have coffee." I looked at Nikki to hear her answer, but she was sleeping. She'd dropped her head against my shoulder and her mouth was slightly agape. Both hands rested lightly on her large belly and I wondered how she could sleep in this position. I lifted my shoulder. "Nikki."

"Leave her, Jen-girl. Another five minutes of sleep will do her good. We all need as much as we can get."

"But she's on my shoulder." And it wasn't bothering me as much as I expected. I knew some people became desensitised with enough exposure to the very thing causing them distress. Was this the case or could it be that my mind was too consumed with this case to register such discomfort?

Vinnie snorted and started making coffee. I watched as my large friend moved around the kitchen. The light was not strong enough to see all his nonverbal cues, but he was broadcasting his deep concern so strongly, it was impossible to miss. He was wearing sweatpants and a white tank top that fit snugly against his muscular torso. I could clearly see the tightness in his neck muscles and how it affected his normal fluid movements.

He brought our coffee and sat on the other sofa, facing me. "Couldn't sleep?"

I shook my head.

"Me neither." He took a sip of his coffee and settled deeper in the sofa. "This is so fucked up, Jen-girl. Not knowing where Daniel is and now Pink fighting for his life is killing me."

I gasped. "Don't use that expression."

"Huh?" He blinked. "Oh. Yes. Sorry." He nodded towards Nikki. "How long has she been there?"

"Thirty minutes or so. I didn't notice when she fell asleep."

His smile was tender. "She's so uncomfortable at the moment, it's hard for her to sleep. She says Eric is pushing on every organ no matter how she sits or lies."

It was impossible for me to imagine what it would be like to have a little human being in my home. The fear settling around my heart was instant and intense. A baby was such a huge responsibility, even though Nikki's fitness to be a mother was indisputable. She was caring, thoughtful and reliable. Even if she was messy.

Eric's father Martin had visited once a week since Nikki had decided to keep the baby. He had shown an uncommon sense of responsibility for a twenty-year-old man. He had a playful nature and a constant, genuine smile, yet had sat us down one evening to discuss his, Nikki's and the baby's futures.

He had a solid plan to build his career and be a part of Eric's life without disrupting the baby's routine. Both Nikki and Martin had reiterated that they were definitely not interested in being romantically involved, but wanted their friendship to be a strong foundation and example for Eric. I respected that. Martin had also deferred to each of Nikki's suggestions and requests. Everyone liked him.

I envied the neurotypical excitement everyone experienced about Eric's arrival. For me, he presented yet another source of overstimulation. And he wasn't even here yet.

"Where's Colin?" Vinnie glanced at our closed bedroom door. "Sleeping?"

"Yes, although I don't know how well. When I left the room, he was very restless."

"Having a party without me?" Roxy walked to the sofa and cuddled next to Vinnie, almost sitting on his lap. Even after seeing her countless times in her pyjamas, I still couldn't help but stare. No matter how many times she tried to explain it to me, I simply couldn't understand how an adult could feel comfortable in a fleecy one-piece suit. She'd called it a onesie. The impracticality of such a garment was staggering. She'd merely laughed and said she'd bought it because of the cute pink sheep floating on clouds. I didn't understand it.

"Want some hot chocolate?"

"No, thanks, snookums." She pushed a few wayward curls behind her ear. "I'll have some coffee in a minute. Just wanna snuggle up to you for a while."

He kissed the top of her head and looked at me. "It's almost five and too early for breakfast, but I feel like I should be cooking some comfort food for us. What do you want, Jen-girl?"

"Chocolate-banana pancake casserole." Nikki didn't even open her eyes or move. "And make enough. I need comfort for two."

I lifted my shoulder and pushed until she sat up. "I thought you were sleeping."

"I was." She rolled her neck and winced. "Until the big punk mentioned food."

Roxy laughed. "Oh, to have the metabolism of a twenty-year-old."

"Twenty-one, I'll have you know." Nikki straightened her legs and wiggled her toes. "Vin, have you heard anything about Pink?"

"I spoke to Claudette just before I came in. She said the doctors are still working on Pink. They've repaired the arterial damage as well as the other internal damage and are now trying to remove the bullet by his spine."

"Oh, God." Nikki hugged her belly. "He must live. He must."

"Doctor Dupont is the best when it comes to spinal trauma surgery." Roxy played with Vinnie's fingers. "I'm not a surgeon, yet I've heard of him. When other doctors talk about him, it's with great respect and admiration. Pink will make it."

But if he survived, what would his quality of life be? I didn't ask the question though. Uttering those words could possibly send me into another shutdown. I wanted to focus on things I could control. Like data analysis.

Roxy didn't give me much chance to continue going through everything I'd learned. She was in a chatty mood. She and Nikki were discussing a recent film that had been released and was rumoured to be a strong contender for the best film Oscar.

Their light-hearted discussion was a pleasant break from

the heaviness of my thoughts. Vinnie got up and, after declaring that he had all the ingredients, started making the casserole Nikki had requested. A few minutes later, my bedroom door opened and Colin came out. He rubbed a hand over his eyes and looked around the open living space. "Good morning."

"Morning, dude." Vinnie pointed at the sofa. "Sit. I'll bring your coffee."

Colin walked to the living area. "Is nobody in this house sleeping?"

"He is." Nikki pointed at her stomach. "And he's lying on my bladder. I have to pee." She pushed herself up, then stopped, glaring at Colin. "Don't take my seat. I'm sitting next to Doc G."

Colin chuckled. "How about I keep your seat warm for you?"

"Deal." She walked towards her side of the apartment. Her gait had changed in the last week. She was walking with considerably more effort.

"Did we wake you?" Roxy's eyebrows pulled down in concern. "We tried to be quiet."

"No. No, you didn't." Colin sat down next to me and took my hand. "I wasn't sleeping well in any case, but didn't hear you until I came out."

"They have that mother of a door that keeps their bedroom safe, Rox." Vinnie put the casserole in the oven and straightened. "Three locks and all."

"Seriously?" Roxy stared at my bedroom door. "Not a bad idea."

Vinnie took his smartphone from his sweatpants' pocket as he walked to the living area. "Huh."

The change in his posture was instant. Dread tightened around my heart. "What?"

"I just got this really strange SMS from Francine."

"What does it say?" Colin asked.

"She wants me to check the apartment for bugs. And she says that they're leaving her place now. They'll be here soon."

Adrenaline surged through my body and my mouth went dry. "You told me you frequently check for surveillance devices. Have you not been doing so?"

Vinnie put his phone back in his pocket. "I check twice a week. The last time was two days ago."

"Better get to it then, Vin." Even though Colin hadn't moved from his relaxed position on the sofa next to me, his muscle tension had increased exponentially. He was ready to jump up and take action.

From experience, I knew that Francine would explain in detail when they arrived. She loved conspiracy theories and creating the most outrageous scenarios, but she would never send an alarmist SMS at this hour in the morning. Not if she didn't have concrete evidence that necessitated a search.

We sat in silence for the seven minutes it took Vinnie to go through every room in our extended apartment. He was proud of the device he used looking for devices that didn't belong in our apartment. Security teams of numerous world leaders used exactly the same device. Vinnie had invested in it not only to ensure our safety, but also because it was fast, thorough and reliable.

He came out of my room, relief and concern evident on his

face. "There's nothing that shouldn't be here. Now I'm really worried why Franny would send this SMS."

A ping from the front door alerted us that someone had entered the security code at the front door of the building. A limited number of people knew the complex code. "Didn't Francine say they were leaving her apartment?"

"Yup." Vinnie took his phone from his pocket and looked at the screen. "It's been nine minutes since her SMS. There's no way they're here already."

"Unless it's something that would get Millard to drive like the devil is chasing him." Colin got up. "Even then, that's a stretch."

Vinnie and Colin shared a look and nodded. They both walked to the front door, their arms away from their torsos, their body language communicating their readiness for confrontation.

Colin stopped next to the small coffee table flanking the second sofa and reached under it. I knew they stored a weapon there. I didn't like it, but appreciated the possible need for it. Vinnie took a gun from behind one of my books on the shelf closest to the door. He nodded at Colin. "Ready?"

Colin nodded once and rolled his shoulders. A soft knock at the door brought added tension to both his and Vinnie's muscles. Francine and Manny had keys to our apartment. They wouldn't have knocked.

Vinnie leaned forward and looked through the peephole. He jerked away. "Motherfucker!"

Colin raised his gun, but frowned when Vinnie pulled the door open. I couldn't see past their bodies and got up in time to see Colin lower his weapon, the muscle tension in his body disappearing. I stepped to the side so I could see between Vinnie and Colin. I gasped, my hand flying to my throat.

Daniel was standing in the hallway.

"Dude! You look terrible." Vinnie pulled Daniel in for a hug, but gentled his hold when Daniel groaned. "You're hurt."

"Come in, come in." Colin put his weapon on the side table and pushed Vinnie away from the door. "Both of you, come in."

Both? I wanted to move to get closer to the door, but my feet didn't obey the signals from my emotionally overwhelmed brain. My strong reaction to Daniel's kidnapping had surprised me, but this surprised me even more. Feelings of happiness, relief, deep concern and fear warred for dominance in my mind.

Vinnie stepped to the side and Daniel walked into the flat, followed by a petite woman. She looked to be in her mid-fifties. Her black hair was cut in a short bob with a straight fringe. I wondered if the wrinkles surrounding her eyes were exacerbated because of the stress clearly visible in her micro-expressions or whether she was older than I estimated.

Daniel exhaled deeply as Vinnie locked the door behind them. "God, it's good to be home."

"Daniel!" Nikki came from her side of the apartment and waddled as quickly as she could to where everyone was still standing close to the door. "You're back. Oh."

She burst out crying the moment Daniel folded his arms around her. He rested his cheek on her head, tears running down his face as well. "I'm okay, Nix. I'm here."

Still my feet wouldn't obey my mind. Roxy got up and held out her hand to the woman. "I'm Roxy."

"I'm…" The woman glanced at Daniel, but he was reassuring Nikki that he was well. She glanced at me, at Colin, then took Roxy's hand. "Amélie."

"Oh, my God!" Roxy grabbed her hand and pulled her into a hug. "We were so worried about you. I'm so glad you're okay. Oh, my God. I'm hugging Amélie Didden. *The* Amélie Didden."

Roxy's enthusiastic welcome affected Amélie. Most of the fear and stress on her face disappeared as she hugged Roxy back. "It's good to be safe."

Colin introduced himself and herded everyone to the table. Roxy ran off to Vinnie's room to get her medical bag and Daniel waited until Nikki was settled before he walked towards me. I still hadn't moved. He stopped in front of me and I inhaled sharply at the numerous bruises and lacerations on his face. His expression softened as he looked at me. "Hey."

It took three tries before I could push any sound past my lips. "Hey."

He waved his hands down his body. "I'm here. Apart from a few cuts and bruises, I'm fine." He narrowed his eyes. "How are you?"

"Relieved."

He chuckled, then winced as he held his ribs. "You and me both. It's been a hard few days."

"You're dirty."

He laughed again. "Yes. Yes, I am. I don't know what I want more right now. To sleep for a month, to have an hour-long shower, to find the bastard who orchestrated all of this or to eat whatever is baking in that oven."

A soft ping sounded from the front door as someone entered the security code. Three seconds later keys scratched in the door and Francine rushed into the apartment. Manny followed behind, his expression relaxing slightly when he saw Daniel. "You made it."

"That I did." Daniel groaned loudly when Francine threw her arms around him and hugged him. "The ribs, the ribs."

"Ooh, sorry." Francine leaned back and held his face in both her hands. "I'm so glad you're here. Oh, God."

"Doctor Roxy's in the house." Roxy pointed at the large black leather bag on my wooden dining room table. "Who's first?"

"Daniel." Amélie shook her head when Daniel inhaled. "Don't argue with me. They didn't see how you could barely walk straight when we escaped."

"Come to mama." Roxy looked ridiculous in her pink onesie waving Daniel towards her. Had I not known her, I wouldn't have trusted her to give anyone medical care.

Daniel winked at me and walked to the table. I wondered if I'd ever told Daniel that I appreciated the respect with which he treated me. He never acted as if I was an inconvenience or impolite. The fact that he'd come to talk to me without any of the emotionality surrounding his return not only made me respect him even more, it also calmed the chaos in my mind. I walked to the table and sat next to Colin.

"Your bag is going to damage the wood." I raised an eyebrow when Roxy blew through her lips.

"No worries, Jen-girl." Vinnie walked to the kitchen and

came back with three dishtowels. He lifted the bag, then put it down on the open towels. "Fixed."

"You're going to need stitches for this one." Roxy's soft comment drew my attention away from my table. Daniel had taken off the ill-fitting winter jacket and his shirt. He was muscular, similar to Vinnie, which indicated a lot of time with gym equipment. Roxy was busy cleaning a wound on his shoulder.

My heartrate increased when I looked at his torso. In three places, large bruises confirmed the rough treatment he'd received. The worst was his entire left side. I narrowed my eyes to confirm that in one place what I saw was indeed the outline of a boot print. It was likely the place where his ribs were hurting most. Roxy put the bloodstained wipes in a plastic bag Vinnie had put next to her medical bag. "Are you sure this is the worst laceration you have?"

"Yeah. It only stopped bleeding a few hours ago. The cuts on my face stopped days ago."

"Well, this is going to leave a nasty scar."

"Pah!" Francine widened her eyes in a way that warned me she was going to say something inappropriate. "Nothing sexier than battle scars. You'll score with the ladies."

"Gee, thanks." Daniel winced when Roxy injected close to the wound.

"Where were you?" I needed to know data, not listen to their bantering. "How did you escape?"

"I'll tell you everything. Can I just have a glass of water first?"

Vinnie jumped up. "I'll get it. Amélie, would you also like water? Tea? Would you like something to eat? I've made enough for one helping for all of us, but will put more in the oven now."

My question went unanswered for the next ten minutes while Vinnie moved Roxy and Daniel away from the table, thoroughly cleaned it and got Nikki to help him set the table and make sure everyone had something to drink. By the time the chocolate-banana pancake casserole came out of the oven, Vinnie had prepared another one to go in. Roxy had finished stitching Daniel's shoulder and cleaned all the other injuries that required attention.

I could see on the faces of everyone around the table how important the bantering, food and sense of normality was. I wanted to respect that, give them all what they needed. Yet I could only wait seven minutes into the meal. "What happened?"

Chapter NINETEEN

"Amélie has quite an impressive list of acquaintances," Daniel said. "It only took her two phone calls to organise a plane to get us here."

I shook my head and held both hands up to stop him. "No. No. You have to do this chronologically."

His smile was genuine. "No problem."

"Just a moment, Doc." Manny lifted one finger, then looked at Daniel. "On the phone you said you didn't know Fradkov's end target. Do you have any intel on *when* he plans whatever he's planning?"

"I would not be sitting here, eating this divine food if I knew." Daniel leaned back in his chair. "I didn't hear much and I definitely didn't hear any deadlines."

Movement caught my attention and I looked at Amélie, but was too late. Whatever her reaction to Daniel's words had been was gone. I studied her closer, looking for any warning signs that she should not be trusted. There were none.

"Okay, let me start from the beginning." Daniel took a bite of his food and swallowed it after chewing only twice. It was not healthy. "I knew something was off as soon as the seatbelt signs went off after we took off from Paris. It was maybe ten or fifteen minutes into the flight. I was sitting in business class in the front of the plane."

"As was I." Amélie looked at Francine. "Did you find out that both our tickets were bought by Paporotnik?"

Francine nodded. "Yes, we did. I also found out that Paporotnik is the Russian word for 'fern'. But that's not important now. Just interesting."

"Tell them what else you found about the Papa company," Manny said.

"In between the plane, the paintings, Fradkov's house and"—Francine paused and swallowed—"everything else, I only got to hacking Paporotnik's account late last night. I've managed to create quite a profile on it. Even though I couldn't find concrete proof that it belongs to Fradkov, there are so many fingers pointing to him that even Genevieve would agree that Paporotnik is all Fradkov."

"I would not agree to any such thing."

Francine looked askance at me. "Really? Well, explain to me how the money in the account with Isabelle's name—which was opened only two weeks ago, by the way—came from Paporotnik. Or how this account is over a decade old and has countless transfers to criminals in all fields, from drug dealers to hitmen to government officials in countless countries. Or how it has a gajillion transfers *from* these criminals. More than sixteen million euros have passed through this account in only the last twelve months."

I inhaled when she paused, but held back when she raised both index fingers. "I'm not done yet, girlfriend. I was able to trace payments in the last months to four known forgers. I bet those are the people who did these Renaissance paintings. I also traced payments to all the names Nikolai gave—the names of the hijackers.

"But that's not all. Once I was on a roll, I figured out that Paporotnik, or actually Fradkov, organised both Daniel's exchange as well as Amélie's symposium. We already know Paporotnik paid for the tickets, but not that he organised the events. Now tell me all of this is mere coincidence."

I couldn't. She was right.

"Amélie and I compared everything we knew to try to figure out the who, what, when, where and why." The smile Daniel gave Amélie was small, but sincere. This event, the time they had spent together had forged a bond. "It's good to know we were right in thinking that the company belongs to Fradkov. Amélie received the invitation to speak at an event the same week I received my invitation. He had somehow set it all up and bought our tickets to make sure we were on the same flight. Her seat was two rows behind mine.

"Three of Fradkov's thugs were sitting in business class as well. I'd noticed them when we'd boarded and kept an eye on them for a while, but they appeared as bored and uninterested as everyone else, so I started going through my notes. When the seatbelt sign went off, all three of them got up." He looked at me. "The change in their body language was significant.

"It was clear that they were about to take some form of violent action. My phone had been in flight mode and I turned it back on. But they'd already blocked all signals, which told me that that the plane had also lost contact. These thugs had everyone in the plane under control within a few minutes. A group of teenage girls gave them a hard time, but that only lasted a minute before they were crying quietly. Once the passengers realised that they were not going to be murdered and that they would possibly live through the experience if they were quiet, the flight continued quite smoothly."

"At first Fradkov's men ignored me." Amélie put her knife and fork down. "For a moment, I had thought they were there for me, but when they grabbed Daniel and didn't even look in my direction, I was relieved."

"They grabbed you immediately?" Vinnie looked at Daniel with wide eyes.

Daniel nodded. "They tied me up and put tape over my mouth. I didn't resist at all. They had assault weapons and I wasn't going to risk the lives of everyone on the plane by putting up a fight and having a bullet puncture the body of the plane."

"But they still beat him up, even though he was just standing there," Amélie said. "Only the five other business-class passengers saw this. The flight attendants had closed the curtain between the two classes a few minutes earlier. I was very upset to see them hit Daniel so brutally and I was not the only one. The other people in business class were very scared. Fortunately, the people in the back didn't see this. I think they would've been less co-operative."

"And we think this was all part of Fradkov's plan." Daniel leaned over to look at the empty serving dish. "Damn, this was really good."

"Another ten minutes and you can have more, dude." Vinnie took the empty dish to the kitchen. "The second casserole is bigger than this one, so there'll be enough for Eric too."

"Who's Eric?" Amélie asked.

Nikki pointed at her stomach and smiled. "He likes chocolate-banana pancake casserole."

"Ah." It was the first time Amélie smiled. "When I was pregnant with both my kids, I ate enough chocolate for seven PMS-ing women."

"Oh, my God. Do your kids know you're okay?" Nikki leaned towards Amélie.

"I phoned them as soon as we phoned Francine." Amélie lifted one shoulder. "They know me well. They know I'll tell them everything as soon as this crisis is sorted out. For now they're just happy that I'm safe."

Her voice hitched on the last word. I studied her expression for two seconds. "You're not convinced that you're safe."

"I am." She stopped when I shook my head, and inhaled deeply. "Look, I've been dealing with threats my whole career. When I chose nuclear science at university, I never anticipated that I would be such a great commodity to the world's psychopaths. Then there is the work that I've done in numerous countries—countries that have enemies.

"I'm used to distrusting everyone. I've been with Daniel for the last three days and since we've survived a plane hijacking and kidnapping together, I trust him. But I don't know you. Daniel has assured me that I can trust you, but…"

"You don't know us," Nikki said when Amélie didn't finish her sentence. "But that's no biggie. You'll get to know us and realise that we're like totally fabulous and you can trust us all."

This time Amélie's smile was smaller, but just as genuine as the first time. "You remind me of my daughter."

"See." Nikki threw her hands up. "You're already seeing the fabulous in us."

"It's all you, little punk." Vinnie sat down and ruffled Nikki's hair, then looked at Amélie. "I get that you find it hard to trust a bunch of strangers, but if you trust Daniel and he brought you here, that should already tell you something."

"I'm trying to tell myself that."

"Okay. Enough." Daniel put his hand out towards Amélie, blocking us from her. "We can deal with trust issues as soon as we're debriefed."

"Where did they take you?" Manny asked.

"Once we landed, two of the thugs used me some more as a punching bag. I blacked out for a few minutes and when I came to, they were dragging me to an SUV. That's when I saw they also had Amélie."

"I wasn't really surprised when they came for me when we landed," Amélie said. "They even allowed me to take my handbag, but they did take my phone. I wasn't threatened or beaten, but being the size I am, I think they knew that there wasn't much I could do against their guns and muscles."

"They took us across the border into Belarus." Daniel pulled his plate closer when Vinnie got up and went to the kitchen. "We drove for about four hours to a farm surrounded by woods. In the car, I blacked out a few more times."

"Each time he came to, they would punch him again to make sure he wasn't gaining strength." Amélie's *depressor anguli oris* muscles pulled the corners of her mouth down. "I've never been in such close proximity to that level of viciousness. The violence. I don't know. Those people are not normal."

"Oh, they certainly enjoyed punching me." Daniel rubbed his hands when Vinnie put the serving dish with the second chocolate-banana pancake casserole on the table. "When we got to their compound, they threw me in a bare room. There was a mattress on the floor, so at least I had something softer than the floor to sleep on."

Amélie nodded when Vinnie offered the casserole to her and watched him dish two spoonfuls onto her plate. "In the car, they told me what my role was to be. They had polonium-210 and they wanted me to weaponise it. I put up the token resistance and they threatened my family and everyone I had ever met. I agreed to their demands in less than ten minutes."

I held up my hand. "Stop. Explain what you meant with 'token resistance'."

"Oh, I was never going to do anything they wanted me to do." Her nonverbal cues revealed her horror at that thought. "I'm one of the best in my field. I know how to weaponise anything nuclear-related. I worked on their polonium-210 and made them think that I'd weaponised it. I made sure that the scientist they had there to supervise me was convinced that I had weaponised it, but it's mostly harmless."

"Ooh, I like you." Francine pointed at Amélie.

"Yeah, she can be our new best friend." Roxy nodded at Nikki and Francine, her curls bouncing. "Then I will have two genius friends."

Amélie smiled, but I didn't want to be distracted. "What do you mean by 'mostly harmless'?"

"Polonium-210 is the most poisonous substance available. Even though it needs to be ingested or inhaled to have any effect, it's still extremely dangerous. A microgram can mean death."

Her expression gave her away. "What did you do?"

"Chelation."

"What's that?" Nikki asked.

"Ooh, that's brilliant." Roxy leaned forward. "Chelation therapy is used to remove heavy metals from the body. It binds to the metal and prevents its absorption and is then eliminated from the body."

"A short and sweet explanation." Amélie smiled at Roxy. "My method to do this outside an organism wasn't very elegant, but it is one hundred percent effective. Not only did I do that, but I made sure that it would be even harder for the polonium-210, which is now chelated, to travel more than two centimetres when airborne."

"What?" Manny held up one hand. "Airborne?"

"Yes. I was told to make sure the polonium-210 will travel when airborne and will cover as large an area as possible." She shrugged. "I was lucky that the scientist watching over me is not as big an expert as Fradkov thinks. He thought what I was doing was a miracle. The stupid man should know that polonium-210 loses energy the moment it travels through air. It would never travel further than a few centimetres."

"That's it." Nikki moved her chair closer to Amélie's. "You're my hero."

Amélie's expression relaxed. "I didn't have much time to do what they wanted, but it's amazing what one does when surrounded with guns. As soon as we got to the compound, I asked them to take me to their lab. They did. It has top-of-the-range equipment, completely unused. I think Fradkov must've bought it just for this event. That's when I was told that I had twenty-four hours to weaponise the polonium-210. That was thirty-six hours ago."

"We think this is because Fradkov is planning something this weekend," Daniel said. "If Amélie had finished on time, he could've shipped it out to any corner of the world and it would be there by now or within the next few hours."

"I thought you finished." I had surmised that from her retelling.

"Oh, I finished everything I needed to. But I told them the polonium-210 needed forty-eight hours before it was ready to be airborne. I used all the right terminology and the scientist believed me."

"Do you have a timeframe in mind?" Manny asked. "Did you get any inclination of when Fradkov is supposed to use this polonium-210?"

Daniel shook his head. "Like I said, I would not be sitting here if I'd known. That being said, I think Fradkov is planning something for this weekend. Possibly even tonight."

"Motherfucker." Vinnie pushed his chair back. "We need to do something."

"We're doing it, big guy." Manny lifted one eyebrow. "We're debriefing, putting our heads together to get to the bottom of this."

"Listen to what else Amélie has to tell." Daniel nodded towards the older woman.

She took a sip of coffee and put the mug down. "I spoke to Fradkov on a video call. He became scary quiet when I told him that I'd already been told what was expected of me. When he spoke again, I realised he was livid that I'd interrupted him. He wanted to repeat all the instructions to make sure that I knew exactly what he expected of me. And he was very precise with his instructions. I was to weaponise the polonium-210 in a way that would magnify its reach. Those were his exact words."

Icy fear brought goose bumps to my skin. I'd heard that quiet anger. I'd tried my best to put that phone call out of my mind in order to focus on the case. Amélie had brought Fradkov's soft-spoken threats back with great intensity. I rubbed my upper arms and tried to pay attention to what she was saying.

"Fradkov knows quite a lot about polonium, but not as much as I do. He was arrogant and even boasted how he expertly got Daniel, me and the paintings all on one flight. He said something about how gullible neurotypicals were. I asked him what he meant by that and again he went quiet. He stared at me for what felt like hours, then repeated in an almost-whisper how he would torture and kill everyone I know if I didn't follow his instructions to the letter.

"I tried to calm him down and asked where he got the polonium-210 from. It kind of backfired. He went quiet again and I had to explain very quickly why I needed to know. Polonium-210 has a half-life of a hundred and thirty-eight days, which means that in a bit more than four and a half months it will be at half its strength. Four and a half months later it will be half of that and so on. If I was expected to create dirty bombs, I needed to know what I was working with. Well, I needed to know how old it was. That would determine how powerful it is. Fradkov told me that the polonium-210 was twenty-seven months old and that it had proven very potent seven months ago."

"That's confirmation that he has the leftover polonium-210 that was used to kill Gallo and poison the Italian president and the German chancellor." I was relieved that this was the same batch. At least we didn't have to look for even more of this dangerous nuclear material.

"Fradkov repeatedly said he wanted the polonium-210 to go wider than it normally would. He had this sick half-smile when he said he was going for mass casualties."

"Bloody hell!" Manny scowled. "That means any public place. Train stations, shopping centres, concert halls, schools, office buildings. This is impossible."

"Amélie is not done." The concern on Daniel's features brought a tightness to my chest.

"Fradkov didn't say much more during our video call, but I overheard a lot of conversation between the two men who were in the car with us." She picked up her coffee mug, then put it down again. "It was a long drive to the compound. Daniel was unconscious for most of the trip, so I pretended to sleep. I was hoping they would relax and start talking. Then maybe I could hear something that would help us escape.

"I wasn't disappointed. They were stupid enough to buy my act. They were talking about Fradkov being uncharacteristically paranoid. It sounded like they've worked for him a few years and knew his behaviour. The driver said that he'd heard rumours that this was Fradkov's last job. Apparently, the payment is millions and Fradkov didn't want to fail. He was reeling after he failed his last job."

"That would be when he tried to kill a few world leaders with his polonium-210." Roxy shook her head. "Now he's trying to kill masses the same way."

"What else did they say about Fradkov?" The more I knew, the more accurate my analysis would be.

Amélie looked to her left, recalling a memory. "They talked about the art that was taken from the plane. They'd heard that Fradkov was using this as a delaying tactic, but some of them believed that he had these guys take the paintings because it was part of some bigger plan. They were joking about taking the art for themselves, but since there were no naked women in the paintings, they didn't see the value in it.

"They also said that this was the first time he got different people to work together. Usually, none of the people responsible for different parts of his plan ever met. No one knew who did what. That way he had more control and no one could conspire against him.

"This was another reason why they thought the rumour about this being Fradkov's last job was true. He was breaking his usual way of working. He never worried about people asking questions. If someone got too close to his operation, he would make them disappear by setting them up for some crime. Not this time."

Daniel reached over and put another serving of the casserole on his plate. "Listen to this. Very interesting."

"The driver said Fradkov had killed a Volyntsev person," Amélie said.

"Aleksei Volyntsev." Daniel looked at me. "Do you know about his death?"

"Oh, do we ever." Roxy straightened in her chair, her

curls bouncing. "He died in my hospital from radiation poisoning."

"Polonium-210?" Amélie asked.

"The one and only. When I heard there was someone in the hospital with symptoms exactly the same as the victim seven months ago, I just knew. But he'd waited too long before seeking medical help. He died a few hours after being admitted to the hospital."

"The strange thing about this is that Volyntsev contacted me six weeks ago." Daniel rubbed his chin. "I still don't know what he wanted. His email only said that he wanted to set up a meeting with me regarding an urgent matter. I replied and gave him my number and told him that I was available any time. He never got back to me, so I left it at that."

"How did he contact you?" I was most disappointed that we had not known this. "We didn't find any connection between you and him."

Daniel's eyes widened. "Oh, God. You investigated my life. Of course you did."

"Yup." Francine leaned forward and whispered loudly, "Puppy videos? Seriously?"

Daniel closed his eyes for a second and pinched the bridge of his nose. He inhaled deeply and looked at her. "With all the shit I see on a daily basis, I need a palate cleanser. Watching puppies playing and being cute makes me smile."

"Volyntsev." I didn't want to waste time with bantering now. "How did he contact you?"

"Did you guys find my second work email?" He nodded once when Francine shook her head. "That explains it. I have a second work email that is only used by my superiors. It's for highly classified or sensitive communication only."

"Fradkov was watching Volyntsev and must have figured out that he had contacted you." Francine tapped her manicured nail on her lips. "That's how he saw that email address. And then he, or Joe, most likely hacked GIPN and he got all your other info."

"Shit." Daniel interlaced his fingers and rested his hands on his head. "Fradkov hacked into GIPN? Wait. Who's Joe?"

"We'll get into that later," Manny said. "First, tell us everything you know about Volyntsev."

"That's it." Daniel lowered his hands and shrugged. "Before my trip, I was busy and didn't think to check out this stranger who contacted me. Until Amélie told me his name came up in the conversation between Fradkov's thugs, I'd forgotten about him.

"But this would explain why I was targeted. I was trying to figure out why on earth they would kidnap me. Not once did they ask me anything about anything related to GIPN"—he glanced at Amélie—"the president or his security. They didn't ask me anything."

"The president?" Amélie lowered her chin and stared at Daniel. "Which president?"

Daniel didn't hide the regret on his face when he looked at her. He turned to me. "Can we trust her?"

I studied Amélie. "Do you intend to kill people?"

"What?" She jerked back. "No."

"Do you work for Fradkov?"

"No!" The corners of her mouth pulled down in anger.

"What is this?"

I looked at Daniel. "She's being truthful. You are very astute in your observations of people and you spent the last few days with her. Do *you* trust her?"

"Yes." Daniel turned to Amélie. "I'm truly sorry I didn't tell you and I'm counting on your work on many confidential projects to help you understand. I didn't tell you that I consult with President Godard on his security and that these people don't only investigate art crimes. They work directly under the president and work with many sensitive cases like this."

"That's why she didn't trust us." Francine threw her hands in the air. "Art crimes. Pah! We do so much more."

"But really?" Daniel rubbed the back of his neck. "Fradkov got me beaten up for an email this Volyntsev person sent me? I don't get it."

"We also don't know how Volyntsev fully fits into this," Colin said. "We do know that he worked with the Russian Consul General to organise the exhibition and that they were good friends. They started Unity Through Art, a foundation trying to unify countries by exchanging artists and organising art exhibitions like the one in Belarus."

"Man, I have a lot of questions. Since we're talking names, have you guys come across a Markov?" Daniel narrowed his eyes. "Clearly you have. Tell me about him."

"What do you know about him?" Manny asked.

Amélie cleared her throat. "The two men in the car were worried about not finding him. It sounded like he was on the top of Fradkov's hit list and Fradkov was losing patience because his people couldn't find Markov. They made it sound like Fradkov was desperate to have this man killed."

"What intel do you have on Markov?" Daniel asked.

"Lev Markov is pals with the Belarussian president despite being sent into exile many years ago. He's also one of the biggest sponsors of the art exhibition." Manny rubbed his hand over his short hair. "How the bloody hell does he fit into this?"

"Tell me what you have so far." Daniel picked up his coffee mug and leaned back in his chair. Manny and Colin spent the next thirty minutes telling Daniel and Amélie everything that had happened so far. They started with Joe Pasquier sending Otto to Francine, Otto's assassination, the paintings sent to Alain, the numbers on the Fibonacci spirals, Justine's intel on Fradkov's strange behaviour and the meeting with Russian Consul General Nikolei Guskov.

Daniel was horrified to find out that he had been connected to first lady Isabelle Godard through transfers that made him look not only corrupt, but also like an assassin and traitor. "This is not true. You know this is not true."

"We've already proven it." Francine waved impatiently. "All those transfers had been added to your account and backdated when you were in the air. It was a bad hack job, but would've been enough to cast you and Isabelle in a bad light."

"To what end?"

"I'm leaning towards destroying your and Isabelle's credibility, which would directly affect the president," Colin said. "If his wife and a trusted security advisor conspired to his benefit it would make him look incompetent at best and corrupt at worst."

"This all has to do with the bloody peace talks between

Russia and the EU." Manny grunted. "For some reason, Fradkov is trying to set Russia up for these dirty bombs and also to make President Godard lose credibility and honour. We are trying to find that reason."

"But we knew those transactions were bullshit, dude." Vinnie slapped Daniel on his uninjured shoulder.

"Thanks, guys." Daniel swallowed. "What else?"

Colin and Manny continued retelling everything we'd uncovered. When Colin talked about the paintings found in the panic room in Fradkov's house, my throat felt as if someone was strangling me. Colin hadn't had time to study the artwork and determine how many of the sixty-one paintings were authentic. Colin looked at Vinnie when he talked about our arrival at the Fradkov's flat.

"This is where things get bad, dude." Vinnie pushed his fists against his thighs. "There's no easy way to say this, so I'm just going to say it as it happened. The flat was cleared by the bomb squad. We went in and looked around for more clues. The fucker had two assault weapons rigged in a hiding space in the wall. He controlled it remotely and shot the shit out of the flat. The old man's shoulder was grazed, but…" Vinnie's nostrils flared. "Pink was badly injured."

"How bad?" Daniel's voice cracked, his face void of any colour.

"Bad."

Daniel pressed the palms of his hands against his eyes for a few seconds, his jaw moving as he tried to control his breathing. "Tell me."

"I'll check in quickly." Roxy took her smartphone from a fluffy pocket on her hip. We listened in silence as she received an update on Pink's condition. She ended the call and put the phone on the table. "He's out of surgery. They've managed to remove all bullet fragments from his spine. The next twenty-four hours will be critical, but Doctor Dupont is optimistic."

"That he will walk again?" That was great news.

Roxy shook her head once. "No. It's far too early to determine this. All his internal injuries will heal without any long-term effects. Doctor Dupont believes that Pink will have full mobility from his waist up. He warned me that we need to be very cautious about Pink's ability to walk again. If he does walk, it might have to be with crutches."

"He'll walk again." Vinnie stated it as fact. "That is one tough mother. He will not let this get him down."

"The rest of the team is in the waiting room," Colin said. "They wouldn't leave until they knew Pink was going to be okay."

Daniel nodded. He tried to speak, but couldn't get past the emotion overwhelming him. Tears ran down his cheeks and he wiped them with the back of his hand. "Let's get this sick fuck off the streets. Then I'll be with Pink."

It was quiet around the table for almost two minutes. I still had plenty of questions for Daniel and Amélie, but it was clear that Daniel needed this time to process everything. Not only the devastating news about his friend, but also the information about the case. I used this time to reflect on what they'd told us. If Fradkov's plan was indeed for this weekend, we were running out of time to find connections between the elements to this case.

"Ooh!" Francine's exclamation caused Nikki, Roxy and

Manny to jump. She chuckled. "Sorry. I just forgot to tell you that I checked that computer that we found in Fradkov's panic room. And at first I only found loads of files filled with rubbish. I almost thought the only useful information was the videos we found that led us to Fradkov's flat."

"You found something else." I studied her face. "And you are confused."

"Well, yeah." She lifted her tablet from the table. "I don't know what this is supposed to mean." She swiped her tablet a few times, then handed it to me. "It was a file hidden in another file hidden in another file. Only photos, no video. There are seven images."

I took her tablet and frowned when I saw the screen. "This is taken from the surveillance camera in Fradkov's home office."

"Yup." She shook her head. "And it's of Fradkov sitting at his desk, so I'm pretty sure he didn't capture those images."

I pulled my attention away from the discussion around the table and looked at the first image. Fradkov was at his desk, speaking on his phone. One by one, I studied each image and couldn't find anything obvious in these photos that could lead us to Fradkov's plan or his location.

Each photo showed a generic-looking middle-aged man sitting at his desk. From the higher angle, the slight loss of hair on the top of his head was visible. In the first photo, he was working on his computer, his brow furrowed, his focus intense.

In the second photo, he was wearing a suit that reminded me of the bespoke suits Phillip wore. It was of obvious quality, as was his tie. He was holding a pen against his lips, deep in thought. The other three photos were similar. In all of them, his posture was erect, his focus strong and his appearance well-groomed.

Keeping my eyes on the last image, I allowed Mozart's Fugue in G minor to narrow my focus. My mind had registered something and I needed it to come to the fore. It didn't take long, but when it did I gasped. My hands and feet felt cold and my mouth dry.

"Jenny?" Colin's warm hand rested on my forearm. "What do you see?"

It was quiet around the table, everyone watching me. I swallowed away the fear and anger, and zoomed in on the left corner of the desk. "Look."

"Talk to me, Doc."

I shook my head. I couldn't yet verbalise how manipulated I felt.

"Shit." Colin jerked, then zoomed in even closer. "Is this one of those magazines you've been receiving?"

I nodded.

"What the hell?"

"What magazine?" Daniel asked.

"Jen-girl has been getting academic-type mags delivered to Rousseau & Rousseau one or twice a week for a few months now." Vinnie's fists clenched. "Are you telling me that fucker sent them to you?"

"It appears so." Colin swiped the screen and zoomed the next image. "The five photos I've looked at all have a magazine that was either addressed to Jenny or that I know she's received."

The deep disappointment in myself that I had been so

easily tricked felt heavy in my chest. Since the first journal had arrived, I'd become increasingly more resentful of the art crime cases that had been taking my attention away from my academic career. That had spilled over into the way I felt about the people in this room.

How had Fradkov known that I would've been susceptible to such manipulation? That the articles in the journals would skew my perception of my team and my work? I felt ashamed of myself.

"Fradkov knows where I work. He knows my interests." I swallowed. "He knows that I would read these magazines."

"You couldn't have known, Jenny." Colin handed Francine's tablet to Daniel, not taking his eyes off me. "There was nothing suspicious about those magazines."

"There was." Why had I not followed up on my initial thoughts that there had been something strange about the deliveries? "I told you I never ordered those journals. I should never have read any of it."

"What damage did reading them do?" Roxy's expression was gentle. She was trying to comfort me.

Being around neurotypicals had taught me a few things. The most important of those at the moment was that I would cause unnecessary hurt if I shared with them that I sometimes felt paralysed by the emotions connected to their friendships. It wasn't often that I curbed my responses, but I was glad that I was taking time to consider my answer. I didn't want to cause my friends any emotional distress. So I forced myself to tell only half the truth. "I allowed him into my life, into my mind."

"Did he write those articles?" Nikki asked.

"No. The journals were real, the professors who wrote the articles and the research they'd done were all real." I could see no one understood my distress. I bit my bottom lip and wondered if Colin would understand.

"Huh." Manny looked at me.

Francine took her tablet back and swiped the screen a few times. "All the files on Fradkov's computer were created four days ago. They were made to look as if they were created over the last four years. But I'm not the queen of all things digital for no reason. I didn't have to dig too deep to figure out that the computer and all its files were less than a week old."

"Doc?"

"What?"

Manny's lips tightened. "What are your thoughts on all of this, missy? On this computer nonsense?"

"It's not nonsense." I pressed my lips together to stop myself from continuing and also to organise my thoughts. "It's too convenient."

"My thoughts exactly." Francine nodded as if she approved of my assessment.

"I feel the need to qualify that what I'm about to say is not based on concrete evidence, but rather circumstantial evidence."

"Duly noted, Doc. Now talk."

"I'm having doubts as to Emad's role in this case. He's been presenting himself, not only now, but also when we first met him in the last case, as a villain. But now he's also presenting himself as a victim. I don't doubt that he smuggled numerous shipments of contraband across borders for many criminals. What I'm having trouble with is him claiming to have been under Fradkov's control, that he was under Claude's control and that he is a victim of his childhood and other circumstances."

"Do you think he's working for himself or someone else?"

I thought about this. "Someone else. Emad doesn't have the same ambitions as Fradkov. Unlike Fradkov who takes work that will give him more power, as well as money, Emad is doing this for a higher purpose."

"What the fuck can that purpose be?" Vinnie crossed his arms. "What is 'high' about killing people?"

"Hmm." Colin leaned back and looked up at the ceiling. "People who go undercover often suffer from identity loss. They're so busy being someone else that they forget who they really are. I'm assuming that Emad has had to take on quite a few identities over the years being a spy. That would confuse anyone, but someone who doesn't have a very strong sense of self would suffer even more."

"I've heard that some actors also struggle with this," Nikki said. "Especially actors who play in a television series for many years. They're in character eight or more hours a day and find it harder and harder to distance themselves from that character."

"Doc?"

"I need to speak to Emad again." I really needed to. "I need to re-evaluate how he used the app to send messages to Alain, the paintings, the computer we found in Fradkov's house, the numbers, all the clues he used to give us insight into and information on Fradkov. Looking at it holistically, it is too neatly laid out."

"Well, then we'd better get to the office." Manny put his hands on the table to push himself up.

"No, wait." Nikki raised both hands to stop us. She turned to Daniel. "You didn't tell us how you escaped."

"That's all Amélie." Daniel smiled at the scientist.

"Daniel makes it sound much more than it was." She shrugged. "All I did was use science."

"Do tell." Roxy's smile was excited.

"I was taken to the lab the moment we arrived. I had just enough time to have a look at what it stocked when I had the call with Fradkov. Then I met Fradkov's scientist. Quite a clever man. He left as soon as I told him I was done and we had to wait for the polonium-210 to be ready. I had the lab to myself for two hours before I was taken to my room.

"I discovered that Fradkov had stocked xenon in the lab as well. I don't know for what reason, because I was supposed to build a weapon that would infect people, not put them to sleep."

"Xenon is a very expensive general anaesthetic," Roxy said. "It's not used often, but is considered to be a very safe alternative."

"It can also be used in liquid form to measure gamma rays." Amélie shrugged. "It could be the reason Fradkov stocked it. I didn't care. I was just glad it was there. It didn't take a lot of time or effort to use it for our escape. Once I rigged it, I took the masks from the lab as well as hydrochloric acid. I used a few drops of that to burn through the lock on Daniel's door."

"I was barely with it when she came into my room. All I remember is the mask over my nose and mouth and this tiny woman almost carrying me outside."

"How did you get out?" Roxy asked.

"I opened the door." Amélie shrugged again in a gesture that she seemed to use a lot. "I put the gas into the ventilation system and trusted that everyone in the building was affected by it. It worked."

"No." Francine raised one finger. "What I want to know is how you carried that big man. I mean, he's twice your size."

Amélie raised one shoulder. "Yoga. And adrenaline, I suppose."

"You're like totally MacGyver." Nikki looked at Roxy and Francine, her smile wide. "A female MacGyver. So cool."

"Who's MacGyver?" Did this person have anything to do with our case?

"A TV character, love."

"Oh." I got up. I was no longer interested in the light conversation between Nikki, Roxy, Francine and Amélie. I wanted to have a quick shower and then go to the office. I wanted to check a few things in preparation, but most of all, I wanted to speak to Emad.

Chapter TWENTY

I paused the footage and leaned closer to the fifteen monitors in front of me. On screen, Emad had just proclaimed that he'd been under the control of Fradkov and, before that, Claude. A few clicks later, I replayed those forty-seven seconds in slow motion. I was seeing deception cues I had not caught before. There were so fleeting and well-disguised, even the most exceptional specialist would've missed it. But I wasn't letting anything go unnoticed now.

"Doc, you're going to get a video call." Manny walked into my viewing room and lifted one eyebrow when I turned around, making sure my irritation showed on my face. "This is more important than re-watching those interviews."

"What could possibly be more important?" Colin put down one of the journals I'd been receiving. Or rather, one of the journals Fradkov had been sending me. While I'd watched all the footage we had on Emad, he'd been reading about the influence of cultural background on nonverbal communication. I hated that there was value in things I'd received from Fradkov, things I'd started looking forward to.

These distressing thoughts were the reason I'd put all my focus on the footage of Emad. I'd isolated portions, played them again and again at different speeds, looking for every nonverbal cue Emad displayed. I'd learned a few things, but not as much as I had hoped. Emad had mastered deception.

It had taken us less than thirty minutes to get ready to come in to our team room. Nikki had taken Amélie to her room to shower. She'd been very pleased that her pre-pregnancy clothes fitted Amélie and had been happy to loan her whatever she needed, including shoes.

Vinnie had insisted that Roxy and Nikki also prepared to come with us. Daniel and Manny had agreed that, given the situation, they would be safest with us. I was glad they were here. I would've been distracted with concern had they not readily agreed to join us.

"Doc!" Manny sat down on the chair to my left and knocked on the desk. "Answer the bloody call."

I turned back to the monitors and clicked on the icon to answer the incoming call. Even though I was most vexed that Manny was interrupting my viewing, I trusted him not to waste my time. The face that filled the monitor in the centre confirmed that. I raised both eyebrows. "Nikolai."

"Good morning, Genevieve." Russian Consulate General Nikolai Guskov's expression caused me to jerk back.

"What's wrong? Why are you terrified?" What I was looking at was not fear. It was stronger. Much stronger.

"My life is in danger." He swallowed.

"Is that why you are in what looks like a hotel room?" Colin straightened in his chair. "Good morning, Nikolai."

"Morning. And yes, that's why I'm not going in to my office today and also why my family is now at a secret location."

"Where are you?" Manny looked behind us to the door. Daniel and Vinnie were standing in the door, outside the view of the camera. Daniel was wearing Vinnie's tracksuit pants and a long-sleeve t-shirt. Both were loose on him, but fitted well enough until he could get his own clothes. Manny turned back to the monitor when both Daniel and Vinnie nodded. "We can come and get you."

Nikolai shook his head. "It makes me very sad to admit that I've prepared for a day like this. I'm still in Strasbourg, but no one will find me."

"Are you sure all your devices are untraceable?" Francine pushed past Vinnie and Daniel into the room and stood behind Manny. "I'm Francine, by the way."

The distrust on Nikolai's face was immediate. His eyes shifted as if he was inspecting the monitor of his computer. He was most likely making sure there wasn't anyone else in the room.

I loathed having to reassure people. "We've all been working on this case. Not just Colin, Manny and I. Our whole team. If you trust us, it is rational to trust my team too."

Nikolai's internal struggle was evident on his face. He sighed. "Okay, who else is there?"

Francine waved Vinnie and Daniel over. "Daniel and Vinnie."

"Monsieur Gusko—"

Nikolai interrupted Daniel. "Please call me Nikolai. I can't handle any formality at the moment."

Daniel nodded. I recognised his expression. His eyes and mouth always contracted in this manner when he had made an astute observation and was about to suggest something potentially controversial. "Would you like to defect, Nikolai?"

"No." His answer was immediate and genuine. But he closed his eyes, his lips pressed together to reveal only a thin line. Manny inhaled to speak, but I held up my hand. Nikolai was having difficulty verbalising a decision he had made. He needed time. A few seconds later, he opened his eyes. "I might not have any other choice. For the safety of my wife and children, I might have to do the very thing I've judged so many others for doing."

"Whatever security you need, we'll provide it," Manny said.

"Like I said. I've prepared for this. No one will ever find my family's location. Once I'm done here, I'll disappear as well. At least until I'm sure it would be safe for my family if I defected." His *depressor anguli oris* muscles pulled the corners of his mouth down. "My dream of showing the true beauty of Russia is going to disappear with me."

He was losing focus and I needed to know what had caused the terror in his eyes. "Why did you call?"

Nikolai took a deep breath, then rolled his shoulders and straightened. "Lev Markov called me three hours ago. He's devastated. He said that he never intended for this to get out of control like this. He admitted he naively thought only a few key people would be affected."

"What the bleeding hell are you talking about?" Manny leaned forward, his frown deep.

"I need you to know that I've known Lev almost as long as I was friends with Aleksei."

"Aleksei Volyntsev?" Daniel asked.

"Yes. But Al and Lev were closer. I didn't spend that much time with Lev, but I knew that Al held him in very high regard. When Lev phoned, he begged me to make sure everyone understands why he did what he did. He never imagined that so many people might be affected by his actions."

"What actions?" Manny nodded his head impatiently. "What did Markov do that has gotten out of hand?"

"Lev was exiled from Belarus because he was too rich and had too much influence in high society. Russia didn't like it, because Lev has always been extremely liberal. He was never a supporter of communism and when Belarus gained its independence from Russia in 1989, he was delighted.

"By then he already had two moderately successful businesses. Within five years, those two companies grew to multi-million-dollar companies and he expanded into Western Europe. It was around that time that Russia took note and leaned on the president to get rid of Lev.

"Pyotr Grekova, the current president, was friends with Lev even then. He was also on the then-president's staff and was able to intervene. Lev agreed to leave Belarus as long as he could take his businesses with him. It was ultimately Russia who had to sign off on this, since they were the ones who wanted Lev gone.

"Russia agreed and Lev took his family and left Belarus. That was eighteen years ago. He has not been back since then. Even though Russia no longer has as strong a hold on Belarus as it had immediately after the end of the Soviet Union, Russia still controls most of what happens in that country. Lev is unlikely to return to the country of his birth in his lifetime."

"And he wants to go home." Colin looked down from the ceiling. "So he hired Fradkov to set Russia up. If Russia was involved in an international scandal that made all the NATO countries ready their militaries, it would be easier for the current Belarussian president to take steps to move away from such a controlling power."

Nikolai nodded. "That is almost exactly what Lev told me. He had two reasons for hiring Fradkov to frame Russia. His strongest motivation was to return to his home country. He longed to once again walk along the river on the farm where his grandparents lived. The second reason was to help his very good friend, President Grekova.

"He knew that Grekova wanted to be less dependent on Russia, but was powerless to change anything. With Russia on the defensive for their alleged actions, he could discredit Russia to Belarussians who would not give the West any consideration."

"Oh, wow." Francine tilted her tablet for Manny to see what she was working on. "Lev Markov most definitely had the cash to fund such an ambitious political project."

"Is this right?" Manny looked from the tablet to Nikolai. "Lev Markov is worth ninety-three billion dollars?"

"It sounds about right." Nikolai crossed his arms tightly over his chest. "That kind of money can warp a man's mind. I honestly didn't think it happened with Lev. The times I'd met him with Al, he always seemed so down to earth. The two of them met at an art exhibition soon after Lev had come to France.

"Their relationship started very strained. Al was working for the country who had taken Lev's home away from him. But it was their shared passion for the arts that kept them together. It was also this that brought me to the friendship.

I'd admired Lev's ability to move on and make the most of his life outside of Belarus. He seemed genuinely happy."

"This idiot hired a psychopath to destabilise a country, but didn't think it would affect many people?" Manny uttered a rude noise. "How can you admire someone like that?"

"I didn't know about any of this." Nikolai blinked a few times as if to gain control over his emotions.

I pointed at his forehead, forgetting for a moment that he couldn't see exactly where I was pointing. "Your expression is revealing intense grief. What happened?"

"Last night, all three of Lev's children were murdered."

"Oh, my God." Francine slapped her hand over her sternum. "That's horrible. What happened?"

Nikolai rubbed his hand over his mouth a few times. "They were executed. There was no attempt to make their deaths look like accidents or suicides. It was clear these were assassinations."

My mind immediately went back to Otto's lifeless body next to me in the restaurant. I grabbed Colin's hand and focused on his fingers tightening around mine.

"They killed his son in London, his other son in Minsk and his daughter in Paris. All three were shot in the head." Nikolai pressed his fist against his mouth for a few seconds. "Lev called me as soon as he got the news. And I sent my family away immediately."

"Tell us exactly what Lev told you." Manny's jaw muscles were tense, his hands fisted in his trouser pockets.

"Lev contracted Fradkov to put Russia in an extremely compromising position. Fradkov was quite excited about the idea, but demanded complete autonomy in executing the plan. Lev was pleased with this, because it would give him deniability. He didn't want any of this to come back to him. He also paid the ten million euros up front without any question."

"Ten million?" Francine asked.

"That was only the deposit. Fradkov was to receive another forty million as soon as things started falling apart for Russia."

"Holy saints." Manny shook his head. "That's a lot of money. A lot of motivation."

"Lev didn't mind spending it if it meant he could go to his homeland. And he has the money." Nikolai shifted in his chair. "But he didn't know that money would buy so much trouble. He didn't know that Fradkov had his own agenda."

"What agenda?" Daniel asked.

"He wouldn't say. All Lev told me was that he contacted Fradkov about a year ago. Their original plan was to frame Russia in an indisputable manner so all the NATO countries would push back. Lev would then get President Grekova to side with NATO. Lev knew it would take time before he could return to Belarus, but he was willing to wait. He just wanted Russia to lose power in a country it had no business controlling."

"Well, things certainly didn't work out as planned." Vinnie walked back to lean against the doorframe separating my viewing room from the team room.

"Lev realised this after the radiation poisoning a few months ago." Nikolai shook his head. "He said that he'd spoken to Fradkov, wanting to back out, but Fradkov wouldn't. Lev said that he'd never met a man who had scared him as much as

Fradkov. And that's when he asked Al for help.

"Lev thinks that Al wasn't careful enough when he looked into Fradkov. Lev warned Al that Fradkov has people everywhere. Maybe Al didn't take it seriously enough. Maybe Al was very careful, but Fradkov found out anyway that Al was looking into him and whatever he was planning."

"So Fradkov poisoned Al with polonium-210." Colin nodded. "Easy way to get rid of a threat."

"You didn't know any of this?" Manny's tone conveyed his scepticism.

"Not about this." Nikolai shook his head vigorously. "Not about Lev's plans, not about Fradkov and this plot to set Russia up or any other plots."

"You're truthful about not knowing about Lev and Fradkov, but then you hesitated." I wouldn't need to replay this. His hesitation had been quite obvious. "What do you know?"

"I didn't know about Fradkov's plot."

"That's true."

Nikolai sighed. "But I knew something was going on."

"Speak." Manny slouched deeper in his chair.

"Roman, my assistant, has quite the knack for finding out all the gossip. It doesn't matter if it's personal, professional or political, these rumours always find their way to Roman. And he tells me.

"About two months ago, he told me that he heard rumours that some man was exchanging paintings in Lev's Strasbourg house for forgeries. I immediately told Al who told Lev. Back then, he promised us it was impossible. The exhibition paintings he had in his house were under twenty-four-hour protection. When I asked him about this now, he told me it had been Fradkov. Apparently, he'd threatened Lev's business and family and also promised to reveal Lev's conspiracy against Russia if Lev didn't turn a blind eye while Fradkov entered the secure room with the paintings. Lev said he didn't have a choice. He also said that all the paintings were inspected before they were shipped and there were no red flags. All the paintings were accepted as authentic."

Manny shook his head. "Idiot."

"Roman told me about another interesting rumour. A few weeks ago, he came to me and said that there are a lot of grumblings in the Kremlin about some conspiracy to either slow down or put a complete stop to the peace talks between Russia and the EU."

These were the talks President Godard and Isabelle had attended in Brussels a few days ago. The same talks Isabelle feared any scandal connected to her or the president would damage. A scandal that could've come out had someone found the fictitious transfers from the offshore account in her name to Daniel's account.

"Roman also heard that the Kremlin was extremely happy that they'd managed to turn some spy."

"What spy?" Manny asked.

"Roman didn't know whether it was CIA, MI6 or any other agency. He only knew that Russia was paying this man a lot of money to get rid of Fradkov. And yes, Roman was quite sure it's a man."

I thought back to our visit to Nikolai's office and my impression of Roman Kuvaev. "How much do you trust Roman?"

"I believe this information to be true, but I don't trust Roman to keep any of my conversations, actions or even visitors confidential. He's the kind of man who's only loyal to himself. He's said enough to make me doubt his loyalty to Russia. He would pretend strong nationalism, loyalty if that would get him promoted, but not because he truly cares for Russia."

"Not like you do." It was clear on his face.

He nodded. "I love my country. This is really hard for me. I can understand why so many officials are willing to pay personally to fund this spy."

"The Kremlin is not paying this spy?" Manny asked.

"They are. But Roman said quite a few officials offered bonuses on top of the fee if Fradkov is killed."

"What's the bet these are the officials under Fradkov's control?" Francine tapped her finger on her lips. "If Fradkov is gone, they will also be free."

"Bloody hell." Manny rubbed his hands over his face. "I just hope we can stop Fradkov before this turns into a world war."

"What else did Lev tell you?" I asked.

"That's it. I've just betrayed my country by telling you all of this." The corners of his mouth turned down. "But I don't know if anyone else can be trusted at the moment. Not to do the right thing. It seems like everyone has a dog in the race. I'm counting on you to look at the bigger picture. Please don't let there be any more bloodshed than there's already been."

"Do you need our help, Nikolai?" Daniel asked.

"No. I will clear out here and go to my family. You won't hear from me again. Not soon anyway."

Manny and Daniel tried to convince Nikolai to remain contactable, but he was resolute. I didn't know why Daniel didn't see the stubborn expression around Nikolai's eyes and mouth. He was not going to put his family's or his life in any more danger. He ended the call.

I turned to Colin. "There aren't any dogs or races that I need to think about, right?"

"What?" Colin's frown quickly turned into a smile. "No, love. That was just an expression to say that Nikolai was worried about everyone's motivation being self-interest."

"Talking about self-interest." Manny lowered his chin and stared at Colin. "I saw you drooling over the paintings. How many are real?"

Colin rolled his eyes. "Of the sixty-one we brought from Fradkov's panic room, only thirty-two are the original artworks. Add that to the six that we got from his house the first time gives us thirty-eight original Renaissance masterpieces that should be on that plane. Thirty-eight. My God, the value is just hard to imagine."

"What about the others?" Daniel asked.

"Good forgeries, but they would not have passed muster." Colin looked at me. "They would easily have been identified as forgeries."

"Doc?" Manny studied me. "What do you think about this?"

"If you're talking about Nikolai's revelations, I think it gives us better insight into the catalyst for Fradkov's plan. The profile I built on him makes me doubt that the money is his only motivation—significant as the amount might be. Not only is this kind of political game is an exciting challenge for Fradkov, it would also give him the perfect opportunity to find new ways to gain control over more key people."

"And he's willing to go to extremes to eliminate anyone from stopping his plan." Francine rubbed her arms. "Killing a man's children is beyond cold."

"Aleksei Volyntsev sent me another email." Daniel waved the new smartphone Francine had given him. "I checked my second work email and there is an email from him. He sent it the day before I got on the plane." He looked at his phone. "He said he was worried about his safety and his health. He thought he was poisoned and that he was most likely going to die. And if anything happened to him, I must look into Ivan Fradkov."

"Why did you not see this email earlier?" Manny asked.

"This address is only used by my superiors. Whenever there's an email about a sensitive or top-secret issue, I receive a coded SMS. Only then do I check my email. I got that SMS for the first email. Most likely because one of my superiors gave Volyntsev my email address and knew I might not check that address unless prompted. But I didn't receive an SMS for the second email."

"Got it!" Francine did a little dance and winked at Daniel. "It wasn't too hard finding your second email account. At least not too hard when I looked for accounts with only numbers in the address."

"Supermodel." Manny sounded tired. "Stop hacking law enforcement agencies."

"Pah!" Francine froze. Her smile disappeared, replaced by an expression I seldom saw. "I just got an email from Joe."

"Hacker Joe?" Manny asked before I could. Although I

would not have referred to the man who'd sent Otto to Francine as 'Hacker Joe'.

Francine didn't answer Manny. Instead she pushed her way past Vinnie and ran to her computer.

Chapter TWENTY-ONE

"Come on, Joe!" Francine's *corrugator supercilii* muscles pulled her professionally shaped eyebrows together. "Don't do this to me."

Manny moved closer, but wisely didn't say anything. I was standing with everyone else behind Francine. She was typing frantically on her computer, her breathing fast, her body tense. I looked at her computer monitor again, even though I knew that I would not understand any of the codes running across the screen.

"No!" Francine typed for another thirty seconds while uttering phrases that made even Vinnie raise his eyebrows. Finally, she brought both her fists down hard next to her keyboard and screamed in frustration.

"Speak." Manny pulled a chair closer and sat down next to her.

"If I ever find this piece of shit, I swear I'll harm his family jewels so badly, he'll curse me every single time he has to pee."

"What do a man's family jewels have to do with his ability to urinate?" My shoulders dropped when the men groaned and the women laughed loudly. I had once again interpreted some ridiculous expression literally. At least my question had lessened the tension in Francine's body. "Don't answer that. Rather tell me why you are so angry."

"I was trying to get Joe to come in and talk to us, but he

refused." She gestured angrily at her computer. "Then he got all pissy and logged off. *After* he told me that I'd just have to make do with what he sent me and that he was bowing out."

Colin squeezed my hand. "He is withdrawing from hacking." He frowned and looked at Francine. "Did he mean he was retiring from hacking completely or just from talking to you?"

"Hacking. He said he's done with it." She leaned back in her chair and rubbed her temples. "Because of Fradkov. He's so scared of Fradkov that he has set himself up with a new identity and will never be found. And believe me, Joe is a brilliant hacker. No one will find him if he doesn't want to be found."

"What did he give you?" I asked.

"Huh?" She blinked a few times. "Oh. Yes. He gave me a frigging mile-long list of IP addresses. And no, girlfriend, it's not really a mile long. I'm just pissed off, so forgive me if I exaggerate a little."

"You seldom exaggerate 'a little'." I sighed when her mouth dropped open in faux outrage. "Your hyperbolic statements are at best unbelievable and at worst fantastical."

"Yeah, yeah. I love you too." She rolled her eyes. "Joe told me that he's been working for Fradkov on and off for the last three years. The money has been spectacular, which made it easy for him to look past the things Fradkov was doing."

"As if this Joe isn't committing crimes." Manny pushed his hands in his trouser pockets. "Tell me more about the IP addresses."

Francine turned to her computer. "Joe said that Fradkov is planning something huge this evening and that these addresses will lead us to the what, where and when. He didn't have time to look into that. And he said that he's not really interested in looking into that. He didn't start hacking to save the world, but he couldn't sit back and let all these cities get blown up."

"Hellfire." Manny straightened. "What cities? And what did he mean about 'blown up'?"

"I don't know if he meant it metaphorically." Francine flipped her hair over one shoulder. "I did ask him, but the twit didn't answer."

"What cities?" I didn't apologise when the words came out loud and impatient.

"Let me see." Francine scrolled back on the coded conversation she had with Joe. "Here it is. Los Angeles, New York, Washington. These are the only US cities. Then there's Birmingham, Munich, Marseille, Lyon, Milan, Kiev and Warsaw."

"With the exception of Kiev in Ukraine, these cities are all in NATO countries." Colin counted on his fingers. "US, England, Germany, France, Italy and Poland. All NATO members."

"Do you think NATO is playing a role in this?" Daniel frowned when his question was interrupted by a video call from Tim.

Francine clicked on the icon to answer the call. Tim's eyes widened as soon as he saw all of us. "Well, hello, everyone." He narrowed his eyes, then smiled with recognition. "Daniel. You have a lot of people here looking for you."

The tension in the room rose. Manny glared at the monitor. "Who the hell is looking for Daniel?"

"Oh. Oops. I should've phrased it differently." His smile was apologetic. "Daniel, your team is here with me. Should I send them up?"

"Yes," Vinnie said before anyone else could.

"Done and done." Tim wriggled his fingers in an unprofessional wave and ended the call.

One of the countless things I disliked about working with other people was the constant interruptions. I had rushed to the office this morning to prepare myself for interviewing Emad to confirm my suspicions. That had been interrupted by Nikolai's call, then Joe's communication and now Daniel's GIPN team. I was becoming impatient. I wanted to speak to Emad.

The next five minutes reiterated the importance of allowing interruptions. Everyone in the room relaxed as Claudette, Bonnard, Gautier, Cosse and Meslot came into the team room. After an emotional initial greeting and the team inspecting Daniel to assure themselves he was indeed not injured too badly, they asked about our progress.

"First tell me, how's Pink?" Daniel looked at Gautier. "What's the doctor saying?"

"It's a waiting game now." Gautier looked regretful. "I wish I had better news, but we won't know for the next twenty-four to thirty-six hours. The doctors told us that we could do nothing more and we should go home."

"There's nothing for us to do at our homes." Claudette smiled when the other team members nodded their heads. "We want to do something to catch this bastard."

"Good. We might need more hands." Francine pointed at her computer. "A lot of info to work through."

Manny walked in from my viewing room. I had been so busy observing the GIPN team's nonverbal cues that I had not seen him go into my space. He put his smartphone in his trouser pocket. "Just got off the phone with Louis Bellamy."

"Who's that again?" Cosse, the newest GIPN member, asked.

"The secretary general of Interpol," Manny said. "He wants us to confirm that the threat is real before we inform these cities. And he wants us to do this within the hour."

"Joe already sent info to all these cities." Francine scrolled through her coded communication. "He hacked the FBI director, the MI5 Director General and the heads of all these countries' federal law enforcement agencies. That's his way to show how vulnerable they are."

"And to make bloody sure these people take note." Manny tried to hide his approval, but I'd seen it. "We still need to confirm that the threat is real though."

"What else did Joe tell you?" I needed all the information before I could proceed.

"Let me see." She scrolled down. "He said that he got a look at Fradkov's emails and he's convinced Fradkov is planning to kill tens of thousands of people, if not more. He also suspects that Fradkov doesn't trust him and that's another reason he wants to disappear."

"Holy hell!" Manny got up. "He saw Fradkov's emails? We need to speak to him, supermodel."

"I tried, handsome." The corners of her mouth pulled down. "I really tried, but he wouldn't budge."

"How many IP addresses did he give you?" I asked.

"Thirty-eight."

"It will take too long." I lifted one hand when I saw Francine's reaction. I had not been clear in my communication. "I want to speak to Emad and if I'm going to help looking into the IP addresses, I will have to wait even longer before I can interview him."

"Is it essential that you speak to him now?" Colin pointed at Francine's computer. "Won't it help if you have even more data when you do speak to him?"

I thought about it. "That makes sense."

Colin winked at me, then looked at Francine. "We'll take half of the IP addresses."

"Give us some of it as well." Claudette sat down at the large round table next to the windows and opened a laptop. "I'm not as good as Pink, but I know how to get as much information as possible from an IP address."

Manny cleared his throat and waited until he had everyone's attention. "If this Joe person is right, then we have less than ten hours until Fradkov's plan is executed. We need to find out if Fradkov is planning bombs other than the weaponised polonium-210, who else might be involved and where exactly. All these cities are huge with too many opportunities for mass casualties."

"Especially with today being Friday. Any of the transportation or entertainment hubs would be like shooting fish in a barrel." Daniel looked at me. "An easy target. Manny and I will co-ordinate with the other countries. You guys get everything you can from this new intel."

It turned out to be more time-consuming than I had

anticipated. Francine was the only one with the hacking skills to procure the true identities of the owners of the IP addresses. While she worked on that, I finished watching the footage I had on Emad. I was convinced now that nothing he'd told us was to be trusted as the absolute truth.

An hour later, Francine had a list of thirty-eight addresses linked to the IP addresses. Some of the addresses were in apartment buildings, which took even more time to ensure that we had the correct person. Francine was happy to take those. She thrived on the challenge.

Colin and I took the IP addresses located in houses. With our resources, we were able to find sufficient information on each person. Claudette took all the names and ran a search for mentions of their names as well as postings of photos on all available social media. Together we built profiles on the owners of each of the IP addresses.

When Colin and I got to the sixth name on our list, I frowned. "I recognise this name."

"From where?" Colin stopped typing and turned to me.

"Give me a moment." I closed my eyes and mentally played Mozart's symphony no.28 in C major. My eyes flew open. "The money."

"Huh." Colin pushed the keyboard towards me and stayed quiet while I opened a few files until I got to the right one. Francine had refreshed the list of names with any connection to Paporotnik and had emailed it to me three hours ago.

I highlighted two lines. "Paporotnik bought tickets for Robert Barnes six hours ago."

Colin turned to look through my open door. "Francine!"

From my seat I could see Francine completely focused on

her computer monitor. Colin called her again and she turned to him with a frown. "What?"

"Can you hack Paporotnik's account?"

"Again?" She rolled her eyes when Manny groaned. "I'm just about done with all the IP addresses. Give me a few minutes and I'll have access to that account."

"Bloody hell."

I couldn't see Manny, but his tone was enough to know that his censure was not sincere. I would never have imagined that I would be grateful that someone could break the law to give me more data.

In the beginning I had resisted Colin, Vinnie and Francine's actions which were mostly borderline, but often indisputably illegal. Now I knew they would continue regardless of my disapproval. They had, however, proven themselves never to abuse their power.

Colin and I continued with the other IP addresses until Francine rushed into my viewing room. "You struck gold there, girlfriend. Ooh, look, just look at this."

She fell into the empty chair to my left and grabbed my keyboard. I sighed heavily and pushed the computer mouse over to her as well. Usually she asked before she invaded my space, but the excitement on her face made me forego my usual lecture.

"What's going on here?" Manny walked in and stood behind her chair.

"We have payments, handsome. Lots and lots of payments." She pointed at the monitor to the far left. "Last night Paporotnik's account only showed that tickets were bought for Daniel, Amélie and the men who had hijacked the plane. And of course the transfers to Isabelle's fake account in St Kitts and Nevis." She highlighted lines as she spoke. "Here is the transfer to Robert Barnes. But look at the last twelve hours. There are ten transfers, each one a whopping fifty thousand euros."

"Could be a deposit," Daniel said from the door. He walked in when Vinnie joined us. "These might be the people who are going to do Fradkov's dirty work in the other cities."

"And they'll get the rest of the money as soon as the dirty bombs do their job." Vinnie crossed his arms. "We need to stop this."

"Can you cross-reference all the names we got from the IP addresses to…" There was no reason for me to continue. Francine was already comparing the thirty-eight names to the owners of the ten accounts that all received fifty thousand euros.

"Bingo!" Francine did a little dance in her chair. "So, Robert Barnes is in New York. Then we have Roy Young in Washington, Paul Marley in Birmingham, Walter McGee in Los Angeles, Olivier Duhamel in Lyon, Jerzy Balce"—she frowned—"let me try this again, Jerzy Balcerowicz in Warsaw, Anatole Plaviuk in Kiev, Hermann Grünewald in Munich, and Charles Mathieu in Marseille. They're all here."

"Claudette." Daniel walked back into the team room. "Get us everything you found on these names. Anything and everything on social media." He turned back and looked at Manny. "It's time we contact these cities."

Manny left my viewing room, his phone already in his hand. I turned to Francine. It wasn't the determination or focus on her face that concerned me. It was the familiar glee that brought tension to my shoulders. "Don't hack from my computer. Do it from yours."

"But I'm here." She winked at me without pausing her typing. "And I'm already in Robert Barnes' Gmail account."

"Millard's going to have an apoplectic fit." Colin didn't look concerned about this. He leaned back to look at the monitor. "What did you find?"

"Nothing yet. I haven't read any of Robbie's emails. I'm busy getting into Roy Young's account." She paused for a second, then continued. "Why don't you guys go through the emails and see if you can find any clues about Fradkov's plan?"

I didn't like it. This was a gross, unacceptable invasion of privacy. Yet I carefully aligned my keyboard in front of me when Francine rushed to her computer. I pulled up the email account she'd accessed and scanned each email for anything that could help us stop the attack Fradkov was planning.

Robert Barnes from New York had received twenty-three emails yesterday alone, a few of which referred to previous conversations. It took longer than I preferred to carefully go through each email. Colin pulled his computer closer when Francine gained access to Roy Young's account and started analysing his emails.

With each new email address, Francine delegated it to someone else to go through. Roxy and Nikki were more than happy to help. It felt like a mere hour later when Vinnie grabbed my keyboard from my desk. "I have food on the table."

"I'm not hungry." I glared at my keyboard, then at Vinnie's

face when he hid it behind his back. "Let me work."

"The old man wants us to debrief and I think you need to eat."

"I could eat." Colin got up and held his hand out to me. "It's been seven hours since Vin's casserole."

My eyes widened and I looked at the clock on my computer. It was twenty-seven minutes past twelve. I had been about to ask for the next email account since I'd learned everything I'd been able to from Robert Barnes and Charles Mathieu's accounts. I got up without taking Colin's hand. Then I thought about it and took his hand before I walked out of the room.

Someone had added more chairs to the round table to accommodate Roxy, Nikki and Daniel and his team members. I didn't like the change, but refrained from commenting. There was less space around my chair, but I didn't mind sitting close to Colin. Nikki always invaded my personal space and this time was no different.

"Let's compare notes." Manny took one of the fresh bread rolls and proceeded to make himself a sandwich with the selection of cheeses, hams and sliced vegetables laid out in the centre of the table.

"If you mean we should compare our findings, I can report that I found two emails mentioning seventeen hundred hours today." I'd found the use of twenty-four-hour time interesting. It was more common for the average person to refer to five o'clock in the afternoon.

"Huh. Mine is an hour earlier." Roxy added an extra slice of ham to her sandwich. "Paul Marley said that he'll have everything set up for sixteen hundred."

"I have a different time frame." Claudette's eyebrows drew together. "Roy Young confirmed that he'll be ready at eleven hundred."

"Walter McGee's email showed that they are planning it for oh-eight-hundred," Francine said.

"Then it will happen at the same time." I reached for a bread roll. "Four o'clock in the afternoon in Birmingham is eleven o'clock in the morning in New York and eight o'clock in Los Angeles. This is a co-ordinated attack."

"Where?" Manny had his smartphone in his hand.

"Grand Central Station," Claudette said. "It was mentioned twice in Young's emails. It makes sense. At any time of the day, that place is filled with people coming in and out of New York."

"Union Station in Washington," Nikki said.

"München Hauptbahnhof in Munich."

"Gare de la Part-Dieu in Lyon and the central train station in Warsaw." Both cities were in the same time zone, which made it rush hour on a Friday afternoon. "Gare de la Part-Dieu is a very busy train station. It serves up to a hundred and forty thousand passengers a day."

The others reported the main train stations in Birmingham, Marseille and Kiev. No sooner did Francine receive the location she'd found in Marseille than Manny got up and tapped his smartphone screen. I put two slices of cheese on my bread roll while listening to Manny's side of the conversation.

It was clear that he was talking to the secretary general of Interpol. It was also apparent that the secretary general had been in contact with the other law enforcement agencies and everyone was ready to deploy. Now that they had the names of Fradkov's contacts in each city and the possible locations, they could take action. Manny reassured the secretary general that we were still looking for more information, then ended the call.

I looked at Amélie. "What would you have done to reach as many people as possible with the polonium-210? Taking into consideration the locations that we've found."

She didn't hesitate. "The ventilation systems. That's the most effective way to release the polonium-210."

"You think it will go along with a big bang, Doc?"

"A type of explosion? Very likely. Fradkov would want to draw people's attention to this co-ordinated attack. He can't do that if the polonium-210 is spread unobtrusively."

Manny's phone rang and again we sat quietly listening to his side of the conversation. All the cities had sent out all their specialised units to these locations as well as to arrest every person on our list. He ended the call and asked Amélie to explain more options of getting mass casualties with weaponised polonium-210.

I stopped listening. I finished my sandwich and closed my eyes. I continued mentally listening to Mozart's Symphony No.28 in C major. For the entire Andante, I allowed myself to not think about the case. I just luxuriated in the beauty of the strings, the complexity of the harmonies building to an exciting crescendo. When the last notes filled my mind, I exhaled and opened my eyes.

"I need to speak to Emad. Now."

Chapter TWENTY-TWO

"Madame Godard." Phillip took Isabelle's hand in his and shook it gently. "It's an honour to have you here. I wish it had been under different circumstances."

I waited impatiently in the hallway. Isabelle and her security detail had just stepped off the elevator. Even though I was glad she had immediately agreed to come in and rushed to get here, it had still added another forty-three minutes of waiting before I could speak to Emad.

"I want to once again state that I'm completely against the first lady being here." Luc was in charge of Isabelle's security, but had also been her friend since their university years. I liked him, if only for his genuine and proactive concern over Isabelle's safety. He turned to Manny. "Since when do we give in to terrorists' demands?"

I stepped closer. "I'm no longer certain that Emad fits in that category."

Luc jerked. The look he gave me was not friendly. "Is Emad Vernet not the same person who's in bed with Fradkov? The very man planning to let off dirty bombs all over the world?"

"I have no knowledge that Emad ever shared a bed with Fradkov."

Isabelle snorted. "Luc's being overprotective again. And he was using a silly expression."

"That bastard doesn't have any weapons and hasn't been

out of our sight since we captured him yesterday morning." Manny pointed at the conference room door where Emad was waiting. "The room is secure. I would never let my people in there if it wasn't safe."

"Why does he want to talk to me?" Isabelle stepped closer to me. "You didn't say when you phoned."

I hadn't said much when I'd phoned her. Manny had been most displeased when he'd found out about the call. I had only told Isabelle that I needed her to come to Rousseau & Rousseau immediately and she'd agreed without asking for information. "I went into the conference room to interview Emad, but he refused to co-operate. He said that he would only speak to me if you were there as well."

"How strange." Isabelle shrugged. "Why do you want to interview him again?"

"I no longer believe what he told us before to be the complete truth."

"Well then, let's go."

"The president is going to have my job and my head for this." Luc turned to Phillip. "Please tell me you have coffee in this place. Very, very strong coffee."

Phillip smiled and gestured toward the front desk. "Timothée will bring everyone coffee. I assume you will be in front of the conference room door?"

"I'm going in with Isa… the first lady."

"Only Isabelle and I are to go in." I found the fury on Luc's face interesting. "Being angry is counter-productive. It won't result in anyone agreeing to your demands."

Isabelle laughed. "Get your coffee and wait for me, Luc. I'll be fine."

I couldn't wait any longer. I walked to the conference room and exhaled in relief when I heard Isabelle's footsteps behind me. I had been deeply disappointed when Emad had refused to speak to me. I had seen his deep concern and his desire to talk, but I had also seen his determination to have Isabelle join us.

"Doc." Manny rushed to my side. "We'll be out here. I've got the security camera feed on my tablet and will come in whenever I deem it necessary. Just try to get as much from this bloody arsehole as possible."

I nodded and put my hand on the door handle.

"Wait, wait." Isabelle put her hand on the door as if to prevent it from opening. "What am I supposed to do?"

I thought about it. "Trust your intuition."

"I'll do my best." Isabelle took her hand from the door and nodded. "Let's do this."

I opened the door and stepped inside. Emad was still in the same place he'd been when I'd left the room less than an hour ago. The coffee mug on the table in front of him was empty, as was the plate that had held two sandwiches. His eyes widened when Isabelle followed me into the room. "I didn't think you'd come."

"Monsieur Vernet." Isabelle sat down two chairs from him. I sat down across from her, also two chairs from Emad. She appeared completely relaxed, but I wondered if Emad also noticed her increased pulse beating in the carotid artery in her neck. "I'm intrigued. Why do you want me here?"

"To the point. Good." Emad put his hands palms down on the table and leaned towards Isabelle. "I don't know who to trust."

"And I'm worthy of your trust?"

The small smile lifting the corners of his mouth was genuine. "It's more a matter of elimination than true trust. Although"—he glanced at me—"I do trust Doctor Lenard."

"Then why do you need me here?"

"Because I know how much you have at stake. I know how hard you've worked to support your husband and how hard you've both worked to make the peace deal with Russia a reality. I also know how much the last scandal set you back and the effort you put in to prove every single allegation false. It took you less than three months to regain the trust of France and the rest of Europe."

Isabelle's eyes widened. "You know an awful lot about my life, Monsieur Vernet."

"Emad, please." He shrugged. "We're way past formalities. And yes, I do know a lot about you. It's my job to know things about people. You've proven yourself to be a woman of integrity. I can only hope that you will not bury what I have to say under mountains of paperwork. Or use it to your own advantage. I know Genevieve won't. But I don't trust any of the people outside that door. You two are the only ones I believe will take action."

"Okay." Isabelle also placed her hands on the table. This mirroring action revealed her willingness to listen to Emad. "I'm here. I'm listening. What do you need us to hear?"

"No. Not yet. First I need to know that both of you will use every bit of power and influence you have to get me out of this mess. I'm tired of everyone thinking they can control me. I want my life back." He pulled his shoulders back. "I want to live in Wyoming. I want a small farm, or like the

Americans call it, a ranch, where I can have a few horses and a lot of peace and quiet. I don't care if the French government knows where I am, as long as everyone just leaves me be. I'm done with this life. I'm done serving masters who change loyalties all the time."

"I don't know if I can make any of this happen, Emad." There was censure in the look Isabelle gave him. "You swore an oath to serve this country when you agreed to work for the DGSE. You knew the life of a spy was not going to be easy."

"But I didn't know that I would completely lose control over my own life. All I ask is to be left alone."

Isabelle leaned back. "As far as I understand you've been involved in countless criminal activities. I don't know if any law enforcement agency would let you live with your horses on a ranch as if you've never done anything wrong."

"Just give me your word that you'll try to make it happen for me."

Isabelle glanced at me, then looked back at Emad. "I will try."

"What about you?" Emad looked at me.

"I don't have any influence over such a decision."

He smiled. "You honestly don't know how much power you have, do you? Of course you don't. Just tell me that, if you are asked, you will give your honest assessment of me. And that you'll tell the decision-makers that I would benefit from a peaceful life away from all these political games."

"I will never give anything but my honest assessment." I glanced at the clock above the door. It was twenty-one minutes to two. We were wasting time. "Do you have any useful information?"

He looked at me for a long time before he lifted one shoulder. "I don't know what will be useful to you or not. Simply because I don't know what you've discovered so far. I'd hoped that by sending you enough clues, you'd figure it all out and Fradkov would already be arrested. Or even better, he'd be dead. That way he will never know that I stabbed him in the back and I would be free from him. But alas, here we are. I hope that at least by now you know that Fradkov is planning an attack in"—he glanced at the clock above the door—"less than three and half hours."

"We know about that."

"Do you know which cities he plans to attack?" He huffed a humourless laugh. "Sorry. I shouldn't have asked. Of course you won't answer that. But I don't know if you've been able to find out that a few of those cities are red herrings."

It took a few seconds to remind myself that he was not talking about fish, but I needed clearer information. "Explain."

"Fradkov wants you to run around chasing your tails. He's only interested in embarrassing and hurting Russia's most obvious enemies."

"And who might that be?" Isabelle asked.

"The US, Ukraine and Poland."

"What about the UK? Germany?"

He started shaking his head before she finished her question. "Those countries are influenced by the US. Poland has always had a contentious relationship with Russia, even more so in the last few years. Ukraine is quite obvious. Russia wants more power over their neighbour, but the western part of Ukraine is not willing to listen to the loyalties of the poor eastern part. If Kiev suddenly suffers the results of a deadly dirty bomb, even the East will take up arms against Russia."

"To what end?" All I had was a hypothesis. I was most interested in Emad's answer.

"There is a piece of land in Siberia that Fradkov wants. He has offered the Russian government millions for that land, but they refused. Then he threatened to reveal damning evidence on eight strategic Russian officials, but that also didn't work. And when he threatened to create irrefutable evidence that General Sokolov is a traitor, they still wouldn't give him the land."

"Who's General Sokolov?" I asked.

"He's the person in control of that land. And he's a very powerful man in the Kremlin. And he wasn't intimidated by Fradkov. That made Fradkov livid and now he wants to show them exactly what he's capable of."

"By killing thousands of innocent people." The horror on Isabelle's face was real.

"He doesn't care. And he sees the deaths of these people as incidental, collateral damage. This is just part of him making his point to Russia."

"For a piece of land?" I studied every single micro-expression Emad exhibited. The footage had made me familiar with his deception cues. Now I would know when he was lying.

"Not just any piece of land." There was no calculation or falsehood visible on his face. "It's in the far north of Russia, in the Siberian Federal District. The land he wants is rich with nickel. A few of the mines in the area are in financial trouble or facing other obstacles preventing them from modernisation. General Sokolov is old school. He doesn't believe in pouring money into maintenance. And these mines seriously need maintenance. They've fallen into dangerous disrepair. Fradkov wants control of the land and the mines. He'll use part of the forty million to upgrade the mines. It will be an investment since that land and the mines will belong to him."

"A lot of power and money." It fitted Fradkov's profile perfectly.

Emad nodded. "So when Lev Markov came to Fradkov with his plan, Fradkov thought it was the perfect opportunity for him to force the Kremlin to agree to his demands."

"Does Russia know that Fradkov is trying to set them up?" Isabelle asked.

"Yes." His micro-expressions were most telling.

I pointed at his face. "They approached you, didn't they?"

"They did. Somehow they found out that Claude had gotten himself, and therefore me, involved with Fradkov. After Fradkov's failed attempt a few months ago, they put all their spies to work and found me. I was in Paris a month after Claude died when they came to me. I was still pretty angry that my brother was dead. I was angry with Claude, Fradkov, Gallo, that Daniel person who killed my brother, and your whole team.

"So, when they laid out their case and offered me ten million euros to find out Fradkov's plan and get them access to him so they could kill him, I was very happy to aim all my anger at one person."

"Why would Russia want to kill Fradkov?" Isabelle's blinking increased. She looked shocked that she'd asked that question. "I mean, why wouldn't they ask you to do it? You had physical access to him."

"They wouldn't trust anyone else to do the job properly. Two of the generals who are under Fradkov's control said they wanted to make sure Fradkov was truly dead. Apparently they've had assassins collaborate with their intended victim to fake that person's death. I was glad for this. I'm not an assassin."

"Is this the reason you stayed in that house even though you have the skills to have left and most likely disappear?" I had wondered about Emad's motivation for being a captive.

"Partly." He shrugged. "I was also trying to figure out a way to stop him. He's grown too powerful, his reach too long and too far. Someone needs to end the control he has over the dozens of decision makers." He paused for a moment, looking at me. "A few of those he gained with initial contact, like sending magazines."

It felt as if my heart stopped beating and all my body heat escaped. It took all my inner strength to control my reaction and my voice. "How did you find out about the journals he was sending me?"

"He boasted about it." Emad looked down for a few seconds as if conversing with himself. When he looked up, determination lined his face. "I found a way to access his security cameras. You found the stills I took? Ah, good. I wanted you to know that he was fucking with you.

"When Claude was alive and Fradkov still trusted me, he would often boast that he would study his newest quarry until he was sure he could find a weak point. I have no idea how those magazines could exploit your weaknesses, but he was as giddy as a freaking teenager when he sent you that first magazine.

"The last two months, he stopped talking to me about anything important. Sometimes he let something slip, but he kept our communication to orders and threats. That's when I found a way to hack into his system to see what he was up to. And that's when I discovered the shit he was planning. I might no longer be France's favourite little spy, but I couldn't let this fly."

"Where are your loyalties at the moment?" Isabelle lowered her chin and stared at Emad.

"With my father." He swallowed. "And France. My loyalty has always been with France."

"Even when you were smuggling contraband?"

"My superiors knew about this and approved. As long as there were no deaths, it gave me access to a high-end criminal element the DGSE had never been able to infiltrate. At first I was surprised how many politicians and billionaires bought art, diamonds and other valuables on the black market.

"But everything became so convoluted. It's true that being a spy is like living in a forest of mirrors. I reached a point where I didn't know whether my handlers at the DGSE weren't just as corrupt as the other people I dealt with on a daily basis. Then Fradkov happened."

His expression was revealing. I leaned forward. "He made you doubt even more."

"After Claude's death, I had no one to go to. That document leaked with President Godard's emails." He looked at Isabelle.

"It really made it look like he was receiving benefits for almost every treaty, bill or new contract signed."

"I know." Isabelle had lost weight in those first few weeks and had looked exhausted every time we'd met for lunch. It had taken three months before the last allegation had been proven false.

Emad pushed his fingers through his hair. It was the first time he had acted on his distress. "Fradkov was there. He knew just what to say and do to make me second-guess everything I believed in. And he got me to trust him. I suppose it worked both ways. It was three or four weeks after Claude's death that he told me about his plans for Russia."

"Was that before or after you were approached by Russia?" I hated it when people relayed events non-chronologically.

"A few days before." He thought about it some more. "Yes. It was a few days before. That's why I wasn't surprised when they told me that they knew about Fradkov's plans and that they wanted me to stop him from starting a third world war."

"Did they know about the polonium-210?" I asked.

"Oh, yes. They knew about that as well as Fradkov's plans to weaponise it. Although they found that out only two months ago."

I frowned. "Your nonverbal cues are telling me you deceived them."

"If the omission of the truth is a lie, then I suppose I did." He tilted his head back and looked at the ceiling for a few seconds. When he looked back at me, the exhaustion around his eyes was more prominent. "Look, I don't know if I can trust anyone in the DGSE anymore, but I'll be damned if I'm going to see Russia take forcible action on French soil. Or any European soil for that matter."

"What forcible action?"

"If I told Russia that Fradkov was planning the dirty bombs in LA, New York and the other cities, they would not have acted subtly. Russia would not just sit back and trust these countries to deal with it on their own. They're so desperate not to be tied to the bombings that their actions would've tied them to it."

"Why didn't Fradkov kill you?" This question had been bothering me for a while. "You said he distrusted you so much. Why not just eliminate the threat?"

Emad's smile was genuine. "Because he couldn't afford to. See, being a spy taught me to always cover my ass. From the moment Claude started dealing with Fradkov, I made sure to gather as much damning evidence on that psycho as I could. I recorded our conversations, found out about quite a few of his residences, figured out his bank accounts." He stopped. "Hey, did *you* figure out his bank accounts?"

I didn't answer him. Manny would be furious if I revealed any of our discoveries.

"Of course." He snorted. "You're not going to tell me what you know. Well, let me just make sure you know that he has that Russian-registered company Paporotnik and that he has an account in St Kitts and Nevis. Ah. You know about that. Good. Good. I was worried that someone would stumble across that shit and think that Madame Godard did things she didn't do."

"It still doesn't explain why Fradkov wouldn't just kill you."

"Ah, yes. The first time he accused me of working against

him, I told him about all the intel I had on him. And that all of that was set to be delivered upon my death. If I don't stop that scheduled email from being sent, it will wait twenty-four hours and then off it goes."

"Addressed to whom?"

"My father, of course. Although I didn't tell Fradkov that."

We were silent for a few seconds. It was an interesting feeling of satisfaction to know how Emad had gained the knowledge about all the things he used as clues. I thought of everything else he had revealed.

"But why the games?" I didn't understand why he didn't just come to us earlier with all this information. "Why the app on your father's phone? You wasted a lot of time with your games."

He was quiet for a long time. "I didn't know if I could trust you. I needed to see how you were handling my dad. And how you were handling the intel I was sending you."

"You weren't sending us a lot of useable information."

"And yet you managed to learn a lot." Brief concern flashed across his face. "I knew Fradkov would be waiting for you at his flat, but I didn't know how to warn you. I was counting on your team being smart enough to not step into his traps."

Again I remained quiet. Not because I didn't have anything to say. My throat was too tight with concern over Pink to push any words out.

"And in case you wonder, I haven't seen Fradkov in three days. The last time I saw him, he was excited about his plan at last coming together. That's when I realised I had to act."

"But why now?" I didn't understand. "We captured you

yesterday. Why only give us this information now?"

He pressed his lips tightly together and took a few deep breaths. "I only decided two hours ago to trust you." He glanced at the clock again. "Time is running out fast and I didn't know if you were actually going to stop Fradkov." He huffed a humourless laugh. "I still don't know if you'll stop him."

"Then give me something I don't already know. Give me something I can use."

Emad thought about this for a few seconds. "Fradkov planned for Doctor Didden to make the polonium-210 airborne, so that it can travel long distances. He wanted to get to each of the cities, but was realistic enough to assume that there will only be enough polonium-210 for five cities. So he chose the cities."

"The three countries you mentioned?"

"Yes. It will be New York, Washington, Los Angeles, Warsaw and Kiev."

"I understand the significance of all the cities, except Los Angeles. It doesn't have the same political power as the other cities."

"Fradkov hates Hollywood and everything it represents." He closed his eyes for a second. I wondered if he'd slept at all in the last thirty-six hours. He sighed and looked at me. "I can't remember how many times he ranted and raved against neurotypicals. According to him, me and the rest of the world are stupid idiots. Only a select few non-neurotypicals would ever understand his work and appreciate it. He especially loathes how Hollywood is run by and catered for the lowest levels of neurotypicals."

He leaned towards me, his expression conveying his alarm. "If you know everything I've told you and you managed to stop him, he'll be coming for you. For you, your team, your family, anyone and everyone who stands in his way."

My heartrate increased when I recognised the truth in his expression. I didn't know what to say to that and looked at Isabelle. She looked as concerned as I felt.

The door flew open and Manny stepped in. The deep scowl pulling his eyebrows together and the tension around his mouth increased my muscle tension until it felt like my whole body was being strangled. Manny pointed to the hallway. "Doc, we have a situation."

Chapter TWENTY-THREE

"If I get my hands on that motherfucker, he's dead." Justine's angry voice greeted us when Colin, Manny and I stepped from the elevator into the team room. Vinnie was standing by Francine's desk, nodding at the smartphone in his hand. It was obvious that Justine was on speakerphone. "I swear, Vin. He's not taking anyone else from me."

"We'll get Alexis back." Vinnie put the phone closer to his mouth. "And Fradkov will never see the light of day again."

Manny stopped next to Vinnie, then looked at the phone. "Stay on the line, Justine."

"I'm not going anywhere." Justine's tone was hard to analyse. There was so much emotion in those words, it was difficult to identify how much of it was fury, how much fear and how much sadness.

"Tell us everything."

Manny had only told us that Justine had information that we would want to hear. Dread outweighed the curiosity I experienced.

"That motherfucker Fradkov kidnapped my Alexis. He took her while we were shopping. She was waiting for me outside the fitting rooms in *Galeries Lafayette*. When I came out to show her the pants I was thinking of buying, she was nowhere to be seen. She does that sometimes, but never when she could have a say over my choice of clothes." She took a shaky breath. "When I phoned her, Fradkov answered. That evil son of a bitch answered my baby girl's phone. He told me that he had her and that he would tell me later what he wanted."

"When did this happen?" I asked.

There was a moment of silence. "Twenty minutes ago."

"What else did he say?"

"Nothing. I shouted that I wanted to speak to Alexis, but he laughed and ended the call." Her voice cracked and she cleared her throat. "I phoned back a million times, but he's not answering. I don't know if Alexis is okay, if she's injured or… if she's still alive. All I know is that Ivan Fradkov is a dead man."

"Where are you now?" Vinnie asked.

"In my fucking car." It sounded like she hit the steering wheel. "I don't know where to go. I don't know what to do."

"Give me Alexis' phone number and I'll track her phone." Francine leaned closer to Vinnie's phone. "My name is Francine and I'll be right behind you to end Fradkov."

"Thank you, Francine." Justine recited Alexis' number. "You won't be able to track it. Alexis turned off the GPS and any other location indicators on her phone."

Francine snorted. "Oh, I'll find that phone. Just give me a… hold on… I got it!"

"Where is she?" Justine's desperation was evident in the volume and pitch of her voice. "Where's my baby girl?"

"Don't." Manny grabbed the phone from Vinnie's hand and held it close to his mouth. "We'll handle this. I'm not having senseless citizens running around on vigilante missions."

"Fuck you and everyone in your street." Justine exhaled loudly. "Vinnie?"

Vinnie lifted his middle finger when Manny held the phone out of his reach. Vinnie grabbed Manny's wrist and spoke into the phone. "Come to us, Justine. We'll bring Alexis back and you can join us when we bring Fradkov down."

"Where are you?"

Vinnie gave her Rousseau & Rousseau's address. He released Manny's wrist when Justine ended the call and shrugged. "I suppose she's on her way."

"What is the location of that phone?" Daniel walked to Francine's desk.

"I think Fradkov might have dropped it in a rubbish bin." She pointed at the map on her computer monitor. "It's in the middle of Parc de L'Orangerie and it's not moving."

"That park is huge." Daniel turned to Claudette. "You, Bonnard, Meslot and Gautier go and look for that phone. I want it back here in twenty minutes or less."

"It will take ten minutes just driving there." I knew this from experience. The traffic in the city centre during the day was bad enough, but on a Friday afternoon it would most likely take them longer.

"It will take us less than that." Claudette nodded at the men. "Let's go."

"What can I do?" Isabelle was standing next to Roxy. "Do you need more personnel? Luc?"

"I'm not going anywhere." Luc sat down at the round table and glared at Isabelle. "I suggest you sit down as well."

She ignored him and looked at me. "Can I help?"

"No."

"What Genevieve means is that she doesn't want you to put your life in danger." Roxy gestured at the table. "It might be best if we get out of their way. I wouldn't mind catching up with you."

It wasn't what I had meant, but I didn't want to waste time pontificating, not when Isabelle appeared pleased to sit with Roxy, Amélie and Nikki at the table. I walked to my viewing room. I needed to process everything that was happening. Alone.

"They've cleared New York, Warsaw, Kiev and Los Angeles." Manny walked into my viewing room and sat down on the chair next to me. "Just spoke to the secretary general. They've locked down most of the public transport in those cities."

"That must be causing a terrible disruption." Colin sat down on my other side and put a mug of coffee on the coaster next to my keyboard.

"But it's better than thousands dying." Manny slumped deeper into his chair. "Only five of the thirty-eight people from those IP addresses have not been arrested or taken into custody yet. Everyone is being interrogated as we speak."

"This seems too easy," Vinnie said from the door.

"It's not been that easy, big guy." Manny turned to look at him. "There were scuffles in Birmingham, Marseille and Munich. Four officers and agents have been injured."

"What about—" I pressed my lips together in irritation when Manny held up his hand to prevent me from speaking.

He took his ringing smartphone from his trouser pocket and answered it. He didn't say much, just listened for almost three minutes. The tension in his body and the concern on his face gained intensity. "There was an incident in Washington."

"The bomb went off." I had surmised it from his side of the conversation.

"Anyone hurt?" Daniel was standing next to Vinnie.

"No." Manny closed his eyes for a second. "They found the dirty bomb, evacuated the station as well as a six-block radius. I doubt they got everyone out, but there was no one in the station when the bomb squad guys started working on it. The idiot working for Fradkov in Washington turned out to not be such an idiot after all."

"Roy Young." I had memorised all their names.

"Yes, him. Like we found out, he was in the army and from his social media it's easy to see how pissed off he is with the government. What we didn't find out is that he had training and quite a bit of experience in explosives when he was in Afghanistan."

"His bomb had a trip switch." Daniel winced.

Manny nodded. "The bomb squad guys saw it, but it was too late. It detonated."

"Did it disperse the polonium-210?" Amélie asked from the team room. She was standing behind Vinnie and Daniel, but didn't look worried at all.

"Yes, but they were prepared for it." Manny got up and looked past Vinnie and Daniel. "They had some kind of suction system going to act like a huge vacuum cleaner in case the thing went off. It was running when the polonium-210 was airborne. The bomb squad people were all wearing masks. They reckon that most of the polonium crap was sucked up and they'll spend the rest of the day making sure the area is completely clean before they allow anyone close."

Amélie folded her arms. "It wasn't a good plan."

"What do you mean?" Manny scowled at her.

"It would've been more effective had it been put into the water supply."

"That was Fradkov's previous attempt." Roxy narrowed her eyes. "They say the definition of insanity is doing the same thing hoping for different results. I suppose this is more confirmation that Fradkov is insane."

I shook my head in annoyance. "That is not the definition of insanity or any way to diagnose Fradkov."

"Well, I think we all agree he's completely bonkers, Doc." Manny frowned when Tim's voice sounded from the team room. Vinnie and Daniel walked back into the room and I saw Tim's face on Francine's computer monitor.

"Hi, everyone. I have a Madame Justine with me." He glanced away from the camera. "She…er… doesn't have a surname."

"I choose not to give you my surname." Justine's face appeared in the corner of the screen at the same time as Tim leaned away and glared at her. "Am I coming to you or are you coming to me?"

"I'll come for you." Vinnie didn't even bother to move closer to Francine's computer. He looked at me. "You can convince the old man that Justine is trustworthy."

I walked to the team room just as the elevator doors closed behind Vinnie. Everyone turned to me. I pointed at Luc's face, then at Manny's. "Your anger at me is misplaced. Your energy would be best spent on finding a strategy to deal with

Fradkov when he makes contact. Justine can be trusted. Her need to avenge the deaths of her sons and their wives won't allow her to betray the trust of people helping her. She won't reveal anything she learns here today."

"You sound very sure, Doc."

I thought about it carefully. "I am."

We stood in silence for a few seconds. Then Isabelle shrugged. "Does it really matter who joins in? We need to stop Fradkov's plan. The treaty is going to be signed tomorrow. It has taken us months of intense negotiations to get to this point."

The elevator doors opened and Justine walked in, followed by Vinnie. She was wearing jeans and a maroon knitted sweater, a thick blue winter coat draped over her arm. Her steps slowed down when she noticed Isabelle. "Isabelle Godard?"

"In the flesh." Isabelle got up and shook Justine's hand. "I'm so sorry about your granddaughter. You need to know that the people in this room are the absolute best at what they do. If anyone will get Alexis back, it will be them."

"Thank you." Justine turned to Manny. "You're the big boss around here? Tell me where that phone is. Where my granddaughter is."

"I tracked the phone to Parc de L'Orangerie," Francine said before Manny could answer. "We have people there now to retrieve it."

"What about my granddaughter?" The tension around Justine's eyes and mouth increased.

"I searched all the cameras in the area, but couldn't find anyone fitting Fradkov's or Alexis' descriptions." The regret on Francine's face was genuine. "There isn't a camera aimed at the location of the phone, but I checked all the cameras in the immediate area. There were too many people walking along those paths between the time Fradkov took Alexis and the time I located the phone. I think Fradkov paid someone to dispose of the phone. I doubt he or Alexis were anywhere near the park."

"Fuck!" Justine walked to the table, sat down, but got up immediately when the elevator doors opened.

Claudette rushed into the team room, followed by Bonnard and Meslot. The elevator was too small to hold more than three people. Claudette walked straight to Francine, holding a phone in her hand. She handed it to Francine. "It was in the rubbish bin, just like you said."

Francine took the phone and activated the screen. "Oh, goodie. Not password-protected. Hmm. Interesting."

I stepped closer when Francine held the phone out to me. There was only one icon on the home screen—the message icon. A little red number one on it indicated a new message. I took the phone from Francine and tapped the icon. The message opened and I inhaled sharply.

"What is it?" Justine rushed towards me, but Vinnie caught her arm and held her back. She put her hands on her hips, her thumbs pointing to the back. She was ready for combat. "What's on that fucking phone?"

"Only a text message. No photo. It only says, 'Genevieve, phone me.'" I swallowed. Fradkov had known I would have access to this phone.

"Are you going to phone him?" Amélie asked.

I nodded my head without looking up from the phone.

My finger hovered over the number while I forced Mozart's Symphony in D major into my mind. Months of dealing with the fallout from Fradkov's last plan as well as looking for him had led us here. I was a tap on a screen away from speaking to the man who had unnerved me with the surprise phone call and before that had taken up most of my mental energy for far too many months.

"Give me a sec, girlfriend." Francine took the phone from me and tapped the back of hers against it. "I'll track the call and hopefully get a location on him."

I took the phone back and took three deep breaths. No one was speaking. For that I was grateful. Another deep breath and I called the number that had sent the SMS. I immediately turned on the speakerphone. It rang only twice.

"Doctor Genevieve Lenard." Fradkov's quiet voice triggered an immediate response. I forced the fear to the back of my mind and stared at the phone. "It gives me such joy to speak to you again."

"Why?"

"Why is it a pleasure?" He laughed. "Oh, because I'm like a cat. I like to play with my prey before I destroy them. And you've proven to be a lot more fun to play with than my usual prey."

Daniel held up a piece of paper with Alexis' name written across it. I nodded. "Is Alexis with you?"

"She is." He paused. "Say hello to the nice lady."

"Fuck you, you motherfucking fucker!" A pained scream followed Alexis' outburst. Something that sounded like a scuffle came over the speaker. My heartrate increased and I had to concentrate to even out my breathing.

"Well, there you have it." Fradkov cleared his throat. "She is quite a feisty little kitten."

"What do you want?" I had to determine his end goal.

"You."

"You can't have me."

"Then I'll just kill the kitten after I've blown up the world."

"We've located your polonium-210 bombs. Your plan will no longer work."

Silence followed my statement. Going on Amélie's and Emad's accounts of conversations with Fradkov, I wondered if I'd succeeded in angering him. Were the lengthy silence an indication of the level of his fury?

"All of them?" His question was almost a whisper. Yet he sounded relaxed.

"Yes."

"Hmm. That's not good." It was there. Barely audible, but the tension that tightened his vocal cords was there. I closed my eyes to listen even more carefully to his next words. "You've destroyed my plans twice now. Twice. How dare you of all people do this to me? I wasn't surprised when Doctor Didden and the Mister Cassel escaped. What else can you expect from these neurotypicals? They can't see the bigger plan. But you? You?" Not once did he raise his voice. If anything, he sounded more unperturbed. More dangerous. I had just taken away his hope to gain the territory in Siberia. That would enrage him. He sighed as if bored. "If you ever want to see this beautiful young girl again, you will come to me. I want you, Doctor Genevieve Lenard. And I want you alive. I will phone you with instructions."

I inhaled to very clearly tell him that I would never work

for him, but he'd already disconnected the call. Sounds erupted around me. Justine was arguing with Manny and Vinnie, Roxy and Amélie were talking to Daniel. I didn't move.

I thought about everything I'd heard and ignored the feelings of frustration and helplessness threatening to overwhelm me. I would've been able to learn so much more if only I'd seen Fradkov's face during our conversation.

"Hey." Francine nudged me with her shoulder. "Whatcha got?"

I turned to her. "Did you find his location?"

"No. He very effectively rerouted his location. I would've found him, but I would've needed about twenty or thirty minutes." She raised her eyebrows. "What did you make of the conversation?"

I turned to Manny. "His anger is dangerous."

"He didn't sound very angry. Just totally psycho." Francine raised both shoulders. "What? We all know he's sick in his head."

I thought about his reaction. "For some reason he expected me to support his plans. I don't know what action he'll take now that he thinks I've betrayed him as well."

"These bloody idiots are always most dangerous when they think they have nothing to lose. Or when their plans are completely screwed."

"What are we going to do when Fradkov phones again?" Cold fear flooded me just thinking about it. "He wants me in exchange for Alexis."

"No way." Vinnie walked closer, his posture aggressive. "There's no way you're giving yourself to that psycho."

"What other solution is there?" I certainly couldn't see any other way.

Francine was back at her computer, typing furiously. She turned to look at me, then continued working. "He must've removed the battery from the phone he used earlier. I can't even turn it on remotely. And I definitely can't find his location. But I'm not giving up. I'm widening my facial recognition search for anyone remotely resembling him or Alexis."

An unsurprising argument ensued between Manny, Vinnie, Colin and Daniel about using me to draw Fradkov from wherever he was hiding. Luc also became involved in the argument and became the one who turned it into a discussion about strategy. Isabelle looked proud.

"Love?" Colin touched my forearm. I hadn't noticed him sitting down on my other side. "These guys are talking about using you to lure Fradkov out. How do you feel about it?"

I considered my answer. "Rationally, it is a workable plan."

Colin squeezed my forearm. "That wasn't my question."

"I know." The resentment that had been building for the last few months, my shame at being manipulated, and the constant and overwhelming concern for my friends made me hesitate. It was not easy admitting weaknesses. "I don't know how reliable I am at the moment. Daniel's kidnapping and Pink's injuries have affected my control. I can't guarantee that I won't shut down at a strategic moment."

"We're never going to let it get that far, Genevieve." Daniel's expression revealed the confidence in his team and this plan. "You know Fradkov. Where do you think he'll want to meet you?"

I thought about this. "Somewhere public. He will use Alexis' and the other people's safety to control my behaviour."

"That's what we thought." Daniel glanced at his team and they all nodded. "We have a very good plan."

"What we need you to do is agree to whatever Fradkov demands when he phones." Manny pushed Alexis' phone across the table towards me. "But first put up enough fight to make it believable."

Daniel lowered his brow, his concern sincere. "Will you do this?"

"You don't have to." Colin took both my hands in his. "If you have any doubts, just say no. We will find another way."

I swallowed at the tightness in my throat. What other way? I was confident that I had the ability to get more information from Fradkov. His need to have my support, to have me work with him was something I would use. He wouldn't have this vulnerability with anyone else. How could I not agree to this plan?

An unfamiliar ringtone jerked me from my thoughts. Alexis' phone was ringing. I looked at Manny, Vinnie, then at Colin. He squeezed my forearms again. "Only if you want to."

I nodded stiffly and picked up the call. Again I put it on speakerphone. "Hello?"

"Ready to work for me, Doctor Genevieve Lenard?"

"No."

Fradkov laughed softly. "Oh, you will. I have so many interesting projects. You'll love getting your hands on all the data to analyse it. We'll make a great team."

"I don't want to be on your team."

"Wait until you see what I have to offer. You'll change your mind."

"I doubt it." I ignored Manny's gestures to engage more with Fradkov.

"Then I'll just have to convince you." Underneath Fradkov's calm tone was a smugness that I hoped to use against him. "Little Alexis is ready to go home to her granny. Are you ready to change places with her?"

"No." I made sure my sigh was audible. "Do I have any other choice?"

"Of course you do." He made it sound as if we were having a quiet chat. "You always have a choice. You can miss out on the opportunity to work with me, but that would mean I will take my time with Alexis. I will start with her fingers. One by one. When I run out of fingers to cut off, I'll go for her toes. Then I'll leave her as a nicely tied up gift in a conveniently abandoned building. I'm sure the local rats would love something warm and fresh to snack on."

"Why should I care about Alexis?"

"I suppose you shouldn't. But she is a very smart girl. Twice I've had to tie her up again after she managed to almost free herself. She's quite frustrated with me at the moment." He chuckled. "But she's only one of the thousands who will die today if you don't join my team."

"Thousands?" What other plan did he have apart from the dirty bombs?

"Join me." The trace of impatience in his tone was revealing. "I'll bring Alexis to our meeting. But please know that I'm not inviting anyone else but you. If you bring some friends along, many people will die immediately. Understood?"

I was silent for a few seconds. "I understand. Where do you want to meet?"

"There is a concert at Zénith de Strasbourg. They've already started the opening shows. The headline concert will start in an hour. I think that will be a good time for us to meet. Keep this phone with you. I will let you know exactly where to meet." He lowered his voice. "Don't for one second think I won't see if you bring an entourage. I have a nice little trigger in my jacket pocket. I just have to press the red button and boom. Come alone."

The call disconnected and I stared at the phone. "He knows I won't come alone."

"But he won't know who or how many will join you." Daniel got up and looked at his team. "We have work to do."

They walked with him to the elevator. Manny joined them. "Let me know when you have everyone in place."

"Doc G?" The fear in Nikki's voice pulled my attention away from the elevator doors.

I turned to her and studied her pallor. "You will be safe here until I return."

She shook her head. "It's not that."

The micro-expressions on her face had my heart racing. I got up and sat down next to her. "What's wrong?"

"I…" She glanced at Luc and Isabelle. The vulnerability in her tone had drawn everyone's attention. The hint of hysteria when she giggled sent a rush of adrenaline through my system. She sighed, groaned, giggled again and put her hands over her blushing cheeks. "My water broke."

Chapter TWENTY-FOUR

"But I promised." My voice was hoarse from the emotion tightening the muscles in my throat. Not only did I loathe breaking the promise I'd made to be with Nikki during her giving birth to Eric, I despised the internal conflict bringing me closer to a complete shutdown.

Nikki's announcement had caused a moment of panic in the team room. I had barely registered that it had only been the men who'd lost colour in their faces and looked like they were entering a gunfight without any weapons. My focus was on Nikki and only on her.

"I've got her, Genevieve." Roxy put her arm around Nikki's shoulders. She looked excited. "You know I can take care of her."

"I'll be there as well." Isabelle got up and snapped her fingers at Luc. "Get the whole security detail. We're taking this girl to the hospital and keeping her safe."

"Doc G?" Nikki's eyes were wide in her pale face.

I imagined my expression mirrored hers. I didn't know what to do. I thought about how Phillip would handle the situation, but my mind was pulled in too many directions to settle on a strategy. I stopped breathing when Nikki winced. "Are you in pain? Have your contractions started?"

"No." She breathed through her nose loudly a few times. I watched in panicked wonder as she blinked a few times and pulled her shoulders back. She patted Roxy's hand on her shoulder. "I'll be okay. Roxy and Madame Isabelle will be with me. Everything will be fine."

Tears blurred my vision. "You're lying."

"No." She pulled her shoulders even further back and lifted her chin. "I'm convincing myself. It's like totally different."

My breathing was erratic and darkness was pushing its way into my peripheral vision. I looked at Colin. "I don't know what to do."

I jerked when Alexis' phone vibrated in my hand before Colin could answer. I had forgotten that it was still in my hand. I dropped it on the table and glared at it.

Manny took the phone and tapped on the screen. "It's Fradkov."

"Jenny, look at me." Colin sat down on my other side and tugged at my hand. "Look at me, love."

It felt like an impossible task to take my eyes off the phone in Manny's hands. Too much was happening all at once. Too much stimuli. Too many emotions.

I turned my back on Manny and the phone, and faced Colin. I tried to speak, but my mouth refused to form words. I grabbed Colin's hands and focused on the strength of his grip for a few seconds. "I don't know what to do."

"It's an impossible decision, love." He moved closer until his nose almost touched mine. "But we're all being brave. I don't want you to walk into that insanely dangerous situation. I want us to go with Nikki and wait for Eric to join our family. But that is not a real possibility now."

"We need you, Doc," Manny said from behind me. "Fradkov

is saying in this SMS that he will blow up the Zénith and all the concertgoers if you don't keep to your agreement to join him."

I had to keep to an agreement I made with a psychopathic criminal, but I wouldn't be able to keep my promise to Nikki. The emotional toll this was taking on me was outrageous. Had this been five years ago, the decision would've been instant and easy. Then I hadn't had the people in the room who were now ingrained in my life and emotions.

I inhaled deeply and turned to Nikki. She was sitting quietly, leaning into Roxy's embrace. I lowered my chin and studied her face. She was scared. But the determination visible in her shoulders and jutted jaw was evidence that she was going to face her fears. Again tears filled my eyes. She was much braver than me.

Her smile was soft and genuine. She took my hand and pressed it against her stomach. "I will wait for you, Doc G. Just maybe, Eric will also wait. Or he'll already be there when you join us."

I swallowed. I didn't want to leave her. And I most definitely didn't want to enter a crowded venue with blaring rock music to confront Fradkov. But if Nikki was willing to enter this new phase of her life differently than we'd been planning for months, I would find it within myself to face Fradkov. I took a shaky breath. "I love you, Nikki."

Roxy lifted one shoulder to wipe tears from her cheek and glared at Nikki when she snorted. Nikki rolled her eyes. "Doc G is being all irrational and like overly emotional. It's not like I'm the first woman in the history of mankind to push a ginormous human being out of my hoo-hah."

"Oh, bloody hell!" Manny slapped both hands on the table. "Stop this nonsense right now. Roxy, get this silly girl to the hospital." He scowled at Nikki. "Go to the hospital and behave yourself. No embarrassing the doctors and nurses." He straightened and turned to me. "We have to get this show on the road, Doc. Fradkov is only giving us twenty-five minutes to get to the Zénith de Strasbourg."

"Go, Doc G." Nikki sounded surer of herself. "The president's wife is going to be with me. It's going to be epic."

"Our people will be in place in another fifteen minutes." Daniel walked closer, putting his smartphone in his pocket. "Even before we get there."

I was still shocked at Nikki's earlier observation. At first, I was going to refute it, but I realised that I was being irrational. Only a few times in my life had my emotions been so overwhelming that they overrode my usual rational behaviour. I mirrored Nikki's behaviour and pulled my shoulders back. "I wasn't paying attention when you were working on your strategy. You'll have to brief me on the way there."

"Done." Manny pointed at the elevator and turned his attention back to Nikki. "Are you going to sit there all day or are you going to the hospital?"

Her cheeks gained colour, then she shrugged and got up with Roxy and Isabelle's assistance. "I was going to wait until there were fewer people to see my wet pants, but what the heck. Soon half the country is going to stare at my hoo-hah while Eric is…"

"For the love of all that is holy, get her out of here!" Manny's lips twitched when Nikki blew him a kiss and winked at me. His body relaxed marginally when the elevator doors closed behind Nikki, Isabelle and Luc. Roxy was tapping her foot, staring impatiently at the doors. The elevator was too small for her to join them.

"The old man and I will brief Jen-girl on the way over." Vinnie walked to Roxy and hugged her. "I'll go down with Roxy and get suited up. I'll meet you guys at the SUV."

The next twenty minutes were excruciating. I tried pushing my favourite Mozart compositions into my mind, but my thoughts were too chaotic. As much as I tried to focus on the plan Vinnie and Manny were laying out, my mind kept returning to Nikki. It was only when we drove by the parked cars towards the entrance of the large, circular concert venue that I managed to gain control over my thoughts.

Daniel opened my door as soon as the SUV stopped. "Everyone's in place."

"Stand still for a sec." Claudette approached me, holding something small between her thumb and index finger. "Your coat is perfect for this camera. Can I attach this to your breast pocket?"

I looked at the silver device and was grateful for the advancement in technology. I nodded and she stepped closer.

"This camera is top of the range and we have full control of it. The whole team has similar cameras. It gives us more intel and more control over the situation. Yours is also for the unlikely event that you get separated from us." Daniel glanced behind him. "Francine's in the truck and will turn the camera off if someone checks you for electronic devices. She'll turn it on again obviously, but after a few minutes. Unfortunately, we have no other alternative. But the rest of the time, we'll have visual as well as audio. You won't be alone. We've got your back." Claudette narrowed her eyes at the button on my coat pocket, then nodded and stepped back. "We decided against an earpiece. It's too risky that Fradkov will see it."

I exhaled in relief. Not only did putting something in my ear cause me great distress, I found someone's voice speaking directly into my head most disconcerting.

Manny jerked and took Alexis' smartphone from his pocket. "Another SMS." He tapped the screen. "He wants you to enter the building alone and go to staircase twenty-five to the left of the hall. You should leave this phone out here. Someone will meet you inside and escort you from there."

I wished I had time to close my eyes and mentally write Mozart's entire Symphony in D major. I didn't have that luxury. Instead I mentally turned it on and let it flood my chaotic mind.

"We have people placed everywhere in the entrance, the auditorium as well as numerous other places." Daniel glanced at the main doors. "There's already a strong police presence because of the heightened terrorist threat in Europe and all of them have received notification to be on alert for communication from us. We have an army in there." He pointed at the GIPN truck parked a few metres away. "I'll be in there with Francine."

I nodded. I was glad Daniel wasn't one of those men who felt they had to prove their masculinity by ignoring their physical limitations. He was still favouring his side and numerous times I'd noticed pain marring his expression.

"Let's do this." Vinnie looked at Justine. She'd won the

argument when Manny had insisted she stay at Rousseau & Rousseau. She had given her word not to get in anyone's way, but she wanted to be here when Alexis was freed. Vinnie winked at her. "I'll bring Alexis back to you."

"And kill him, Vin." Hatred dominated her face. "He should not share the same air as any of us."

"No one is bloody getting killed today." Manny pointed at the GIPN truck. "Go with Daniel. We'll let you know when we need you."

"You won't see all our people, but know that there are a lot of us looking out for you today." Claudette adjusted the strap of her assault rifle. "Are you ready?"

"No." I pulled at my coat. The bulletproof vest caused my coat to sit much tighter than usual. It was not comfortable. At least I knew that part of my torso was protected. As was Colin's, Vinnie's and everyone else's. Colin had only a handgun, but it was in its holster on his belt. He hated weapons and I hoped he wouldn't have to use it at all.

We walked through the front doors and I took a shaky breath. Francine had hacked the security cameras. She would follow me wherever I went inside this enormous building.

The hall before the auditorium was large with numerous entrances leading into the concert hall. All those doors were closed, yet rock music overwhelmed me. I made my way to the sign with a large twenty-five on it, knowing that Colin was following a few steps behind me. There were a surprising number of people milling around, as well as many security guards. I wondered if any of them were the police officers looking out for me.

One of the guards narrowed his eyes as I came closer to

the staircase. An almost invisible nod to himself alerted me that he'd recognised me. He reached into his jacket pocket and fear rushed through me. I came to a complete stop, my eyes on his hand.

The loud sounds of rap music drowned out the rock music behind the closed doors. The next moment a large group of people joined in a line and started a well-choreographed dance. More people joined, filling the entrance hall within seconds to a very crowded state. I looked behind me, but could no longer see Colin. I also couldn't see Manny, Vinnie, Claudette or any of the other team members. My throat felt dry and tight, my breathing shallow. Fradkov had been prepared for my team joining me.

Most of the young women in the entrance hall were identically dressed. Jeans, red coats, blue scarfs and blue gloves. The exact outfit I was wearing. My team would never find me in this crowd of impersonators.

I turned back to the staircase and barely suppressed a shriek when the guard who had reached into his pocket was standing in front of me. He held a phone. "This is for you, Doctor Lenard."

The moment I took the phone, he turned around and walked away. Before I could call out to him, the phone in my hand rang. I took off my gloves and swiped to answer the call. A video filled the screen and I gasped.

Alexis was hunched over in a chair, groaning and swearing.

"Look up, Alexis. Say hello to the woman who's going to save you."

The sound of Fradkov's voice sent a rush of adrenaline through my system. He was in the same room as Alexis. The décor was modern and rich. I had never been to this concert venue, but was willing to guess they were in a VIP room or an extremely well-furnished office.

Large abstract paintings decorated the battleship-grey walls and a beautifully carved red door with three silver locks was all I could see behind Alexis. She was tied to an executive office chair, her cheek bleeding. She looked up, strongly resembling her grandmother in that moment. Their anger looked the same. "Fuck you!"

"That's not nice." Fradkov chuckled. "Doctor Lenard, you have exactly five minutes to get to the VIP lodges. Once there, I'll direct you further. For fun, I'll keep this line open. You know, so you can see what happens to this pretty little girl when you don't get here on time." He laughed when Alexis spat at him. "Such a feisty little thing. Oh and by the way, I'm splitting the screen on your phone so you can follow the directions towards us." The video shook as he worked on the phone. Then the image of Alexis became smaller and moved to the top right of the screen. Behind that a map of the building appeared. "Just follow the red arrows and you'll be here in no time. You'd better get moving, Doctor Genevieve Lenard. Your five minutes start now and you have quite a distance to cover."

He was right. I would have to run up stairs, along three different corridors and another set of stairs to get to the room indicated on the map. I estimated it would take me more than ten minutes to walk. I started running.

I reached the top of the first set of stairs when I remembered the camera on my left breast pocket. I lifted the phone a bit higher, so Francine and everyone else could see what I was looking at. And where I was. I wondered how Justine was dealing with seeing her granddaughter being beaten up and restrained in an office chair.

The physical activity warmed me up and soon I removed my hat and scarf. Was this Fradkov's plan all along? Not only would he be able to see anyone else running with me, he would also have me at a disadvantage being out of breath from running. I was grateful that I had always found jogging a way to calm my mind. I might not be fit or fast enough to compete in a marathon, but running through the halls of the Zénith was not an extreme test of my physical condition.

The true challenge was in my mind. I ran down the second last corridor and focused on following the red arrows. If I were to think about all the people and emotions surrounding this moment, the darkness pushing in on my peripheral vision would completely take over.

"Ooh, look." Fradkov's quiet voice over the phone echoed in the empty corridor. "You're almost there. But you can stop and catch your breath first, Doctor Genevieve Lenard."

I stopped, but didn't need to catch my breath. I hated that he used my full name, but wasn't going to respond to that. There had been a tone in his voice that made me realise he was playing a game with me. I waited.

"You're still there, Doctor Genevieve Lenard?"

I lifted the phone and breathed as if I was winded. "I'm here."

"You made good time. Now you can follow the new map." A different image filled the phone's screen. I was certain Fradkov had this phone's camera on and was watching me, so I frowned and looked deeply worried. It wasn't that difficult to exhibit concern. In the top right-hand corner, Alexis was clenching her jaw so hard her *masseter* muscles were bulging. She was fighting tears.

"Should I follow the blue arrows?" I tried to sound breathless.

"Aren't you just a genius." He laughed. "You have four minutes. This is a little closer."

I disagreed. The distance between where I was now and the final destination appeared to be further than the distance I'd just run. I turned around and started running again.

I was running towards a row of rooms that the map indicated were artist lodges. I assumed that was where the performers would ready themselves for the concerts. I reached the stairs I had just ascended and ran down them as fast I could. When I reached the level surface of another corridor, I lifted the phone to check on Alexis. She seemed to have gained control over her tears. Her anger was back.

I turned left into another corridor and skidded to a stop. I turned around and walked back to the previous corridor and stopped in front of the second last door on the left. There was a short carpeted entrance before the door.

The red, beautifully carved door.

I reached for the door handle. There was no doubt in my mind that Fradkov was in this room, terrorising Alexis. The door handle lowered and I pushed the door open.

Chapter TWENTY-FIVE

"Doctor Genevieve Lenard." Fradkov was leaning against the large dark-wood desk, his thin lips pulled into a fake smile. His nose dominated his face, his deep-set eyes small, his teeth crooked.

His tailored suit and handmade shoes would lead a person to the rightful assumption that he was rich. But it would not make him attractive or give him class. The malice in his smile and his nails bitten to the quick revealed the person under the expensive veneer.

He was holding a smartphone in his hand aimed in my direction. He was still transmitting. I lifted the phone in my hand to make sure my breast pocket camera would catch this. Francine would be able to locate me. I was surprised—and quite concerned—that Manny, Vinnie and Colin had not caught up with me. I didn't allow myself to consider the numerous reasons why they might not be close.

Instead I glanced one more time at Fradkov before I focused on Alexis, sitting with her back towards me. "Alexis, are you well?"

"Never better." Her tone and what I could see of her body language belied her statement. Taking into consideration her grandmother's penchant for rudeness and sarcasm, I dismissed her answer as such.

"Come in. Join us." Fradkov tapped the screen on his phone

and put it on the table. He reached into his jacket and brought out a handgun. And pointed it at my chest. "Now."

The blackness I feared and had been fighting crept into my peripheral vision, the safety of a shutdown beckoning me. How was I supposed to protect this vulnerable young woman, my team and all the people at the rock concert when my mind wanted to close down under stress?

With more effort than I'd ever put into something, I pulled my eyes away from the barrel of the handgun. I looked up at Fradkov and forced myself to analyse his features. His nose was slightly crooked and he'd had a haircut since Emad had captured him on those photos, but there was nothing that would make him stand out from a crowd.

I registered the small smirk lifting one corner of his mouth and the intelligence in his eyes as he studied me back. On a deep inhale, I put the phone in my pocket and stepped deeper into the room, but stopped when he nodded at the door.

When I didn't do anything, he rolled his eyes and sighed as if highly inconvenienced. "Would you please close the door behind you? And do remember to lock it up nice and tight."

I hated turning my back on him, but to make the idea that had flashed into my mind work, I had to do it. I walked the three steps back to the door, closed it and took a step to the right, obscuring his view of the locks. I had the same locks on my bedroom door as well as the front door to my apartment. Hoping Fradkov wouldn't suspect anything, I turned the first lock's turn button once to the right, then back to the left.

These locks were top of the range and with two rotations would secure a door against the pressure of a hundred and fifty kilograms. Two such locks would make the probability of a breach highly unlikely. But one rotation to the right and one to the left would give my team the possibility to reach us.

I turned back to Fradkov, more in control of myself. "Let Alexis go. You have me."

"Not yet, Doctor Genevieve Lenard. Not quite yet." He tilted his head to the side and smiled. It was genuine. "I just knew you wouldn't run past this room and go all the way to the artist lodges. So what did you think of my strategy to get you to come to me?"

"It was exceptional." Complimenting him would serve two purposes. Firstly, being truthful was less stressful for me. But more importantly, people like Fradkov thrived on reassurance.

I wasn't disappointed. His chest lifted with pride. "Once that pathetic loser Emad confirmed my suspicions that he was betraying me by making sure you caught him, it was fun watching you work. Oh, but just so you know, I've been watching you for a few months. I wanted to know who managed to destroy the plans that had taken me years to put into place. I was pleasantly surprised that it was you.

"And watching you try to solve Otto's sad demise and then visit my homes was also a pleasure. You're beautifully predictable. Your behavioural pattern was another fun thing to observe. For example, this winter you've only ever worn this red coat when the temperature was between five and ten degrees. Closer to zero and you wear your dark blue coat.

And you confirmed it this morning by wearing this beautiful coat. It was easy to get my people in place."

"You anticipated that I would not come alone."

He snorted. "Of course I did. There was no way you would come to me if you weren't protected. And there was no way those men hanging around you would let you come alone either."

The micro-expressions when he talked about Manny, Vinnie and Colin elicited a strong fear response. I took a deep breath. "Have you hurt them?"

"No." His malicious smile was back. "I'm just playing with them a little bit."

The darkness returned and I took a few deep breaths to push it back. "What are you doing?"

"Scrambling signals. Everyone relies on technology so much today." He glanced at the phone on the desk. "One tap and I disabled all transmissions."

"No." I shook my head. "You did that less than a minute ago. What did you do before that?"

"Delayed them." He sobered and looked at me for a few seconds. "See? This is why you need to be here. Away from that distraction."

"What distraction? Why me?"

He leaned a bit back as if he was indulging in daydreaming, but the grip on his weapon did not relax. "I want you to join me. Together we can do great things."

His micro-expressions and the change in his gentle tone alerted me that there was more to his words. "Clarify what you mean by joining you."

"What I mean by joining me is that I want you to partner

up with me. I don't want you to work for me. That's banal and, frankly, far beneath us. I want you to work beside me." He shook his weapon towards the hallway. "All those neurotypical idiots will never understand us. They will always resist our plans, undermine our greatness and try to make fools of us. You're not like them, Doctor Genevieve Lenard. *We're* not like them."

"We're different." I needed to know how he categorised himself as well as me.

"You see it." His smile was sincere. "I knew that you would. At first, I was worried that you'd been sucked into their ridiculous world of friendships and hugs. It surprised me when I discovered that you hadn't published any new research in years. That's why I sent you those magazines. I wanted you to know that I understand. I know what it's like to hunger for more knowledge, for more power. Together we can be unstoppable."

"Did you truly believe I would agree?"

He gave a half shrug. "No. But I hoped that you would be smart enough to know that I will kill Alexis right now, right here if you don't come with me. But if you do come with me, I'll leave her here for your pathetic, confused team members to find. And as a bonus for becoming my partner, I won't detonate the thirteen other bombs I have planted."

It took all my focus not to react. Fear constricted my lungs and throat as I thought about spending any more time with him. I wanted my team to come through the door and end this. I wanted to be with Nikki. I wanted to be anywhere but here. But to do that I would have to call on all the knowledge I had to be convincing.

I made sure my nonverbal cues conveyed my anger. As well as my reluctance. "I'll come with you."

His tongue protruded for a millisecond. Victory. He schooled his expression and nodded sagely. "You will not regret it, Doctor Genevieve Lenard. We're going to be great together."

I didn't respond. Even though I had agreed to go with him, I hadn't agreed to work with him. And I had lied. I did not plan to leave this building with him.

Deception was never easy for me and required concentration, but I had convinced Fradkov. He lowered the handgun and straightened. "Well, let's go. I won't be able to keep your people busy and confused for hours on end."

Against the wall to the right of the desk were two beautifully carved cupboards. The style resembled the door. Fradkov walked to the two cupboards and twisted both door handles on the one cupboard. The hiss of a hydraulic lock sounded and the cupboard slid to the side, revealing a wide doorway. And stairs going down.

I had lost count of the times Manny, Vinnie and even Colin had warned me never to leave with someone I didn't trust implicitly. During the many years I'd learned self-defence, I had also learned never to be taken to a second location. I stood frozen.

"Having problems, Doctor Genevieve Lenard?" The muscles around his eyes contracted and dread settled deep in my stomach. Casually, he walked to Alexis and, while keeping his eyes on me, slapped the young woman hard across the face. So hard that the office chair rolled a few centimetres to the left. Fradkov raised one eyebrow. "Coming?"

I walked around the office chair and looked into Alexis' face. Her lip was bleeding and there was a fresh cut on her cheek. Tears ran down her cheeks, but it wasn't from fear. Even though I could clearly see the fear in her expression, it was anger that made her cry. I leaned forward and studied her for another two seconds. I straightened when I was satisfied. "You're strong. You'll be fine."

She huffed a laugh, then winced when more blood trickled from the cut in her lip. I wondered if I should say anything else, but didn't know what, so I turned around and walked past Fradkov. I hesitated in front of the stairs.

My mind was at war. One part of me wanted to give in to the comfortable shutdown beckoning me. That way, I would not have to deal with any of this. It would be someone else's problem. The largest part of me agreed that humouring Fradkov was the best possible decision available at the moment. There was no one else to deal with him. There was no one to overpower him, take his weapon away from him and take him into custody. Not here and not at the moment.

This was up to me. I swallowed and took the first step down. I lingered on each step, hoping that I was giving Manny and the team more time to reach me. A shudder shook my body when the light from the office was cut off by the cupboard sliding back into place. Soft yellow lights lit the staircase, at the bottom of which was another red door.

"Your people aren't going to reach you in time, Doctor Genevieve Lenard," Fradkov said from behind me. Something hard pressed against my shoulder. "I don't have a problem shooting you in a place that can heal quickly. Mind you, you don't need your shoulder to work with me, so I don't even have to be careful where I shoot."

I moved faster. Not because he'd ordered me to. I needed to get away from the gun pressing against my coat. I inhaled deeply and tried to focus my mind, tried to find a strategy. I reached the red door before I came up with anything.

"Open it."

I didn't want him to get close enough to push the weapon against me. I opened the door and quickly stepped into a brightly lit garage. My eyes widened at the exclusive space. I had not thought about what was behind the door, but had not expected a garage designed for at most four vehicles.

There were only two vehicles parked, one a black Mercedes Benz, the other a white Ford Mondeo. The latter was one of the most common cars on European roads, perfect for an escape. I walked to the Mercedes and waited at the passenger side.

Fradkov laughed as he twisted both the locks on the door to the staircase. "You're trying to delay the inevitable. You know we're not taking the Merc. Far too conspicuous. Get into the driver seat of the Ford, Doctor Genevieve Lenard. You're driving."

"After you answer a few questions." Not only did I need the answers, I also wanted to give Manny more time to reach me. But more importantly, Fradkov would become suspicious if I became too agreeable.

"You can ask me three questions." He glanced at his watch. "You have a minute for each. We need to get going."

I closed my eyes, when he walked around the Mercedes and pointed the gun at my chest. I wasted twenty seconds calming my mind before I opened my eyes and analysed every muscle contraction in his face. "Are there more bombs? Here and in the other cities?"

"Yes. Oh, yes." His shoulders relaxed. "This would not be as much fun if I wasn't going to blow more people up."

I pointed at his face. "You're lying."

"You hope I'm lying."

"No." I shook my head. "You've been watching me, observing my behaviour. And I've been studying you for months. On top of the profile on you that I built, I also have spent the last ten minutes learning your nonverbal cues. You are lying. There are no more bombs."

He blinked a few times, then a genuine smile lifted his cheeks and wrinkled the corners of his small eyes. "This is why I want you to work with me. You're even better than I'd expected."

Yet he was everything I had expected. Ivan Fradkov was not the first psychopath I had observed. Even though people like him were known for their pathological lying, they still revealed themselves with nonverbal cues. Not quite in the same manner as neurotypical people, but the clues were there and easy to identify if one knew what to look for. I did.

"You enjoyed the fear and chaos you caused with the bomb threats." I nodded when he smiled. "There were only the five polonium-210 bombs."

"Yes."

Again his expression gave him away. I narrowed my eyes. "Your arrogance made you miscalculate the probability of failing yet again." I almost smiled at the flush of anger on his face before he controlled it and leaned against the Mercedes, his entire body relaxed. "You didn't have a backup plan."

"I did." A small smile pulled at the corners of his mouth. "You."

"Me?" I made sure to look surprised and a bit flattered. I was anything but flattered. I wasn't Fradkov's backup plan. I was his desperate attempt not to fail again. And I was the cause of that failure. What better revenge than making me suffer for his defeat. "I won't be able to secure that piece of land in Siberia for you."

"Don't be so sure about that." He glanced at the weapon in his hand and smiled. "After watching you, I've come to believe that you are the missing ingredient to my plan."

"So, you wanted to play this game with me and then have me agree to work with you." I realised now how important it was to him that I went with him willingly. He didn't want to force me to become his partner. "Why?"

He put the handgun in a holster on his hip. "You are so much more than what you're doing at the moment. It took me merely one day to realise how much of your talent is going to waste with these people you call your friends. They distract you. All that emotion, all that attention you have to pay to what you say and when you say it. It's leagues beneath you."

An uncommon anger rose in me. Yes, the emotional chaos that reigned in my friendships was most distracting, but I had analysed the pros and cons. The benefits of having Colin, Phillip, Vinnie, Francine, Manny, Nikki and now Roxy in my life outweighed the distress. And this man, this *criminal*, had succeeded in making me doubt the value of the people in my life. Never again.

"I can see I have not yet convinced you." Fradkov smirked.

"So tell me, Doctor Genevieve Lenard, when is the last time you published an academic paper? You're like me. You need cerebral challenges. There is nothing that excites me as much as doing research into a new project."

"Your so-called projects are illegal." They were plans to overthrow governments.

"But much more challenging than your little art crime cases. If that does not convince you, how about this: When is the last time you travelled? The last time you learned something new that didn't have to do with useless relationships? When is the last time you felt alive because of your work and not on the verge of a breakdown?"

There was much truth in what he was saying. But he was presenting a one-sided argument. I didn't respond. There was no sense in justifying my life choices to this man. Seeing him and everything he represented sent an overwhelming sense of gratefulness for the people I knew were fighting to get to me.

"Come with me." Excitement around his eyes and mouth indicated that he thought he'd swayed me. "You will never again suffer from too much emotional stimulation."

I thought of Nikki in the hospital, very likely telling Eric to wait for me and then saying the most inappropriate things in front of Isabelle and the other doctors. I thought of Phillip and his gentle patience and firm correction whenever my social skills weren't appropriate. Colin's unfailing love, Vinnie's protective friendship, Francine's unconditional acceptance, Manny's stability, Roxy's bubbly nature.

Could I truly imagine my life without these people? They'd brought a facet into my life that I would not have experienced had I continued living my isolated life. I might never be as emotionally open as Nikki and Roxy or as tolerant and patient as Phillip and Colin, but being on the receiving end of their neurotypical behaviour had enriched my life.

Fradkov sighed. "I'm so disappointed." He took the gun from the holster. "I had expected you to be a true peer. Far superior to these plebeian emotions, ambitions and limitations. Now I'll have to—"

The door blasted towards us, followed immediately by a loud flash. I fell to the ground, and not because this was what Vinnie and Manny had repeatedly told me to do whenever there was gunfire. No. I fell to the ground because my leg muscles simply refused to obey any more signals from my brain.

I curled into a foetal position and became aware of a burning sensation on my upper arm. Around me the garage filled with gunshots, shouting and more gunshots. Darkness filled most of my vision and for a single heartbeat I considered giving in to it.

Then I thought of the way Nikki had pulled her shoulders back to face childbirth without me.

I started fighting.

I focused all my energy on pushing Mozart's Violin Sonata No. 20 in C major into my overwrought mind. Note by note, I mentally wrote the Adagio. And for the first time in my life, I simultaneously tried to maintain awareness of my surroundings. I didn't want to lose myself to Mozart. I wanted to be in control when the shooting stopped. I wanted to rush to the hospital to be there before Eric arrived.

For two seconds, silence filled the garage. I wrote another

three notes before lifting my head and looking towards the door. Colin ran to me and fell on his knees beside me. "Jenny! Are you okay?"

I tried to speak, but couldn't. I barely managed a nod and looked past Colin. Manny and Vinnie was standing next to Fradkov's prone body. A pool of blood was growing around his torso. Manny was shouting into his phone for the rest of the GIPN team. And for a body bag. Fradkov was dead.

"Jenny." Colin took my hands and squeezed until I looked at him. "Are you okay?"

"Yes." I remembered my shoulder and looked down. "No."

"What's wrong?" Colin's eyebrows shot up when he saw the bloodstain on my shoulder. "You're hurt."

"I don't think it's anything serious. I want to go to the hospital."

"Bloody hell!" Manny walked over. "Why the blazes do you need the hospital? How bad is the injury?"

"No. No, no, no." I swallowed away the panic when I realised that doctors and nurses would be touching me. "I want to go to Nikki."

Manny pointed at my shoulder, a scowl pulling his brow down. "Then what the bleeding hell is that?"

I shrugged, then groaned. And then I smiled.

I felt the pain. I was sitting on the dirty floor of a garage, looking at Manny's scowl deepening and Colin's confusion. This had been a traumatic event, yet I wasn't in a shutdown or, even worse, a meltdown.

Colin pressed my hands against his chest. "Jenny?"

"Take me to the hospital."

Chapter TWENTY-SIX

"Colin, can you take Eric for a moment?" Phillip walked to the sofa and carefully handed the tiny human being to Colin.

Two weeks had passed since Fradkov's death. Two weeks since Eric's birth. The race to the hospital hadn't given me enough time to prepare myself for what was to come.

I had managed to keep my shutdown at bay throughout the confrontation with Fradkov, Vinnie's frightening driving through the city to reach the hospital in time and even the doctor insisting on cleaning the flesh wound on my upper arm. Not even the three stitches he had put through my skin had caused me to shut down.

But the moment Nikki had screamed in pain as another contraction hit and I'd seen the absolute agony on her face, everything had gone dark. I'd had no control. And I'd missed Eric's birth. Colin had managed to put me on the sofa in the corner of Nikki's luxury birthing room where I'd stayed curled up, rocking and keening long after the nurses had taken Eric away and brought him back.

When I'd eventually come out of my shutdown, Nikki had been asleep with Eric resting on her chest. I'd gone home. The deep disappointment still bothered me. Nikki had assured me numerous times that my physical presence had been enough to give her strength. She'd been truthful.

That night I'd blurted out to Colin how I'd come to resent the emotional limitations surrounding my friendships. A few times my voice had completely disappeared when I'd admitted my shame.

He'd been shocked. Not at my resentment, but that I'd felt so ashamed. He'd touched my forearm and told me everyone, neurotypical and not, had to find their own place within relationships, find their own balance between their needs and the needs of others. And he'd laughed when he'd said that he didn't know if anyone ever found that balance. Apparently, it was very difficult.

Now I was challenged to add another person to the dynamics in my life. Even though Eric had been born two weeks premature, he'd weighed a healthy four point six kilograms. Nikki had trouble breastfeeding him, but he'd shown no signs of distress feeding from a bottle. He was an easy baby and was sleeping quietly in Colin's arms.

I kept reminding everyone that the books insisted that babies should sleep in their beds, but no one heeded my warnings. I'd been the only one who'd accumulated a collection of books and had studied them vigorously. The others insisted they were going on natural instinct.

Colin settled deeper into the sofa and looked at me. "Maybe today?"

"No." I still hadn't had the courage to hold Eric in my arms. I'd touched his soft skin and had stopped breathing for a few seconds when he gripped my index finger three days ago.

His complete vulnerability and dependence scared me. Only when I'd been four years old and my parents had left me alone at the hospital for more tests had I been more terrified. I'd learned to deal with that fear and was determined to overcome this as well.

"When's dinner?" Nikki walked into the living area and sat down on my other side. "I'm starving."

"Patience, little punk." Vinnie turned away from the stove to look at us. "My Auntie Helen's lasagna will take another ten minutes or so."

"I'll come and help you. I'm sure you forgot to add lemongrass and rosemary." Francine started getting up from the other sofa, but Roxy grabbed her arm and pulled her back down.

"I'll keep her here and protect your cooking, snookums." Roxy threw both legs over Francine's lap and exaggerated the hold she had on Francine's arm. "I've got her. You're safe. Your cooking's safe. Auntie Helen is safe!"

Nikki laughed and leaned over me to look at Eric. "I'm sad his wrinkles are disappearing. He no longer looks like Gollum."

I had researched that name the first time Nikki had called Eric that. I'd been utterly appalled when I'd seen online images of the fictional creature from a popular book and movie. Nikki had only laughed and told me to think of it like Francine calling Manny 'handsome'. We'd then spent twenty-three minutes in a strong disagreement about her comparison. She'd giggled more than argued.

"How's Marty?" Roxy let go of Francine's arm, but didn't move her legs. She was wearing bell-bottom jeans, a flowy top and running shoes. Francine glared at the footwear with her top lip curled in disgust.

"He was here this afternoon." Nikki settled back in her space and I exhaled in relief. "He says hello."

"Did he take Eric out?"

"Yeah." Nikki touched her hair. "Gave me three hours to have a long bath and clean up our room. It feels like all I'm doing is cleaning."

Martin had visited Nikki every day at the hospital and had been here every second day to take care of Eric for a few hours. Today was the first time he'd taken Eric outside. I'd made sure he knew about the importance of keeping Eric wrapped up while out in the winter temperatures.

I'd had to remind myself numerous times that I should trust Nikki's judgement. She'd been watching Martin handle Eric and was confident that the baby would be completely safe with his father. I still had my doubts.

"I hear it gets worse as they get older." Roxy widened her eyes as if horrified. "They go through five or more sets of clothes a day and make a mess wherever they go."

Francine slapped Roxy's leg, pushed both legs off her lap and looked at me. "Eric will be fine. No messes."

"You don't have to protect me from a baby, Francine." I looked at the small body resting in Colin's arms and wondered if I'd just told an untruth. In many ways I felt threatened by this little human being, even if the threats were mostly irrational and related to my emotional equilibrium.

A soft ping sounded from the front door and both Colin and Vinnie became more alert. Vinnie put the wooden spoon down on the holder next to the stove and walked to the front door, his body language aggressive. The tension in his muscles relaxed marginally when keys turned and the door opened to reveal Manny and Daniel.

"Waiting at the door for us, big guy?" Manny gave Vinnie a sideways glance and walked to the sofas. "If you're hoping for a hug, ask Roxy."

"Screw you, old man." Vinnie bumped his fist against Daniel's. "How's Pink?"

"The doctors say there's increased brain activity, but he's not waking up yet." Only the bruise on Daniel's left cheek remained after his kidnapping. The lacerations on his face had healed well and he no longer favoured his side as he walked.

Daniel had left the Zénith only after the police had evacuated the concert hall and the bomb squad had declared it clear of any explosive devices. He and Manny had made sure that all the cities had searched all public areas. There hadn't been any more bombs. Fradkov had indeed lied about more bombs.

But he'd been truthful about delaying the team. During the surprise dance performance in the entrance hall, another three hundred people had flooded the area. They'd all worn black clothes that closely resembled the GIPN uniforms and had crowded the real GIPN team, limiting their movements.

Colin had told me Manny had been so furious, Colin had expected him to start shooting at the group crowding him. Vinnie hadn't shot anyone, but the people crowding him had quickly dispersed when he'd punched and broken the noses of two men.

This show of force had been enough to scare off a lot of the others. But by this time, I'd already disappeared. Fortunately,

Francine had been able to follow me. She'd directed them to the room with the red door. Panic still tightened my chest when I thought of how they had almost been too late.

Daniel's team had waited with him until everything had been cleared. Then they'd forced him to go the hospital. It had been the next day. Daniel had had his injuries treated and examined and had visited Pink. I had not been to visit Pink. My mind was still fragile after the confrontation with Fradkov. Many things he had said were still mulling around in my thoughts.

"Three more minutes and the food's done." Vinnie walked back to the kitchen. "You might as well grab your seats."

Colin looked down at Eric. The reluctance to put the baby down was clear on his face. He looked at Nikki. "Can you fetch his blanket? Then I'll put him on the sofa. He'll be with us when we eat."

"Okey-dokey." She jumped up and walked towards her room. The first three days she'd been back in the apartment had been difficult. She'd been uncomfortable after giving natural birth and had been worried about Eric not breastfeeding.

I had immediately bought books on bottle-feeding the moment the doctor had told Nikki that she was not producing enough milk. I'd read through them all and quoted the numerous studies to Nikki. It had calmed me to see her relax when I told her about the countless adults who hadn't been breastfed and had shown no long-term effects.

After that, she'd recovered much quicker. I still smiled every time I thought about her shouts of joy two days ago when she realised she could see her feet. And that her feet weren't swollen. She was also excited that she could be wearing 'normal' clothes soon.

Nikki rushed back to the sofa and put the soft cream blanket next to me. I got up and watched as Colin gently laid Eric down without waking him. I had wondered how my sleep was going to be interrupted by a crying baby, but so far I had only heard him a few times. His crying sounded to me like prolonged hiccoughs. And he stopped the moment his mouth latched onto the teat of the bottle.

I followed the others to the table, amazed at how such a small being could dominate the thoughts and conversations of everyone now settled around the table.

My dining room table comfortably seated eight people, but today Vinnie had set a place for Daniel as well. Francine didn't seem to be troubled by sitting so close to Roxy. Not even when Roxy accidentally knocked over the salt shaker. I stared at the spilled salt until Francine put a napkin over it and smiled at me.

"I set up that account." Francine looked at Daniel. "So you can tell Pink's doctors they can go ahead with the treatment."

"Oh, goodie." Roxy exhaled in relief. "Doctor Lenoir and Doctor Falco are really the best of the best when it comes to spinal injuries. Their treatments have helped many people."

"But it's bloody expensive." Manny leaned away to give Vinnie space to put the large serving bowls on the table. "Do we have enough money?"

Francine snorted and rolled her eyes. "Oh, my naïve handsome cop. Yes, we have enough money."

Manny's eyes narrowed and he turned to Francine. "Firstly,

I'm not a cop. And secondly, is all this money you're so proud of legal?"

Francine ran her manicured nail down his sleeve. "I'll tell you later tonight, after we—"

"Supermodel!" Manny leaned away from her, his frown deepening. "Is that money legal?"

"Of course it is, Millard." Colin handed the serving dish to Phillip. "Now shut up and enjoy Vin's food."

Francine took a bite and gave an extravagant shudder. "Oh, this is horrible. It needs rosemary. Lots and lots of rosemary."

The next twenty minutes were chaotic. Vinnie and Francine quarrelled non-stop about spices, cooking temperatures, cuisines and everything else. Phillip, Roxy and Manny discussed Pink's recovery and treatments. Nikki and Colin talked about the complex process of returning all the Renaissance paintings we'd recovered.

Russian Consul General Nikolai Guskov had disappeared. Julien hinted that he'd been in contact with French intelligence services and that France might know where he was, but Julien had refused to give any details. I hoped Nikolai and his family were safe.

I'd been surprised to learn that Nikolai's assistant Roman had taken over the Unity Through Art project. He'd shown unexpected enthusiasm for making sure all the exhibitions that had been organised were going to take place.

Emad was still in custody of the French authorities, but would soon move to Wyoming. His most powerful weapon had been all the recordings of Fradkov he had. Not only that, he also had memorised a list of people Fradkov had blackmailed, killed and controlled. Interpol valued such information so highly that it had pressured France into giving Emad what he wanted as soon as they had those lists. Alain had told Phillip that Emad spent twelve hours a day writing down everything he knew.

It had been most interesting to learn that Emad had known that Fradkov was not only blackmailing General Sokolov, but he had also built an entire case against him. Fradkov had opened an offshore account in General Sokolov's name from which he'd made transfers to and received money from numerous criminals.

The biggest transfer had been to an estate agent for a property in Malta. The most impressive feature of that mansion was the art gallery that could host at least three hundred works of art. Fradkov had created connections between the general and the hijackers so it looked like the heist had been arranged by the aging military man. Apparently, Fradkov had told Emad he was going to make sure General Sokolov took the fall if he didn't receive the Siberian piece of land.

The conversations shifted a few times and I spent most of the time listening. It gave me pleasure to see the people I cared about relaxed. The days following Otto's assassination in the restaurant had been trying for everyone. At least Fradkov and the danger he'd posed to everyone on my team and to global peace was no longer a threat. I wondered if we had to worry about the assassin. He had still not been identified or captured.

"And Otto's two girls are the cutest." Francine picked up her tablet and started swiping. She never went anywhere with at least two of her devices. She tilted the screen to show Roxy. "See? I got these pics from their mother's Facebook account. This is Jordyn and this one is Grace. Cute, right?"

It had taken Francine five days to locate her hacker colleague Joe Pasquier. She'd intimidated him into giving her access to Otto's finances and had transferred everything to his ex-wife. None of it had been done legally. Manny had been furious and proud.

"Let's take this party to the sofas." Vinnie got up and reached for his plate. "Roxy and I will clear the table and bring the desserts."

"Ooh, dessert." Nikki jumped up and gathered a few plates. "I'll help clear the table. I need something sweet."

"What excuse is she using now?" Phillip stopped at the sofa and gently touched Eric's cheek before he sat down on the opposite sofa. "She's not eating for two anymore."

"I have to keep my energy up," Nikki called from the kitchen. "It's hard work being a mommy."

Nikki had told me last night she was planning to return to her yoga classes this coming week. She pretended to indulge a lot, but was careful with her diet. A few times I had observed her staring at her reflection in the mirror.

"What happened to Amélie?" Phillip watched Daniel bring a chair from the dining room table and sit down. "I exchanged only a few words with her, but she made a good impression."

"She's in Minsk. The lectures she was supposed to give at the symposium were pushed back. She's speaking there this week as well as at two universities." Daniel got up to give Vinnie more space to bring in the tray of coffee mugs. Roxy followed with a large chocolate cake, small plates and forks on another tray.

"Justine sent this cake." Roxy put her tray next to Vinnie's and straightened. "She came by the hospital this afternoon. Alexis has chosen a university and is doing well. She's also in therapy. Justine looked tired but happy."

I'd received seven emails from Justine thanking me for the role I'd played in keeping her granddaughter safe. I hadn't responded until Vinnie insisted that Justine thought I'd been kidnapped. I'd sent her a one-sentence email wishing her and Alexis well.

Daniel sat down and watched as Vinnie cut the cake and put a piece on a plate Roxy was holding. "At least the peace deal went through."

"I read about that in the news." Phillip smiled and accepted the plate from Roxy. "This is a remarkable move, especially with the upheaval in global politics the last year. After Russia and China voted against the UN's bid for a ceasefire in Syria, I was surprised that Russia signed this agreement."

I wasn't surprised. Isabelle had invited Francine, Roxy and me for a private lunch last week at the presidential residence. One of the topics we'd discussed was the hard work that had gone into making that agreement happen. There had been many compromises and negotiations, but it had been Fradkov's death and President Goddard's acknowledgment that Russia had not been complicit in any of the events leading up to the Zénith confrontation that had convinced Russia to sign the agreement.

Isabelle had been greatly entertained by Francine's

conspiracy theories and Roxy's bubbly sense of humour. Like now, I'd also been more withdrawn than usual. Fradkov's words continually came back to challenge me.

Yesterday, I had started research for an academic paper. I was excited about the topic and hoped the books I'd ordered would be delivered tomorrow. I had done a lot of introspection to ensure my decisions were not to prove anything to the now-deceased Fradkov. His arguments had merely been the catalyst. I wanted to write this paper.

I looked at the baby sleeping next to me on the sofa and made up my mind. This was something else I wanted to do. But this was much harder.

Conversation around me stilled as I twisted and gently pushed my hands under the soft blanket. I had bought it for the only reason that the texture didn't aggravate my senses.

Eric jostled a little as his warm weight rested in the palms of my hands. He was so small. I lifted him and was surprised at how light he was. Just like Nikki did every day and Colin had done earlier, I settled him in the crook of my arm and stared at him.

All the books I had read had been written by neurotypical people. Most of them had talked about the wonder of holding a baby and the warm emotions flooding your being as you looked down at the little being.

I felt none of it. What I did experience was an amazement at biology and evolution. And fear. Paralysing fear. That was the emotion that flooded my being. Fear that I would do or say something that would harm this little boy. Fear of the threat that the changes in society and social media posed to his emotional wellbeing. Fear that…

"Jenny?" Colin put his arm around me and pulled me against him. "Are you okay?"

I was keening. I cleared my throat and nodded once. I didn't look away from Eric. "Take him."

Nikki sat down next to me and took Eric with the ease of a mother who'd had many children. "Doc G held you, my little Gollum. Now you gotta watch out. Next stop is hugville."

I leaned away from Nikki, deeper into Colin's embrace. I didn't want to get involved in another inane discussion. Everyone laughed and the room filled with the sound of light chatter.

I was relieved. I had faced another fear and held Eric. It hadn't been easy, but I was determined to try again. Maybe next time my autistic mind wouldn't be overwhelmed by his warm weight and his distinctive scent. Colin tightened his arm around me in a strong one-armed hug. I rested against him for three seconds, then I straightened.

It was time for me to make the next decision. Already I had taken the step to develop my academic career. And I had held Eric.

I looked at the people in the room and again thought about how wrong Fradkov had been. Not all emotional demands and distractions were negative. They could enrich one's life. They could give one enough strength to take steps that had previously caused paralysing fear.

I waited until there was a lull in the conversation. "I want to go on holiday. Abroad."

~ ~ ~ ~ ~

Be first to find out when Genevieve's next adventure will be published. Sign up for the newsletter at
http://estelleryan.com/contact.html

~~~~

Look at the paintings from this book (also with the Fibonacci spiral fitted over a few) and read more about hacking planes, Uccello and the Fibonacci spiral at:
http://estelleryan.com/the-uccello-connection.html
~~~~

Other books in the Genevieve Lenard Series:

Book 1: The Gauguin Connection

Book 2: The Dante Connection

Book 3: The Braque Connection

Book 4: The Flinck Connection

Book 5: The Courbet Connection

Book 6: The Pucelle Connection

Book 7: The Léger Connection

Book 8: The Morisot Connection

Book 9: The Vecellio Connection

Book 10: The Uccello Connection

and more…

~ ~ ~ ~ ~

Please visit me on my Facebook Page to become part of the process as I'm writing Genevieve's next adventure.

and

Explore my website to find out more about me and Genevieve.

Made in the USA
San Bernardino, CA
02 September 2018